ALSO BY WILLIAM SHATNER AND JEFF ROVIN

ZERO-G: Book 1

ZERO-G

A NOVEL

GREEN SPACE

WILLIAM SHATNER
AND JEFF ROVIN

SIMON & SCHUSTER
New York London Toronto Sydney New Delhi

Simon & Schuster
1230 Avenue of the Americas
New York, NY 10020

First Simon & Schuster hardcover edition September 2017

For information about special discounts for bulk purchases,
please contact Simon & Schuster Special Sales at 1-866-506-1949
or business@simonandschuster.com.

The Simon & Schuster Speakers Bureau can bring authors to
your live event. For more information or to book an event contact the
Simon & Schuster Speakers Bureau at 1-866-248-3049
or visit our website at www.simonspeakers.com.

Interior design by Lewelin Polanco

Manufactured in the United States of America

1 3 5 7 9 10 8 6 4 2

Library of Congress Cataloging-in-Publication Data

ISBN 978-1-5011-1158-7
ISBN 978-1-5011-1160-0 (ebook)

This novel is dedicated to my wonderful family, my glorious wife, my three delightful daughters, their handsome and charming husbands, and my five brilliant, loving, extraordinary grandchildren. What a team. And I would be lacking in judgment if I didn't also note Cappuccino, Espresso, and our never forgotten Starbuck.

ZERO-G

GREEN SPACE

PROLOGUE

THE VINE SHOULD not have existed on board the space station. It should not have existed anywhere at all.

The stubby protuberance was a gnomish thing, about two feet long, with a large, lumpy knot protruding from the underside. The stunted limb did not even look as if it belonged at the end of this particular trunk; it would have been more at home on a terrestrial kapok tree somewhere in the Amazon.

The tree had begun its existence seven weeks earlier as a clean, trim, paper-thin ribbon of deep-green Echeveria-Cyborg six inches wide and, as it grew, the thick base had retained the delicate, elegant quality of a broad and twining frond that had grown to a prodigious height and character—before suddenly budding the chunk of dark, blighted pulp.

The tree was the only object inside the high, narrow Vault. Located in the Agro Center of the space station *Empyrean,* the opaque enclosure provided not just security for the classified experiment but also room for it to grow. "Merlin"—code-named after the Arthurian wizard who, according to some legends, was entombed inside a tree—was the first of a new generation of SROs, Self Replicating Organisms. The SROs were so called due to the vast population of cell-size nanites patrolling, perfecting, and expanding the tree from the carbon-nanotube lattice that stretched from root to tip. They were doing the same macroscale work that genetic engineers did, substituting manipulator spikes for a biologist's pipette. Using that molecules-thin framework, they snagged and applied external biological materials that had been synthesized and replicated in the soil, fed by the element-enriched wash of gases flowing through the Vault.

The tree stood out in the darkened, otherwise empty chamber because the deep pine-green bark of the SRO glowed with a dull, internally generated sheen, due to an electroluminescent impurity created by the nanites in the vine's electrocharged nanotubes. Unlike the rest of the greenhouse, which had a system of misters and sprinklers to keep the foliage watered, the contents of the Vault required very little water, giving the interior a dry, almost brittle feel.

"Impurity, my eye," the Individual Cloud belonging to Agricultural Officer Lancaster Liba had once suggested. "I'm thinking the little bastard robots invented little nanoheadlights so they can see."

It had been a somewhat flip comment, programmed into the personality of Liba's IC; nanites did not need to see. But there was some truth in the observation all the same. The cell-size robots could perfect themselves in any way necessary, just as easily as they could alter any raw material within reach of their microscopic manipulator spikes . . . change it to any image, atom by atom. Left alone in the soil with their programming, and nothing more, the hundreds of nanites had constructed the tree's foundational nanotube ribbon with elegant precision—rolled hexagons of carbon atoms into a weave of extraordinary tensile strength. Once that framework had been completed, a new mandate was triggered into their logic systems, a more complicated morphology, a shakedown to test their abilities: they were tasked with knotting together contractile proteins to form bellows and bladders like those that uncurled a spider's leg. They used those to create plant photocells, chloroplasts, to feed on the sharp, unobstructed sunlight of the lab. Simultaneously, the nanites grabbed and reshaped more and more raw material.

The one thing the nanites could not control was the tilt of the tree. Even before the emergence of the freakish branch, the stalk leaned nearly ten degrees toward that side, coming nearer to the Earth-facing wall of the Vault as it grew. Liba believed it was a natural tendency to want to go "home." Whenever he entered the Vault to take readings, the stalk reminded him more and more of a Christmas tree that had started with the best intentions but found itself weighted to one side by too much tinsel.

Only in this case, the scientists at NASA assured him it wasn't weight that bent the stalk; the lean was caused by centripetal force that effectively flung the knitting-needle top in that direction and kept it there because the tree—along with the rest of NASA's space station *Empyrean*—was turning in a retrograde arc to generate anything from a near-zero to a three-quarter gravity tug throughout any given radial arm. The near zero gravity in the greenhouse that contained the Vault could not fight that force.

The stalk had grown just over six inches each day. Though the programming in the nanites could be altered to accelerate or decelerate the process, they were working at a pace that allowed Liba and Zero-G medic, biophysicist Dr. Carlton Carter, to assess the progress and any changes which might be required. On their own, the nanites could not suddenly change speed. They could not stop.

And until now, they could only improvise if it served the parameters of the SRO design. There was no leeway to show creative initiative.

The solitary mutated branch began to shimmer and change as the knot spit particles into the air. Instead of rising to the pointed top of the tree, as designed, the nanite-borne cells added nearly a foot to the ugly, twisted end of the branch. Within moments, the knot knit back into its previous shape. Minutes later it erupted again at the tip, expanding another dozen or so inches to the branch.

And then it did so again, and again, until it poked the electronic wall of the Vault.

■ ■

An alarm sounded in the head of Lancaster Liba.

Actually, the pleasant chirp alerted him in his Individual Cloud;

hooked directly to the cerebral cortex, responsive to eye movements or hand gestures, the IC was equipped with SimAI—simulated artificial intelligence—which anticipated the needs of its user. An unexpected event in the greenhouse, in the Vault, loudly required the man's attention.

For the verbal-syn of his IC, Liba had used his father's voice, sampled from an old analog recording. The elder Liba, a Budapest-born sugar beet importer, had died in 1994—broken by the agricultural drought and recession in Hungary the previous three years. But his no-nonsense attitude lived on.

"Hey! *Csöppsége!* Kid!"

Curled in a stiff, narrow cot in his small residence adjacent to the Agro Center, Liba opened his eyes on absolute darkness.

"There's an emergency!" Zoltán "Butch" Liba's cigarette-roughened voice shouted at him. "Get out of the bed!"

The gaunt-faced septuagenarian scowled like he did when his father told him to get up for school. When there were still classrooms to go to.

"I'm getting out, I'm getting out," he assured the IC.

Liba waved a finger to turn on his heads-up display and blinked on the room-light icon. His 240-square-foot living quarters filled with a green glow that complemented the deep, nostril-filling scent of pollen from the many potted plants. There were times when the agricultural genius, the man who had made both Death Valley and China's Gobi Desert flower, wasn't sure he *could* get up. He felt certain he'd wake one day and find himself rooted to the ground. The older he got, the more he felt kinship with the foliage he so loved.

"Where's the emergency?" he asked the IC as he sat up in the half-gravity of the cubicle. Usually, problems in the Agro Center involved some kind of mechanical failure that caused one of the greenhouses to leak water, gases, plant food, or all three. Components that were designed and built on Earth did not always fit correctly after being rocketed to space.

"It's in the Vault, boy," the voice informed him.

"You mean *at*?"

"I mean in, *in*," the voice said, scolding him.

A crisis in the Vault was not good. It meant that Assistant Agricultural Officer Douglas Cameron, who lacked appropriate security clearance, would not receive the alert. Liba would have to go this alone. The Vault was one of the most secretive areas of the station, second only to the Space Intelligence Force section of the Drum, the spy "wedge" located in the *Empyrean's* command center.

There was a good reason for that, Liba thought.

Liba rose slowly so that he wouldn't shoot toward the ceiling, at the same time already half-walking, half-reaching toward the door; it was like sinking in a pool. In space, the swinging motion of one's arms was often more effective than one's legs when it came to covering distance, though the combination gave Liba a kind of loping, Bigfoot gait.

The door of his quarters was very narrow—space in space was costly—and he had to turn sideways to exit. It deposited Liba just outside the largest of the four greenhouses. The first greenhouse was rectangular, with a slightly convex roof and bulging sides; the remaining greenhouses were clear domes. All were equipped with windows that were large, transparent solar panels, and situated to take advantage not only of the constant, aggressive sun but of light reflected by the station's massive solar sail.

The entrance portal recognized Liba's IC encephalogram ID and opened as he arrived. As fast as it closed, the sodden windows nonetheless began to drip themselves clear from the motion of the stirred air. Almost at once, the heavy, humid vapor restored the normal opacity of the windows.

Blinking out the moisture that clouded his tired eyes, Liba started toward the Vault. Given the thickness of the air, he actually felt a tingle from the electrical charge that comprised the opaque walls of the Vault as he neared.

The twelve-foot-high structure resembled a classic bank vault, though that was simply an aesthetic choice Liba had made; it could just as easily be made to resemble a jack-in-the-box, an old milk pail, or anything else he wished. NASA had rejected most of his suggestions as lacking dignity.

"It appears I have zero gravitas," Liba had joked to his old friend Sam Lord, director of the FBI's Zero-G unit.

The electric field was active camouflage, an illusion created by the volumetric screens to conceal what was inside, a top-secret project funded by NASA and safeguarded by *Empyrean* security—

The thought of the ill-fated security team caused Liba to wince and collapse a little inside. He hadn't known many of those people, but he'd seen them about the station. Their enthusiasm, energy, and stoic professionalism were missed. He forced his mind from the recent disaster to address the matter at hand—whatever it was.

Liba stopped and looked around the exterior of the Vault. He was still winking away dampness that had pooled on his forehead and filled his eyes. He moved his eyelids carefully so as not to activate the icons in his IC. It was a skill most people learned, now, when they were young— like the art of texting when he was a youth. To look around without interacting with the drop-down IC panels required chicken-heading, using a slight forward thrust of the head while blinking. It was another skill most people learned when they were very young.

"*There* is a problem, though it's not *the* problem," the IC said unhelpfully as Liba scanned the barrier.

"You want to take another swing at that?" he asked his IC. "What's wrong?"

"Earthward side, top quarter has been breached, if you'd bother to look there. Still trying to understand the cause. Materials not submitting to analysis."

Liba did not have to ask why. The Vault was high-security. Whatever was inside was not logged in any public database. The botanist stepped off the very narrow rubber walkway that ran from the greenhouse door to the Vault. He pushed to his left, moving easily in the near-Earth gravity through the thick leaves and watermelons underfoot. He brushed aside avocados and peaches, all of them rich and plump in the perfect growing environment of zero gravity and continuous, misty sunlight. Just by breathing, he inhaled the fragrances of each as he passed.

As he rounded a patch of grapevines—paid for by a private wine grower on Earth who had the only "space" vintage on the planet—Liba saw the problem high on the side of the black Vault.

"Crap."

"Eloquently spoken, boy," his IC told him as it captured and analyzed the image of the branch tip protruding from the wall.

"Open the Etheric," Liba said. "Password Lancastersayso."

At once, an Etheric Blueprint opened in his IC. There were no details beyond the level of his security clearance. But this broad outline was enough to tell Liba what he hadn't wanted to see.

"That configuration is not in the programming," Liba muttered.

"Nor is the chemical composition," the IC replied. "The Etheric-listed ingredients have formed new compounds. What you have here is a mutation made of I-don't-know-what."

"How can you not know?" Liba asked.

"Too damn small, whatever is causing this," the IC told him. "I don't have a built-in magnifier, boy. If you remember, it made you dizzy—"

"Yeah, I remember," Liba said, still eying the fracture. "How the hell did it even penetrate the electrical fence?"

"My guess is that something inside the bark is interrupting the charge, redirecting it with what would have to be metalized shells," the IC replied.

"You're sure it's metal?"

"I'm sure. If you'd take the time to check the intrinsic impedance, ηs—"

"I'm a botanist, not an engineer," Liba said. "Go to sleep," he ordered, cutting the IC off.

Now he knew what the problem was. He had known what the experiment involved—he had to, to help with the botanical components—but he did not know what the catalytic element was. But there was a new metal alloy . . . it was in the vine . . . and the man who did have highest clearance, Dr. Carlton Carter of Zero-G, was a biophysicist, emphasis on the physicist.

Nanites. Tiny robots, nanobots, used as an extreme growth trigger. The achievement was remarkable and, given what it was apparently engaged in at the moment, also terrifying.

As the agriculturalist watched, the protruding section of limb shivered and swelled. A node popped, sending a cloud into the air. The green mist writhed along the limb toward the tip and gathered around it like swarming bees. A piece of molted bark chipped off when the branch shook and Liba picked it up, scratched at it. The thing was dry and seemingly lifeless but he knew it was alive: he could feel it wriggling, like when he used to peel bark from a termite-infested tree.

It only looks lifeless, he thought with sudden realization. *The cells are shielded, metallicized.*

He looked up. The limb was still twelve feet or so from the nearest window that formed the exterior of the greenhouse—but he had no idea what the growth rate or accelerated growth rate might be. If it struck the glass, the fragments would likely hold for an unknown period depending on the location and nature of the fracture. But if the limb pierced the pane of the greenhouse and then moved on toward the glass that protected the Agro Center from space, the climate would be sucked from the structure and everything inside would perish. That amounted to just over sixty percent of the home-grown foods on the *Empyrean.* Supplies would have to be rushed to space on the small shuttle fleet, putting all other shipments on hold.

He winked on his IC to notify the staff of the *Empyrean.* As Liba did so, the branch shivered and forked.

"Oh damn," he said.

"Yeah, this isn't so good," his IC agreed.

Lancaster Liba loved this place, and he would be damned if some top-secret beanstalk—destined for great things, but still just in the experimental stage—was going to jeopardize his greenhouse. Shifting his eyes to his drop-down contact box, Liba blinked it open and rotated his head slightly to enlarge the image of Commander Stanton.

ONE

A DOZEN PEOPLE DEAD. *Good people, people who trusted my judgment—* Retired General Curtis James Stanton, civilian commander of the space station *Empyrean*, lay on his smartfoam cot and peered into the darkness of his relatively spacious cabin. His IC was set to emergency alert only, yet in this rare moment of quiet his mind was anything but at rest. Eyes open, his memory vivid, Stanton's brain whipped him with pain he could only allow himself here, in private. He dared not display weakness or distraction while he was on duty in the Drum, and there was no one he could talk to, no one who would understand.

There was doubt enough about tactics that his military brain attached to the failed mission. But there was, as always, the chaser: the human component. The first one got a quick, fixed reaction from the brain. It ran down a checklist, compared the results to the protocols.

That move was right . . . that one wrong . . . right . . . wrong . . . right . . . chancy . . . .

Those decisions never got any better or worse. The other, though, the human toll: that took a while to seep into his soul and there it got uglier and more suffocating. He saw once again those twelve faces focused on their mission—young and middle-aged, eager and professional, all prepared and eager to serve. They trusted his judgment completely. Stanton's tortured mind could only scroll back as far as the unit's preparation for the recon. He saw again and again the bulk of his security detail rocket off and then perish conducting recon of the Chinese space station *Jade Star*, which had lost control of a particle weapon and was spewing death across near-space. He could not stop seeing the soundless explosions out the window of the Drum, hearing the cries in his IC—

"Stop!" he muttered wearily, helplessly, squeezing his fingernails into his palms. "*Please*, stop."

Commander Stanton's shoulders moved and the mattress adjusted to hug in him place. He bunched his fists against his forehead but he didn't bother to shut his eyes. Open or closed, it was equally dark in his cabin. And either way, there was his security team once again making their preparations, once more sledding into the void.

Einstein said that time and space were illusory, that they changed with one's perspective. Commander Stanton had latched onto that idea during his six months of training for this assignment, but even Einstein didn't prepare him for how elusive a quality time really was in space. Without day or night to mark its passage, sleep was actually the only real measure—and the lack of it did change one's subjectivity. For the past week, Commander Stanton hadn't had much rest. Everything that had happened—the loss, the failure, the personal shame, the way others avoided eye contact—was immediate and ongoing. It did no good to remind himself or NASA that what he had ordered was a standard by-the-book deployment.

Fourteen single-occupant vehicles, all piloted by veterans, but only two returned.

And one of those survivors was not even a member of his team. It was Sam Lord's man McClure.

That was the other thought that plagued Stanton. Samuel Lord was the head of the FBI's six-person Zero-G unit based on the *Empyrean*. His man had not only survived, it was Lord—just two weeks up from Earth—who had succeeded in personally shutting down the lethal Chinese device with a maneuver that was anything but by-the-book. And unlike Stanton, after the battle, the octogenarian former flyboy was the same tutelary saint he had been before.

Only now with more halo, the fifty-three year-old thought bitterly as he tried in vain to sleep.

Nor was Lord's cool triumph merely the fact that he stopped the Dragon's Eye. Compounding Stanton's sense of failure, Lord had also fulfilled the role he had been sent to space to accomplish. He had found the traitors who helped the Chinese build the weapon. That had given momentum to Lord's reputation as a go-getter who just wouldn't quit. Meanwhile, Stanton's career up here, just nine weeks old, was the subject of doubt and subtle derision in the newtiae. These news minutia summaries collected, cross-referenced, and analyzed every public mention of a name or situation to provide an N-rating. In the immediate aftermath of the loss, Stanton's superiors at NASA had backed the retired army general publicly. After all, they were the ones who had written the white paper he followed. Then they went silent for six days as the newtiae numbers eroded like the orbit of the United Arab Emirates' ill-fated DubHigh Hotel a year before.

The commander was no longer in free fall and that was only because there wasn't much distance left *to* fall. He didn't expect to be replaced anytime soon, since there was no one on deck: at least there was time to try to rebuild his reputation. Yet that plagued him too because he didn't know how. He had been sent here because he wasn't a Sam Lord. He did things in a conservative, traditional manner.

Stanton couldn't get the man's round, open face out of his brain. He saw the attentive eyes and thoughtful brow topped with gray steel-wool hair, the easy roll of Lord's big shoulders as he walked. He heard the newtiae praise, replayed in his exhausted brain the interview with Hiromi Tsuburaya, the Japanese chief operating officer of Consolidated Bandwidth of Asia, where Lord was a hero for avenging the attack that had devastated the nation—

"It was a team effort," Lord had said.

"But you were the leader of the team," Tsuburaya had responded.

"*'A'* leader," Lord had replied modestly—with intentionally boastful *false* modesty, Stanton was sure. Because then he went on to talk about the teams he had served with in two wars, in test piloting, running through his credentials as if they were talking points on a campaign trail—

Dammit! Enough.

Stanton dug the heels of his palms into his exhausted eyes. He found himself envying Blake Tengan, the forty-eight-year-old commander of NASA's Armstrong Base on the moon. She had a PhD in astrophysics to go with her credentials as a decorated military veteran. Not only did she make all the right calls up there during the Dragon's Eye crisis, but she had breadth that he lacked. Inferiority on top of failure was a deadly, paralyzing combination. The hell of it was, he had lost personnel before. There had been thousands of deaths among his elite troops during the War on Narcotics and the Pan-Persia Occupation. But those situations had been volatile. They had been classic terrestrial problems fought with traditional weapons—if a neutron bomb that killed people without destroying property could be considered traditional. This was outer space, the final frontier, God's backyard. His command on the *Empyrean* was only supposed to be about organizing science and engineering projects with selective political surveillance on the side, electronic intelligence gathering paid for by agencies like the CIA and run by two specialists in the Drum. The threats beyond Earth's atmosphere were supposed to be radiation, micrometeoroids, structural fatigue, centripetal gravity distortion.

They weren't supposed to be old global conflicts carried beyond the atmosphere by old global lunatics, he thought bitterly. *NASA and capitalism were supposed to have things under control up here. They should have been supporting him, not scapegoating him with silence—*

Stanton angrily punched the air and, with a pop of the foam, the motion carried him several inches off the mattress toward the wall on his right. He met it with open palms and pushed himself back. The residences in Radial Arm Five had from one-quarter to three-quarters gravity; the artificial pull was strongest toward the outer reaches of the structure.

"That's where stuff gets flung by centripetal force," was how team physicist Dr. August Bird had dumbed it down for Stanton during his orientation briefing. Bird was also the man who had explained Einstein to him.

In order for him to be close to the centrally located Drum, Stanton had to take one of the lesser-gravity cabins. Until this moment, it hadn't been a challenge. He had mastered everything from showering to shoving a foot in his boot without becoming a human cannonball.

At least Isaac Newton and his third law aren't against you, Stanton thought as he settled back. The wall had simultaneously exerted a force equal in magnitude and opposite in direction from his fist. Otherwise, thanks to Newton's first law, he would have gone sailing away, a body in motion continuing to be in motion.

Science, bless it, was reliable.

The "urgent" IC ping from Lancaster Liba was both welcome and not. It allowed Stanton to stop thinking about past disasters and turn his attention to whatever this new emergency might be.

"Go," Stanton said, engaging Liba's icon with a wink.

"Commander, the SRO is misbehaving," the agricultural officer said from just outside the Vault. "Misbehaving very badly."

"Coming," Stanton said, rolling his shoulders so that he was immediately sitting upright. The light came on automatically as the commander stood. "Are you contacting Dr. Carter?"

"My next call, commander," Liba said.

Stanton winked on the "out" icon, an exit sign. Even though the biophysicist was a consultant on the Merlin project, he was FBI and not on the *Empyrean*'s emergency alert list. Notifying the Bureau's resident medical officer would also cause Sam Lord to get a heads-up. That was fine with Stanton. This was not Lord's jurisdiction. If he showed up, he would have to wait outside the greenhouse, just like anyone else who rented space on the *Empyrean*.

Like most of the crew, Stanton slept in his U-wear, underclothes made of antibacterial and odor-eliminating, antistatic and flame-retardant cotton and polyester. It did not have to be cleaned for at least two months despite constant wear, thus conserving resources. The commander hurriedly jumped into his trousers and pulled on his shirt, but not the rest of the uniform. He did not want any crew members to think that he was on duty and bring him small problems. Not when there was trouble in the Vault.

The low gravity of the radial arm allowed him to cross the room in a single, long-legged stride. After two additional steps he was out of the radial arm and into the main corridor of the residential wing. Three short elevator rides took him to the start of the green line that brought him to the Agro Center, which was located at the bottom of the *Empyrean*'s nearly five-hundred-foot-long central column, two levels below the Drum. In addition to growing an increasing percentage of the food consumed on the *Empyrean*, this was where water vapor and waste liquids were recycled.

The descent was slightly disorienting, not only because of the near zero gravity along the hub of the station—which required the use of handrails and artful stepping—but because the elevators generated their own slight but disorienting motion-induced gravity as they traveled. A passenger had simulated weight, then didn't, then did; that was the reality of movement throughout the *Empyrean*. It was also the reason the U-wear was waste-absorbent, since the body did not always react sympathetically to the more dramatic shifts elsewhere in the station.

The trip took nearly two minutes, during which Stanton tried to imagine what could be wrong with the project. Merlin was a prototype for one of the greatest undertakings in human history. If it had simply stopped growing, Liba would not have alerted the commander. He and Carter would have had to go back to the original design and find the problem.

There was a sudden sizzle in Stanton's audio feed.

"Liba, what was that?" Stanton asked.

Liba did not respond. Stanton accessed the station's eyes-only medical database. The man's vital signs showed up with a SimAI assessment: *Subject unconscious.*

Stanton reached the primary greenhouse; the door read his IC ID and popped open. The wave of humid heat washed over the commander as he shouldered his way in, the glass panel shutting behind him. He wiped his eyes with his fingertips as he looked around.

"Liba!" he shouted. Stanton's voice had a muted quality in the thick air, as though he were shouting into a quilt. The moisture-prismed sunlight was bright, almost blinding, and he walked tentatively through the mist-shrouded leaves toward the Vault. Halfway there, he shouted again.

Stanton did not hear Liba but he heard the sizzle again, much louder than the last time. Before making his way any farther he paused to send a message to his immediate subordinate, Mark Winters, leaving him in command until further notice. Then Stanton shut his IC entirely. It was strange to have no icons in his field of vision, not even the handful of emergency images, but if that sound had an electrical origin, then interaction with his IC could have been what took Liba down.

Stanton saw the deformed branch jutting through the top of the Vault before he saw Liba sprawled on his back among the cantaloupes below it. He took a moment to study the situation, watching as the limb expanded again, trembling faster than the eye could see and crackling audibly as it pushed through the sensor-impenetrable Faraday wall of the Vault. The branch stood some four feet above Liba's head. It was just two feet from the top of a dwarf coconut tree Liba had bred and five feet from the wall of the greenhouse.

Not a lot of room for continued expansion, he thought with rising horror.

The branch wasn't just replicating rapidly, it looked nothing like the slender structure that presumably still supported it inside the Vault.

Stanton absorbed all that in moments. He began moving toward Liba, sweeping his way with both arms through the tightly clustered vegetation. Arriving at the Agro officer's side, he bundled the light-weight man in his arms and hurried back to the door of the greenhouse. He was hoping the cooler air would revive him.

Dr. Carter was hurrying forward as they emerged.

"What happened?" the forty-six-year-old physician asked, immediately using his IC to scan Liba's vital signs.

"Merlin has sprouted some kind of deformity that's pushed through the Vault and is apparently causing electrical interference," Stanton answered as he lay Liba on the rubberized white flooring outside the greenhouse .

"A *deformity*?" Carter asked, bending over the agriculturalist. He began gently feeling for broken bones, looking for thermal blips indicating breaks in the skin, bleeding.

"Yeah. Grotesque looking, fast growing," Stanton told him. "When it replicated it sounded like someone was running lightning through a sieve."

"The growth itself was diffuse?" Carter asked, using his IC to scan Liba.

"I'm not sure if that's the word— "

"Like a little shot of static electricity? Not arcing anywhere, just . . . jagged?"

"Basically," Stanton said.

"That's a rending caused by the Vault wall being breached, most likely," the medic said.

"I figured, but how is that possible?" Stanton asked.

"I have no idea," Carter replied.

"Not what I was hoping for from the lead scientist on this project," Stanton said angrily.

"On this *experiment*," Carter reminded him. "I'll look when I'm done here."

As the doctor spoke, his narrow face was composed, his pale eyes moving in sync with the thermal, systolic, diastolic, and other medical data. Though Liba was unconscious, that did not stop his IC from transmitting.

Suddenly, Liba did stir, opened his eyes. He didn't seem startled, didn't recoil—suggesting that the last thing he saw was not an assault. This was an accident.

"I—*ow*," Liba said, reaching for his forehead. He winced when he moved his arm, pain snapping through his shoulder. He stopped moving and Carter helped him ease back down.

"Lancaster, do you know where you are?" Carter asked.

It took a moment for the man to answer. "I do, and also where I've been," Liba replied.

"Where?" Stanton asked.

"Damnedest set of particulars," he said, frowning as he thought back. "I was right under the limb when the hole in the Vault wall started screaming. *Screaming.* Knocked me on my ear. Maybe my IC transmitter overloaded and caused my brain to short."

"There would be a log of that," Carter said.

"Nah, I shut my IC off after calling you and the commander," Liba said. "He was annoying me."

Stanton took Carter by the arm and pulled him gently toward him. "How could he have heard screaming?" the commander asked. "He must have been hallucinating."

"Not necessarily," Carter said quietly, easing his arm free. "It could have been the nanites."

"How?" Stanton said. "They're not alive."

"There are nine thousand of them in the Vault," Carter said. "A significant number of them would have begun vibrating as the expanding branch carried them through the wall and the current passed over."

"Do I have to worry about them having migrated to Mr. Liba?" Stanton asked. "Was it reckless to go in?"

"They'll try to stay with the vine," Carter assured him. "That's what they're programmed to do."

" 'Trying' is not very reassuring," Stanton said.

"That's all I can give you right now," Carter said.

"Just want you to know, I heard that, Commander," Liba said. "I'm hurt, not deaf."

"I wasn't accusing you of a protocol violation," Stanton assured him with only partial conviction. "Just trying to establish threat parameters."

"Mr. Liba, do you have any digital tingling, fascillation?" the medic asked.

Liba just stared at him. "IC is off, Doc."

"Are there any unusual sensations, movement in your fingertips?" Carter asked.

"There's only good humus under my nails," Liba replied, winking his IC on.

"Heartbeat normal and I don't see any burns," Carter said, checking Liba's clothes and areas of exposed skin. "No apparent contusions."

"Maybe I got stunned smart," Liba said.

"*That* didn't happen," his parental IC informed him.

"Headache?" the medic asked.

"Unh-uh." Liba opened his eyes carefully. "But now that you mention it, I have light sensitivity too, Doc. You better have a look at the back of my head where—"

"You have a bump, that's all—no concussion. The light sensitivity is from waking in sunlight after having your eyes closed. What about neck pain? Nausea?"

"No and no," Liba replied. "I just went to sleep for a couple of minutes. The commander carried me out here—thanks, by the way."

"You're welcome," Stanton replied, still annoyed that security protocols had been ignored. Certain that secret information would no longer be discussed, the commander turned his IC back on and, after summoning the *Empyrean* EMTs, accessed the various surveillance positions inside the greenhouse. The branch seemed to just hang in the air, thrusting forward.

Just then, there was another static sound from inside the greenhouse that caused Liba to wince. Stanton rose and Carter's eyes shot toward the top of the greenhouse. The noise was followed by a loud cracking sound that was not electronic.

"That was my poor coconut tree," Liba said. "I know it."

"What the *hell* is that thing doing?" Carter wondered aloud, glancing up as he finished his examination.

"We're in trouble if you're asking that," Stanton said.

"Doc, can I get out of here?" Liba asked. "The sounds—PTSD."

Carter looked down at the man. The way he was looking at him made Liba feel very uneasy. It was almost like the doctor was a human MRI, scanning him from top to bottom.

"As soon as the team gets here, you can go," Carter said.

"What were you just looking for?" Liba asked.

Carter didn't answer. He raised his eyes and looked ahead.

"Commander, I'm going into the Vault," Carter said.

"If you think it's necessary," Stanton said. "And safe."

"It's the former," Carter said.

"All right," Stanton said. "Do you want anyone to go with you? If they've already got high-level clearance, I can give them a temporary bump—"

"What about me?" a smooth-as-cream voice asked.

As one, three sets of eyes shifted to a figure standing with his arms straight at his side, his legs slightly athwart, his sparkling gray eyes peering at them from under a swath of steel-wool hair. He was standing on the other end of the green line that helped visitors find their way to the Agro Center. The man was dressed in a collarless blue suit over a dark red tunic and retained the healthy suntan that had been burned into his flesh from decades spent walking across tarmacs around the globe.

Associate Deputy Director of Earth Operations Samuel Lord smiled as he came forward with a big, easy stride.

TWO

LIBA'S LEATHERY FACE scrunched out a smile. "Howdy, Director Lord," the botanist said.

"Hi, Lancaster," the Zero-G director replied, the smile drifting into a half-smile. "Hit your coconut on a coconut?"

Liba returned the grin. "What hokes me is the shell probably sustained more damage than me."

"Mr. Lord, if you'll excuse us, we have an emergency," Stanton said, turning toward the greenhouse.

"Of course," Lord said, but Stanton was already gone. Dr. Carter followed him, giving Lord a parting "be patient" look as the EMTs arrived. Lord acknowledged Carter's admonition with a nod then squatted beside Liba while the EMTs broke out a stabilizing gurney: canvas with a tight mesh cover and neck brace to keep patients fully immobilized as they moved through different pockets of gravity.

"What's going on?" Lord asked Liba quietly.

Liba motioned with a finger and Lord turned an ear to the man to hear the response.

"Merlin's gone haywire." The agricultural engineer whispered so the others wouldn't hear.

"In what way?"

"Growth . . . out of control."

"How is that possible?" Lord asked.

Liba shrugged and winced from the pain.

"Watch it," Lord said.

"Thanks," he said, relaxing. "To answer your question: I don't know. It popped the Vault, headed toward the greenhouse ceiling."

"I see."

Lord backed away as the EMTs went to work. He not only knew about the top-secret project, he knew it from Liba. Unknown to Stanton or anyone else at NASA, the agriculturalist—code-named the Gardener—was an FBI informant on the *Empyrean*. A former associate of FBI Prime Director Peter Al-Kazaz, Liba had worked closely with him during the Southwest Water Rebellion of 2024. On the *Empyrean*, because Liba was charged with overseeing the care of the planters scattered throughout the station, it was easy for him to linger, hover, and provide HUMINT—human intelligence—by eavesdropping on staff and visitors. Like pilots and waiters, gardeners were invisible to most people. If the function weren't entirely ethical, it was nonetheless essential. The politician Al-Kazaz, the environmentalist Liba, and the retired military man Lord all agreed that space should be protected from terrestrial squabbles by any means necessary.

"It will find its own unique troubles soon enough," the PD had cautioned Lord when the retired pilot accepted this post. It had taken all of two weeks for that to come true with the madness on the Chinese space station.

There was a crash of glass behind them as the tip of the branch cracked through the greenhouse wall. The pieces didn't shatter as they came loose but floated to the ground like falling leaves.

The EMTs looked over with alarm. Liba squinted out at the sun-bright exterior glass of the Agro Center. It was about ten feet from the tip of the branch.

The EMTs finished hurriedly and Lord motioned for them to wait a moment. They didn't answer to Lord but the two station workers respected his request. They stepped back again as Lord squatted beside his friend.

"Next stop, space," Liba rasped, "unless they take a chainsaw to that sucker. But even that might be like bailing a sinking boat."

"Can you at least describe what went wrong, Liba?" Lord asked quietly.

"Oh yeah," Liba said. "It's like a tumor just budded and went wild. Bad-wild," he added for emphasis.

"What was it doing? Thrusting? Whipping?"

"The first," Liba said. "Like a toe coming through a torn sock."

"Thanks." Lord smiled down at him and stood. "Remember when fabric tore?"

"I miss those days too," Liba said. His eyes were still narrowed as they looked Lord up and down. "Say, what are you all dressed for this time of night anyway?"

"I had a date," Lord replied.

"Truly?"

Lord nodded.

"I'd've guessed another newsia interview about how you thumped the *Jade Star*," Liba cracked.

"I do those to promote *our* work out here, *not* me," Lord said.

"Yeah, well, a lot of folks don't understand that," Liba said.

"I can't answer for them, only for me," Lord replied.

The Zero-G director gestured to the EMTs, who hoisted Liba up.

"You had a date," the Gardener said as the EMTs took him away. "Anybody I know?"

"Don't make a big thing of it," Lord said. "It was just an IC date with an old friend."

"Old? Do you mean 'former' or 'aged'?" Liba asked as he vanished along the green line. "With you, it could be both."

"With me, it *is* both," Lord said softly, wistfully.

A quiet settled briefly on the Agro Center, the kind of quiet to which one became accustomed in space: the localized background knocks and hisses of any enclosed system surrounded by the utter absence of environmental background noise. It wasn't the kind of muted embrace one experienced in a submarine or isolation tank, both of which Lord had experienced. It was infinitesimal sound and fury that eluded the senses, that existed on a plane life was unable to hear or see or process. Yet it was not nothingness, Lord knew. It was not the nonexistence that had existed in the instant before the Big Bang. It was the active, great mystery of the universe . . . the reason he was out here . . . to start to hear, to see, to learn.

The moment filled with fleet, disconnected impressions passed as Lord became aware of his own breath, his heartbeat, his life. Whatever insight, whatever grasp he thought he had, or was on the verge of having, evaporated.

He was back in the "now," where he was and where he had been just a few minutes before.

When he received the alert, Lord had been sitting in the *Empyrean*'s smallest, coziest bar, the Explorer, and he had literally lost track of time. The Explorer wasn't as busy as the big, central tavern, the Scrub; this one was exclusively for quiet virtual dates with loved ones at home. Lord wanted to catch up with General Erin Astoria, his last and brightest flame, on the occasion of her engagement to a small-town mayor. Their virtual goodbye was still very much on his mind minutes after she evaporated from her holoseat. It wasn't so much that Lord had wanted to marry her, or anyone; he'd done that once, raised some fine children with the woman, but ultimately the kids were all he and Consuela Lord had in common.

Still, the idea that this was "it" with him and Erin left Lord feeling a little raw. His relationship with Consuela, a meteorologist, had initially been mostly lust and infatuation. And Lord had enjoyed his recent time with Dr. Saranya May, who was stationed on the moon. But neither of those women, or any others, had the common language he and Erin shared. The fact that she would only be a platonic friend going forward made his uniform feel less like a bond and more like something that was just holding him together.

What a piece of work is a man, he thought with a self-deprecating nod to Shakespeare. To go from cosmic philosopher to wounded lover in the space of seconds.

Apprehension followed as the rogue limb splintered again, thrusting forward amid the self-generated green cloud. It was a large surge, cutting in half the distance between it and the exterior pane. Lord stood on the opposite end of the green line that helped newcomers find their way through Argo, looking up at the branch, a hybrid fist of carbon in what looked like a parody of tree bark. He hoped Carter and Stanton had a plan. The SRO had already punched through two barriers, the Vault and the greenhouse. This last one, the Agro Center itself, was the strongest constructed of cyanine-derived organic salts with a thin coating of transparent protective polycrystalline. The entire structure was four inches thick, as was the one beyond; the fact that the structure kept space out did not mean the window was impenetrable.

The feeling he had now was just like the old days in the ready room: stand down until you're told otherwise or find yourself under attack. Lord's eyes drifted to the greenhouse. He could make a case for possessing the emergency authority to go inside and forcibly involve himself— only the Vault was off-limits—but that might be counter-productive at the moment. He didn't want to intrude on Stanton's territory any more than he already had.

That was when he heard a sharp crack from against the inside glass of the Agro Center, almost like a rifle shot. His eyes snapped up. The forked branch had not penetrated the pane but the top finger had cracked the thin UV filter that coated the interior. This development was not good. If the windows themselves were breached, the area would decompress. Though airtight walls would slam down—hence the name "Slammers"—he and his subordinate Dr. Carter were now potentially in danger. He had the authority and obligation to get involved.

Lord's IC opened the greenhouse door and he eased inside, the panel shutting softly behind him. He unbuttoned the collar of his uniform as he moved through the damp heat. Despite the humid blanket of air that dulled sound, he could hear Stanton and Carter conversing—loudly.

"... not my call," Lord heard Stanton say.

"It *has* to be," Carter replied. He pointed up at the break in the greenhouse and the branch pressing on the glass that stood between the *Empyrean* and the void of space. "That limb is not going to stay bent against the glass forever."

"It may grow down from there," Stanton said. "We don't know. *You* don't know."

"I'm telling you, it won't," Carter said. "The nanites won't *let* it."

"Doctor, you are outside the secure zone."

Carter held up his hands in apology.

"Further," Stanton continued, "you have *no* idea what this thing will do, you said so yourself. You can't talk to it. The thing is running its own plays for whatever reason. You're not even sure you can shut it down."

"Maybe not the ordinary way, no, since I don't know what's happened to them," Carter admitted. "But if I hit the kill switch, the nanites—and therefore, I expect, the tree—will go to sleep."

"You 'expect,'" Stanton said. "Not reassuring."

"That's why this is called an 'experiment,'" Carter said.

"I've signaled NASA," Stanton said. "That's all I can do."

"No, you can pulse the Vault interior," Carter implored. "A limited electromagnetic burst in the station *is* within your jurisdiction. They will stop."

"So will the systems in this section of the station," Stanton said.

"IC says that's a sixty-forty likelihood," Carter replied. "The glass breaking in the next quarter hour or so is worse and far more likely."

"*That* can be contained," Stanton replied.

"With the loss of our food supply, water recycling, and other facilities," Carter said.

"I didn't say it was *good*, I said it was *better*," Stanton answered. "You send an EMP through Agro, breakers will kick in and the NASA manual says we go dark. There is *no* simulation that gets us up-and-running again before we freeze and/or suffocate."

Carter was shaking his head. "If I can shut one down and do a postmortem, that may enable me to fix the others and start them up again."

"No responsible course of action begins with 'if' and 'may,'" Stanton said. "NASA has been notified and we will await instructions."

Lord crossed the studded rubber walkway that ran through the foliage. "Forget NASA and your little robotic ant farm," Lord said. "What would it take to shut the branch down, Doctor?"

"Not your concern," Stanton replied angrily. "And how do *you* know what this is, anyway?"

Lord shrugged. "If it acts like an SRO, chances are it *is* an SRO."

"Why don't you go back to whatever you were doing?" Stanton said.

Carter stepped between them, facing Stanton. "Commander, please just listen. The best option is I hit a kill switch and the nanites instantly go silent. I reverse the switch, they come back. We buy time and NASA still has veto power."

"That will be all, Carter!" Stanton said.

Lord nodded. "Carlton, I suggest we allow Commander Stanton to wait for his response."

The doctor turned. "Sam?"

"It's his command, Doctor."

Carter was openly surprised by Lord's response. The Zero-G director was not known for his patience with bureaucracy.

The branch surged again, only this time in three directions: the arm thrust forward, deeper into the coating, while two fingers stretched out through a fresh green mist, up and down.

Carter was more agitated than Lord had ever seen him.

"Commander Stanton," the doctor implored, "Merlin has mutated for some reason but it's following the original—"

"Doctor!" Stanton roared. "*Everything* about this project is classified!"

Lord's hands opened compassionately. "Commander—Curtis—I can *see* what's happening. But we seem to have one advantage."

"What's that?" Carter asked.

"The limb doesn't have intelligence, just mechanical symbionts," Lord pointed out. "For some reason the experiment has jumped its parameters and is aggressively moving toward the gravity center of the station."

"All the foliage in here does that," Carter said.

"Yes, but this one is doing a 'Davy Crockett,'" Lord said to blank looks. It was an intentional ploy: he wanted them to slow down, listen, think. "The limb has adopted the same basic tripod configuration as the recoilless gun the United States deployed during the late 1950s to fire tiny nukes," Lord went on. He wagged a finger at the broken greenhouse glass. "Your tree is literally branching out to brace itself for a big push and—I suspect—is in the process of reinforcing those fingers to support that thrust."

Stanton's eyes were fixed sharply on Lord. Carter said nothing. The medic merely confirmed the gist of what the Zero-G chief had said with an expression of quiet respect.

"You are very observant, Director Lord," Stanton replied. His eyes shifted between the men. "Please wait outside the greenhouse, both of you. I will let you know when I have my instructions."

Carter hesitated. He did not report to Stanton, but Lord gave him a look and he complied. Lord regarded the station commander a moment longer then he turned as well. Lord couldn't tell if it was mist, perspiration, or both on the man's forehead and cheekbones. Lord had done his homework, he knew that Stanton was more than a capable leader—cautious but not indecisive. When his convoy came under sniper fire in the jungles of Xalapa, Mexico, during the War on Narcotics, Stanton famously led a patrol that jumped into the fast-flowing Filobobos River, got behind the shooters, and picked them off. The Dragon's Eye mission had immobilized the man.

It would do that to anyone, Lord thought.

But that was as far as Lord's charity extended. Being fearful of responsibility—a natural post-traumatic response—was not the correct response.

Lord turned and joined Carter. As the men emerged in the white corridor outside the greenhouse, the air crackled again and Lord jabbed off his IC lest he end up like Liba. They did not have to look back through the shattered glass to know that the fingers were thickening and the central branch was expanding outward.

They stopped just outside the greenhouse door.

"Why didn't you back me in there?" Carter asked.

"It wouldn't have helped," Lord said. "What are your thoughts on what *can* be done? Or more important, what's gone wrong."

"Like I told Stanton, I just don't know," Carter said, scrolling through his IC. "I don't even know where to start. To replicate bio-cybernetic material this fast, the nanites have to be transcending their program by a factor of tens of thousands."

"So they were reprogrammed."

"Clearly," Carter said. "But I'll be damned if I know how."

"Intentionally?"

Carter shrugged.

Lord was surprised at how little Carter knew about his own creation. But then he thought back to all the test planes he'd flown. Often, aeronautical engineers didn't know why a subtle result or effect happened until they reverse-engineered the data.

"Where are they getting the raw material to build?" Lord asked.

"From the soil, the air, everywhere, as they were designed to do," he said. "Other plants—I saw a few that looked like they were being drained of key elements. Sam, these things are the smallest factories ever built. And judging from the growth rate of that . . . that *thing* in there, the increased productivity in those factories is becoming exponential."

"A Marxist's dream," Lord said.

"All I know is what's obvious," Carter said. "We have to shut them down."

"If they are not shut down, I assume the branch will just grow again if we cut it," Lord said.

"It appears the mutation is systemic, so, yes," Carter replied. "It no longer has a top but a direction. And we don't know if the severed section will keep growing independent of the rest."

"The Sorcerer's Apprentice," Lord said.

"What?"

"The old story about the enchanted broomstick that gets axed to splinters and each one of them comes to life," Lord said. "What if we get a tether around the branch and lash it to the stalk?"

"The nose of the limb will turn outward again pretty quick," Carter told him. "What you said before—a small correction."

"What do you mean?"

"That branch probably isn't headed toward the gravitational center of the station, Sam."

"No? Where is it going?" Lord asked.

"Where the much slower-growing tree, the *original* experiment, was designed to go," Carter said ominously. "Into space. And then toward Earth."

Lord flicked a finger to turn his IC back on. It took only a moment for the implication to sink in, as Lord's SimAI helpfully offered a motion visual of a nonclassified Jet Propulsion Laboratory holostudy of a living space elevator. It was three years old and showed a theoretical vine stretching from a not-yet-completed *Empyrean* to the upper atmosphere. Passenger buses rode the vine from hyperplanes that flew to the stratosphere.

Lord shut the video. He stood in the cooler air of the corridor facing the biophysicist.

"You've got to do something, Sam," Carter said.

"Me?" Lord said.

"You've got vocal, public support because of the *Jade Star*."

"What you're saying is I could survive a full-frontal attack," Lord said.

"We don't have a lot of time to let this play out," Carter said.

"No," Lord replied.

"Which part are you 'no'-ing?" Carter asked. "That we don't have a lot of time or that we shouldn't intervene?"

"The latter," Lord said. "It's not our mission yet. If we're attacked, that changes."

"Did you not see what happened? An attack by attrition will likely destroy the Agro Center," Carter warned.

"I'm very aware of that," Lord replied calmly, "which is why I need to understand the enemy. Do the nanites have SimAI?"

With open, visible impatience, Carter settled into a professorial mode. "No. They're programmed to do a task. A complex task, but they can't simply 'decide' to change that."

"So the task was changed *for* them? So we're back to—was it done intentionally? Remotely?"

"Possibly the former; the latter—very unlikely," Carter said. "Especially with the security system of the Vault." He went silent for a long, thoughtful moment. "You know, it's also likely that local impurities somehow affected their operating matrices."

"What kind of impurities?"

"Very small particles, not more than one hundred nanometers in diameter, or else something gaseous," Carter said. "These nanites are externally hardy but internally very delicate little robots. The tree is designed to provide a protective staging area as well as access to elements from their own environment. The nanites process those into new cells and guide them into position."

"So the tree or the nanites could've eaten something they weren't supposed to," Lord said.

"In a manner of speaking," Carter said. "My concern is that NASA will treat this like a scientific crime scene. They'll want to lock everything in place by hibernating the entire tree."

"What's wrong with that?"

"The farther we get from the precipitating biomechanical incident, the colder the trail," Carter said. "We need to see what the tree itself may be doing, which requires it to be active at a cellular level."

The men fell silent as Stanton emerged from the greenhouse.

"They want us to freeze the limb," Stanton said.

Carter shook his head. "That is *exactly* the stupid idea I was expecting," he said.

"Well, at least someone decided quickly," Lord remarked.

"What's wrong with the plan?" Stanton asked. He had looked as if he wanted to bark something back but thought better of it.

"The nanites are designed to function perfectly in the -450 Fahrenheit conditions of space," Carter replied, ignoring Stanton, who was practically snarling at another breach in security. "You *can't* freeze them."

"A block of CO_2," Stanton said.

"Dry ice?" Lord asked.

The commander was reading from his eyes-only IC feed now. "NASA says that that composition should lock everything in place, hibernate the thing."

Lord felt a chill hearing the words Carter had just warned him against.

"God help us from people who just know a little about a lot," Carter said. "Commander, it won't work."

"Why?" A flick of Stanton's eyes showed that he was having Carter's response transcribed and sent to Houston.

"The nanites have a sublimation function, to protect themselves from the cold of space," Carter said. "They will turn that dry ice back to gas and we may all end up with hypercapnia—too much CO_2 in the lungs. It'll probably kill everything in the greenhouse *except* the SRO!"

"NASA says the Vault will contain the release," Stanton said, continuing to read from the top-secret encoded IC feed. "They just ran the simulation."

"But the wall has been breached," Carter pointed out.

"Their top scientists believe the entire tree will hibernate, including the section outside," Stanton said. "It can then be broken off, like an icicle."

"Commander," Lord said, " 'believe' is on par with 'if' and 'may.' "

Stanton appeared undaunted. "Houston is sending settings so the electromagnetism will enhance the greenhouse effect inside, raising the CO_2 levels as high as we need."

"That will take more time than we have," Carter said thickly. "Commander, you're refusing to hear me—"

"I hear you perfectly, Doctor, but it is *not* our call."

The laminate on the window cracked again as Stanton was speaking.

"There's no time for this," Stanton said urgently. "We have to make this happen."

The commander went on his IC and ordered the station's stores of CO_2 brought to the greenhouse, then woke Assistant Agricultural Officer Douglas Cameron and told him to report to the Agro Center control closet at once.

As Stanton was finishing his IC communication, the window of the space station cracked harder than before. Three sets of eyes turned upward as the jagged break spread across the door-size pane.

"You've got about three minutes to the next surge," Carter said. "The branch cannot be frozen in that time."

Lord's eyes snapped to Stanton. The Zero-G man did not have to say anything. His stern but encouraging expression said it all.

"Doctor, kill the nanites," Stanton said with quiet authority. "Immediately."

Carter's eyes moved in his IC. His cloud was not linked to the nanites directly but to the solar generator that remotely fueled their batteries. The power cells were not built to retain energy; cutting the signal was designed to stop the experimental technology in under a second.

It did not.

"What's wrong?" Lord asked, reading Carter's expression.

"I can't believe it," Carter said. "They appear to be drawing their

instructions *from* the Vault. My access is being rerouted there and . . .
stopped!"

"How?" Stanton said. "Is there someone inside?"

"No, there must be a cluster of nanites working as some kind of ad
hoc central processing unit."

Even before Carter made the announcement, Stanton was back on
the IC link to the assistant agricultural director.

"Mr. Cameron, prepare to seal the Agro Center for imminent
breach," he said. "Lord, Carter, evac at once. Mr. Winters?"

"Sir?" said the *Empyrean*'s second-in-command.

"Initiate Vault Shutdown Protocol at once."

"Confirming Vault Shutdown Protocol."

"At once," Stanton replied.

Lord checked his FBI eyes-only IC. That procedure would take at
least ten minutes. It wasn't just a matter of cutting the power: as a fail-
safe, the Vault was linked to the *Empyrean* grid. The secure area could
not be turned off without shutting down the entire station. It would
have to be isolated and then depowered.

Lord was staring at the glass and at the cosmos beyond. "Doctor,
why is the branch headed to that part of space?"

"Shortest distance to its programmed target."

"Lord, get out of this sector now!" Stanton ordered.

The Zero-G director ignored the commander. "Shortest distance
based on what data, Doctor? What are the nanites reading?"

Carter was about to answer when he suddenly brightened. "Yes.
Yes. They're using visual references triangulated through the computer
link they still share with my database," the scientist said, his eyes already
shifting around his IC. "Absolutely, *that* can be shut down!"

"What can be shut?" Stanton asked.

"My computer, which is where they're getting their directional
coordinates," Carter said. He killed the connection, shutting down
the nanite guidance system. The branch did not stop moving—but it
stopped thrusting forward. Its next move, which came just over thirty

seconds later, was now perpendicular, toward the gravity center of the station.

"Damn," Carter said, exhaling loudly. "I've got to reestablish control. Sam—you just bought us the time we needed."

The three men didn't realize how tense they were until they suddenly relaxed.

Stanton's eyes were on Carter. "Do we still need the Vault shutdown?"

"Yes, sir. I have to get inside to turn off whatever neo-brain is operating inside. But we can scale back the time frame. We have at least twenty minutes before the branch reaches the floor."

Stanton nodded. "Cameron, stand down on the seal-off, get yourself in here at once." He moved his eyes to another icon in his emergency response file. "Chief Engineer Archer, we need a repair team in the Agro Center now."

"Yes, sir," Judy Archer replied.

Stanton stood tall, as he always did, it was in his DNA; but he seemed to have deflated somewhere behind his eyes. Lord noticed and hurt even more for the man.

Stanton finished giving instructions to the team then turned to Lord.

"Thank you, Sam," the commander said.

"I just stumbled into that one, Curtis," Lord replied casually. "It's like the SimAI self-guidance software in the last Vampire I flew for the air force. That's the only reason it occurred to me."

"You're being uncommonly modest," Stanton said. "But nonetheless, I'm glad it did."

The two men stood facing each other for what seemed a very long time. Carter was forgotten until he turned to go.

"I'm going to have a chat with the nanites," the biophysicist said. "I'll keep you apprised, Commander."

Stanton nodded in acknowledgment then turned to Lord. "You should leave too. It's not safe here.

"At once," Lord said.

Lord started off but Stanton stopped him, grabbing his elbow. "I appreciate what you just did. I truly do."

"I was doing my duty."

"If you say so," Stanton went on. "But I also don't appreciate what you've *been* doing."

"Oh? And what have I been doing?" Lord asked.

"Wake-riding," Stanton said. Wake-riding was a military term coined in 2033 to describe the free ride Remora missiles took on airborne targets by feeding on the chemical residue in their vapor trails. "You always seem to be there, right behind me, whenever I screw up."

"These *are* relatively close quarters," Lord pointed out.

"I never see Adsila Water or Janet Grainger on my tail."

"They like the comm. That's their post. I've always been free-range. Blue skies, open air, all of it. Comes from growing up in a dark Hell's Kitchen walk-up."

"Yes, I've seen the interviews you've given, heard the glib patter," Stanton said. "I just don't believe you're *that* self-possessed."

"Well, it's true," Lord replied. "You're also not eighty. The world—the universe—seem more joyous than grave, even in their darkest aspects. That's what you see in me."

"Optimism?"

Lord shut his eyes and nodded.

The emergency repair team had arrived, along with Douglas Cameron. Lord stepped aside so Stanton could give them their instructions before following them toward the glass wall of the Agro Center.

"To be continued," Stanton said as he turned to go.

Now it was Lord's turn to take his arm. He regarded the commander without reproach. "Curtis, this is a giant job you're doing. First time in history anyone's tried it, so go easy on yourself—and on the rest of us. We really are only trying to help."

Stanton regarded him sharply. "To be continued," he repeated as he followed his team.

THREE

ERO-G ASSOCIATE DEPUTY Director Adsila Waters awoke with a smile. She had had the dream, again, for the fifth time since she had been on the *Empyrean*: the one where she was an owl-winged cougar rising, diving, gliding low over mountain and cloud, utterly free. The dream faded quickly but the smile lasted; she was that wondrous chimera, the glorious, soaring hybrid.

She lay there, allowing her human body to embrace its own "wings" in the just-over half-gravity of her quarters in Radial Arm Six. It was never truly quiet here, with walls and doors made of lightweight alloys that were cost-efficient to launch into space but not soundproofed. For that, occupants relied on Ineffs: Interceptor Filters built into the IC that snagged and eliminated sounds as they entered the ear. Only pre-programmed noises were admitted, like automated alerts or the voices of key personnel such as the Zero-G team and Commander Stanton.

There were no urgent calls, so there was no rush to get up and she reveled in her dream-state return to Earth.

Adsila's family elders had always told her that skin walking was not a Cherokee tradition, that assuming animal form belonged to the Navajo, the Hopi, others. Yet whenever they would go into the woods to camp, the night skies would cause the young girl to channel the spirit of her animal-sister, Tivdatsi. She would feel compelled to move on all fours, to hold her head low, bobbing, to seek out the small and helpless.

Over his pipe, her father once told her, *"The cougar and the owl are special as you are special. Of all the animals, only they remained awake to witness the Creation of all things."* Then he blew smoke and stared into it and said, *"One day you will take wing."*

Adsila had never been guided by his prophesy, not to the point of seeking this career on board the *Empyrean*. But when it was offered to her, she was neither surprised nor hesitant.

If only it were not eternal night in space, and the Wahuhu-Tivdatsi could rest, she thought.

The urge to fly and hunt was strong. She did both now, every day, but differently than any Native American who had ever come before her. The dream seemed to encourage her to look back. In addition to expressing her own nature—her own duality as a pangender—Adsila believed that the dream had to do with renewal, a way of plugging into her roots in the family's native Oklahoma.

And the precious elements you left behind, she reminded herself. Earth, fire, water, air.

Except in dreams and an occasional, off-duty hallucinogenic indulgence of a cannabis-mushroom blend in the Scrub, up here the spirit of the great open plains was nowhere in evidence. The canned, recycled air tasted even dryer than the winds that blew across those great expanses. It wasn't pleasant, though after some initial raspiness she had gotten used to it. The nights were never peaceful, punctuated by the systemic noises of the *Empyrean* fine-tuning its orbit or the frequent stumble of someone outside her cabin door trying to negotiate the awkward gravity; though in that respect the room wasn't much different from the noises at her Rhode Island Avenue NW apartment in Washington, DC, where she worked for the Data Intercept Technology Unit at Hoover Command in Washington before being sent up here.

Her reverie did not last long. Awake and alert, and having given the spiritual experience all the conscious analysis she cared to apply, the twenty-eight-year-old did not like being away from the Zero-G Command center in Radial Arm Two, with its friendly but dignified camaraderie and comfortable, Earth-like microgravity. There, her IC was hijacked, on full alert, plugged into the known universe. In her cabin, she was lo-jacked and alone. The Waters family was very closely bonded; "alone" was not a state Adsila enjoyed.

It was still early, though. No one would be at the command center. She *should* try to rest a little longer. Given her job, there was no telling when a crisis could emerge that would keep her awake through several sleep periods.

The pangender tried switching to her male form. Occasionally, the chemical alteration from one sex to the other released tension and relaxed her. The shape-shifting fluids and differently firing chemicals effected the switch within seconds; all they did was change how the blanket held him in place, and its casein adhesive fabric adjusted its self-knit function to the form-fitting mattress. Adsila did, however, smile when he thought about how his great-uncle Diwali was about to sell a large herd of cows a dozen years before, in 2038, due to the rise in the use of hemp milk. That was when DowMont Chemicals found a way to create the self-sealing formula using milk protein. There were jokes about clothing "made of cheese" and how it would overtax the functions of deodorant, but the odor-causing chemicals were baked away, leaving only the casein. Diwali became wealthy and it was he who gave Adsila the gold milk bucket he used as a planter for his lilacs. His great-uncle had paid a small fortune to send the memento into space. Engraved on the inside lip was: *Trust the universe: it will show the way.*

Shifting back to female, her dominant form, Adsila glanced at her IC clock in the far right bottom of her vision. It was the equivalent of 2 a.m., Earth Time. Clocks on *Empyrean* were set to Central Standard Time on Earth; for NASA's Johnson Spacecraft Center *Empyrean* Command, based in Houston. Biorhythms were balanced by using blackout shades to keep out the constantly blazing sun, or by having no windows whatsoever in all-hours places like the Scrub and the athletic center.

It was no use trying to sleep, so she dressed and headed to the Zero-G Command Center. When the team first arrived at the *Empyrean*, Adsila's subordinate, Janet Grainger—the associate executive assistant director and Zero-G communications director—had asked Lord why they needed a physical comm at all, since the facility was vacant an average of four hours a day and she had found a way to securely divert alerts directly to their ICs.

"Because teamwork is about more than a joint response to crisis," Lord had replied. "It is about knowing the habits, likes, and strengths of your comrades-in-arms."

They had all seen those qualities in their first serious challenge. Perhaps, without his colleagues united in the comm, Special Agent Ed McClure of the Laboratory and Space Science Division would not have found the added resolve he needed when he was stranded in space. Perhaps their tech agent, Michael Abernathy, would not have engaged heart and soul with mind to find his solutions to logistical problems. The long history of her own Cherokee people was rich with both strengthening the skills of the individual and then melding them with the abilities of others.

Adsila strode down the corridor in broad, vaulting steps. The ninety-two-second elevator ride carried her four levels to Radial Arm Two. She made the trip in the company of Stephen, a young bartender at the popular Scrub. He was just coming off his shift and had the contented look of someone who had taken a long dissolve on a roomer, a tablet made from a genetically modified, mood-anesthetizing mushroom grown in the Agro Center. Unlike hallucinogenic mushrooms, there was no physical or spatial disorientation. Just bliss. He looked at her and smiled.

"Perk of the job," he said knowingly.

The Scrub was a close-quarters, highly stressful place and interacting with a challenged, disoriented public was a difficult task—especially

when supplies were scarce and VIPs were always expecting him to reserve them something choice. She nodded back but let him have his
moment without conversation.

The *Empyrean*'s small, windowless command center, officially
known as the FBI Off-Earth Investigative and Intelligence Unit, was
more familiarly known by the designation Zero-G—a somewhat cheeky
reference to the old slang "G-men" for FBI agents. Adsila's post was by
the door, facing in. Here she could observe the others and, even more
important, could see the 1/100th-size, transparent, 3-D projection of
the space station. Lord had insisted that there be a communal view,
since he found the "dollhouse" views in their linked ICs uninvolving
and trivial. The private and public sectors were clearly marked, as were
the shuttles coming and going from Earth and the moon. Privacy laws
forbade them from constantly tracking staff or visitors to the station,
but they were allowed to access security scanners as a situation dictated.
There were more than three hundred of them on the *Empyrean* and they
appeared as red dots.

Except for "night" shift personnel—the word had little meaning
up here, since it was based on a clock and not an environment—very
few people were to be found at this hour along the route to the comm.
Most nights, Adsila would come upon Lancaster Liba tending to his
planters and they would exchange a few courteous words. He seemed
to sleep even less than she did. There was a familiar, comforting quality to his earthiness; up here, that quality took on special significance.
She wondered how soon it would be before people who grew things
in space had not been born on Earth, never even visited the home
world.

But Liba was not around. Adsila's IC immediately connected with
the Zero-G comm and the door slid open to admit her. She instantly
accessed all the terrestrial observation links.

Adsila watched all the updates from the *Empyrean* and from
HooverComm. She saw at once why Liba was not making his usual
rounds. There had been some kind of emergency in the Agro Center,

but it was being handled by the *Empyrean* staff and Dr. Carter. There were no further details, other than an *Empyrean* medbay report that Liba was in quarantine. There was no further explanation. Adsila wouldn't bother asking Carter. Though he was a member of the Zero-G team, the biophysicist was also engaged in outside research that was off-limits even to Sam Lord. Some of that work, involving nanites, had recently helped to protect Adsila from a microbot infestation. She noticed in the log that Director Lord had gone to Agro but had not filed a report.

Of course he didn't, she thought. Like the fighter pilot he had been, Sam Lord simply left his handwriting across the heavens, like a contrail, where it could be read by all.

Adsila turned her attention to matters over which she had some jurisdiction.

The world below the *Empyrean* was relatively quiet. The disaster in Japan had inflicted a calming effect on strife zones and finance, had stirred up the climate in such a way that no one was sure, yet, where it would come to rest. There were early murmurs that the massive destruction in Asia, including changes to the Japanese coastline, had created permanent shifts in ocean and air currents. It had already caused hundreds of dead whales, porpoises, and other marine creatures to wash ashore all over the Pacific. Navies were too busy with cleanup to threaten one another.

Awful as it all was, Adsila seemed strangely disattached from events on Earth.

Is this how it starts? the woman asked herself. *Loyalty to a new home? You disengage from the old one, become increasingly fond of the new one, and finally there is a tipping point—*

The Outer Limits Array pinged. Adsila read the report. The geostationary satellite ring was located nearly forty thousand kilometers above the Earth's surface and had been designed to watch for incoming asteroids and other massive deep-space objects. It had detected an unscheduled rocket departure *from* high Earth orbit into the solar system.

The only indication of the launch was a reflection in the atmosphere, like a flashing pebble entering a pond and then vanishing. A Stealth Signature Flare—a pixel-blinding digital flash, invisible to the eye—obscured the object and its rocket throughout the burn. Its trajectory could not be determined from the launch, other than that it was headed toward the inner solar system. That much the OLA was able to determine from the direction of the atmospheric reflection.

The only launch-capable facilities in that region were the *Empyrean*; the largely disabled Chinese space station *Jade Star*; and *Red Giant*, the former International Space Station now owned and operated by Moscow. Except for a dozen or so severely dated missiles, the Russians had nothing onboard that was known to be spaceworthy. The operative term in this case was *known*. During his final years in office, when Americans no longer needed Russian spacecraft to ferry them aloft, Vladimir Putin had thrown a Cold War–style cloak of secrecy around all space endeavors. NASA and Department of Defense intelligence agencies were convinced it was to hide the fact that the nearly bankrupt nation was doing nothing other than routine maneuvers in Earth orbit.

"Can you provide further information about object OLA-305?" she asked her SimAI.

"That information is not available," the neutral male voice told her.

" 'Not available' or eyes-only?" she asked.

"Not available."

"Has OLA or any other entity recorded other launches from this location?"

"Yes," the SimAI replied. "Thirteen."

"Since what date?"

"September 14, 2048."

"Recorded by whom?"

"NASA, the Chinese National Space Administration, Armstrong Base, and at least four independent telescopic installations, all of them amateur."

"And we knew nothing?" she said, amazed.

"We didn't ask."

"What can you tell me by collating information from these other sources?" Adsila asked.

"None of the launches went to the moon since the SSF could not have obscured a landing or crash," the SimAI said. "None of the launches orbited the Earth since celestial displacement and obscuring would have been noted. They had to have left the translunar region."

"Were any of the launch observations planned or were they accidental?" Adsila asked.

"Unknown."

That was naggingly little information for the FBI to possess about a total of sixteen launches from off-Earth into space.

"Specificity on my eyes-only question," Adsila said. "Is there any file marked confidential or top security that *might* pertain to these launches?"

"The space kite reported seeing a UFO visually, not on instrument, correlating to launch number eleven," the IC replied. "That report is sealed but not yet closed. Eighty-three percent likely overlap."

"Who is investigating?"

"The UATB," it replied.

Adsila frowned. The Upper Atmosphere Transportation Board was essentially a corrupt, bribe-run licensing bureau for the operators of private space kites and hyperplanes. As long as the mysterious projectile or object did not intrude in its suborbital space, into its "lanes," then the "Bored"—as it was euphemistically called—would not expend very many resources investigating. For all she knew, they were paid *not* to look into it.

Adsila sent the file to Lord—not that he would necessarily read it. Her superior entertained hard targets, hard objectives. He was not a man who bothered with "what ifs" and "maybes." He told her he had never liked writing white papers, since it was impossible to anticipate every nuance of every threat. He much preferred for himself and his people to be well trained and able to react to events.

"I am guessing," a voice sounded in her ear, "that the Russians are firing their old Scud Fs."

It was Sam Lord, either up uncharacteristically early or else he had found a way to inhabit her mind and thoughts.

"Director Lord," Adsila said with surprise. "Where are you?"

"Right here."

A door opened in the rear of the comm. That door was the sole access to the LOO—the Lord Only Office—the director's tiny private space. It was the size of a closet and held a chair, a low hoverlight that floated in the microgravity, and absolute silence. The LOO was the only place on the *Empyrean* where communications were not just secure, they could survive an electromagnetic pulse or a solar flare. Before the FBI came to *Empyrean*, it was designed to be the station commander's "panic room" in the event of a catastrophic emergency.

Lord came out slowly, like the moon emerging from eclipse. "We had a little problem in the Agro Center, as I'm sure you saw."

"There were no details, just the 'all clear,'" she said. "Is there anything I should know?"

"It's a secret NASA project," Lord replied. "I came here to call down and wake up PD Al-Kazaz. I have to brief him, since Dr. Carter is involved. Not that he or I had much to contribute. As for the launches, the Russians have—or had—sixteen Scuds that had been sent up to threaten Armstrong Base if we went military on the moon."

"Those were designated as military—" she began, then stopped. That's why they weren't showing up in her IC. Those fell under Department of Defense jurisdiction, not as eyes-only but as FBI "non-jurisdictional."

"Two of those Russian missiles exploded minutes after firing," Lord said, "and there have now been a total of sixteen launches that fit the general Scud profile. My guess is that the Kremlin is using them for something else."

"Solar research?" Adsila asked. It was an area of increasing interest on Earth, ever since several severe solar flares in 2047 had threatened communications networks in space.

"Possibly," Lord said as he quickly read through the file Adsila had sent. "But then why would even the Russian government have suppressed information about the launches? And why send all the rockets, retaining none for their original purpose?"

"New Russian leadership between then and now," she suggested.

"A good guess," he said, with an emphasis on *guess*.

"Right," Adsila agreed. "Should we investigate? It's a little out of the Zero-G orbit—"

"Not if we relabel it a potential threat to the *Empyrean* from a foreign nation," Lord said with a crooked smile. "Secretive enemies are always presumed guilty until proven innocent."

"I'll check the amateur astronomers at 2Ms," she said, referring to the Maxim Mirrors. "They noted four of the launches."

Mirrors were the heirs of blogs and tweets, virtual recordings of everything that happened in people's personal or professional lives, sometimes both. Algorithms automatically bunched them together in percentage-based matches, creating Maxims: hall after hall of synergistic Mirrors for like-minded voyeurs.

Lord reached Adsila's desk. They both stood beside it, the director looking directly at her while she initiated the 2M search.

"Now tell me, EAD—why are *you* here?" he asked. "Dreams still waking you?"

The woman looked past him at the empty comm. She wasn't surprised that he knew; Dr. Carter was obligated to file health status reports with the director. But it was nonetheless slightly embarrassing to someone as private as Adsila.

"My dreams are elusive, they do not surrender to study," she told him. "I am very comfortable when I'm at my post."

"You like puzzles for which there are concrete solutions," he said. "I understand that. You're much more relaxed when you're on duty than when you're trying to relax."

Adsila looked back at Lord and he noticed her eyes look him down, then up. He was puzzled at first and then he understood.

"My attire?" he asked.

"Puzzling," she said. "Not your usual comm wear. Special assignment?"

"I didn't put on a dress uniform to go to Agro, no," he said. "I was talking to a dear old friend when duty beckoned."

"I see," she replied, without probing. "I'm glad you were relaxing, sir."

"It wasn't quite that," Lord said. "She's getting married. This was goodbye."

"Oh. I'm sorry, sir. I didn't mean to intrude—"

"That's all right. You're young. You should learn from my mistakes," Lord told her. "The truth is, I'm the one who is sorry. She was mine to lose, and I did. Grandly. Red," he addressed his SimAI, "you were eavesdropping back there—"

"I was recording at your request, Sam."

Red was named for Elsa "Red" Wayne, Lord's devoted wingman who saved him from a Lanza missile in the Battle of Vera Cruz during the War on Narcotics. Lord had very recently found a declassified recording of her cockpit-to-ground communications from the day his fire-haired colleague died, testing a Berylline ultrasonic aircraft. After reflection—sorting through the pros and cons of bringing her back "to life"—he had ordered his SimAI to replicate it. That included the backtalk she occasionally gave her superior cockpit-to-cockpit.

Lord ignored the rebuke. "What's the best quote to describe what happened with Erin? Please share it with the EAD."

The SimAI replied with a crackle in her voice, "George Eliot wrote, 'Only in the agony of parting do we look into the depths of love.'"

Lord considered that. "A little strong, but I accept it," he said.

"And to accuratize the record, now that it has been entered into the comm log," Red went on, "you ordered me to record the parting with General Astoria, in contradiction of General Surveillance Order 732:915."

"Delete from log," Lord ordered.

"That is against—"

"Command code Alpha January three-five."

"Log deletion confirmation," Red replied. Coldly, Lord could swear.

Lord regarded Adsila. "Contrary to what some people apparently think, I like to be reminded of my failures as well as my successes," he said, then used a finger to brush the SimAI off. He preferred that motion to blinking, which made his eyes tear and blur. "Perspective is essential."

Adsila had been uncomfortable with the admission of both the personal surveillance and the deletion of same, though there was no point arguing the illegality of what Lord had done using FBI resources. The director was a master deflector; his personality was too big for censure to stick. What he did, right or wrong, he did with absolute conviction that it was necessary.

A voice that didn't belong to Red sounded in their ears.

"Director Lord?" It was Carlton Carter.

"I'm here," Lord said as he took his IC private again.

"To the sick bay, please?"

"On my way," he replied.

Adsila stepped aside and Lord moved around her.

"You'll leave your IC on, sir?" she asked.

"It's on now," he said as he left the comm.

Adsila scowled. That was an answer, but it wasn't an answer to her question. Lord had a knack for appearing to tell someone what they wanted to hear then doing what he wanted anyway. As in the past, if he decided to isolate himself, Adsila would have to physically seek him out if he were needed.

But that was all right, she knew. The *Jade Star* crisis had taught her to trust this man. Like dealing with the elders in her tribe, deference was typically a frustrating experience, one that often ran counter to her own needs and intuition. But she had learned a great lesson from him about being open and accessible—very few people in his position would have opened up about a failed romance—and also about the value of independent action. As she turned back to the feeds, and started going through the 2Ms, she resolved that there was one goal she was determined to meet.

She also wanted the director to learn something from her.

FOUR

EXOBIOLOGIST DR. GAVRIIL Borodin floated freely in the snug, instrument-cluttered cylinder that used to be the Japanese Experiment Module *Kibo* on what was once the International Space Station. Patchwork IC interfaces protruded from the panels like the prickly skin of a cactus and were just as painful when he accidentally brushed them. Replacement hardware that didn't fit the original design hung in the air like detritus from a sunken submarine. It was altogether a *lusus naturae* of a module, as one of his professors used to call mutations—a deformed freak.

But it was outer space, and for that Dr. Borodin was profoundly grateful.

The Russian Federal Space Agency, Roscosmos, had taken possession of the ISS in 2047, when its orbit had decayed and it was just months from burning up in Earth's atmosphere. Financed by the criminal consortium *Спутник*, "The Satellite," the Russians quickly repurposed old Vostok boosters to push the dated station back into a high Earth orbit. Of course, the consortium had not operated for the good of Mother Russia. The Satellite now occupied what was formerly the United States laboratory module *Destiny*. As far as any of the seven permanent occupants of the station knew, the two-person team was a pure-science group, though everyone on board was aware—from the chemicals and equipment they ordered—that the science they were pursuing was the manufacture of new and powerful drugs to fill the void left by the collapse of the Mexican and South American cartels.

"It's one thing to defeat an evil," Dr. Borodin's colleague Dr. Vasilisa Nevsky had once written of The Satellite's contribution to the space program. "It's another to leave the wound open for others to fill."

The physician was found on a street in St. Petersburg shortly after, her head crushed very flat by a truck tire.

Borodin did not like working beside The Satellite or being forced to fraternize with their personnel, but he liked working in space. Even the chronic surliness of the most attractive woman on board, pilot Svetlana Uralov, could not sour him. Most of the last three years had been spent up here on a project that had required his constant attention. He expected to be up here for much longer, however: now that that first phase of the project was nearly at an end, the real work was just beginning. Especially if the head of the Faculty of Biology at Moscow State University confirmed the final research Borodin had been conducting up here. That IC alert was due at any moment.

It was rare that the forty-nine-year-old had nothing to do, so he just allowed himself to enjoy the zero gravity—a panacea for his natural, tense state—while he watched the old Russian cartoon *Zhiharka* on his IC. He spent so much time looking out the window at Earth, looking through a telescope at other worlds, even watching his long gray hair floating freely like sea anemones, that he needed to connect with something else. His childhood favorite was based on an old fable about a boy who outsmarted a very canny fox. Borodin grew up wanting to be that child. He had succeeded, which was why he was selected for this assignment over nearly two thousand other highly qualified applicants.

The view mode was set on cathode ray, color, so Borodin could replicate as closely as possible the experience he'd had watching the film in his Moscow apartment more than forty years ago. He had just reached the part when the cat and sparrow chased the fox with scimitars when his IC beeped. Borodin paused the image. His insides burned with anticipation as he accessed the contact, not even minding the prick of the IC pins as he rushed to switch channels on the makeshift system—

"*Pazdravlyayoo!*" the voice of Dr. Ivan Cherkassov exclaimed with barely contained excitement. "Congratulations!"

Borodin allowed himself a moment to take that in. "Then it's true," he whispered.

"It is," Cherkassov went on, "and before you ask, as you must, the answer is yes. I am certain. You *have* one, Doctor. You most definitely *have* one!"

The truth was still seeping through all the mental roadblocks, scientific caution, alternative explanations.

"Thank you, Ivan," Borodin finally replied. "Now—my God—*now* what do we do?"

"Happily, that is neither my problem nor challenge," Cherkassov replied. "I assume you will go there?"

"I will," Borodin quickly agreed. "I must."

"Will you publish first?"

"I don't know if that will be permitted," he said. "The Kremlin '22 Doctrine is still strictly enforced. And . . . consider the repercussions, Ivan! It is my field, this is my dream, but I must still be very careful how it is handled!"

"I know, and I wish I could advise you. This is so important, but I understand what you are saying." Cherkassov was thoughtfully silent for a moment, then said, "I hope you receive help *and* guidance from enlightened sources."

"Up here?" Borodin snickered. "Ptushko may defer to me if I walk him through it step by step. But down there?" He shook his head. "Greed and jealousy are more likely."

"Perhaps the cosmos will advise you, as it did Galileo and many others," Cherkassov said. "Or your discovery may inspire you. This is all undiscovered country."

"On which we now have a beachhead," Borodin replied with renewed awe.

The two men chatted a moment more and then Cherkassov signed off. Borodin looked at the frozen cartoon image of the little girl who had fled the fox. She was bending over the carrot she had dropped, not quite touching it. He advanced the image with IC blinks until she grabbed it. Then he smiled broadly and shut the film.

The exobiologist continued to float, continued to contemplate the meaning of what the MSU scientist had just informed him.

Seven months before, modified Scud missile thirteen had been sent to Venus with a robotic passenger to collect atmospheric samples at the level where the components for the new project were about to be delivered. The collection was not for Borodin but for the construction effort, to ascertain what parts of the thermosphere and exosphere could be used for human survival. Before sending them to Earth, he ran a routine scan on the quarantine content. What he found caused him to send the scientists at Roscosmos searching back into records over eighty years old, to the early days of the Venera program. They were searching for specific procedures, specific materials, everything they could find about the construction of a series of spacecraft that had been launched toward the same target.

Borodin's own research revealed that the original launch protocols had been sound, and that they had been scrupulously followed on every flight: those fourteen spacecraft and their robotically assembled cargo had been clean, absolutely free of contaminants. Borodin had scanned this new sample in every kind of light at every available level of magnification, using techniques that ranged from Rutherford backscattering spectrometry to elastic recoil detection. Cherkassov had examined those breakdowns for any hint at an atomic level of the metals, plastics, mineral, or silica that had been on board the original launch vehicle, the satellite, the probe, or any of the probe's subsystems. Cherkassov had confirmed what Borodin had found: the comparisons found zero matchups.

Nothing in the microscopic sample that Borodin had stored in magnetic suspension in a sterile container had come from any of the spacecraft launched between 1965 and 1983.

The particle found in the atmospheric sample that had been returned from Venus had not been produced by any of the pioneering Venera spacecraft that orbited or landed on Earth's sister world. The biological object just five micrometers long and .4 micrometers in diameter had originated on the second planet from the sun.

After a long period of quiet breathing—and after considerable thought—the still-smiling Borodin had put in a secure IC call to *Red Giant* commander Admiral Boris Ptushko. He requested immediate permission to contact his Earth-based superior, Dr. Aleksandra Ivashova, chief of Extraterrestrial Biology Research at the Russian space agency. As much as he wanted to go to her directly, and immediately, this had to go through channels lest Borodin be punished for breaking the chain of command. And he did not want to be punished. He did not want this to be taken away from him.

Permission had been granted by the half-asleep Ptushko and Borodin immediately placed the IC call. Borodin had not paid any attention to the hour on Earth until Ivashova answered.

"This had better be nothing less than first contact," she said groggily as she answered with voice-only.

Borodin took another calming breath and replied softly and clearly, "Dr. Ivashova—I am pleased to advise that is exactly what this is."

FIVE

D R. CARLTON CARTER met Sam Lord at the door of the smaller of the space station's two medbays. This facility, which had been assigned to Carter and Zero-G, was located forty floors below the comm. Despite the distance, it was a relatively quick, direct elevator ride.

They stepped inside the small foyer that opened into both the medical treatment center and the small lab beyond. Carter never showed what he was feeling, or thinking. Even now, he was calm. But there was a look in his eyes that Lord had not seen in the few months they had known each other. It reminded him of an old watch face: steady but ticking.

As soon as Lord was inside, Carter shut the door behind him. The doctor was not a suspicious man, and from the vagueness of his call Lord knew he was being unusually cautious.

"How is Liba?" Lord asked, nodding toward the screened-off area to the right.

"Resting," Carter said, also vaguely.

Lord frowned. "Not very informative."

"He's fine, Sam. Patient records are confidential, you know that," Carter replied.

"I do." Carter did not know that Liba was also a subordinate of sorts and Lord did not enlighten him. "So why am I here? Do we still have a situation in the greenhouse?"

"We do," Carter said. "I'm still trying to find a way to shut the nanites down ASAP because they'll be a bear to contain otherwise."

"Did you mean what you told him, that they'd stay close to the limb?" Lord asked.

"I meant it when I said it," Carter told him bitterly. "Now? I don't know what they've become. We have to find that out, and also how it happened."

"Assuming you can still talk to them," Lord said.

"I'm relatively certain I can establish communication with the brain center," Carter replied. "One of the nanites I MaGloved from Liba gave me the direct frequency."

Lord glanced at a heavy work glove in a Q-pac resting on a small instrument table. The glove was sitting in the clear quarantine pouch with its magnetic surface facing up. It was covered in what looked like smoky black mist from wrist to fingertips.

Carter noticed Lord's gaze. "You asked a moment ago about whether the nanites would stay close to the limb," Carter said. "Sam, that cloud is comprised of 203 nanites."

"All from Liba?"

Carter nodded.

"*Nu-da-nv-dv-na!*" Lord exclaimed, employing a mild epithet he'd learned from Adsila. "Does Stanton know?"

"He does now," Carter replied. "He wasn't happy."

"Understandable. But it's good news that you have the frequency, yes?"

"It will be when I get to use it," Carter replied.

Lord had been watching him carefully. "All right, but I'm guessing that's not what you called me here to tell me," Lord said. "To help you wait."

"No," Carter acknowledged. That was all he said for a long moment.

"Your sudden knack for espionage and finagling intrigues me, Doctor," Lord said with a little grin. He had hoped to take the edge off the moment. It did not, for Carter.

After weighing what he was about to reveal, Carter said, "I called you here because there's a loophole in what I can and cannot tell you. Please bear with me."

Lord would—to a point. Cockpit-trained, he was accustomed to bottom lines, not recitations.

"Mr. Liba was complaining that the flesh under his fingernail hurt," Carter said. "I assumed it was because the nail was pulled from the skin, or something like that."

"It wasn't," Lord said.

"It was not," Carter replied.

Lord waited, but only a second. Now he was getting impatient. He didn't have to say it: his upturned palms and coaxing expression said, *And?*

"I located a microscopic particle of tree bark under the nail of the right index finger," Carter said. "And in that sliver was a nanite."

"Still functioning?"

"Still functioning, Sam. No reason it shouldn't have been. And no reason it shouldn't have been there. It's small enough, and Liba wasn't wearing gloves when he went inside."

"Are you saying the nanite was starting to build *bark* on Liba?" Lord asked. "A new tree?"

"No, the foliage sample I recovered under the fingernail was inert," Carter said.

"Why?"

"The nanite had turned to other business," Carter replied. "Faced with a choice—and with the self-upgraded SimAI to make that choice—the thing defaulted to what I originally designed it for, when I still called them bio-nanites. That nonclassified work was created to build new skin for grafts."

Lord was impressed. "You designed the nanites to make synskin?"

"Not synskin," Carter said. "My nanoflesh tissue was—*is*—stronger, more durable, more natural, and more versatile. It's superior to that plastic stuff they slapped on your cybernetic leg."

Carter was referring to the hip-to-knee replacement Lord had been given in 2021, after an Israeli tank in which he was riding overturned in a river during a training mission with the Pan-Persian Occupational Forces. Jerusalem had given Lord a free upgrade in 2040, though the human-cell-and-spider-silk skin—which had sensitive mechano-receptors sandwiched between layers to simulate "touch"—had to be replaced every five years, or "one hundred thousand steps," as Lord joked.

"I commend you, Doctor," Lord said. "What's the rest? Assuming it's not classified."

Carter was silent. In the relatively short time they'd known each other, Lord had learned to read his expression and tone of voice. Right now, both said there was bad news.

"Doctor?" Lord pressed.

"The skin I found on Liba, the skin it was producing, did not belong to him," Carter replied.

"Are you saying it was a mutation?" Lord said. "A variation on Liba?"

Carter shook his head. "The cell the nanite was replicating came from someone else."

"Do you know who?"

Carter nodded.

"Someone on the *Empyrean*, which is why you are—why you *can*—tell me this," Lord said, catching up.

Carter nodded. He leaned closer so Liba wouldn't hear. "According to our DNA data base, the skin sample belonged to his assistant, Douglas Cameron."

Lord did not know the agriculturalist and his IC immediately brought up his dossier. He swished it away with a cock of his head.

"I'm guessing that Cameron would not—or should not—have been inside the Vault," Lord said.

"That is correct."

"We shed skin cells all the time," Lord said. "Could a cell sample have come free in the greenhouse or somewhere else in Agro and floated in there?"

"The humidity of the greenhouse would have weighed it down,"

Carter said. "Discarded skin cells actually comprise .02 percent of the compost in the greenhouse, to your point about people shedding."

"I see. I'm further guessing that there's very little chance his DNA would have come into contact with a nanite out here."

"There is no chance at all," Carter said. "Cameron had to be in the Vault. And something about him caused the nanite to want to make more of him."

Which was where the FBI could legally enter the picture. Still, it was another jurisdictional twilight zone for him. Cameron reported to Stanton. The only way Lord could intervene was if they suspected a crime had been committed. Just entering that restricted zone was an internal matter for NASA.

"Vault security is an *Empyrean* matter and I cannot investigate that unless Stanton asks," Lord said. "Were any of your nanites missing *from* the Vault?"

Carter gave him a puzzled look. "Sam, there are thousands of—" he began, then checked himself. "Right. Yes. It appears I'm not getting signals from several of them. They could be inactive *or* they may have been stolen."

"Are you reporting a potential crime?" Lord asked. "A theft from the Vault?"

"I certainly cannot rule it out," Carter said.

That was close enough. "Very well. We will look into it," Lord assured him.

"Hold on," Carter said, raising a hand. "Incoming message."

Lord waited while Carter listened to the update. The weight on the man's shoulders seemed to lessen.

"Well, hallelujah," Carter reported. "Stanton just got the formal kill order from NASA."

Lord smiled thinly. *The accountants and insurers probably told them losing the space tree was more cost-effective than losing the station,* he thought.

The Zero-G director watched as Carter made careful eye motions in his IC.

"There," the doctor said. "The nanites are—"

He paused as his eyes moved from side to side, watching the data stream.

"Huking damn," Carter said. "*Damn.* They're not responding, Sam."

"Rewrote itself more than you expected?"

"Apparently," Carter said, winking all around his IC. "Advanced intelligence compounding advanced intelligence exponentially . . . it's never happened." He swore again. "The signals are being generated— they're just being ignored."

"Blocked or consciously disregarded?"

"I don't know."

The distinction was significant. The first suggested a program. The other suggested what Carter had just described: evolving artificial intelligence.

"Should I start to get security clearance for McClure and Abernathy?" Lord asked.

"Not yet," Carter said with an impatient wave as he headed toward the lab.

"Doctor!" Lord called after him.

Carter turned impatiently.

"Good luck," Lord said.

His voice, his calm demeanor, the break in Carter's charge toward the lab—all had the effect Lord was seeking. It stopped the biophysicist long enough to allow him to catch his breath. He nodded and turned, moving with urgency but less agitation.

There was nothing more Lord could do here, so he checked on Cameron's location. The agricultural associate was still in the Agro Center with Stanton and several sanitation workers who had been trying to keep the mutating limb within the greenhouse while they repaired the fractured glass. The commander was not permitting anyone inside the Vault. Then Lord contacted Adsila, whose three-dimensional likeness hovered in the upper-right corner of his IC.

"EAD, would you please get in touch with Judge Yakima Hinson and obtain a search warrant for the quarters of Assistant Agricultural Officer Douglas Cameron?"

Adsila was silent for an instant. "The judge's IC is off, sir. It *is* three a.m."

"Enter emergency code Archimedes," Lord instructed.

Adsila spoke the word without question. The warrant appeared, filled in with Cameron's name and residence.

"Sir, you have more magical codes than anyone I have ever known," Adsila said.

"Nothing supernatural about it: authorized and quite legal," Lord reassured her, reading her expression and anticipating the question his number two was obviously reluctant to ask. "Meet me at his quarters with the warrant."

"Of course, sir."

Hinson had been Lord's divorce attorney decades earlier. The judge respected the fact that Lord had not done flyovers to spy on his wife and her new beau, or to buzz them. The future judge felt a man who did not stalk a legal adversary could be trusted.

Lord left the medbay and headed back to Radial Arm Six. His chat with Erin Astoria seemed like it had taken place a full day before. He pinched suddenly tired eyes as he walked. There was also a slight dizziness as Lord moved from gravity system to gravity system. Yet, while his lids were heavy and everything below the chin was on the verge of revolt, Lord's brain was overactive. It reminded him of how he used to feel on long-haul flights, experiencing the dichotomy of exhaustion and hyperalertness caused by extended viewing of his heads-up display.

Lord wondered how Stanton and his people would contain the nanites and the vine they were building—along with any severed pieces, some of them microscopic—if the nanites couldn't be corralled. The only thing Lord could think of was opening the Agro Center airlock and allowing everything inside to be sucked into the void.

Except Carter had said the nanites could function just fine in space, Lord thought. *Never mind Newton or the first law of thermodynamics or any other part of the science canon. This is exactly the kind of Frankenstein monster that science fiction has been warning us about since Day One.*

Lord hurried ahead, hoping he could be done in Cameron's room before the man returned. A showdown with one of Stanton's people—or the commander himself—was not something he cared to have right now, either personally or politically.

SIX

L ORD REACHED CAMERON'S small room in less than five minutes. At this early hour, the hall was still empty. Though day and night were just words in space, *Empyrean* functioned as closely as possible to a twenty-four-hour clock.

The Zero-G director scanned the door and its frame for alarms by layering the original blueprints on the current physical, electronic, thermal, and biological content. Even Fleas, lighter-than-air microdrones that were the forerunners of Carter's nanites, would be detected. They could only be airborne in an empty room, due to the danger of inhalation.

When the readings came back negative, Lord used his Skeleton IC Key to pop the lock. He quietly thanked Judge Hinson for his trust . . . and foresight.

The room was ten feet deep by six feet wide, with images of living wheat fields that immediately surrounded the occupant and seemed to expand the walls endlessly. These were actually haptic-feedback screens comprised of the same material that filled the windowless corridors of the *Empyrean* with changing views of sea and sky, mountain and valley, desert and plain. They were made volumetric, magnetically contoured microvoxels that actually had the physical texture of the objects they displayed.

Lord used his Zero-G system override to shut the image down. They could be used to hide contraband in plain sight; a 360-degree image of a jeweler's shop, for example, would make it extremely difficult to find a diamond embedded in a wall.

The white walls of the room stood stark and unadorned. There was very little to personalize the room. The toiletries in the tiny lavatory consisted of a programmed razor, sonic toothbeam, and a hairbrush; the utensils and products in the even smaller, open kitchen quadrant were all station issue. In the closet were mostly work-related gloves, bootlets, and trousers. There was one *Empyrean*-standard dress uniform for official receptions; from Earth there was one leisure outfit, one workout suit, and one "airful"—a white whole-body suit that did not require pressurization but, like a space suit, contained a sealed environment within, fed by oxygen generators. Lord also spotted a palm-size mirror and nodded knowingly.

Clever, he thought, pocketing the highly polished glass.

Lord eliminated all drop-downs from his IC that were not related to the mission at hand. He scanned the clothing for anything that wasn't floral matter from the *Empyrean*. The result was negative. Then he scanned for minerals. There was nothing that could not have come from the post-decontamination shuttle trip to space, the space kite trip to the *Empyrean*, or the *Empyrean* itself. He had been hoping for something telltale from a visit to a private shuttle or from smuggled contraband.

Still facing the closet, Lord switched the scan to DNA, without labels, and his IC lit up like all the stars in space seen through a prism, as he expected. Everyone on the *Empyrean* came into contact with a great many people, both permanent residents and visitors. In addition to those, Cameron's possessions were covered with vegetal particles.

"Red, remove *Empyrean*-indigenous persons and material and show whatever is left," Lord said softly. Immediately, the molecular cosmos shrank by roughly ninety percent. The remaining lights looked more like a Christmas tree now than a starry sky—blue for biological, red for mineral, yellow for hybrid. "Visual ID," Lord said. At once, images were superimposed in his field of vision, hovering transparently over the lights. "Is there anything here that has a match in the FBI database?"

Lord had not made that his first request because, at trial, it was more effective for a judge or jury to witness the process of deduction and investigation rather than simply be shown the end result. He'd learned that the hard way, from testimony he had given at courts-martial of subordinates. Stripping away layers also suggested impartiality rather than a supposition of guilt going in.

All but one gently pulsing blue light disappeared. It was located on the pocket flap of one of the Agro Center's green coats. Lord shut his IC and looked at the area in visual light; unmagnified, unenhanced, nothing was visible except the fabric of the jacket. Whatever the object was, it was either very small or visible only in ultraviolet or infrared. He winked the IC back on, tried just those light sources, but neither showed anything. He restored the original search setting and the blue light reappeared. He used an index finger to poke at the icon and expand it. The particle was not just microscopic; it was tiny beyond the visual acuity of the IC.

"Red, what am I not looking at?" Lord asked the IC.

"I cannot ascertain from direct observation," Red informed him, "but tracking downward from the ripple effect of spin quantum number, intrinsic parity, and charge conjugation, that there are millions of defective hadrons present, clustered in a small atomic mass."

"It would 'appear'?"

"As I said, that is a conclusion based on surrounding energetic reactions, since I cannot see a hadron." Red added, "I would also infer, from the uncharacteristic ripple configuration in supersymmetry, that the hadrons are defective, since said patterns do not fit any of the recognized or predictable theory."

Which led to Lord's next question. "Explain hadrons and *defective* hadrons."

"A hadron is a bundle of quarks and antiquarks, which, in sufficient number and specific cohesion, are otherwise known as protons or neutrons, the component matter of atomic nuclei," Red replied.

"So Cameron's got broken nuclei in his pocket."

"Yes, in effect," the voice crackled.

"That's what made him so tasty to the nanites," Lord thought aloud. "He was 'daddy.'"

"Sorry, Sam?"

"Nothing, Red," Lord said. "Based on your reading of what is roughly equivalent to describing a pebble thrown in the pond based solely from the waves it produces," Lord said.

"Simplistic but also essentially correct."

"Are broken hadrons typically found up here?" Lord asked, indicating "space" with a circular gesture.

"Not as far as we know," Red replied. "We have detected exotic hadrons, which are naturally occurring as part of the P matrix of—"

"Thank you. Is it possible that Cameron—that *we*—have stumbled on a new particle out here?"

"No, Sam."

"Then I'm confused, since the particles are obviously here."

"You asked about space. Defective hadrons are known to exist artificially on Earth."

Lord forgave Red's penchant for literal answers. Sometimes he forgot she was just a SimAI. "All right, where on *Earth* are they found, Red?"

"There are at present only three places where quark-gluon research could produce such particles," Red informed him. "The Fontana Collider in Geneva, the Livnot Collider in Idhna, and the Pushkin Collider in Putingrad."

"Any idea which?" Lord asked.

Lord's initial thought was Idhna and that Ziv Levy was behind this event. Ziv was an infamous Israeli cyborg who had a private shuttle, spent quite a bit of time on the *Empyrean*, and played all sides against one another in order to acquire intel and influence. He also possessed crude but efficient nanobot technology.

"I lack the sensor sophistication to be certain," Red replied, "but a classified FBI file from Pushkin, document 10520.15, contains a lengthy request for funding upgrades in 2033. The document cites the need to improve strong-force research—the glue that bonds quarks and antiquarks to produce hadrons. The Russian word *поломанный* appears seventeen times. It means 'broken.'"

"Just to be clear, there are no faulty hadrons from Switzerland or Israel?"

"That appears to be accurate," Red remarked. "According to classified data as well as published reports, that research has produced healthy specimens."

"The Russians, then," Lord thought aloud. "They also have limited ways and means to reach their space station. They would have a good reason to want Merlin."

"Merlin is a likely 97.4 percent fictional magician who has no relevance to the current—"

Lord silenced Red's response with a blink, though he knew that he shouldn't be saying anything aloud about a top-secret NASA project that the FBI itself was spying on. Even his team did not know of it—yet.

"Director Lord?"

To his point: it was Adsila. She had heard all of that. He was glad he trusted all his people.

"Yes, EAD."

"Thank you for keeping me linked," she said. "Sir, there is no indication in his file that Douglas Cameron has ever been to Putingrad. In fact, it doesn't appear that he's ever been to Russia."

"Like Burnam Wood to Macbeth, Putingrad may have come to him," Lord said. "Has he been to the *Red Giant*?"

"That is not showing up in any flight records."

"Does any nation have laws against conveying defective hadrons, inadvertently or not? Quarantines?"

"None," Adsila replied. "It would be extremely difficult to enforce a program enacted to bar particles that are everywhere, anyway."

"Thank you," Lord said.

Lord turned his IC back on. He did not want to stay in Cameron's room any longer than he had to, but Lord also did not want to confiscate evidence without cause.

"Red, give me any intersect between *Red Giant* staff or known visitors and Mr. Cameron," Lord said.

The IC flashed images. Lord watched, looking for anything that might register subliminally. Red not only searched through flight records but all available video surveillance on Earth. The Ring of Steel, designed to protect Lower Manhattan in the years after the World Trade Center attack, had been expanded and adopted by most cities on Earth, a linked network of official and private surveillance from traditional building cameras, Fleas, tiny wall-crawling spidercams, satellites, socialnets, and ordinary IC eyes—what everyone saw, which could be automatically recorded.

"Closest proximity was two hundred and eleven kilometers apart, four years and three months ago," Red crackled.

"That's no help," Lord said. "Check Cameron against KGB or Russian criminal elements."

"None," Red replied.

"Cameron and any Russian," Lord asked patiently.

"Same location, nine weeks and one day ago, International Exobiology Summit, Zurich," Red informed him. "Cameron spoke with Dr. Aleksandra Ivashova, chief of Extraterrestrial Biology Research at Roscosmos. The symposium was Theoretical Exoflora."

At Lord's request, images from the meeting—also from a dinner reception—flashed before his eyes. There was physical contact between Cameron and Ivashova. As Cameron turned away, the botanist's right hand slipped into his pants pocket.

"What was Cameron holding?" Lord asked.

"Judging from the bend evidenced by the back of his hand, something akin to a ring box."

"So it could be anything," Lord mused.

"That would fit in a ring box," Red added.

"Anything else in the files?" Lord asked.

"Before that, ninety-eight days ago, Dr. Sergei Trutnev, surgeon, was present at Punjab Agricultural University, where he and Cameron were attending a class reunion."

"When did Cameron receive his *Empyrean* commission?"

"Eighty-seven days prior to the class reunion," Red said.

"Adsila, his income?"

"No immediately apparent infusion of funds," she replied.

"Thank you," Lord replied. He winked at an icon. "Mr. McClure?"

There was a moment's delay; the science officer was probably still asleep. "Sir?"

"ELEG, Radial Arm Six, Room 359."

"Right, sir. Coming now."

"No need to dress up," Lord added. "I want this done fast."

"Yes, sir."

The ELEG—Electromagnetic Lyophilization Evidence Generator—was able to preserve the integrity of delicate, nonbiological matter without damaging it. The ELEG was a key tool of the trade and Lord understood, at least in a rudimentary way, how a sphere-like field was formed that instantly analyzed, replicated, and contained all environmental factors while at the same time generating an electromagnetic field that prevented electronic activity within. Where the workings of the device lost him—and fortunately, he did not need to understand these—had to do with the cosine ratio of gravity, inverse square laws, and volume elements. All that mattered was that the field could not be broken until it met a matching environment. The two ELEGs would then merge and the transporting beam could be shut.

While he was waiting, Lord checked to see if Dr. Carter was available. The biologist did not answer his IC page. Lord was beginning to get the same adrenaline surge as he did in combat, one that flattened his exhaustion like a sonic boom over a wheat field. An idea—more than that, a solution—was beginning to form. He punched in the emergency override to Carter's IC.

"Carlton—"

"Can it wait, Sam? I'm in the middle of—"

"Doctor, would a defective hadron screw up your nanites?"

There was the briefest hesitation. "What?"

"You know, a broken atomic nucleus," Lord said, as if he had always known what one was.

"I know what a defective hadron is, Sam."

"Good. Suppose one of those contaminated the Vault?"

Carter took another moment. "If it affected a nanite, any nanite, one corrupted system could theoretically impact all of them like an old-school computer virus," Carter said.

"Would—could—the nanites rally their wits, so to speak . . . look for a way to reject or assimilate the particle?"

"Again, I suppose it's possible. Why?"

"Because I have a cluster of those particles," Lord informed him. "On a jacket."

"You have an atomic nucleus comprised of defective hadrons?"

"I do. And I have an ELEG on the way to secure it."

Carter took another moment to process that, then said, "I will prepare a quarantine field. Get it to me, please, ASAP."

SEVEN

UNSHAVED AND WEARING tight U-wear topped by baggy yellow work-out shorts that undulated like poured honey in the weak gravity, Special Agent Ed McClure arrived at Cameron's room prepared and attentive.

"The adaptability of youth," Lord remarked as he came through the unlocked door.

"Sir?" McClure and Adsila said at the same time.

Lord didn't respond. He simply stepped aside, remembering the "scramble" days of the War on Narcotics, when he would jump from a deep sleep on a cot in a ready room and be taxiing along a tarmac four minutes and thirty-five seconds later. Then, he was able to shuck off sleep like a dog shedding hose water. These days, it took him that long just to go from bed to the lavatory.

"That duty jacket," Lord said, pointing at a garment in the closet. "There's subatomic evidence in the pocket."

The special agent's eyes narrowed with intrigue. He didn't ask how Lord knew; the director was like that. He found things out. McClure stood a foot from the jacket and lifted a white-gloved right hand, fingers raised, palm facing the garment. The glove reached to his elbow and was made of flexible rubber infused with metal ions for conductivity. McClure used his own IC, plugged into Red, to identify the target. An

ELEG icon appeared in his vision, over the spot. McClure fixed his eyes on it and blinked twice. Then he blinked a third time to activate the microsystems in the glove. That created a powerful electromagnetic stasis field that locked the garment on an atomic level. When the icon turned from red to white—the all-clear signal—he gripped the garment at the collar.

Lord felt an invisible little push against his entire body when McClure turned from the closet. It was like the invisible force that comes from trying to shove opposing magnets together, only covering a wider area. That buffer was the fringe of the electromagnetic field, the beginning of a filtration process that not only kept the contents fully stable but kept foreign elements out. The cotton and stainless steel fibers that comprised McClure's glove provided full resistivity both to protect his flesh and allow access to the contents of the field.

As McClure made his way toward the door, Lord scanned the room for weapons, utensils, tools, rope, wire, communication devices, or any other physical tools a spy might need. There was nothing. Like Liba, Cameron appeared to be a man who was primarily about his work. Lord shook his head at what seemed on the surface to have been a stupid, stupid choice.

"Our destination is the lab in the smaller medbay," Lord informed McClure as he caught up to him in the corridor. "Let me know if you need to stop."

"I should be fine, sir," McClure assured him. "The gravity along that route and the weight of the impound are well under my ELEG certification."

Part of the training that preceded using this technology was the very practical need to keep one's arm extended during transit, lest the ELEG field buffet the agent. On Earth, the conveyance time was brief, usually to a waiting van or gurney. In space, the challenge was less arm weariness than keeping the object from swinging in all directions due to centripetal fluctuations.

McClure was very good at that. Throughout the six-minute passage he moved like a participant on *Dancing in the Stars*, the zero-gravity ICvision oldie, weaving this way and that, high-stepping, ducking, always maneuvering to keep his "partner" from hitting something. Though the ELEG contents were secure, the field itself could have damaged any person or system it came in contact with.

Dr. Carter met them in the corridor outside the medbay. The biophysicist still seemed calm, if uncommonly focused.

"Doctor?" Lord said with a concerned look.

"They're having a time of it below," he said, nodding in the general direction of the Agro Center. "Share secure 826," he instructed his IC.

As the others went ahead, Lord stopped to look at Stanton's feed from the greenhouse, the area outside the Vault, which was bound by security restrictions. It showed the small makeshift Agro team among the plants and trees of the greenhouse. The group was spearheaded by Cameron, supervised by Stanton, and they were physically moving the protruded section of vine to change its direction. The gold stars superimposed on their images indicated that all of them had been granted emergency, mission-specific top-level security clearance by NASA to enter the Vault, if necessary. Some of the crew were aloft on the thickest parts of the vine, others were maneuvering to grab the ends of each now-massive fork like space Tarzans, hanging there until it sprouted so they could pull it in a different direction. The resultant growth was like a massively disfigured pretzel, twisting in and around itself. Lord realized at once the greater danger: if the vine wasn't shut down, the ball of space foliage would become so thick it would simply bulge through the Agro Center on all six sides. Ducts, vents, electronics, and other life-support functions would be crushed and compromised.

"Red?" Lord said.

"Yes?"

"Let me have a threat assessment to *Empyrean* in the event of Agro breach," Lord said calmly. He noted that Adsila was still connected to his own feed, and made a point of suppressing any alarm he felt.

"Decompression can be contained and structural components are threatened, but there is the more immediate problem of the solar sail," the IC responded. "It's already struggling to maintain equilibrium."

"Diagram, please."

The massive solar sail was affixed to a sun-side tower on the *Empyrean*. A 255-foot-wide, square, ultrathin sheet coated with liquid crystals in the light-absorbent orange, yellow, and gold end of the spectrum, the sail added and subtracted other colors, which caused it to slowly move. The shifts of prismatic light were functional as well as beautiful: adding or subtracting absorbed light created pressure that adjusted the position of the sail. That sustained the altitude and attitude of the slowly spinning space station. Red generated a visual showing the intrusion of the vine into conduits in the greenhouse. As they expanded, they would continue to squeeze data flowing to the sail and other systems, taxing the ability of the sail to adjust to the normal challenges of the station. Its failure would send the *Empyrean* into a tumble that could not be braked.

"Within roughly eighteen minutes, based on present growth acceleration, the *Empyrean* will go from being smoothly proactive to abruptly reactive, which will cause structural stress," Red informed Lord.

"Understood," Lord said. Starting to move slowly toward the medbay, the Zero-G director checked the latest sail data. The flux was indeed crawling closer and closer to the structure's theoretical limit. And there was no guarantee the expansion of the vine would maintain at its current rate.

Lord checked the newtiae as his pace increased. The "rainbow riot," as it had swiftly been dubbed, was already creating buzz on Earth. Houston crafted a lie to explain it, a terse statement about experiments with higher-density crystals for deep-space missions. Very few scientists in the media were buying that.

Lord had not received any queries from Al-Kazaz. Apparently, the prime director had gone back to sleep. That was understandable: as far as he knew, this was a problem for NASA, not the FBI. Lord did not bother updating him. There was nothing the PD could do except warn Lord not to exceed his authority. Again.

Arriving at the medbay, Lord found McClure waiting outside the lab section, the ELEG glove still on his hand but deactivated.

"Evidence delivered," the young man said.

"Thank you, Agent."

"You're welcome, sir." The special agent gave Lord a questioning look.

"Sorry, I can't tell you anything," Lord told him. He cocked his head toward the outer door. "Get dressed and report to the comm. Keep the ELEG with you, in case we need it."

"Yes, sir."

"Oh, and check to see if there were any unexplained light flashes outside the station in the last three hours," Lord said. "Anything not sunlight or earthlight reflecting from the hull, sail, a spaceship—"

"Right away, sir."

Lord was sorry he couldn't confide in the boy. He *was* proud of the twenty-three-year-old. McClure had been a green, largely untested science wunderkind when he'd arrived. Having survived the frontal assault on the deadly Dragon's Eye—an attack that killed a dozen members of the fourteen-person team—McClure was already a confident, poised Zero-G agent.

As he passed the medbay screen, Lord waved at the drowsy Liba, who was resting on one of the two cots. The botanist grabbed his sleeve as he passed. "I just want you to know something, Sam."

"Yes?"

"My avocados . . . crushed too."

"Sorry?" Lord said.

"I was growing avocados just for you," Liba murmured. "There's not enough . . . fish up here for sushi . . . but avos and rice? I . . . hope some . . . can be salvaged."

"I love you." Lord winked then turned to enter the lab.

"Sir?" Red said.

Lord scowled at the modern age. The wink had activated the IC's communication mode. "Sorry, Red. I was talking to Mr. Liba."

"Should I add him to your amorous connections?"

"That's a negative," Lord replied.

The pocket door whooshed aside to admit him. Lit by just the glowing tabletop, the lab was the size of a lavatory stall on Earth. Cameron's coat lay on the table, locked in a transparent electromagnetic field. Carter was using a long, hollow, needle-like probe to study the sample. Lord marveled at how steady the man's hand was. Though the room was comparatively warm, Carter wasn't perspiring. Like the cool veteran he was—though Lord did not know of what—he had adjusted to this situation. Carter was a longtime colleague of Al-Kazaz, and neither man had brought Carter's background up to Lord. Most of that information was classified, even to Lord.

Numbers and values scrolled by in Lord's IC as he plugged into Carter's feed.

$1\ GeV/fm3$, $T=1/(aN\tau)$, ~$103\ km{\approx}R$, and similar equations appeared in side-by-side columns. Lord was about to blink it away when he noticed that patterns in one repeated in the other.

"This data is coming from your original programming, the other from a nanite with a defective hadron inside?" Lord guessed.

"That's correct," Carter told him. "Once I find the fingerprints of the hadron, I can hopefully send a corrective update."

"Can't you just send the correct coding?" Lord asked.

"I could, if I could get in," Carter said.

"What's preventing you?"

"Quantum speed bumps of some kind that cause my data to scatter."

"Put there intentionally?" Lord asked.

"God, I hope not," Carter replied.

Lord watched the flow flash by. "That's a lot of data."

"There are a lot of mollies," Carter said.

Mollies were molecular microprocessors. Lord had learned about them when he was at the end of his test-piloting days. They were supremely fast chemical systems that were literally 1,022 times faster than the last of the traditional 10 GHz chips.

"And they are apparently vulnerable to our defective hadrons," Lord noted.

"Very," Carter said as he worked. "When I first designed the nanites, I shielded the mollies from everything but what we frankly couldn't anticipate. At that subatomic level, we're still learning. We've got this magnificent quantum-dot processor in which entangled spin-states of single electrons perform amazing feats of computation due to a quantum overlay where you can simultaneously have a zero, a one, and an indeterminate state between both of those—"

"Doctor, I'm a flight jockey who *happened* to hear of mollies," Lord said. "I'm not a physicist."

"I'll put it another way," Carter went on doggedly. "It helps when I run logic out loud. Imagine a vintage processor as a checkerboard and think of a molly as a game of multidimensional chess where all the boards are being played simultaneously."

"*That* I understand," Lord said.

"But the molly system is also very delicately calibrated," Carter went on. "Bring defective hadrons from the quark-gluon process near the mollies and there's a near certainty that they'll disrupt this entanglement, addle the processors."

"Which is what happened here," Lord said.

Carter nodded. "The first corrupted nanite contained the 'latest' update, which caused the entire system to clone itself in that new, corrupted form. As soon as I have the full mathematical statement of the particle and its corresponding influence on the nanite, I should be able to adjust the equation and broadcast that to the others."

"Might there be other unwanted hadrons floating around in the Vault?"

"Quite possibly," Carter said. "But they will probably be of the same type as this one. I will immunize the nanites and the other rogue nuclei won't be a problem. The damn particles will pass right through them without a trace. The only conceivable impediment is if they create some kind of electrical filter to block my signal."

"Is that something they can do?" Lord asked.

"They're merged with biological material, the most basic instinct of which is to survive. I have no way of knowing what kind of synergy they might have developed."

"Lovely," Lord said. "We may have natural-selected ourselves out of existence."

"I have always wondered if biology is only an interim intelligence, born to create superior machines," Carter said.

The data stopped scrolling and Lord waited as Carter asked the IC to create a new code that would block the defective matter from impacting the nanites. The accompanying graphic that appeared beside the master nanite column showed the skin of Carter's creation being struck, in very slow motion, by an infinitesimal comet. Rapidly, and piece by piece, the tail of the comet vanished, taking contaminated formulae with it. Soon there was only the head of the comet. The column was gone. Carter reset the original program.

"Send it," Carter instructed, "then shut all the nanites down."

Lord waited, Carter standing stiffly beside him. The wait was not a long one.

"The nanites are no longer active," the neutral-voiced IC informed them.

Both men exhaled loudly, then again. Carter set the needle on the small lab table. "Thanks, Sam."

"Glad to help," Lord replied. "Tell me—what happens now to all the nanites that may still be on the skin of the people who were in the greenhouse?"

"They're essentially like any of the thousands of species of microbiota that inhabit the flesh and mucosal areas of the human body," Carter said. "Without conditions suitable to their survival, they will go dormant and, by design, turn to slag within a designated period of time."

" 'Conditions,' meaning—?"

"Electronic activity, their stuff of life." He frowned. "Their batteries were designed to live a finite period, long enough to build the vine. But out there, in space, who knows what influence that dark energy could have on their altered systems? That was one of the things we hoped to study with when our carefully controlled construction project went to the next phase."

"I understand, I think," Lord said just as McClure signaled him from the comm. His search for a "glint" had come up negative.

Carter opened a secure line to Commander Stanton. Lord would not be able to hear Stanton's side, so Carter put his IC on audible. Lord thanked him with a slight nod.

"Commander Stanton, the nanites in the Vault have been powered down," Carter said. "The vine should stop growing immediately."

"It appears to have done so, and none too soon," Stanton said.

Lord did not hear Stanton's response. Other than by primitive hard-wiring, there was no way to override the secure NASA lock on the rest of the data, so Lord had no idea what was going on. Conversely, Stanton would have been able to hear him, so the Zero-G director stepped away so he wouldn't be heard. Then he spoke to the comm.

"Adsila, meet me in the Agro Center at once," he said. "Come armed."

EIGHT

A DSILA MARCHED SMARTLY to the equipment storage unit to the right of the LOO. Her IC unlocked the traditional-looking steamer trunk that had been constructed from materials collected during the ORP of 2048. The Orbital Reclamation Project was created because it was less expensive to recycle and repurpose metals, glass, and plastics already in space than to launch them from Earth.

Like the Vault, it was nothing more than an electromagnetic barrier that came down when she opened it. The locker concealed a grip board, a surface infused with a van der Waals adhesive—a molecular bond that was secure but not as permanent as a chemical bond. Just two months after it was installed, the board had a kind of outmoded quaintness: newer models were based on the *Streptococcus pyogenes* bacterium, using the same chemicals the microbes used to invade and adhere to human cells.

On the grip board was an array of weapons. Adsila retrieved her Gauntlet, a sturdy, FBI-issue glove that reached to the elbow. Activated by pressure from the palm, the plastic-rubber alloy launched single or multiple two-stun-level arcs of electricity from the back of the wrist. The wearer's IC controlled the voltage based on threat assessment. There was a Gauntlet for each agent in their quarters and in the comm. Adsila's DNA released it from the panel.

She was not overly fond of firearms—she had seen them too easily abused in a moment of rage or misguided passion—though she was extremely proficient with them. On Earth, she had excelled on the target range with everything from traditional guns to palm-size SPLS—Smart Projectile Launch Systems, which used the IC to target the bullet, not the weapon, allowing it to be discharged without physically aiming the gun.

Adsila shifted to her male form as she left the comm. It wasn't voluntary; she received a testosterone jolt from the prospect of conflict and didn't resist the change. She also didn't analyze it deeply. All through her life, the slightly broader shoulders had an intimidating effect on adversaries and she simply accepted that. Both forms were her/him, and she enjoyed these fringe elements that did not overlap. As long as someone did not court old stereotypes and request one over the other, Adsila was fine.

He arrived to find Lord standing outside the elevator right by the start of the green line that terminated in the Agro Center. The Zero-G director did not show any reaction on seeing the fit young man who arrived. Lord simply turned and started toward the greenhouses with Adsila a step behind him. But the director's casual demeanor concealed a personally disconcerting reaction he always had to the change: the fact that he felt no differently toward Adsila as a male than he did when she was a female. He had always tried to keep an inviolable personal distance with all his professional colleagues, rarely letting a relationship cross the line into physical intimacy. Despite his Cybernetic Human Abstract Individual or CHAI hip, as it was commonly called, he was still mostly human. He found Adsila attractive and was confused that even without the pleasing contours, the fuller lips, the subtle but unmistakable aroma, he still felt an attraction to "her" as "him."

The Western world had long ago made peace with personal sexuality, but Lord had been raised in a time before sweeping societal change, and in a professional environment of inviolable machismo—even among the women.

I think that makes me a more enlightened human being, he had told himself the first time he acknowledged the nontraditional appeal. But the admission had a kind of whistling-past-a-graveyard quality because it required him to rewrite some sixty-seven years of sexual conditioning. Lord was still trying to understand it, and had spent some time upon his arrival reading psych testimonials about how couples with a transgendered member had been addressing these topics since the early part of the century.

The voices of Stanton and his makeshift team reached them just before Lord and Adsila rounded the corner. Lord and Adsila stopped.

"... decon scan finds no electrical activity on any of us," Stanton was saying.

"Very good," someone replied.

"Put together a detail from the remainder of the Agro workers, sanitation personnel, and station mechanics," Stanton went on. "Have them report here but wait outside the greenhouse. I'll need to get security clearance for Vault access once I have their names."

"Yes, sir," the same someone replied again.

Lord's IC told him that the "someone" was Cameron. Lord looked at Adsila, whose IC had also informed him that their quarry was on the way.

Lord remained standing just a few paces from the corner. He saw Cameron as he hurried forward. The botanist was leaning ahead and toward the inner wall to compensate for the outward centripetal force of the station. The assistant agricultural officer slowed but did not stop when he saw the two Zero-G officers.

Adsila stepped so that he was shoulder-to-shoulder with Lord, blocking the narrow corridor. Now Cameron had to stop and he leaned back to do so. His youthful face seemed perplexed.

"Excuse me, Director Lord," Cameron said, "but I'm on an urgent—"

"You *were* on an urgent," Lord said, leaving the expression unfinished. "Mr. Cameron, please come with us to the Zero-G command center."

Cameron's gray eyes shifted to the Gauntlet and then back to Lord. "What's the difficulty here?" he asked. It was a painfully improvised, obviously strained effort at being casual.

Before Lord could respond, Commander Stanton charged briskly around the corner. Seeing Lord he stopped, also wobbling a little from the suddenness. "I thought I heard your voice—again," he said pointedly. "What the hell is going on?"

"Zero-G business with Mr. Cameron," Lord replied bluntly.

Stanton saw the weapon on Adsila's hand. "Do you intend to interrogate one of *my* people at Gauntlet-point?"

"No," Lord replied. "I intend to book Mr. Cameron in our comm and *then* question him."

Stanton grew sterner and Cameron suddenly seemed to grow visibly frailer.

"Question him about what?" Stanton demanded.

"Interplanetary felony," Lord replied—feeling no pride in the fact that it was probably the first time that phrase had been uttered in the line of duty.

"You'll have to give me more than that," Stanton replied.

That wasn't true, Lord knew. The Zero-G charter—of which Stanton was a signatory—specified that the commander of a space station did not have to be consulted about an arrest and could not countermand one, even when it was one of his crew members. However, he had the right to ask about it. For the sake of maintaining even a threadbare relationship with Stanton, Lord decided to answer.

"We have a probable violation of *Empyrean* Code 910, unlawful entry of a security zone," Lord informed the commander.

"The Vault?" Stanton asked.

Lord nodded slightly.

Stanton's eyes snapped to the botanist and remained there. "Your proof, Director Lord?" the commander demanded.

"Currently under analysis by a member of my team and obtained, by warrant, in Mr. Cameron's quarters—the result of having obtained said evidence being the nanite threat deactivation you just witnessed."

Stanton's gaze burned into Cameron. Nothing was a higher priority to him than the safety of his station and its personnel. "What did you do, mister?" Stanton demanded.

"There is no need to answer," Lord said, inserting himself between the men and raising a hand to stop further interrogation. There were strict rules of action and they had to be followed. The exact wording of the FBI process dropped down in the ICs of all four with a gesture from Lord:

During an interview with a witness, suspect or subject, under no circumstances should it be stated or implied that public sentiment or hostility exists toward such person. . . .

Stanton reluctantly took a long step back. Lord turned to face him.

"Thank you, Commander," Lord said.

"Director Lord, I will want an *immediate* update on any verifiable code and/or legal infractions and your team's assessment of future threat potential," the commander said.

"Of course," Lord assured him.

Cameron shifted from one to the other of the men. "This is huking nonsense," he swore.

Stanton's eyes remained on Cameron a moment longer. They seemed, to Lord, to say, *God help you if it isn't.*

"Mr. Cameron, would you please turn off your IC?" Lord said.

Cameron just stood there.

"Mr. Cameron?" Lord repeated.

The distracted botanist obliged with a series of blinks. Lord checked to make sure; when he could not connect with the prisoner, he made a circling motion with his hand, indicating the man should turn around. Cameron turned with uncertainty; his mind was clearly elsewhere. Lord stepped to the man's right. He had not brought magnetic handcuffs, which would attach them wrist-to-wrist. Adsila still had his weapon in his hand. Though it was pointed down, Lord knew—even if the prisoner did not—that he would be unable to get far before Adsila could fire.

With Adsila behind them, the three followed the green line to the elevator.

NINE

THE GROUP MOVED swiftly, purposefully toward the comm.

Lord never took his eyes off the botanist during transit. Not that he expected the prisoner to run off; that was the beauty of space. Vast as it was, there was nowhere *to* run. What Lord was looking for was any tic, any external manifestation of an internal monologue. Lord had been present for dozens of mission debriefings, knew how people behaved when eyes and ears were on them. This man was surely running explanations in his head. If any gestures he saw now repeated themselves during interrogation, Lord would hit that rehearsed line hard.

But the man remained emphatically still and silent. His eyes were mostly downturned, arms swaying only with the side-to-side motion that came from walking in this sector. His lips were still. If the man were thinking—or rather trying to think—it was at a very low level of complexity. His repetitive stride told Lord that he was focusing on appearing at ease, trying not to show any of the panic he surely felt. Any thoughts would be at a high level of abstraction: what big picture would justify treason or how to plead his way out of this by possibly betraying someone else—probably both. Several times Cameron's eyes snapped up; it seemed to Lord as if the man wanted to turn toward him and say something; then he obviously thought better of that and his eyes rolled back down.

Smarter to respond to what the interrogator has to say, Lord thought. *Less chance of offering information that was previously unknown.*

The *Empyrean* morning crew and its guests were awake by now, and they scrunched up to the walls of the narrow corridors in order to let the party pass. Those who didn't know Lord knew, from his stride, that he wasn't stopping.

By the time they reached the comm, McClure was already at his post, the ELEG hooked to his utility belt. Communications director Grainger had arrived moments before Lord did; tech agent Michael Abernathy arrived moments after.

Lord bid everyone a good morning. He maneuvered through the narrow little desks that were designed more for holding mementoes, food, and coffee cups than equipment. While Adsila took his post—still wearing the Gauntlet—Lord extended an arm toward the rear of the comm, ushering Cameron to an empty station there. That was for Dr. Carter on those rare occasions when he met with the team.

Lord faced the botanist. "Sit," he directed.

"I don't think I should say anything without an attorney present," Cameron said. "I waive physical presence."

"Access to counsel, present or virtual, is guaranteed by US law," Lord acknowledged. "However, you are being charged under the *Empyrean* charter, which was modeled after the legal codes crafted by the First Territorial Legislature of 1864." Lord flicked that clause to a holo-monitor above them. He rotated the three-times-life-size document so it was facing down. "Since time is short, I'll paraphrase: in the event of clear and present danger, the right to an attorney is subordinate to the survival threat facing the station. Now, Mr. Cameron—sit."

Cameron looked numb. He obliged without protest, sliding over the stool and folding his hands on the desk. Lord perched on the corner of the desk, his hands on a thigh, and turned to face the botanist.

"This session is being recorded," Lord told him. "Anything you say—"

"I thought you have to arrest me before reciting my rights," Cameron said, marshaling sudden defiance.

"I did," Lord said. "You were processed upon entering the comm." He used a finger to flick that form to the holomonitor as well. "Continuing," Lord said, "what *this* document says is that anything you tell us can and will be used to prosecute this case in a physical or recognized virtual court under the laws and Constitution of the United States of America and the *Empyrean* subscription thereto." Lord leaned closer, his gaze relentless. "This is real, Mr. Cameron. You are not going to experience another day of freedom unless you answer truthfully and help us avert this crisis."

For the first time, Cameron seemed slightly unnerved.

Lord eased back slightly. "Now then—what are you doing with the Russians? And before you answer," Lord held up a hand, "let me add a personal note. We all make miscalculations. Answer my questions honestly and I will do everything I can to help you. Lie to me, waste my time, further endanger this station, and I will come after you hard. If you want to think it over, let me know. I'll get us both coffee. I've been awake a *lot* of hours, thanks to you."

Lips pressed tightly together, Cameron shook his head without considering the offer. It was a contrite rejection, not a rebuff. The man was afraid, but not yet willing to throw himself on the mercy of a good cop or a friend.

"I think I'll have something," the Zero-G director said, rising and walking to the other side of the LOO. A small shelf there had pouches that self-heated when squeezed, due to the plasticized lime case; the lime powder prevented the heating fibers from burning the contents and were non-toxically dissolved in the process, adding their own distinctive "*Empyrean* kick," as it was called. Lord selected a black coffee and held it as he walked back. He sat. When the readout said 150 degrees, he snapped back the cap and sipped.

The prisoner was looking down again. His knit fingers were not red or white, they were relaxed. Cameron was not an angry man, he was beaten.

"Mr. Cameron?" Lord coaxed.

"Yes," he said flatly.

"That offer, my assistance, my charity, does come with an expiration date." The voice of the Zero-G director was quiet but firm. Traitors and sympathy were not a synergistic fit for him.

"I don't know what to say," Cameron replied. "I don't know how this happened, the—the accident, I mean. I swear to God, I don't."

"I'll make this simpler if not easier," Lord said. "Do you admit that you were in the Vault?"

Cameron sat very still.

"I'll ask one more time before terminating this interview along with any hope you have of leniency," Lord said.

Cameron nodded tightly. "I went there," he said.

"Into the Vault?"

The prisoner nodded again.

"Why?"

"I was angry," he said. "Christ, I probably shouldn't say that, but it's true."

"You should always say what's true, whatever the situation," Lord said. "Easier to remember. Go on."

The botanist inhaled deeply to calm himself then exhaled slowly. He looked around the room. "Am I free to speak? About the project?"

"You mean, the one you shouldn't even have known about?" Lord asked.

"I—I don't want to compound my problems."

Lord almost laughed. The man was choosing to be discreet *now* after undermining a top-secret experiment. However, since the conversation was being recorded, and his own staff was not cleared for top security, Lord answered the only way he could.

"No," Lord told him. "No details."

"All right," Cameron said, breathing heavily one more time. "I knew that something of professional interest was going on in there—why else would Lancaster Liba be given security clearance? But I didn't know what it was. I felt I should have."

"Professional pride? Personal hurt? Both?"

"Both," Cameron agreed. "I was at a symposium with Dr. Aleksandra Ivashova, chief of Extraterrestrial Biology Research at Roscosmos. She had heard about it too."

"How did she hear of it?" Lord asked.

There were tears in his eyes.

"From you?" Lord pressed.

Cameron's mouth clapped shut. He was aware that he was about to pillory himself. He shifted uneasily.

"Mr. Cameron—this is a cold pool. Best to jump in."

Cameron nodded suddenly. "Yes. I told her. I mean, when she arrived I told her there was something I wanted to talk about. I thought . . . I wanted to give myself time to change my mind. But I didn't. Damn it, they should have told me!"

"Bureaucracies are deplorably impersonal," Lord said sympathetically. "Go on. You both wanted to know more about this project."

Cameron nodded, then added, "Not just to know."

"To hurt the people who overlooked you?"

Cameron was silent.

"Any other reason?" Lord asked.

"Yes. They were . . . professional. Goal-oriented. A way to make sure I was the most qualified man in any room."

"You lost me," Lord said.

Cameron slowly held up a thumb. "It's CHAI," he said. "They literally gave me a green thumb. It contains a webwork of solar storage batteries that increases chlorophyll absorption by a factor of up to 333.2:1 in both monocot and dicot cells. It also contains a steel skeletal structure that allows me to hold up the fingernail, which provides instant plant analysis on a molecular level."

"Molecular, Mr. Cameron? Or subatomic?"

"I don't know," he said. "I truly do not. The data feeds directly to my IC, gave me an advantage to getting this post . . . and, I had hoped, one day succeeding Liba."

"Supplanting him, you mean."

"He—he didn't show any interest in retiring," Cameron said.

Lord didn't show the annoyance he felt. He didn't ask, *Why should he? He's a senior citizen, he's not dead.*

"Where did you acquire the thumb?" Lord asked, remaining on topic.

"In Finland," he said.

"When?"

"That was 2047," Cameron said.

The date didn't fit with any known contact between Cameron and the Russians. The CHAI also wouldn't have fit in the ring box Lord had seen.

"You were already planning ahead," Lord said. "You received the CHAI from an intermediary?"

Cameron nodded. "A Syriarabian scientist, Dr. Mahdi Bek."

Lord's SimAI drop-down emphasized a connection between Bek and the Minister of Natural Resources and Environment of the Russian Federation. He was annoyed that the original search had not picked up that once-removed connection between Cameron and a Russian. Lord stole a quick glance at Adsila, who nodded.

"Mr. Cameron," Lord said, "did Dr. Bek's presentation come with or without the enhanced fingernail?"

Cameron hesitated. The line was about to be crossed. "Without."

"That was furnished by whom, where?"

Another hesitation, this time longer. "Dr. Ivashova, at the symposium."

Lord gestured to restore Cameron's IC access. "Please turn on your IC viewer," Lord said.

Cameron obliged. Lord winked on an image in his picture file, the photograph from the dinner when the botanist had accepted something from the Russian scientist.

"Was this where and when you acquired the fingernail?" Lord asked.

Cameron's lips were pressed together tightly as he nodded.

"Would you confirm verbally that this image captures that transfer?" Lord said. That was required for jurors or jurists who might be visually challenged.

"Yes," Cameron told him. "That symposium was where I acquired the fingernail."

The botanist was broken; ashamed. Lord waited a long moment before continuing. He wanted Cameron to be collected, attentive. Everything to this point had been known or suspected; this was where the real investigation began.

"I have everything I need for the prosecution of this case," Lord told him. "This is where you can start to do yourself some good."

Cameron brightened slightly.

"Mr. Cameron . . . Douglas . . . are you aware of any other Russian agents on board the *Empyrean*?" Lord asked.

"No, and *I'm* not—I'm not a Russian 'agent,'" he insisted, showing the first signs of fortitude since his arrest. "This . . . this was just something stupid I did, *one* thing, out of desperation. No harm was supposed to be done. I . . . we only wanted to know what was going on. When I saw . . . Jesus . . . I am a *botanist*. How could I not want to know more, get my hands dirty?"

The double meaning stopped his meandering confession. Reasons and context rarely mattered in these cases: treason was clearly and broadly defined as any conduct that undermines the government or the national security of the United States. In any case, that was for a tribunal to decide.

"Your findings were communicated electronically, correct?" Lord asked. "To someone on the outside."

Cameron nodded. "As soon as I emerged from the Vault."

"You met no one here."

"No one," Cameron insisted. "I swear it."

Lord believed him. People are usually insistent when they've done something virtuous.

"When did you first enter the Vault?" Lord asked.

"It was—the same day the Dragon's Eye was shut down," Cameron replied. "Everyone was distracted."

"Did you make recordings of any kind?"

"Readings," he said sheepishly. "I only took readings, acquired data. Chemical. Electrical."

"Which, to clarify, went to Dr. Ivashova."

"Yes. I'm sorry."

If Cameron were telling the truth—as Lord suspected he was—his spying might not have been thorough or detailed enough to detect the nanites.

"Are those recordings still in the CHAI?" Lord asked, nodding at the finger.

"No. Data was erased after fifteen minutes."

"To protect you in case you were apprehended."

Cameron nodded.

"How many times did you enter the Vault?" Lord asked.

"Just that one time," Cameron said. "It was risky and . . . and I had second thoughts after I did it. I'm sure you can understand."

Lord wasn't moved. In fact, his gaze was even less kindly than when he had addressed the man by his first name. Cameron's reckless act not only compromised security, it had endangered the *Empyrean*.

"Is there anything else you want to tell me?" Lord asked.

"No. Nothing."

"Now is the time."

"No," Cameron repeated, shaking his head slowly. "If there were anything else, I'd tell you."

Lord eased from the edge of the desk.

"Mr. McClure—the ELEG," Lord said, without taking his eyes off Cameron.

Cameron's expression shifted to concern, his eyes darting toward the man who was approaching. He was pulling on a glove.

"What are you doing?" Cameron asked.

"The thumb," Lord said to the botanist. "Surrender it."

"Director Lord, it's part of—"

"There is a reject code or you would have had to go through a microscan on Earth," Lord said. "I know. I have a CHAI hip. The fingernail represents a demonstrated security risk to this station. You will give us the thumb or it will be taken."

Cameron's hands remained folded—tightly, now.

"Mr. Waters?" Lord said, motioning him over.

Adsila came forward with his Gauntlet. As the EAD and McClure converged on their position, Cameron held up his hands.

"Okay, yes—I—I have to access my IC and I'll shut it down."

"No you don't," Lord told him. "Hold out your hand."

Cameron continued to sit there with his fingers knit. Many ICs had a "fry code," designed to obliterate cyborg implants or any other personally worn surveillance equipment—as well as other electronic contraband, such as drug manufacturing or distribution data or plans for terroristic activities. Zero-G needed the fingernail as evidence. Lord couldn't afford to trust Cameron, however remorseful he seemed.

"What are you going to do?" Cameron asked anxiously.

"I'm going to give you another few seconds to comply," Lord said. "After that, you will be subdued."

The Zero-G director moved eye and finger to bring up his IC scan code. The results would be analyzed by Shin-Aleph, the FBI's file of Israeli CHAI codes, sourced directly—and without their knowledge—from the Mossad database.

Now Cameron seemed like a cornered boar. He looked from face to face to face, and then at the closed door of the command center.

"Mister Cameron," Lord said, drawing out the first word. "The only way you are leaving the comm is walking and thumbless or carried out unconscious and thumbless. Extend your hand please, palm facing you."

The botanist still hesitated. Then, suddenly, he moved to slam his hand hard on the desktop.

Adsila fired as the hand was in motion. Twin arcs of white lightning flashed into the prisoner's chest, on the opposite side from the CHAI-hand. The descending hand fluttered and went limp as Cameron jerked back, trembling; the Zero-G agent was already moving forward, using his free hand to grab the man's wrist. Adsila held it up high as the rest of the man sagged.

"Impact trigger, backup destruct capacity," McClure theorized as Adsila maneuvered behind the limp but conscious captive for a better grip on the wrist. "It would've blown off his hand to the palm heel."

"Impressive work, EAD," Lord said.

"Thank you," Adsila replied, still in an aggressive posture as he shifted to his dominant female form.

"Mr. McClure, how did the comm not pick up an explosive?" Lord asked.

"Because there is nothing incendiary here," McClure said. "The thumb creates an electrical surge that superheats the oxygen in the CHAI— "

"Which expands, and *boom*," Lord said.

"The search protocols will be expanded at once," Abernathy assured him. It was his responsibility; nothing more was said.

Lord moved closer to Cameron's hand and scanned the thumb, walking around it. When he was finished, a red triangle appeared in his IC.

"Mr. McClure, get ready with the ELEG. If it's as heavy as he said—"

"Sir, I used to catch hardballs barehanded back in Connecticut," the agent replied. He moved the ELEG so that it was directly beneath the thumb and bent the fingers up, like a backstop, in case the CHAI popped forward slightly.

It didn't. When Lord activated the icon the digit dropped like a plumb line, leaving behind a carpo-metacarpal joint with a silvery coating. Though McClure caught the CHAI element, the ELEG dropped a full foot.

"Heavy, as advertised," the science agent said. "Three pounds, two ounces of partial digit."

Lord shuddered slightly inside as he turned from Cameron's hand. He recalled looking at his own holoray surgery images and seeing the biodistribution of silica-coated silver iodide nanoparticles that took the place of human nerve endings. It wasn't quite like witnessing one's own rebirth, since there was nothing of personal genetics in what was about to become a large part of you—in Lord's case, from hip to knee. It wasn't like death, either; it was more like a transformation into some-one—some*thing*—new. In the two years since his operation, Lord was still processing the impact.

"Adsila, Abernathy—take him to his quarters and seal the door," Lord said. "Zero-G access only."

As Abernathy scooted over, Lord anticipated the EAD's question. "I've done a scan, the room is secure," he said.

Still wearing the glove, Adsila took Cameron under one arm, Abernathy slipping under the other, and they walked him from the comm.

Lord watched them go. Then, brushing creases from his tunic, he approached Janet Grainger. The thirty-five-year-old African American had not only been the first hire of the team, she was Lord's personal find. The former director of the FBI's Tampa field office, she had regularly interfaced between the Bureau, Cape Canaveral, and the US Air Force in all aerospace matters. That was where Lord first encountered her, at a reception for the NeoDouglas hyperspace bomber Moonbird. Grainger was as passionate about the US space program and living 26,000 feet above the Earth as she was about having that much distance between herself and her former husband.

"Okay to send the interrogation log?" the woman asked.

"Okay to send," Lord replied, after checking an FBI file for specific data.

The recording, an IC virtual recording, went to Prime Director Al-Kazaz, whose breakfast it would hopefully follow and not interrupt.

They caught him taking a bite from a honeyed biscuit. The PD saw what the message contained and immediately contacted Lord privately.

"Is there anything I need to see right away, Sam?" he asked.

"Not in the log," Lord said. "But I notice there's been a number of secure communications between the *Red Giant* and Moscow today. It's a QP2—first one I've seen them use up here."

Quantum photo polarization encryption programs were both a boon and curse to secure communication. While they were virtually impossible to decode by interception, they also destroyed the data as it was received. Users got one brief pass to see it in a correctly keyed receiver, after which it self-scrambled and was lost.

"Those communications may not be about us," Al-Kazaz said as he looked at the encrypted file. "Could be something else they have going up there."

"Whatever it is, it's important to them," Lord noted. "The question is whether it's important to us as well."

"You mean, whether it has anything to do with Cameron's report or his capture," the prime director said.

"Exactly."

"I want to listen to the Cameron interrogation before I ask the CIA what they have," Al-Kazaz said. "Stay available."

"Yes, sir," Lord said as Al-Kazaz signed off. "Red, give me the current location of exobiologist Dr. Aleksandra Ivashova."

"She is at a meeting in the Kremlin."

"Do you know if it was scheduled?"

"That appears unlikely," Red replied. "She was supposed to be attending a two-day meeting about the militarization of the Chinese space program at the Moscow State Institute of Interplanetary Relations."

"Is *that* meeting going ahead?"

"It is. Dr. Ivashova registered in person but is not present."

"So she was recalled."

"That's a reasonable assumption," Red said.

Lord still believed that Cameron was telling the truth when he said he had not been in touch with any other operatives onboard the *Empyrean*. That would have been in keeping with the historic method of quarantining agents so that the fall of one did not cause the fall of many.

The timing of Dr. Ivashova's meeting may just be coincidental, perhaps having nothing at all to do with the vine, Lord thought. Therein lay the challenge of this job and the reason Al-Kazaz had taken the unprecedented step of giving it to a combat pilot: Lord understood the importance of on-the-fly risk assessment, interpreting enemy interaction during a battle, and finding and choking adversarial supply lines.

"Agent Abernathy," Lord said without turning, "are you able to see the Tsiolkovsky telescope on board the *Red Giant*?"

"I am."

"What are they studying?"

Abernathy scanned the FBI plug-in with the *Empyrean* lenses turned to that sector of the heavens. "The lens is turned toward the direction of Venus," he replied.

"And the—what's the name of their asteroid spotter? What's that doing?"

"The Tereshkova small array," the agent replied, a trace of puzzlement in his voice. "It's watching the area beyond the moon, but also spying on the external activities of Armstrong Base, according to data I'm getting from Armstrong."

"Very good," Lord said. "Thank you."

Lord's IC pinged. PD Al-Kazaz was calling for an immediate meeting in the LOO. That meant he had something secure to discuss. So secure that he didn't want the team to hear even Lord's replies.

Lord shut his IC so he wouldn't forget.

"Knock if there's anything urgent," he said over his shoulder as he headed toward the rear of the comm. "I'll be indisposed."

TEN

LORD EASED SIDEWAYS into the LOO, a room barely larger than the sum of its contents: a comfortable chair—basically a seat attached to the back wall—and a low hoverlight. The Lord Only Office was also silent, without the ever-present sounds of the *Empyrean*: personnel talking to each other and on ICs, plumbing, air vents, elevators, and the movement of various external robotic arm pivots, flexible dish joints, and other hardware that vibrated through the structure. Even the four fans that provided the room with air and kept the temperature at a constant 70 degrees Fahrenheit were quiet, the blades run by frictionless barrel-type bearings. The soundproofed walls were lined with a thicket of Faraday-cage metal to protect internal conversations against eavesdropping.

Settling into the cushiony form-fitting seat, Lord rechecked that he'd turned off his personal IC—which could neither receive nor send data in here—and waited for the door to self-lock and the room-filling secure IC to come on.

At once, the sun-darkened, leathery features of Prime Director Al-Kazaz hovered before him. To Lord's surprise, the PD was in a good mood. That was unusual, given that there was a crisis and that one of his top people had been in the thick of it.

Not that Peter Al-Kazaz was easily shaken; he was usually just focused. The sixty-year-old had been a field agent for Homeland Security, stationed in Dasht-e Kavir before the formation of the Middle East Confederacy. Living among nomads in the great Salt Desert of Iran, collecting intelligence, Al-Kazaz had acquired a fixed expression that was neutral, bordering on grave, like a man who appeared to be burdened by life—but he was, in fact, taking everything in and thinking deep thoughts about whatever mission he was on.

"I watched the Cameron file," Al-Kazaz said. "Very, very impressive, Sam."

"Thank you," Lord said. "It was really a Zero-G effort—"

"I'm not talking about the arrest or the nanite takedown," the PD said.

Lord was perplexed. "What do you mean?"

"I sent you up there to work your magic for me," Al-Kazaz said. "You have. While I was watching the Cameron interrogation, a communiqué came in from NASA. They attached a brief report from Dr. Carter. In light of your actions, both you and I have been granted full security clearance for Merlin. And—*and*—the sec-pro was endorsed by Commander Stanton."

"Well," said Lord. A security promotion was better than the last communication from Stanton to Al-Kazaz, the one that began with "Keep your sonofabitch director from ever bugging my security wedge again." That had been a reference to an advanced eavesdropping device, a Jumper, that Lord had slipped into the secure section of the Drum during the *Empyrean*'s showdown with the *Jade Star*.

"What's really going on there, Sam?" Al-Kazaz asked. "Your interp."

"The Russians specifically targeted the Vault, so they knew months ago that something was *about* to go on there," Lord said. "NASA has a data leak."

"Which they realize now and are scrambling to plug," Al-Kazaz told him. "You know what tipped off the Russians?"

"Knowing the military-industrial complex as I do? I'd say a NASA flight manifest, available to any member of the public who asks, that included foliage without decorative or consumable value?" Lord suggested.

"Impressively close," Al-Kazaz replied. "It was the purchase of a variety of seeds for study seven months before said flight."

"Ah, democracy," Lord said. "Freedom of information, and the only ones who ever ask are our enemies."

"And the newtiae."

"Didn't I just say that?" Lord quipped. "But let's back up a bit first. I'm a little concerned that no one saw fit to share the specifics of Dr. Carter's nanite work with me. He is, after all, on my team."

"But you knew anyway," Al-Kazaz said. "From Liba, as I knew you would. Keeping you in the dark officially was not my call."

"Whose call was it?" Lord asked. "Carter says the nanites were just medical tools when he started out. That's also not in his dossier."

"National Security Agency scrubbed it after the fact," Al-Kazaz told him. "And it may have started out as a medical program, but it had—well, graduated by the time the NSA came calling. They wanted these creations of Carter to burrow into people's epidermis, pull a new blanket of flesh over them, and hide there, sending data."

"Because tatpro worked so well," Lord said.

The Tattoo Program was a CIA initiative in 2031 in which metallic inks were used to record conversations on dermal mollies. It failed when the inked image of a battleship started broadcasting data during a meeting of North Korea's Ministry of State Security.

"This was viewed as a considerable improvement," Al-Kazaz said. "The NSA canceled the plan because the skin corrupted the signals. Actually, it was suntan lotion."

"Hold on," Lord continued. "Does Carter hold the patent for these nanites?"

"You're a step ahead of me, as usual," Al-Kazaz said. "Carter was working for himself, in his own privately funded research lab, at the time he created them. So he's free to customize his nanites for whoever he wants. That's one reason I hired him. I knew he couldn't resist the opportunity to work on them in zero gravity. In exchange, we were to get access to any applications he came up with."

"Or was instructed to come up with," Lord said. "But you said 'were' to get?"

The prime director nodded. "After the NSA departed, NASA beat me to him," Al-Kazaz said. "Flexing their sinews, expanding, never wanting to go back to the lean years of the turn of the century."

"Smart," Lord said. "So he holds the patents, but NASA controls anything he develops while he's on the payroll."

"The best I could do was put him on our payroll as a medic," the prime director said. "NASA didn't see that twist coming."

"Even smarter, which is why I'm not in politics or business," Lord said.

"Don't ever let them corrupt you," his old friend said.

"So, speaking of smart," Lord continued, "amidst all this high finance, crafty bureaucratic maneuvering, and ongoing secrecy in our own government, the Russians managed to sneak in and steal one of our juiciest secrets."

Al-Kazaz frowned. "Intramural competition has nothing to do with espionage, Sam."

"Unless it takes our eye off the ball," Lord said.

"That's not what happened here," Al-Kazaz said. "In any case, Carter assures me that whatever Cameron obtained from the Vault, nanite technology was not in the mix."

"No, they can buy *that* from Ziv."

"Not at this level of sophistication," Al-Kazaz replied. "But the way this unfolded points out a fundamental flaw in our work, an area where you, fortunately, excel."

"Which area is that?" Lord asked. "There are so many."

The comment was only partly in jest. The prime director let it pass.

"Almost everything we do is ELINT, and electronically based intelligence does not have a human observer to react, change, analyze,"

Al-Kazaz replied. "You used to employ your heads-up display in combat, but you also relied on your eyes and your gut. That's what the Bureau is missing. That's what *all* the agencies are missing."

"You're losing me, Peter. How is the FBI's long-standing systemic failure *my* problem?"

"It isn't," Al-Kazaz admitted. "But the sudden, concurrent uptick in communications between Moscow and the *Red Giant* is. What does your gut say about that?"

"I don't think that is necessarily related to what happened up there in the Vault," Lord said.

"An idea that seems to defy logic," Al-Kazaz said.

"Actually, it's the very soul of logic," Lord replied. "Unless Cameron missed some kind of call-in, which I doubt—he was busy with Stanton when we arrested him—the Russians still think they have local eyes on the Agro Center."

"Maybe they still do," Al-Kazaz said. "Cameron wouldn't necessarily have been told if there were another spy. Word of the nanite transformation, of Cameron's arrest, may have been sent."

"Not likely," Lord said. "They communicate by heliograph."

"What?"

"Mirrors," Lord said. He retrieved the small glass from his pocket. "Found it in Cameron's room. Highly polished chrome surface, not glass. Ideal for reflecting."

"*And* for shaving!" Al-Kazaz said.

"Cameron has a prograz," Lord said, referring to a battery-powered shaving device that remembers the contours of the face. "The enemy used these very effectively in ground-to-air communications during the War on Narcotics. I had McClure run a scan for any flashes from the *Empyrean* not attributable to our orbit or axial tilt. Nothing."

"Nice, Sam. Very nice. You'll put that in the evidence locker—"

"Soon as I leave here," Lord said. "I wanted you to see. It's not just clever, it speaks to the almost Luddite way the Russians do things up here. I'm not surprised their high-tech thumb had flaws."

The prime director circled back to the topic at hand. "Which means that the chatter out there is about something else."

"Most likely," Lord said. He began scrolling through warehoused *Red Giant* data with his finger, not his eyes, to keep from getting dizzy. "They've fired every one of their sixteen Scuds over the last few months. Here are the dates. We still don't know why . . . unless you do?"

"They have said, and NASA agrees, that it's solar research."

"Right," Lord said dubiously. "And our Pan-Persia Occupation was an overreaction to finding an Iranian-built nuclear bomb on a Bulgarian cargo plane bound for London."

"It's not the same," Al-Kazaz shot back. "That was an imminent threat. The Russians *do* engage in pure science up there—"

"Just like Dr. Carter."

"*Still* not the same!" Al-Kazaz said. "One Department of Digital Security white paper—you can read it, Sun742—suggests that they are looking at the composition of the cloud cover of Venus for methods of shielding the nation from explosive solar flares that could shut down all electronic activity."

"Possibly," Lord agreed. They were talking about a country that covers eleven time zones and has Arctic and agricultural regions that are heavily impacted by solar activity. Russia was behind the rest of the world by a good quarter century. They were in survival mode, not conquest, and Venus could offer useful low-tech ideas. "But we also shouldn't ignore the fact that the Russians rent space to the criminal Satellite organization. Whatever Roscosmos learns, the bad guys also learn."

"Apples and PCs," Al-Kazaz told him. "The mob contributes considerable monies to the upkeep of the station. Besides, the criminal chatter up there is far better encrypted than the rest of the *Red Giant*. You wouldn't have picked it up at all."

"Janet Grainger's resourcefulness would surprise you," Lord said. "My point is, there's more to the *Red Giant* than solar research. And we don't know enough about that."

Al-Kazaz considered that. "You have any suggestions?"

"Something did just occur to me," Lord said. "I think I should go to the *Red Giant*."

It wasn't just the ensuing silence that made Lord think the communication had somehow been severed; it was the frozen expression on the prime director's face, a cross between disbelief and shock. Finally, face and voice became active again.

"It 'just occurred' to you," Al-Kazaz said dubiously.

"That's right."

"Under what possible pretext would you do that, Sam? What can you possibly say that will get you on board?"

"No pretext," Lord replied. "I'll tell them the truth, that we've got their spy and his CHAI thumb. I'll offer to bring them both over, no strings. How can they refuse?"

"You are the FBI's ranking agent in space and you expect to get permission to board a space station that harbors Russian mobsters?"

"I expect it," Lord said confidently. "I'm guessing they'll *want* to meet one of the guys they're up against."

"Sure," Al-Kazaz said. "And will you drink the poisoned vodka they gift you with because booze in space is so damn costly?"

"What's the upside for them killing me?" Lord asked. "There are plenty of other candidates in line for this job—younger, fitter, angrier, more aggressive. I'm thinking a visit like this actually buys me a little bit of hands-off protection."

"Which you will curry."

Lord grinned. "Who, me?"

The prime director shook his head. "My mind is arguing against this, Sam."

"An outdated, deeply rooted, Bureau-culture reaction," Lord said.

"You have never *been* a field agent."

"All the more reason to go," Lord said. "I won't look like one or feel like one. Peter, we need recon."

"You must be serious," Al-Kazaz said. "You used my first name."

Lord also knew when to be silent. He sat very still until Al-Kazaz stopped shaking his head.

"You're right about that, Sam. Maybe about all of this, I don't know." He snickered. "I'm glad I have someone who challenges me. By the way, did you hear that sound?"

"What sound?"

"The sound of the FBI's weighty, carefully thought-out rule book going out the airlock," Al-Kazaz said.

Lord chuckled. "It's got good company. The air force rules of engagement, the flight ceiling specs on the *Vampire*— "

"You are a storied contrarian," Al-Kazaz said.

"All in the name of getting results," Lord pointed out.

"If I didn't think that, you wouldn't be up there." The prime director's expression resumed some of its earlier enthusiasm as his chest heaved. "What do we lose by giving them Cameron?"

"No loss to us but, more important, no gain for them," Lord said. "Only, they don't know that yet. Cameron gave them a peek at the ingredients of the vine, though they probably have no idea that it went haywire because of his incursion. And being made aware of the dangers of this new biotechnology—corroborated by their own spy—we may actually frighten them off using whatever science they did pick up."

"There's a certain logic to that, though I don't know how it'll play with the Justice Department," Al-Kazaz said.

"It'll play like an early Christmas," Lord said. "Cameron will be one less case for them to prosecute and one less public embarrassment for NASA security."

Al-Kazaz eyed his longtime friend and confidant. "Glad to see I was right."

"About?"

"Sending you up there," Al-Kazaz said. "You slice through posturing and jurisdictions like you did the sound barrier."

"Only at Mach-9," Lord said. His mood darkened as he backed into an unpleasant memory—tripped over it, landing face-first in sadness.

Al-Kazaz saw the change and gave him a moment. "You've said it to me many times, Sam," he said. "Best to go out with your boots on."

"Yeah," Lord replied. "But Red went a little too soon. And the air force never did get that damn Berylline right."

Lord allowed himself another moment to dwell on the aircraft with the hummingbird wings that were supposed to propel it to record airspeeds. It did—straight down, at speeds that caused the ejection mechanism to lock in place.

"Assuming you get permission from the Russians," Al-Kazaz said, resuming the original conversation, "how do you propose to get you and Cameron to the *Red Giant*?"

It was a good question. The *Empyrean's* personal vehicle fleet had been devastated by the Dragon's Eye, Armstrong Base had only one functioning shuttle, and the only other US space transports were the large kites that met hyperplanes in Earth's atmosphere and ferried passengers to and from the *Empyrean*. The final option was a private shuttle, such as the ones owned by Ziv Levy or history's first trillionaire, Maalik Kattan, who planned to expand his globe-girdling gambling empire into space with a private hotel and casino. The problem with hitching a ride from one of those individuals was a potential conflict of interest: the rogue behavior of men and women like that had made them ongoing targets of FBI investigations.

"When there's only one option, you've got to make it work," Lord said. "I guess I'm going to have to convince the Russians to come and get us."

ELEVEN

RIDING THE EXERCISE cycle in the small fitness module of the *Red Giant*, Svetlana Regina Uralov alternated between reading history books and watching her time and distance on the IC digital flash-out. The blue numbers hovered before her like rich blue sky peeking through chaotic gray clouds. Three days ago, she had achieved a personal best for her half-hour "ride"; this morning she had a feeling she was going to best that.

Perspiration soaked her headband as her legs churned. That, at least, felt like it had on Earth. It was familiar, welcome. When she closed her eyes, like now, she could almost forget where she was. Straps held her feet to the pedals and she gripped the handlebars tightly so she didn't go flying off in the gravity-free environment.

Pumping hard, then harder, the thirty-seven-year-old could not remember a day in her life when she wasn't in some kind of competition, starting with her own family.

She was the great-granddaughter of Serafima Balashov, one of the celebrated *Nochnye Vedmy*, the Night Witches, the female aviators of the 588th Night Bomber Regiment who bombed German targets during the latter years of World War II. She was the granddaughter of Yelena Myshkova, who flew high-altitude missions to test the flight equipment worn by the first female cosmonauts in the 1960s. She was the daughter of Ninel Uralov, who piloted the first helium-filled passenger balloons for the revival of airship travel in 2021. Ninel achieved some renown after her highly secret test ship went down on the peaks of Mt. Kangchenjunga in Nepal at an elevation of eleven thousand feet, where she managed to survive for a week before being found by a Sherpa.

Svetlana was not just born to fly, she had no choice. Whether it was on sleds or bicycles or even a unicycle, once, she found herself competing with other children. She learned to fly before she learned to drive and was recruited by the Russian Aerospace Force, where she flew the Kamov Ka-60R reconnaissance helicopter in ways that even the manufacturer had not known its design could support.

And then, the fall. It happened a year and a half before, a long-gestating, inevitable one-night stand with a general who was married to the youngest sister of President Kuzmina. The general was sent to the frozen military base just north of Tiksi, on the ice-covered Arctic Ocean. Svetlana was quickly trained and rocketed to the *Red Giant* to run the repurposed Soyuz back and forth between the space station and the supply balloons her mother had helped to pioneer.

Space wasn't Siberia or one of the gulags where troublesome citizens used to be sent. It was worse. It was an abode without change, without friends, without gravity. It had room, but that was all except for a window, unusable. It teased with a constant view of lost Earth and the so-solid air that used to roll beneath her wings. Here, she went faster than most humans had ever traveled and yet there was no sensation of speed, no adrenaline surge—

Nothing, she thought as she broke her pedaling record yet again and kept going. *Nothing but memory.* And most of *that* was about the general and the absurd price she had paid for a night of love.

A ping in her IC distracted her. The only active function Svetlana bothered with were for calls from her parents or brother, from the general—which she knew would never come—from the military attorney who had appealed her reassignment—which she also knew would never come—and from Commander Ptushko.

It was from Ptushko. Svetlana continued to pedal as she blinked to open the channel, simultaneously snapping her head to the side to fling perspiration into the air. The globules floated like bubbles on Earth, headed slowly toward the vacuum that cleared the air of impurities and recycled its liquid content. A day from now she'd be drinking that sweat.

"Come to see me," Ptushko ordered. He looked her up and down in a way that somehow made her seem defective. "Immediately."

"At once," she said, professionally but without enthusiasm.

Svetlana stopped pumping her legs and grabbed a towel that sat in a clamp behind the seat; otherwise, it would have been sucked toward the filter. She mopped her face, slipped her feet from the straps that held her to the pedals, and let herself drift from the stationary bicycle.

She caught her reflection in the mirror that was there to provide an illusion of openness, which psychologists in Roscosmos had decided was a good thing. All it did was remind her of how sallow her once-bronzed features had become, how the Mongolian-descended cheekbones rose proudly from flesh that seemed too taut, how the epicanthic fold of her eyes now made them seem guarded and tired instead of exotic. Maybe she was defective, she decided—at least, compared to the eagle she once was.

Clamping the towel back in place, the five-foot, three-inch pilot pushed off the handlebars and sailed toward the round doorway, floating through the dining area, making a sharp left turn with the help of a white plastic grip darkened by the hands of many passing cosmonauts. The commander's cabin headquarters were directly ahead. Svetlana reactivated her IC. The door opened as it read her approaching identification. She drifted in and effortlessly executed a ninety-degree turn to face Ptushko.

The *Red Giant* commander was a short, wiry man with an owlish face that looked as if it belonged on a very different body. He was bald, with dark-brown eyes and a proud demeanor that had served him for fifty years on the once-revolutionary 1,009-foot aircraft carrier *Admiral*

Andreyev. Now sixty-eight, he had spent three years in space using those same tactical and managerial skills, trying to keep scientific, nationalistic, and criminal activities from mutually destructing.

Ptushko was strapped into an inflatable seat behind a desk that consisted of a simple plank bolted to one wall of the small cabin. She greeted him with a casual salute and he returned it with an equal lack of enthusiasm for military formality. Svetlana crossed her legs yoga-style and hovered in front him. The man looked even more tired than usual. The top strap of his rust-red uniform was pulled tight; it seemed to Svetlana that the fabric was helping to hold the man together.

Ptushko reviewed the communication in his IC then looked past it at the lieutenant.

"You have an assignment, directly from Roscosmos," Ptushko said. He was watching her carefully and saw her brighten. "That interests you, Lieutenant?"

"Very much, Commander," she said.

"I am glad," he replied. "Freedom does seem like exile when the scenery does not change."

Svetlana was not a philosopher but she didn't entirely agree with that. She was *not* free and she would have given a great deal to feel the pull of gravity again. To be able to hug her mother and father, her grandparents, instead of occasionally communicating with them on her IC. And even that was strained, her mother and grandmother openly distressed at the stain she had brought to the family name.

"After arrangements have been made," the commander went on, "which will be within the hour, I expect, you will take the Soyuz in a three-person configuration to the American space station."

"The *Empyrean*," she said with a trace of disbelief.

"That *is* the American space station, Uralov."

"Yes, of course," Svetlana said. "Thank you, sir." Her heart sped. She had seen the *Empyrean* through the telescope, on those rare occasions that the equipment was not being used. It was a golden gem in the sky with rainbow sails, a beacon of reflected sunlight and promise.

He regarded her with an uncharacteristic smile. "You don't even care why."

"No, Commander."

"You should," he told her. "About twenty minutes ago we had a request from Washington to shuttle two passengers from the *Empyrean* to the *Red Giant*. I have agreed to grant that request."

Svetlana knew that the Americans did not have convenient means of reaching the *Red Giant*; there was no reason to come here, no accommodations if they did and, thus, no readily available shuttlecraft to make such a journey. The round-trip would require the Soyuz.

"However," Ptushko continued, "they have said very little about their reason for wanting to come here and I have reservations about granting them access. What I have decided is that I will agree to bring them to the *Red Giant*, to meet them—but en route you will conduct a threat assessment."

And there was the barb in the brambles.

"Sir," she said, "I am a pilot. Just a pilot. That is beyond my area of expertise."

"You are a military officer who has been involved in surveillance."

"From the air, sir," she said. "I used equipment with which I was familiar in military situations for which I was trained . . . not person-to-person in a potential political minefield."

"I understand," he said. "But you will try?" It wasn't a question.

"Sir, you are asking something—"

"That could have enormous impact on your nation and your career," he said. "*Try*. Or do you prefer your shuttle runs to continue as they have been, with no new responsibilities, or potential new challenges?"

He knew that she did not. She also knew that he did not have another pilot at hand for those "new challenges," whatever they might be. But the admiral knew what her answer would be. She wanted to get out of stasis.

"Admiral, there must be a stated purpose to this visit," Svetlana said.

"There is, one that is long on words but short on actual information."

Ptushko blinked at his IC and shared it with her, the Glossator function immediately translating.

"*Preevyet, Polkovnik* Ptushko," said the speaker, using an informal Russian greeting to precede the commander's Russian rank. "I am Samuel Lord, Director of Zero-G."

The American allowed a moment for that to register, leaving behind a confident but cherubic smile. Svetlana thought the man's expression bordered on smug, but since coming to the *Red Giant* she had resolved to ignore any and all judgments she made about men. She had misjudged the general too, never thinking he would confess all to his wife.

"The reason for this communication is to inform you that I am in possession of a gentleman who was lately in the—well, he was in the rather secretive employ of one Dr. Aleksandra Ivashova of Roscosmos," Lord continued pleasantly. "Rather than create an embarrassing fuss on Earth, I thought you might like to have him back. If you are agreeable, send one of your transports and I will be happy to escort him to you. I have this individual until twenty hundred hours, which is when the next kite leaves for Earth, and I will be required to put him on it. I hope to hear from you before then. *Spasibo* and *dobreye ootra!*"

The recording ended with Lord's passable "Thank you and good morning" in Russian.

Ptushko regarded his companion as though waiting for comment.

"That seems rather forthright," Svetlana said.

"Exactly," Ptushko replied. "Which is why we do not believe it. Moscow's immediate reaction is that the Zero-G will return this supposed 'spy' in order *to* spy. They want to know why—or rather, why *now*. They would like you to collect this individual along with Director Lord."

"I see," she said.

"But you are still unsure."

"I am wary, Admiral," Svetlana said thoughtfully. "I want to go, sir. I want that very much. But what if Lord is coming here to do more than spy? Perhaps he wishes to bug the station, possibly even to sabotage it."

"Then he may ask you questions that will lead you to that conclusion," Ptushko said. "We assume he will at the very least attempt to gather intelligence. That is his job and we are a rich source of information. We have an opportunity to learn their latest techniques and create countermeasures."

"Yes, sir, and you have 'asked' me to assess his capabilities and intentions during our trip. In which case I will be blamed for anything he uncovers, for having brought him here."

"Or you will be rewarded for exposing him," Ptushko pointed out.

"Sir, we both know that any commendations will go to you. But blame for any failure will fall on me."

Ptushko shrugged. "That is the nature of our hierarchy, though I would share the glory with you, of course. You know that, yes?"

She nodded slightly but without conviction.

"But why be negative?" Ptushko went on. "Consider very carefully where a successful mission could take you, Lieutenant. Perhaps another assignment, one more to your liking?"

Svetlana understood. Current success always overshadowed old misjudgments. But she still had reservations. It was like the caution that used to possess her whenever she did a preflight check of her Ka-60R. The lieutenant was always concerned that a male rival, one of the old-school chauvinists who still dominated the Russian military, would sabotage her helicopter just to get her out of the way. For too many men, that high price was worth paying.

He was watching her closely. "You are still not entirely on board."

"Sir, Lord did not name the other man, this alleged spy," she told him. "Zero-G is part of the FBI. Perhaps the director does not have anyone at all in captivity. He may be fishing. If I show up, it will essentially tell him we *do* have an agent on his station."

Ptushko smiled. "That is very good thinking, Lieutenant. Lord obviously considered the point too, which is why he named Dr. Ivashova. He had to have heard such information from her agent, and Roscosmos informs me that she does have someone on board the *Empyrean*—an agricultural engineer named Douglas Cameron. Lord did not name the man because he is trying to find out if there might be others. If you arrive and are cautious, evasive, probing—he will suspect that you are being guarded because there is more than one. But if you arrive and ask for this man by name—"

"Then he will assume that Cameron is the only one."

Ptushko nodded. "Cameron *is* the only one who reports to Dr. Ivashova."

"Lord cannot know if other officials have their own people on board," she said. "That is something he will certainly try to find out here."

Ptushko nodded again.

"Very smart, all around," Svetlana said. Her heart was still thumping hard; she felt scared but also renewed. It was good to be on the cusp of doing something again.

"Have all your questions been answered, doubts resolved?" Ptushko asked.

"The questions have been answered, sir," she said, then smiled. "The rest is for me to resolve."

He nodded approvingly, then waited.

Svetlana regarded her superior. Ptushko himself could order her to go but hadn't, and had kindly allowed her to voice her concerns. *This part is being recorded on his IC and he's insulating himself from responsibility*, she realized. She straightened her legs in preparation for leaving the cabin.

"I volunteer to go, sir, of course," she said.

"Very good, Lieutenant," he said with a celebratory air.

"What time will I be leaving?"

"Soon, I trust, but I am not yet finished," Ptushko informed her.

Svetlana noticed the admiral's eyes flick. He was no longer recording.

"Two weeks ago you retrieved a top-secret parcel carried aloft by space plane Gagarin"—Ptushko checked a printed manifest—"item 101763 from Earth. You attached it to the armpit. Do you recall?"

The armpit was the nickname the crew had given to the joint under one of the two large solar panels, a storage area that did not consume valuable space inside the station.

"I do remember, Commander," she said, suddenly guarded. "The stowing maneuver took longer than expected because of the size of the cargo, but it was executed as instructed and the connection—"

"Please stop," Ptushko said, holding up a bony hand. "You really must learn to relax. The contents are intact, this is not a disciplinary action."

Lieutenant Uralov didn't realize she had tensed until he pointed it out. She let herself float easier in the weightlessness of the cabin.

"The crate you brought up consisted of a zeta-pinch fusion jet engine," Ptushko informed her. "You are familiar with these devices?"

The woman's eyes came back to life even brighter than before. "Yes, Commander, very much so," she said. "Each one is capable of accelerating at one g for as long as necessary, and trajectories are simple and linear because the engine is simply forward, brute force, nothing sophisticated. If you want to go faster, you add more engines, which will require the occupants to undergo two or three Gs for the duration of the journey—"

"You've read the Roscosmos papers," he said. "I am impressed."

"Thank you, yes, sir," she replied. Svetlana did not tell her superior that she suspected her reading was being monitored by the Russian space agency. Svetlana always believed—and hoped—that the highly secretive Scud launchings toward the sun would one day require more than autopilots. She kept up on all the new flight and propulsion developments; she wanted it to be known that she was interested in and ready for any assignment they might care to give the only bona fide pilot they had in space.

"Upon the completion of your round-trip to *Empyrean*, those engines will be attached to the Soyuz," Ptushko went on. "You will assist. The process should not take long as preparations have been under way since the engine arrived. You will rest and then there will be another flight. A longer one. A more significant one. I cannot tell you more than that at the moment, except that I would prefer that *you* fly the mission." He smiled crookedly. "After all, it reflects poorly on a commander if a pilot must be imported to his station. And this mission is momentous, Lieutenant. It is an assignment that will make history." Ptushko wagged a spindly finger at her. His eyes, his tone told her that he wanted this handled by his team. "Succeed in the *Empyrean* mission, help Roscosmos to turn tables on this American operative, and I assure you, that mission is yours."

"I will do whatever you need," she told him.

"What *we* need," he gently corrected her.

Svetlana left with a smile and an easy, enthusiastic grace she had lacked when she first went to his office. She felt free.

Ptushko was partly right. The scenery *was* about to change. But so was something else: this American federal agent was about to feel every blunt or artful blow she had not been able to land on the admiral who was using her.

TWELVE

I T HAD BEEN a very brief incarceration for Douglas Cameron, perhaps the shortest in FBI history: just over ten minutes. No sooner had Waters and McClure placed him in his cabin and returned to the comm than they were instructed to go back and get him.

"I will explain when you get back," Lord told them.

Adsila caught Grainger's glance as she left, a look that told her that Lord had apparently convinced the PD to let him do something that wasn't quite regulation, and a look they had shared quite often in just a few weeks.

Lord was still in his formal wear when they returned. He indicated for the prisoner to be brought to his right and they immediately knew why, even if Cameron clearly did not. The prisoner's IC was automatically linked to that of Lord by the Mindcuffs-S program, which immediately rendered Cameron's eyes glassy, his shoulders relaxed, his manner compliant. Mindcuffs had been employed by law enforcement since ICs were first approved for government use in 2039. Originally called ICuffs because they were controlled by the IC, a major American corporation sued the Federal Government and the name was changed. The technology linked officer and prisoner at two points—the zygomatic and parietal points of the skull—with at least four inches of separation. If the captive tried to move from within a narrow, virtual yellow band overlaid in her or his vision, either to flee or attack the officer, a three-million-volt charge was downloaded into their skull, causing complete muscular incapacitation. Police on Earth found that many criminals would take the hit just to delay the arrest or transport from place to place, so the cuffs were altered to link with the body's capacity to produce serotonin. As a captive's stress levels rose, the electrical hold tightened on that individual's enterochromaffin cells. Escape was only an abstract thought at best, as the fuel to power it was missing.

Except for Adsila, the rest of the team stood at their posts. Though Dr. Carter was rarely present in the comm, the medic was almost always plugged into group discussions when Lord described a mission change or new initiative. That was the case now. While Adsila Waters removed her Gauntlet and stowed it in the locker, Lord explained the new "initiative," as he called it. She stood by the locker while the door self-sealed; when Lord had finished, she stepped up to him.

"Sir, I am the one who should be making this trip," she said. "'In a situation where a highest-command official should be placed in a situation of potential jeopardy'"—she read from the drop-down—"'that risk should be assumed by the second-in-command rather than—'"

"I appreciate your concern," Lord interrupted, "but that applies to a 'mission,' not to an 'initiative.'"

"Sir, that is a linguistic, not a command distinction—"

"Besides, PD Al-Kazaz has overridden 749a," Lord pointed out. "I'm helpless. I must go."

Her expression dubious, Adsila moved her eyes from side to side. "Director Lord—I am reading the bulletin sent by the prime director, and that is not an accurate reduction of the order," the EAD informed him. "What the alert said, sir, is that he will not overrule your judgment if you *elect* to employ 754a, which, and I quote, 'allows the ranking official to ignore 749a and undertake personally hazardous off-station activity if said activity is vital to the survival of the team and its environment.' Director Lord, neither of those conditions applies."

"I take a different view," he said with a shrug.

"For the record," Grainger added, "Commander Stanton has received the initiative profile from the PD and does not approve at all."

"He wants his man to stand trial, of course," Lord said.

"Whatever the reason, he's looking for a regulation to block your docking request."

"He won't find one," Lord said. "NASA authorized full discretionary priority access in criminal matters when Zero-G came up here. And the commander really has more important things to do."

"Sam, I happen to agree with Commander Stanton," Dr. Carter said, joining the debate. "You are too choice an asset to send blindly and alone to the *Red Giant*."

"You two concur? This is surely a sign of *Apokalypsis Ioannou*," Lord replied.

Five drop-downs defined the Greek for "John's Revelation," the End of Days.

"I am very serious," Carter said.

"I have never known you to be otherwise," Lord replied. "Am I medically unfit?"

"You are not."

"Perfect," Lord said. He whisked aside Carter's face to look directly at Adsila. "I respect your concern for my safety, EAD. I do. And I agree that there is risk. Of course there is. But the needs of Zero-G outweigh the needs of its director."

"Again, that statement assumes there is no one else who can go," Adsila countered stubbornly.

"If you were to go, or anyone else, the Russians would have very little reason to let you aboard or to keep you there," Lord said. "If they did, an emissary of Commander Ptushko—and make no mistake, the admiral probably wouldn't bother to meet you himself; it would send the wrong message about your relative importance—would take our prisoner from the Soyuz, turn it around, and send you home." Lord shook his head. "No. If they want to take the time and stress the resources of the *Red Giant* to squeeze anyone for information, it will be me. That will also give *me* time to try and find out more about who else is involved in this breach." He looked around the room at his team, including Dr. Carter in his IC. "And if something *should* happen to me, I am ably backed by my team."

"We all agree that to any enemy, and the mob-infested Russian space program in particular, you are an incredible asset," Carter said. "Less because of your specific knowledge about the FBI, which isn't very old and isn't very deep, but because of what you know about cutting-edge aircraft, about research you now know is *presently* being conducted by NASA on this station, and about Armstrong Base. You have been to the secret research lab there, you know its safeguards."

"All very true," Lord said. "Again, that is precisely what makes this effort possible. The Russians could not say no to a visit, they *did* not say no. Keep in mind, all of you, that the intel I stand to gather just by setting foot on the *Red Giant* is also potentially immeasurable."

Janet Grainger picked up the nay-saying. "*If* you can get the data to us, sir. The Russians will block any uploads."

"Maybe," Lord said. "They're about fifteen years behind us in their IC capabilities."

"We think, sir," Abernathy said.

Lord turned to the agent and smiled. "You see? Just by my going to the station we will learn whether or not *that's* true."

"The Russian Mafia is not so backward," Grainger said. "We spotted them at the Cape, trying to buy flash drives."

"They are also not respectful of nationality, rank, or reputation," Adsila added.

"Again, all of this convinces me that this is a good way to learn more about their operations up here," Lord said.

"Private, please," Carter said. It was not a request, it was an order—the kind that a medical officer was authorized to make, albeit pertaining to patient-doctor privilege.

Lord obliged, moving away from the others so they couldn't hear his side of the conversation. He could have stayed where he was and activated the ICBM—the blocking mode, which projected a powerful signal-to-noise ratio to block the audio, but Lord felt it was rude to stand there and move his lips while people watched. "You have the floor, Doctor."

"All of your stated reasons are subversively valid, Sam, but they are exceptionally thin," Carter said.

"I've survived in thin atmosphere," Lord said.

"Sam, the Russians aren't stupid *or* careless. You'll be lucky if they even let you use the lavatory by yourself."

"Can't imagine what they'd hope to learn there—"

"Dammit, the truth is you *crave* the risk," Carter said. "The word literally glows with pixel dust throughout your psych profile. Absent dangerous aircraft to fly, you court dangerous assignments. Do you want to see the analyses I worked up on your little adventure in the decompressing cargo bay, in the elevator shaft, on the Armstrong mission, or outside the *Empyrean* on the solar sail?"

"What's the point?" Lord asked. "Those are postmortems on successful results."

"Postmortem is a good description," Carter said. "Your actions nearly killed you—four times."

"Doctor, your job is to save lives by investing time and careful, conservative, experienced mental analysis to a problem," Lord said. "Me? I'm a combat and test pilot, impulsive, intuitive—"

"Reckless."

"Call it what you want, danger is inherent in my approach to life. I made peace with that long ago, the first time I jumped into the Hudson River as a kid." The Zero-G director looked at the doctor's inscrutable expression in his IC. "Chuck, you took me private, so there has to be a med component to this chat. So far, all you've talked about is tactics."

"So far."

"Uh-huh."

"Your psychological profile is squarely within my purview," Carter said.

"And you think this is about what—a fractured ego in need of spackle?"

"That's as good a mixed metaphor as any."

Lord snickered. "Okay. Maybe there's a little truth to that. But it beats the hell out of that pasture I was headed to."

"Maybe there's truth in that, for *you*," Carter said. "I have to be convinced that this is the right approach for Zero-G, not for Sam Lord."

"Hey, Chuck—here's more truth. Sam Lord was on a virtual date in the Scrub when this thing with the vine started," he said, indicating his wardrobe with a downward sweep of his hand. "Sam Lord would rather be back there than squeezing himself into a Soyuz 5C. I hear those things are about as comfortable as Ferris wheel seats. By my reckoning, that makes me very sane."

Carter regarded his colleague. "You can't wear me down with dubious logic," the doctor said. "Take one more swing and convince me."

"How about I take aim at *your* qualifications to judge me?"

"What?"

"Chuck, is Cameron entirely free of nanites?"

That caught Carter off-guard. "Shit."

"Yeah."

"I don't know," Carter admitted. "Jesus, I didn't think to check."

"You're tired, busy—obviously not thinking clearly," Lord said.

"Okay, guilty. Don't you see, that's another reason to slow this down?"

"Of course I don't," Lord said. "What can you do to check him ASAP?"

"Sam, you're a pain!"

"And that's not an answer," Lord replied.

Carter exhaled, partly with frustration, partly with disgust. "I can scan his skin using the inductive coupled mass spectrometry," the doctor said. "That will detect a specific nanite component on the skin."

"Clothes?"

"Artificial fibers will not impede the surface scan," Carter said.

"Let's do it," Lord said, "but only if you agree not to try to stop me from going to the *Red Giant*."

"I can do it without your approval," Carter complained.

"Eventually," Lord said. "I can boot this up to Al-Kazaz, he takes it to NASA, all of that slows you down—"

"You're being a bastard," Carter said.

"I prefer the term 'efficient.'" Lord grinned a little. "Come on—work with me here, Doctor."

"Fine," Carter said. "I agree, but under fierce protest."

The Zero-G director returned to the others and asked Abernathy to run the scan. The agent went to the equipment locker, selected a palm-size disc, and ran it over the prisoner. Lord plugged into the device—after struggling to find the icon in his IC. It was buried in the equipment-locker function. Locating it, he linked to Carter. Lord saw a shimmering line encircle the prisoner along with the readouts. Carter input a formula seeking a specific iron ratio of one part in 1,015.

"His skin and hair appear clear," Carter announced after the slow up-and-down scan.

"Thank you, Doctor," Lord replied.

"Before you go—what would you have done if we *had* found nanites?" Carter asked.

"I'd have made the Russians wait, of course," Lord replied.

Carter soured. "I'll say it again, Sam, you are a—"

"Busy man," Lord replied, and took the conversation public again. He looked around, saw Adsila's resolve crumble when she saw Carter's beaten brow.

"Is there anything else?" Lord asked the team.

The silence that followed was not that of an argument looking to regroup; it was the by-product of a unit giving up.

Lord turned to his science officer. "Status of the Soyuz, Agent McClure?"

The science officer was tapped into the *Empyrean*'s secure ADF—the arrival/departure feed. "The craft is forty-eight minutes from docking," he responded. "According to the flight plan filed by the *Red Giant*, the pilot and sole occupant is Lieutenant Svetlana Uralov."

"Thank you. My companion and I had better get to the docking bay," Lord said, cocking his head toward the prisoner. The dulled Cameron responded like a reined horse, following dutifully.

Adsila made a point of turning ninety degrees to let him pass, moving stiffly, like a door opening in an old, dark house.

"Godspeed, sir," she said, using a farewell that was traditional in the early, danger-filled era of the American space program.

Lord half-turned and winked as he left the comm. A drop-down triggered by that action appeared automatically from an old air force instruction manual:

1.2. **Prohibition of Sexual Harassment.**

1.2.1. **Unlawful harassment includes unwelcome sexual advances, requests for sexual favors, or other verbal or physical conduct of a sexual nature—**

Lord brushed it away with the side of his hand. He'd forgotten that the document from 2010 was there. Early in his career he had been disciplined for winking at a female NCO, and the drop-down was his punishment. Lord did not know what disturbed him more: that the IC remembered to do it, or that it had been four decades since he'd winked at a subordinate.

Would it have done that if Adsila were in her male form? he wondered. *Or Abernathy? Probably not.*

With his captive beside him, Lord headed for PriD1. There, with the help of a station orderly, they donned what were called Minnies—minimalist neoprene space suits, airtight garments with a network of air ducts and coolant with hoods tucked into a pack around the neck. Lord wore white, Cameron got prison red. In the event of a leak, the Minnies would provide two hours of air and pressurization. The tightness of the bodysuit also helped to keep blood flowing when the body was subjected to G-forces. A set of underpants received and broke down liquid waste, eliminating resource-consuming plumbing.

There were two private docking ports on the *Empyrean*. Fittingly, they were modeled after the original Russian SSVP system from the old Salyut days—the *Sistema Stykovki i Vnutrennego Perekhoda*, System for Docking and Internal Transfer. The drogue-and-cone docking mechanism, as well as the tight airlock through which passengers maneuvered, were basic enough to accommodate virtually every kind of spacecraft. This was mandated by law so that, in distress, even sophisticated new private craft or unwelcome ships of a hostile nation could dock.

The PriD1 was like a traditional boarding gate at any airport on Earth, save for the fact that it was smaller and there were foot restraints and black aluminum handrails to keep passengers from floating around the gravity-free room. The lack of gravity was for the benefit of the pilots: decoupled from the spin of the *Empyrean*, pilots were only required to make contact with the docking ring. There was no need to keep pace with it in a longitudinal roll.

There was no one in the bay but Lord, Cameron, and the sole crew member. Typically, Commander Stanton would have greeted the arrival of a vessel from another station; however, it would have sent the wrong message via the newtiae if it became known—and the Russians would make sure it did—that two high-ranking US officials were on hand to greet a lieutenant. It might not have elevated Svetlana Uralov's standing, but it would have diminished Stanton's.

Lord paused and gripped Cameron's arm so the prisoner wouldn't wander beyond the range of the Mindcuffs. The crew member, a young man whom Lord knew only by sight, nodded in acknowledgment when the Zero-G director arrived. The man wore nonporous brown spandex and gloves with a small chest pack on the front. In the event a ship did not pass the *Empyrean*'s bioscan—part of the station's guidance beam that auto-initiated at one thousand meters—the crew member would have to enter the airlock and contain anyone who tried to emerge.

Lord used the time to review what Zero-G knew about the *Red Giant* crew. The files weren't extensive, but even in their superficiality they were sufficient. While he read the drop-down, the Soyuz was a pulsing speck in the distance, the alternately red and green lights standing out in a sea of unfathomably distant white lights. Lord felt a wave of nostalgia as soon as he was able to make out the contours of the craft. When he was growing up, in the 1980s, the Russia–United States space race was over—the moon landing had been accomplished a year before Lord's birth—but a new generation of space hardware was being rocketed skyward. The 5-C was one of the last of the upgraded Soyuz crafts, the fifth-generation series having been built in 2033, before Roscosmos ran out of R&D money. The craft looked like all its predecessors—an unshelled peanut with solar panel wings—but it was slightly more spacious than older models due to the microminiaturization of much of the antiquated technology.

The Soyuz came toward the five-foot-diameter docking ring nosefirst, unlike shuttlecraft and space kites, which rose into view like attacking sharks, granting access to the passenger cabins via a hatch on top. The pilot was confirmed in his IC as Lieutenant Svetlana Regina Uralov, height five foot three, weight 120 pounds—information that was required in the event of decompression and if emergency suits had to be broken out. Lord had never heard of her, though the FBI had. According to a recruitment file, there had been talk of approaching the pilot in an effort to turn her after an affair and subsequent fall from grace; however, the Russians cannily put her in space before that could happen.

The thick, ovoid crew compartment of the craft came closer, pulling its larger, slightly flared propulsion section behind it. The solar panels jutted from near the bottom of the larger section; a pair of satellite dishes sat on long thin arms that paralleled them on top. The green and red beacons grew larger, causing flare that made it impossible to see inside the tiny windows of the craft. Now that he'd stopped moving, Lord realized how tired he was; he closed his eyes to block the flashing lights and found himself drowsing, nearly drifting from the foot restraints.

The Mindcuff distance alert sounded in his IC and brought him back. He tucked his toes into the flexible plastic "slippers" and rubbed his eyes with his palm heels.

Power nap, he told himself as he contemplated the nearly hourlong trip to the *Red Giant*.

The four small braking rockets at the rear of the Soyuz flared toward the station like red pennants. They flashed briefly three times below the solar panels and the craft slowed. There was a noticeable bump as the Russian vessel made contact, followed by the clang of restraining flanges as the ship was secured to the station. When the all-clear sounded—three distinct chimes, pitched to cut through any distractions on an IC—the airlock between the hatch and the *Empyrean* hissed dully. As soon as the short passageway was pressurized, another all-clear sounded and the crewman opened the hatch with a palm print.

Lord walked over with his prisoner as the sole occupant of the Soyuz pulled herself into the airlock and then hand-walked through, using the grips on the sides. She pulled her knees to her chest as she emerged and executed a neat tuck-and-roll so that she was upright when she emerged. She steadied herself on the hatch, her eyes immediately finding Lord.

The woman was striking. She was relatively small and thin, a necessity for constant travel in a Soyuz and inhabiting the cramped *Red Giant*. Yet she had poise and a proud stature that Lord recognized: one did not sit in a cockpit or cabin and slouch with inattention. Her black hair was fashionably webbed—threaded through with gold silk and pulled into two braids. She wore these tucked through straps on her shoulders that had been designed to hold a service cap. Lord corralled his thoughts, not guiltily but with comfortable resignation, as the air force drop-down was shown—again.

As long as there are men, sexual response—like anger—is a quality that will have to be suppressed, not fueled.

"Welcome to *Empyrean*, Lieutenant Uralov," he said with a smile, the Glossator translating. He spoke normally, though he knew that her

translator would not work as efficiently as that of the Zero-G unit: powered by SimAI, the Glossator also re-created tone and added intent to
the translation.

"Thank you for allowing me on board," the woman replied with a
small, respectful incline of her head. "I am here to pick up Mr. Samuel
Lord and Mr. Douglas Cameron."

"We are both present," Lord replied.

Even in that brief exchange, Lord had to tamp down the innate
desire to be seductive. The lieutenant, clearly, did not labor under a
similar burden. There were two parts to that, Lord suspected: first, he
was two generations older, which was not a stake in the heart but close
enough; second, from the quick, dismissive break in her salutation, she
had clearly had enough, either of Americans—which he doubted, given
her limited exposure to them—or, he suspected, from reviewing her
history, of men.

The woman's eyes had snapped from Lord to Cameron. The
Zero-G director knew that whatever readings she tried to take would
be blocked by the Mindcuffs. In 2029, Miranda had been extended to
protecting someone not just from self-incrimination by words but due
to body temperature, facial expressions, pupil dilation, heart rate, respiration, and other indicators of anxiety. She would not even be able to
take a picture of the man.

A twitch in her eyebrows indicated that Uralov had not been informed of that fact—proving his suspicion that she was not an Ameri-
caphile. Indeed, as effectively a political exile, she would not have been
given very many briefings of any kind.

"Can I get you anything to eat, drink, breathe?" Lord asked solici-
tously. "Something you might not have on the *Red Giant*?"

"Thank you, no," she replied. "I exited to allow you easier access."

"Of course. Very considerate," Lord said.

"Practical," she answered with a shrug.

The woman was neither brusque nor hasty; whatever other consid-
erations were impacting her manner, like most members of the many

air corps, she was in the middle of a mission and didn't have time for pleasantries.

She extended an arm toward the airlock and, with a nod, Lord moved ahead with his prisoner.

"There will be no independent communication between yourself and the *Empyrean* once we board," she said as he moved by. "They will be blocked. If you have any signals you wish to send—"

"That's fine." Lord smiled. "They hear enough from me as is. And I have other plans for the transit."

That drew a slight recoil from the pilot, as Lord had intended. With a lingering grin he exited the light of the bay for the muddy dark of the Soyuz.

THIRTEEN

NE OF THE things Dr. Carlton Carter was very, very good at was compartmentalizing. No sooner had his discussion with Lord ended than his chronic and severe discomfort with the man's methods went away. He liked Sam Lord, and he also respected him. The man reminded Carter of a faith healer he was once asked to evaluate. Under careful scientific conditions, Carter had pronounced a patient blind. The subject lay hands on the patient's temples; within a minute, the individual could see. Real healing power? Psychosomatic ailments reversed? Profound belief as a curative? It didn't matter. The malady was cured.

Lord invariably made *this* partly blind doctor see things he didn't want to see.

Whatever the driving psychology, unabashed manipulation, or zig-zag logistics behind the man's actions, he achieved good results for a great many people. At virtually any moment, the work Lord did shutting down the weapon on the *Jade Star* could have killed him. The Zero-G director didn't blink, though the Dragon's Eye did.

Sitting on a bucket-seat stool that had been selected for its light-weight transport rather than for comfort, Carter was hooked into a virtual transmission electron microscope, studying the skin-producing nanite on a slide. The scientist was tired but, in spite of that, he was unusually alert.

One of the reasons that the esteemed biophysicist had come to space was because he did not have time for grants and had even less time for agenda-motivated colleagues. He cared about the science, and PD Al-Kazaz had offered him not only a lab in zero gravity but relative autonomy. It was an unprecedented arrangement: as long as he produced innovations that would help the team, Carter could design materials for other agencies as well. NASA had given him the same freedom, along with funds to hire researchers on Earth. It was an enviable position, one most Earth scientists would have jumped at. Within six months, Carter also expected to have a woman working with him on the moon.

Freed from the need to scramble for money or to be the first to publish in some super-political peer-reviewed journal—many of those peers being rivals who were keen to shoot him down—Carter had found himself not just content but focused, filled with energy he had never thought possible. Not exactly happy, since he was constantly frustrated by how much he didn't know. But as close to it as he had ever been.

Part of that had to do with space: the false gravity and centripetal forces kept his body dancing inside, air and blood flowing, organs performing at optimal levels. Having the naked cosmos on all sides kept his mind hopping on a subconscious level. Freed from Cradle Earth, as he called it, and its protective atmosphere, the very matter of which he was formed was subtly reconnecting with its ancient origins. All the body's heavy elements, from carbon to oxygen to iron, were formed in the explosion of second-generation stars.

The net result was that he felt as if he were truly alive for the first time. Here, alone in his lab, he was able to let that feeling flower, to exist in a way that no scientist had ever lived before. Carter maintained a stoic exterior in order to face and process the demands made on any medic. Inside, however, the prospects of what Dr. Carter, scientist, might be inspired to find or do or attempt were wildly thrilling.

At the moment, his heightened attentions were on the nanite he had plucked from Liba, the one that was replicating Douglas Cameron's flesh. An IC scan was reverse-engineering the malfunctioning device—in effect, scrolling time back in a theoretical construct so that Carter could "see" what went wrong. The chaos induced in the mollies by defective hadrons from the nail resulted in those quantum bits becoming entangled with qbits in other mollies, causing decoherence and a shutdown of the program—but not death.

"You look exactly like the electrical state of a comatose brain," he muttered as he paused the three-dimensional image at the moment of hadron penetration. "After decoherence here, you rebuilt toward a new consciousness."

On your own, he thought ominously. It wasn't designed to do that.

"Drawing on what?" he wondered. "Old, overwritten programs? New ones? Based on what input?"

Data floating through the ether? It wasn't impossible. Over a century ago, silver tooth fillings used to pick up radio signals.

This wasn't artificial intelligence or even SimAI, it was something else: the new and little-understood field of artificial evolution.

That was different from the kind of random mutation or natural selection found in nature. The nanite had created a new template "self" around the foreign qbit.

"And then it rewrote the other nanites to follow *it*," Carter said admiringly but quietly—as though saying it too loud the nanite might hear and self-congratulate, try even harder to upgrade. And that group hug wouldn't be as remarkable as the initial evolution; it was simply a matter of the others recognizing that an advanced version had been written and adapted the latest update, however far afield it was from the original program.

There was a theramin-like sound in Carter's IC, a brief pulse wave, that told him there was new electronic activity in the subject.

"Analysis?" he said to the IC.

The IC answered in its default androgynous voice. "They are gamma wave oscillations."

"Origin?"

"The nanite."

"Yes, *where?*" Carter asked.

"Unclear."

"Speculate."

"Qbits firing rhythmically and synchronously in the WOMB." The Wavelength Origin Molly Bundle, the processing heart of the nanites.

"The defective hadrons?" Carter asked.

"No other likely cause has been detected," the voice replied. "The entire system is coming back on-Cloud."

"No . . ." he murmured.

Cameron immediately placed the slide in a dielectric dish made of Teflon-lined glass to block signals from being released. He did not want this nanite communicating with any others until he found a means of preventing the AE from spreading—

"Oh shit."

There was absolutely no indication that the AE had originated here or that this was an isolated development. Perhaps this nanite had been receiving signals from the Agro Center.

Carter rushed from the lab. He rarely ran, even when there were medical emergencies; footing was just too uncertain from section to section. But he ran now.

Communicating with the team working in the Vault would be of no use; it would have to go to the greenhouse and be relayed through to the electronic blocks personally. There might not yet be any physical manifestations of the change. He had to examine a few nanites there, see if the gamma wave oscillation was the same. He was already assuming the worst and trying to figure out how to shut down a system that could learn and adapt.

Carter's IC showed that Stanton was on his way to the Drum. The biophysicist was relieved: he wouldn't have to waste time answering questions—yet. He reached the elevator that would take him to the greenhouse area and spent the longest thirty seconds of his life riding to the *Empyrean*'s lowest level. The elevator made just one stop, taking on a young man. The IC ID gave his name as Flannery Smith and his crisp black uniform identified him as one of the station's three sanitation engineers, the entire complement having been assigned to vine dismantling and cleanup.

Something didn't look right about him and Carter realized at once what it was.

"You changed clothes," he said.

The shorter man turned his squarish face toward the speaker, looked at him for a moment in silence; Smith's own IC was letting him know who Carter was and his security level.

"It's very dirty work in there," Smith said. "And itchy." He used a finger to hook back the collar of his tunic and reveal his U-wear. "I'll sweat like sponge, but I can deal with that."

Carter's brain wrestled with this new information. The doors opened. They stepped onto the green line; Carter stopped the man by grasping his shoulder.

"Mr. Smith, what did you do with your old uniform?" Carter asked.

"Chute."

The Chute was the laundry conduit that served Radial Arms Four, Five, and Six and used the station's rotation to deliver clothing down a curving slide to the automated laundry center. The dry-cleaning units would read the DNA of the wearer and bag the cleaned garment for pickup.

"You already did that?" Carter asked. "Put it down?"

"Yes. Why?"

Carter did not respond as he waved Smith ahead and stopped to contact Stanton on a secure channel. Since Merlin was still a classified operation, Carter activated the ICBM function. He looked around to make sure no one could hear.

Stanton answered at once. "Yes, Doctor Car—"

"Commander, has any of the vine debris left the greenhouse?"

"No," Stanton replied. "We're waiting on NASA's instructions."

For once, Stanton's chain-of-command caution had a positive dividend. "Good. Issue a general order to the vine crew: nothing and no one is to leave the greenhouse until I give the all-clear. Also, close down the LC and ResCat the contents. *Nothing* is to be picked up."

Carter did not have the authority to demand the latter action. But one thing Stanton did know was how and when to listen to experts.

"Doctor, are you sure about the foam?" Stanton asked. "The chute will have to be—"

"Replaced, I know." ResCat was a combination of lunar-dust resin and catalyst foam spray that turned into a rock-solid mass. Released down the Chute, it would immobilize any nanites that might be on Smith's uniform. The ResCat wouldn't destroy them but it would prevent a nanite's pincers from moving.

"What's going on?" Stanton demanded.

"Commander, the nanite in my lab has morphed," the biophysicist told him. "It hasn't become active and may be the only one manifesting a new master program, but I want to check others."

"Goddammit."

"Yeah."

Carter rushed ahead to the Agro Center. Engineers were just completing temporary repairs on the cracked glass; the vine that had done the damage had been removed from within the greenhouse.

No sooner had Carter opened the door than he heard a woman shout. Carter and Smith entered the greenhouse and the door automatically snapped shut behind them. Carter looked ahead. The door of the Vault was open and there were seven workers packed inside. The crew had been dismantling the vine using palm-size laser saws. The cuts the tool made were precise and clean, slicing at a granular level without creating dust. Because the vine was not only thick but dense, the heat-input required by the laser was considerable. However, the high level of power consumed by the solar-powered devices was not a problem in constant sunlight. But none of the saws was in operation as the black-garbed sanitation crew, the green-garbed Agro workers, and the white-suited mechanics watched one of their number back through the surrounding foliage.

The woman—a powerfully built Agro worker identified in his IC as Project Chief Harmony Keen—had been working beside the original, deep-green ribbon-like growth of vine six inches wide. It was still deeply set in the soil of the Vault; authorization to uproot that original section had not been granted. The vine was surrounded by the remnants of its mutant limbs, stacked like kindling around a medieval witch waiting to be burned at the stake. The vine stood still and upright as before.

"What's wrong?" Carter asked her.

"I *saw* something!" Harmony exclaimed, looking at the vine as she backed away. "I walked by, I didn't touch a thing, and—and I don't know *what* happened!"

"Can you describe it?" Carter pressed.

"It was like . . . a kaleidoscope but with wire-frame shapes, no color other than black and white."

"Was your IC on?" Carter asked.

"Can't be, in here," she said, indicating the Vault.

Right, Carter thought, feeling stupid. Security is not always a friend to the scientist. That meant there wouldn't be a data recording to study. He looked from the woman to the rest of the team. "Everyone stand beside the door but don't leave the Vault."

"On whose authority?" asked the woman. "*I'm* the project—"

"On my authority as a station med officer, *Empyrean* Emergency Protocol 355," Carter declared impatiently. "You'll have additional orders from Commander Stanton. Mr. Smith, your gloves, please?"

The crewman quickly pulled them off and handed them over. They were thick worker's gloves and, like the uniform, they appeared fresh.

The crew tromped away through the vegetation while Carter continued moving forward. He focused his IC thermal indicator on a small section of the vine where the woman had been working. It was the area near where he had theorized the brain center might have been . . . if there had been any kind of hive mind. As he neared, Carter searched for residual warmth on the vine, some place she might have made contact. He found a spot that was a shade warmer than the rest and went to it, carefully climbing over the piled, severed limbs, to crouch beside the small heat signature. Carefully, he extended an index finger. He saw nothing. Even when his fingertip touched the vine, nothing happened.

Carter rose quickly and strode through the plants to Harmony's side.

"Did you experience a bilateral event?" he asked.

"I don't understand—"

"Both eyes?"

She thought for a moment. "Now that you mention it, I don't think so. No. It was my left eye."

Carter did not like where this seemed to be going. He tried to contact Stanton, forgot he was in the Vault, swore.

"What is it?" Harmony asked.

He didn't want to tell her. "Please just join the others," he said. "Let me know if you see anything else."

"Am I all right?"

"As long as you stay away from the vine, I believe you are," he said reassuringly, though he was far from certain.

The woman joined the team to the left of the door. They were huddled close and wearing concerned expressions.

Carter turned back to the vine. He bent near to it. He didn't see anything, but then he didn't have a nanite inside his optic nerve most likely receiving impulses from the vine. He didn't believe any of the microscopic robots would have fallen from Smith's clothes on its way to the laundry: their attraction to biological matter was greater than the pull of gravity. Their legs and pincers would do whatever it took to remain close to biorhythms. But he still couldn't afford to let anyone out, potentially releasing more.

If those things are receiving messages again, then the nanite in my lab was not unique, he thought. *It means the hive brain has resumed its activity.* It could also mean that the nanites possess the capability of rewriting the program he created, which was to seek living matter. It would be fatal to the station if the nanites entered ducts, pipes, and conduits and began replicating plastics or metals.

Even if that were not the case, the vine was almost demonically adaptable and quite possibly evolving a form of sentience. Which meant that there was a question he had to answer immediately:

What is our *next move?*

FOURTEEN

A ND I HAVE other plans. . . ."

Svetlana Uralov refused to turn and face the man who had uttered those words, from whom she had expected spirited sparring for information. Instead, she watched him carefully from the sides of her eyes. Almost immediately after informing the *Red Giant* that Mission 716 was underway, the great military figure, the presumed master of espionage, had gone to sleep in the center seat to her right.

Svetlana had completed the undocking protocols and pushed away from the *Empyrean* only to find him resting quietly, contentedly. This flight was supposed to have been about redemption. Instead, it seemed on a trajectory to failure.

Failure because of a smug American—yet another self-impressed officer, she thought. *One more arrogant man.*

Unlike the old Soyuz crafts, which were controlled entirely by an overhead panel and controls stuck between and in front of the seats— wherever they could be fit, in fact—this nominally updated model was linked to her IC. Eye motions did the bulk of the work while her weightless arms occasionally stabbed buttons and flicked switches around her.

And still her mind wrestled futilely with her dilemma, one she had quickly defined as *И совершил Бог к седьмому дню дела Свои, которые Он делал. . . .*

And on the seventh day, the Lord ended his work which he had made....

Whether the American had intended to or not—and she was not sure which it was—he had shut down her ability to question him, even passively. She had hoped to draw Director Lord out during the flight, get him to talk about anything, show her his technique, indicate the areas in which he was interested: the *Red Giant*'s operation? Its personnel? The crime syndicate? The science? She had wanted to be able to point Admiral Ptushko in some direction, *any* direction, once they arrived.

That wasn't possible with a man who had been asleep for twenty minutes and looked as though he would sleep for nearly forty more. If he had wanted to crush her future, he could not have done a better job.

Because these partial-orbital trips she took were somewhat rote, Svetlana's mind typically lost itself in memory, sought *something* hopeful in the future. It remained unusually active on this trip, not with regrets but with her immediate needs. She did not want to return to Ptushko with no information, no insight, just a botanist's warning that "this man is clever." There was too much at stake: her honor, her future, her tattered confidence.

She glanced to her right. Lord's arms floated above his belly, intermittently blocking the man to his right. The prisoner was lying there, staring ahead, his thumbs hooked in his pockets so his arms would stay at his side. The young man had no questions and, when Svetlana had spoken with him a few minutes earlier, he had no answers.

"Why are you under arrest?" she had boldly asked across Lord, in part testing to see whether the Zero-G director was really asleep.

Lord did not respond, made no indication that he had even heard, and the man beside him seemed uneasy with having a conversation.

"Have the Mindcuffs blocked your voice?" Svetlana asked him.

"No," Cameron replied. "I have nothing to say."

"You are beyond recriminations," she said.

"Am I?" Cameron said. "This man . . ." he began and then his voice sputtered to silence.

"This man what?" Svetlana pressed, the Glossator translating her words and replicating her tone. It was a double hit of displeasure for Cameron.

"This man is clever," the prisoner said, finding his voice.

"Clever in what way?"

"In every way I can imagine and some, apparently, that I cannot," Cameron replied. "I am not certain what he's going to do next." He regarded her for the first time but he was really looking at Lord. "I hope—perhaps it's possible that I can save myself."

"Do you believe that?" she asked.

"I want to," he replied. "But it's all I've got. That, and regret."

Cameron's voice had risen, apparently hoping that Lord would hear even if his IC was muted. But if the FBI officer was listening, he still made no sign.

That was the end of her chat with Douglas Cameron.

Because it was the craft's first trip to the *Empyrean*, there had been no template for the undocking maneuver that had carried the Soyuz a few dozen feet farther from the station than the computer had planned. By the time she reached the *Red Giant*, that differential would have expanded to several miles. Svetlana executed a slight course-correction burn of the port rocket. Everything shifted slightly inside, including Lord's floating arms. The little jolt did not appear to disturb him, however. When the maneuver had been successfully completed, the woman used her drop-down to do something there hadn't been time for previously: reading up on Lord.

Samuel Rhodes Lord was a decorated combat squadron leader, a renowned test pilot for the American Air Force Vampire—a fighter jet whose speed and maneuverability the MiG 31 still could not match—and the divorced father of three children, seven grandchildren, and twelve great-grandchildren, none of whom was involved in space and only two of whom had served in the military. The man's dossier from the Foreign Intelligence Service of the Russian Federation was sparse: the reason there was so little information was the "sacrificial lamb" quality of Samuel Lord's appointment to his current position. No one in

Washington or Moscow expected the eighty-year-old to last in the physically challenging environment of space and the politically taxing position of Zero-G director. After just two weeks, Lord had not only fooled his detractors, he had embarrassed them. After disabling the Chinese Dragon's Eye, his position up here was widely deemed "unassailable," despite his "idiosyncratic approach to command"—a phrase that was not elaborated on in the report. The file had a Prime One tab, a red star. That meant additional information was eagerly sought.

Which is why Admiral Ptushko was so keen to have him visit, Svetlana thought. There would be commendations for whoever could flesh out this file. Her usual pilot's cool was being replaced by rising, ugly heat in her neck and ears. The woman looked out the window to her left, at the glistening expanse of the Atlantic Ocean. Unlike the *Empyrean,* the *Red Giant* was not in a geostationary orbit. It circled the Earth at a much lower altitude, which took less energy—and expense—to maintain. It was also easier to make a 261-mile trip from Earth to the *Red Giant* than it was to reach the *Empyrean* nearly ten times farther away.

I live closer to Earth than this man, yet I could not be farther from my home world, Svetlana thought with sudden, miserable longing.

She looked to her right again, at Lord. Her eyes reflected the sudden, angry preoccupation she felt. She wanted to be the one to open that Prime One tab.

You can't ask Lord if this is his first visit to the Red Giant, she thought. *Your IC would have told you that, and he will know it. Short of a rocket misfire that sends us off-course—and needlessly endangers our lives—what can I do or say that is worth waking him?*

And then the obvious hit her.

"Director Lord?" she asked.

There was no immediate answer. She waited a few seconds, then loosened her harness and raised herself slightly. The chair had been designed to snugly accommodate someone wearing a spacesuit and helmet; the straps that crisscrossed Svetlana's chest were all that held her in place.

"Director Lord?" she asked again, loudly.

"Yes?" he answered without a start. The man opened his eyes and looked in her direction without lifting his head from the form-fitting couch. His gaze found the pilot. "Is there a problem, Lieutenant?"

"No, sir," she replied. "I was just wondering if you would care to try the controls. I imagine this is one of the few aircraft you have not flown."

Svetlana's tone was different from before, not quite as flat, subdued, and formal as it had been. It was pilot to pilot, in a way that implied she was being more than just a good host.

"I'm not quite old enough to have flown with the Wright Brothers either." He smiled.

"I hadn't meant that—"

"I know and I thank you, but I'm really enjoying the downtime. I appreciate the offer, though. Very much."

He was still smiling as he looked admiringly around the cramped space before shutting his eyes again; the conversation was allowed to die like a neglected plant.

Svetlana felt foolish and inept. Again. It occurred to her, suddenly, that he may have assumed she was fishing for a list of craft he had piloted. The man was either paranoid, canny—as his prisoner had said— or else he was being lazy. Perhaps it was his age, perhaps he was tired. In any case, she couldn't—wouldn't—leave it there.

"What do you think of our craft?" she asked, struggling to find an even more conversational tone.

He opened his eyes again. "The Soyuz? It's a classic," he replied with genuine admiration. "As the pilot at the controls, what do *you* think?"

"I've found it to be a very serviceable craft," she said. "Surprisingly maneuverable once you get a feel for the rockets."

"And the lack of air friction, I would imagine," he said. "That was what struck me about piloting our shuttle *Grissom*."

"Very true," she said. "I was taught that American cosmonauts had a name for riding in vehicles like this. 'Meat in a can.'"

Lord grinned. "The expression was 'Spam in a can,'" he informed her, "after a famous meat product. And they were—*are*—called 'astronauts.'"

"That is right," Svetlana replied. "We are the cosmonauts. Yet we are all brothers and sisters, everyone who flies."

Lord was still smiling and nodded before lying back and looking up through the window over his station.

Once again, the only sounds in the craft were the occasional click of an auto-switch and her own breathing. Svetlana was tense and on the verge of giving up. The man was intractable, bordering on rude—

And then he inhaled slowly, deeply, opened his eyes, and blinked them wide to keep them open.

"Sorry I'm being such a very poor guest," he said suddenly. "It's been a really long day and I needed a quick kip, as my granddaughter in London says."

"With so many new experiences, new challenges around you?" she asked, pushing him.

"Regrettably, yes," Lord said. "The mind is always willing but the flesh can be stubbornly unaccommodating."

Svetlana didn't know if he had been sincerely unguarded in that moment or if she was being manipulated by a professional who was effortlessly charming. She didn't know if she was being paranoid. All she did know was that talking to this man was like the card game Svoyi Koziri the flight crews used to play at the Air Base Vyazma. The only way to gain information about other hands was by playing.

"Was it something of a personal nature that exhausted you?" she asked, surprised at the boldness of her own question.

"With me, Lieutenant, everything is personal," he replied. "Even my job. I suppose that's true for any of us who spend so much time working. Unfortunately, the older one gets, the eyes and muscles have more of a say in things."

"I understand completely," Svetlana said. "I'm lucky. In between sorties, I got very good at catching quick rests in ready rooms."

"Ah—I used to do that too," Lord said. "It got to a point where I had trouble falling asleep without the smell of burnt coffee and a sweating duty officer nearby."

"For me it was coffee and tobacco," Svetlana said. She felt she was softening him up. She hoped so.

"Dear old tobacco," Lord said. "The Scarlet Letter. I never smoked, but by around 2012 I remember smokers being tucked in dark, hidden corners. Like spies."

Now Svetlana fell silent. Her IC informed her that *The Scarlet Letter* was an American novel and the brand of an adulteress. A sinner. Was that a warning that he was on to her? An overture to become one, like the prisoner? Or was it just an offhand observation?

You've got to get better at this, and quickly, she chastised herself.

"Speaking of spies," Lord continued, surprisingly making her job easier, "the one you were chatting with, my unwilling traveling companion, is one of yours. Forgive me for not having formally introduced you. But you knew him?"

"I knew of him from your communication," Svetlana replied, wanting to distance herself from any intrigue—or suspicion. "I was informed whom I was to collect."

"An unfortunate fellow, he caused some damage while undertaking a mission for your country. Did you ever encounter the poem 'Lay of the Last Minstrel' by Sir Walter Scott?"

"I am not familiar with it, no," she said.

"A truly great work," Lord advised her. "We used to have all kinds of reading material in the ready rooms. I took to reading poems because they were short, memorable, challenging—but usually insightful. If something happened to me up there"—he pointed to a remembered sky—"I didn't want to be thinking, 'Hey, I wonder what happened to Captain Ahab or your own Dmitri Karamazov in the last chapter.' Do you know what I mean? I wanted to have some smart, philosophical idea in my mind."

"I do understand," she said, flummoxed. She had no idea at all where this was going.

"Anyway, this wonderful poem is about a minstrel who stops at a castle and tells a story about an old border conflict," Lord said. "There is a passage that stuck with me: 'Breathes there the man, with soul so dead, Who never to himself hath said, This is my own, my native land!'"

Lord cocked his head to the right. "This man? His soul went dead. Flatlined. I don't care who you are, but—do you follow soccer? Football, I mean?"

"No," Svetlana said, trying to keep up with his—intentionally?—nonlinear discourse.

"Here's the thing," Lord told her. "If you play for a team, if you wear their jersey, you don't send secret signals to the other bench. If you do that, then you have lost your 'native land.'"

Svetlana did not quite know what to make of what Lord had just said—any of it—other than his disapproval of people who betray a trust. But she already surmised that. And then the prisoner's words came back to her: *This man is clever.*

"But I've talked enough," Lord said, interrupting her thoughts. "What about you?"

"Me?" she said tentatively, collecting her thoughts. "I'm just a pilot."

"You don't say 'cosmonaut,'" he noted. "Pilot."

"Yes," she said carefully, suddenly aware that every word she said to this man mattered.

"Me too," he replied, then recited, "'Once a pilot, always a pilot.'"

"Is that by your same poet?"

"No, it's by me," he said, chuckling. "My former wife used to say that the smell of airplane fuel was in everything I wore. I told her she was wrong. It was in my veins."

"I understand that too," Svetlana found herself saying. "Do you like being up here or would you rather be flying down there?" That seemed like a good way to keep the conversation on him.

"Both," he replied. "I've done so much living at every table I've ever been to, I have to resist the temptation to keep on tasting what I really enjoy, to settle for that. I also want to sample what I have not. I'll tell you what the real question is, Lieutenant, if you'd like to hear."

"Please."

"Did you choose to do what it is that you're doing?" he said.

"I believe—mostly, yes."

"Mostly?"

"Obligation and preference do not always agree," she said.

"True. Yet there were times, during combat—and you may be too young to have experienced this—when I did not want to fly a mission. I didn't approve of the target, where there might be collateral damage. Or there were risks I was perfectly willing to take myself, but I was afraid for the safety of the rest of my team. Still, I always went. The reason? Obviously, I had sworn an oath to follow orders. But it was more than that. It may sound corny—does that word translate?"

"*заскорузлый*," she said. "Outdated . . . backward."

"That'll do," he replied. "I went on those missions because '*This is my own, my native land.*' That was always my first choice. A sense of gratitude for everything I had access to, for everything I had the potential to become." He craned to look at her over the lip of the seat. "Does that make any sense?"

The man was either a naïf or a cajoler, she didn't know which: what he had said played squarely to the part of her tongue that responded to "bitter." She could actually taste it in her mouth.

"It makes sense," she said quietly. "Excuse me, but I have some communications to make."

"Of course," Lord replied as, once again, he settled back and shut his eyes.

As if nothing has happened, no tremor under the surface of my life, the woman thought, then decided: *He's a bastard.*

Svetlana began typing into a physical overhead keyboard, a jerry-rigged addition that allowed her to control all of the Soyuz's functions from a seat other than the central position. She wasn't communicating anything, she was just typing the alphabet because she had wanted to end the conversation.

The warmth in her head was gone. She felt a sickness in her belly and an awful taste in her throat. The son-of-a-bitch was right and if he didn't know it, she did: Svetlana no longer felt as if she had a home. The thought made her want to pound the walls of the tiny craft, but she typed instead . . . typed hard, fast, miserably. Her soul was not dead but it was lost, so lost, and she looked out the window as she typed. Tears smeared the view of Earth as the Atlantic met Europe below. And beyond Europe—

My native land, she thought.

She wanted it back, but this man was not going to help her get it. Svetlana sank in her seat, mimicking the way her soul sank in her body. Beside her, Lord appeared to be asleep already. The man beside him was slumped deep in his chair, invisible now.

The faint glow of the *Red Giant* appeared against the vastness beyond. It was a firefly that should have been a diamond. It should have been an accomplishment to be here, not purdah.

And having this man as her companion, a man with whom she should have had so much in common? Svetlana Uralov was alone again, even more so than before.

FIFTEEN

A S THE SOYUZ made its careful approach to the former ISS, there were only routine communications between Lieutenant Uralov and the space station. Lord heard them without listening. As in his flying days, when he used to hitch a ride on a transport instead of piloting himself, he felt alert after having spent an hour not worrying about *something*. The only drawback, today, was that his artificial hip felt a little stiff having been immobilized in the couch, but that would pass when he was in motion again.

The fifty-two-year-old ISS was briefly visible through the tiny window above him, moving out of view as the pilot skillfully rolled the craft into docking position. The *Red "Giant"* reminded Lord of one of those hyperbolic candy bars he used to eat as a kid, the kind that had the word *monster* or *big* in the name: two bites and they were gone.

The ISS was precisely the size of a football field, but a lot of that size was solar panels and structural support. Habitable space was roughly the same as the interior of the Statue of Liberty, about one-quarter that of the *Empyrean*. The name was coined because Russia viewed the former International Space Station as "the head of a giant," as Russian president Anton Novak put it, "with the powerful body to come."

The body never came because Russia did not have the money to expand. Whereas the FBI paid NASA a great deal of money to inhabit a small room on the *Empyrean,* the Russian mob got to control roughly one-quarter of the station for very little money—the financial minimum required to keep the station aloft and functioning. Science was conducted on board because, in a break with the past, President Novak understood that research and development could produce mercantile results as well as military applications. Already, the Russians had developed an experimental, pancake-shaped dirigible named *Kometa*—the Comet. It was deployed from Earth, ascended to the upper atmosphere by way of small rockets, and remained in the stratosphere to rendezvous with the Soyuz or any other craft from the *Red Giant.* Larger and much less expensive to run than NASA's space kites, the Comet would eventually provide a low-cost way station for goods and personnel journeying to and from space.

There was nothing judgmental or pitying in Lord's reaction to the *Red Giant*: he regarded the former ISS the way he felt about vintage aircraft. He loved them all, contextualizing them as magnificent achievements in their day. Those that still functioned were to be admired all the more.

Like me, he thought as the universe seemed to shift outside, not the weightless Soyuz.

He did hold an opinion about the pilot, however. It was part of Lord's job to assess those on the opposite side of any fence, and this woman was extremely tense. Her annoyance was not about piloting; that came easily, her reactions automatic and sure. It was something else. The stress was all in her face, which was the only part of her he could see peripherally. He could guess the cause. She made a point of not looking in his direction; she exhaled frequently, forcibly, through her nose; and she had not just stopped talking to him, she had given up. That was different from the watchful, slightly more accessible woman he had met at PRiD1. Svetlana was still military, very much a Russian, and her current mood suggested that she had hoped to learn more about Lord than colloquial English or his favorite poems.

Her displeasure was not necessarily a bad quality, however. Not for

Lord. He would continue to watch her without actually looking at her. He would see who she connected with, and how, when they boarded the *Red Giant.*

The slow, gentle approach of the Soyuz gave Lord a chance to study the exterior of the station, note improvements that weren't visible in spy satellites. There was a container module attached to the jointed arm that jutted from the module in the center of the station. It was large and it was not where typical supply cargo was kept. But there was nothing to reveal what might be inside.

Docking gave the ship a gentle bump, which gave the occupants a slow, rocking, head-to-toe ride in zero gravity. Lord heard the same knocks and bangs he had heard in the PRiD, only louder, because he was on the inside of a small metal sphere. Faces and hands appeared as soon as the hatch was open. The Glossator indicated that the crew wanted to remove the prisoner first, and Lord released the Mindcuffs. Cameron was carefully pulled out above him, floating into the station like a Thanksgiving Day balloon. Lord experienced a slight moment of euphoria with the loss of his prisoner. Mindcuffs were equipped with electronic baffles to protect against "brain bleed"— the transfer of thought and emotion from one mind to another. As a result, it was like jogging with ankle weights: when they were removed, the wearer felt lighter, stronger. Lord felt a sudden hit of what seemed like expanded brain capacity. But it was illusory and passed quickly. Ironically, a faction of the Russian mob reportedly had been experimenting with a hallucinogenic based on the same science. It was discontinued when a participating scientist's CHAI arm momentarily became autonomous and began tearing off his flesh limbs. With fifty-seven percent of the population over the age of forty possessing cybernetic parts, the risk of widespread injury and an ensuing crackdown was too great.

Lord was helped out after Cameron, followed by Svetlana. There were stern, scruffy faces all around, none of the polished welcome or comfortable receiving facility of the *Empyrean*. The area in which Lord found himself floating was snug, like a subway car without seats, the walls filled with outdated screens, buttons, and gauges—many of which no longer functioned but had not been replaced. Despite the limited room, it was exciting to be aboard the first space station humans had ever sent aloft, the once-great hope for international cooperation in the final frontier.

Cameron was Mindcuffed to a young Russian man in a blue jumpsuit and taken away. A moment later a thin, short man in a Russian naval uniform floated closer. He came through the squared-off connector between the docking module and what Lord knew, from his reading, was the communications center of the *Red Giant*. The Zero-G director recognized the man too, from the general briefing file he'd reviewed upon first going to the *Empyrean*: Admiral Boris Ptushko, an officer in his sixties who was more a man of organizational and logistics skills than of classic military tactics. Lord did not underestimate those qualities: any able soldier would have a rudimentary idea of how to proceed in a given situation. What that individual required was someone who could keep the supply lines open and serve as a buffer between both the bureaucracy above and the enemy ahead. Ptushko was that man.

The admiral's dark-brown eyes found Svetlana Uralov first. There wasn't much to see in her stoic expression. He frowned slightly, which seemed to darken those eyes even more.

"Do you have a flight report?" Ptushko asked.

The woman shook her head.

"See Engineer Fenin and help make the preparations that we discussed earlier," he told her.

"Yes, sir," she replied, and then departed quickly.

Something unspoken had passed between them; something that brought the lieutenant down and failed to lift the admiral up. The admiral seemed to consider, for the briefest moment, what was clearly a disappointing response before turning to the American. The man's frown softened but did not disappear.

"I am honored to welcome the man who put out the Dragon's Eye," the admiral said.

"I had a lot of help," Lord said, maneuvering to face the man.

"You are unduly modest," Ptushko replied, saluting when they were just a few feet apart.

"You are of a minority opinion, sir."

Ptushko smiled politely. "One leads, others follow."

"Then it is a quality we share," Lord replied, returning the salute smartly. The movement nearly caused him to cartwheel from the wall. He had to grasp an overhead fluorescent fixture to steady himself.

"Gravity is a luxury that you have become accustomed to, Mr. Director," Ptushko observed good-naturedly.

"Preferably at one-earth," Lord said.

"Do you not enjoy the moon?" Ptushko asked.

"In a boat on a lake with a thermos of tea," Lord said. Whether or not the admiral suspected Lord had been there, the American had no intention of playing the confirmation game. "As for gravity, I never cared much for pulling eight or nine Gs."

That was Lord's way of reminding the admiral that he still considered himself military, not just a space cop. It could be a useful bond, if not at the moment then in the future.

"I understand, Colonel Lord," Ptushko said. "Before we talk further, we have received a communication request for you from your local command. Audio only. Would you care to patch in through your IC?"

ICs could be hacked by any number of ways through the interface software used by different systems. He did not doubt that the communication would be recorded, but he did not want the Russians to have a permanent base in his head.

"I'd prefer to take it at your communications station, if you don't mind," Lord replied.

"Of course," Ptushko said, extending a spindly arm to indicate that Lord should float via the opening through which the admiral had come. Lord released the fixture and pushed his way into the portal.

The communications module looked just like the docking module, save that a window in the center looked out on a large satellite dish, one of two that were used for transmissions and scientific study. Beyond that was the Earth, looking much larger than it did from the *Empyrean*.

Lord was directed to a station where a wall-mounted stand held old-fashioned headphones with a microphone. Lord had not worn headphones like those in decades and felt a surprising jolt of apprehension as he unfastened the Velcro strap and slipped them on: his last communication with Red had come through a foam-padded headset that felt like this one.

"Sam Lord here," he said, disengaging his Glossator. Not that it would matter, since there were certainly eavesdroppers listening from Earth. He was sure that whoever was on the other side of the call would know that and take it into account as well.

"It's Carter and I'm calling from the Vault," the doctor replied.

Lord didn't ask how he was communicating from a secure section of the station. The only way he could have gotten through was if a line had been hardwired through the electronic field surrounding the area.

"Go ahead," Lord said.

"Sam, they've changed."

He was obviously referring to the nanites. Even allowing for the raspy stridency of traditional radio communication rather than the more immediate, warmer IC, the biophysicist's voice was rich with alarm.

"Frisky again?" Lord quipped. His tone was to deflect the suspicions of any Russians who were listening, belying the immediate concern he felt.

"They are aggressively so," Carter replied. "Stanton has been advised. Sam, the crew and I can't leave Agro until I figure this out. *Anyone who was in here*—"

"I understand," Lord said, hearing between the lines. The Agro crew was in quarantine. The call was about Cameron. "But the test—"

"That was for something on the surface," Carter said. "It appears they are scrolling through and reactivating old, deleted programs. One of those I originally designed. The PD says you know about those."

"Yes," Lord replied. "You're talking subcutaneous."

"I am."

The CIA plan, Lord thought. Deep in the original programming was the capacity for subdermal activity. "Is there a chance your signal won't reach?"

"Yes."

"If you are able to shut the ones over there—"

"That in itself may not stop any hitchhiker who has escaped," Carter replied. "You've got the equivalent of Christopher Columbus and his crew. They may be acting independently."

Admiral Ptushko looked over. Lord could not continue this conversation much longer without arousing suspicion that something was amiss. Unfortunately, something *was* wrong.

Several somethings, Lord told himself.

Leaving Cameron here, Lord would effectively be leaving behind active nanite technology, not slag. The CIA's onetime secret weapon would not only be out of the bag, the Russian intelligence services would study them, replicate them; so might the criminals on board. And there was one other consideration: a nanite had already begun duplicating Cameron's skin cells under Liba's fingernail. If any had come over, what might they do next?

All of this will be on you, Lord reminded himself. It was his idea to bring him here.

"Still, there's a chance nothing came along," Lord said.

"A chance," Carter agreed. "But if they *did*, then any active strays would most likely resort to older programming."

Carter meant that while the nanites in the Vault were back to duplicating vine cells, a nanite that might have come here with Cameron would go with *its* previous default: attempting to build a Halloween-costume version of Douglas Cameron.

Lord glanced over again at Admiral Ptushko, who was talking to the radio operator at a respectful distance. Nonetheless, Ptushko's continued sideward glances suggested that Lord was overstaying his welcome at the console.

"Is there anything I should be looking for?" Lord asked. "Any protocols I should follow if I *do* see something?"

"If I were you, I wouldn't wait for that—"

"I can't just cut bait and return," Lord said.

"Can't you golden-tongue an excuse?"

"Not likely," Lord said. "Will our little friends at least stay put or is there a chance they could be shaken off or transfer to someone else?"

"I don't believe they will migrate as such," Carter said. "They can and will adhere to the source of raw material for whatever pattern it is intent on building."

"But?" Lord said, reading his tone.

"They could come off along with any flakes of new skin that are also dislodged. And in a zero-gravity situation—"

"They're effectively airborne," Lord said.

"Correct. They will keep working on the original pattern, but that will begin to show up, to grow, wherever they land. If they start making patches of skin, and those migrate to vital systems . . ."

Carter's voice trailed off. The ellipsis spoke gigabytes. This wasn't a tree that could be axed. Quickly duplicated skin cells could plug up pores with new flesh. Floating away in zero gravity, they could block air or electrical circuits. Whatever kinds of countermeasures the Russians might use would be toxic to the occupants of the *Red Giant*.

Ptushko was staring now. Lord held up a finger and smiled. The admiral huffed visibly and continued to frown. It reminded him of when he was a kid and long-distance calls cost money and his mother would scowl at him for talking to a friend visiting California.

"I wish the *Red Giant* had forwarded this call before you got out of the Soyuz," Carter said. "The situation could have been contained."

"Maybe not," Lord said. "They'd be justifiably suspicious."

Especially if they knew what this is about, Lord thought. *The Russians like shiny, destructive new toys as much as anyone.*

"I'm running sims in the IC," Carter said. "If I get anything that can rewrite the program or shut down the hardware, I'll let you know."

"Understood," the Zero-G director told him. "Lord out."

Lord removed the headphones slowly, buying himself a little time to think. His brain was quickly confirming what his gut had already decided: he could not withhold some form of this information from Ptushko. He also knew that, contacting Stanton or NASA, he would never be given permission to do so.

Admiral Ptushko drifted over and spoke to Lord. Hearing only Russian, the Zero-G director winked and turned his Glossator function back on.

"Sorry, could you repeat that?" Lord asked.

"Is everything all right?" Ptushko asked impatiently.

"Not entirely," Lord admitted. He made a quick command decision. "Can we speak in private?"

The admiral hesitated briefly; whatever marginal bonhomie he'd exhibited earlier was utterly gone now. No doubt he was suspicious of whatever plan might have been hatched in that radio communiqué.

"My office?" Ptushko suggested.

"Perfect. Thank you," Lord replied.

His arms extended at his sides, Ptushko flew through the module to the next—a science center—then turned and made his way to his office. They passed a module that was closed off by a thick metal door, which Lord suspected was the home of the criminal Satellite: no one else would have the money to hoist such a heavy payload aloft. Svetlana was nowhere to be seen. Reaching the closed office door, Ptushko opened it with a thumb, drifted aside, and allowed Lord to enter first. The Zero-G director chose a spot before the admiral's desk and hovered there while Ptushko entered. The former naval officer shut the door and did a neat pirouette to land behind his desk.

"I'm listening, Director Lord," Ptushko said.

Lord exhaled. At the moment he was both a player and observer: he had no idea what he was going to do or say, and was fascinated to find out. There was virtually no way to discuss this without treading on national security, and that was something he refused to do. Too many people had paid too high a price preserving that ideal.

Still, he had to find a way to define the fact that there was a potential threat. There was a very thin diplomatic path between treason and entente, and he would have to find a way to walk it.

And while he was considering all that, Lord also marveled at how far from his thoughts his *actual* mission had drifted: to try to find out about all the chatter to and from the *Red Giant*.

Like the nanites, events have their own timetable of evolution, he thought.

The Zero-G director decided to explain that Cameron's transgression had put him in contact with a military program possessing a contact-toxic component, something Lord had only just learned; and that steps should be taken to quarantine the prisoner. He would finesse that as far as he could, and hoped that Ptushko would put the security of the station above intelligence-gathering. Lord was prepared to offer to stay behind, though he knew that two extra people would strain the station's resources.

As Lord was about to speak, the men were distracted by a scream that echoed long and loud through the station.

SIXTEEN

THERE WAS NO holding area for prisoners on board the *Red Giant*. The crew had improvised one for Cameron, bringing him to the infirmary, where there was a gurney and straps to immobilize him around the arms and legs.

The restraints were not required when he arrived; they were now. As Lord and Ptushko arrived, the man was tugging to free his arms.

"It burns!" Cameron was shouting. "God help me—*make it stop!*"

The one Russian crew member who had been assigned to watch him was asking the prisoner to turn on his Glossator.

"He's saying that something burns," Lord explained as he entered the module. Easing past the Russian, Lord hovered over the prisoner. "What burns, Mr. Cameron? Where?"

"My hair . . . my scalp . . . they *hurt!*"

Ptushko forcibly moved the crewman aside. He and Lord were just a foot apart in the tight quarters. There was no mistaking the accusatory look in the admiral's eyes as they moved from Cameron to Lord.

"Do you know what he is talking about?" the Russian demanded.

"I believe I do," Lord replied.

Suspicion and anger clouded the admiral's features in equal measure, and Lord didn't blame him.

"You will explain?" Ptushko said. Just then he reminded Lord of Carter. It was a question that was actually a command.

"I will," Lord answered, though he said no more than that. He still couldn't tell the Russian that nanites—it would probably take more than just one to generate this kind of reaction—had probably buried themselves in the man's epidermis or hair follicles and were likely welding new skin cells in place. But there was also reality: either new skin or hair or both would begin to appear on Cameron. The Russians would learn the nature of the threat soon enough. "But first, we're going to have to do two things, and quickly," Lord said. "I need a sedative and a space suit. Get those and then we'll talk."

Ptushko didn't move, his expression unchanging.

"I promise," Lord assured him. "My safety is also very much at stake."

The admiral thawed very slightly and gave an IC order to two crew members. One of them was a name Lord knew from his initial research about the *Red Giant*: Dr. Gavriil Borodin, a world-renowned exobiologist. The suspicion at the FBI was that Borodin was the "storefront" cover for the Russian mob, a legitimate but money-losing scientific operation akin to the New York bodegas and massage parlors that once provided a public façade for gun-running, drug dealing, and human trafficking.

Borodin came quickly wearing a small medical pack strapped to his left arm. The balding, middle-aged man had the sallow look of someone who had been up here a long time. His skillful maneuvering in zero gravity reinforced that impression. Obviously, like Dr. Carter on the *Empyrean*, Borodin doubled as a medic on the *Red Giant*.

"What's the problem?" Borodin asked.

The scientist was floating perpendicular to Lord and Ptushko, pulling reusable rubber gloves from his pack as he moved toward Cameron.

"This man needs to be unconscious and placed in a space suit," Lord said.

"Quarantined?" Borodin said as he regarded Lord. "Why?"

"We'll talk after this is done," Lord said.

"What have you brought here?" Ptushko demanded, his tone simmering.

Once again, Lord did not answer. He watched as Borodin removed a thumb-size syringe from his pack and inserted a capsule. He floated low over Cameron.

"Hold his head still," the scientist instructed the crewman.

"No!" Lord blurted.

The crew member had already been in motion by the time the Glossator translated. He stopped cold, his hands inches from the botanist and looked toward the admiral.

Borodin laid one hand on Cameron's forehead, holding him securely while he jabbed the needle in the man's neck. The botanist went out almost immediately. Moments later, a crew member arrived carrying a soft space suit—a traditional rocket-ride suit, as NASA used to call them informally. With no hard-joint mechanisms or exoskeletonic parts for working outside a spacecraft, this was probably on board in the event of decompression. Lord would have felt better if this was a NASA-issued hazpack, but there was no reason this shouldn't suffice. And there was no need for the men to touch Cameron as they put it on. It would fit cleanly over the Minnie and, like current American suits—no surprise, since the Russians appropriated the patent—it self-expanded from a pack and encased the wearer. Before it was activated, Lord spoke to Borodin.

"That left-hand glove and the needle," Lord said, purposely indicating just the one glove Borodin had used to hold the man down. "You might want to leave them inside the suit, with the prisoner."

Borodin looked at Ptushko for approval, which came as a single nod. The scientist laid the items on the man's chest and looked inquiringly at Lord.

"That's fine," Lord said. "Thank you."

A pair of oxygen tanks with a total of two hours of air was attached to external hoses. These were left floating behind the prisoner.

Cameron was then reattached to the table with straps around his upper arms, waist, and thighs.

At a look from Ptushko, the crew members and Borodin left the module. The scientist exited first, quickly, his right hand hidden from view. Ptushko's eyes held those of the scientist as he left. Lord noticed that something passed between them, and he had a good idea what it was. The admiral remained inside with Lord and shut the module door. Ptushko was as stiff and unforgiving as an Inquisitor.

"Explain this," the admiral demanded.

"You'll have your answer soon, I think," Lord said.

"Another delay!" Ptushko yelled. "What are you playing at? You have a reputation for irrational behavior—"

"Have I? According to whom?"

"I am conducting this interview," the admiral said. "Tell me, is this a carefully crafted FBI plan to undermine this facility?"

"If it were, would I actually confess to that? But in the name of expediency and cooperation—it's nothing like that," Lord assured him. "The only reason I came here was to return your agent, Admiral."

The Russian made a dismissive gesture as the Glossator translated that. The conversation stopped while Ptushko looked away, apparently trying to figure out what Lord was doing. He couldn't know that it was nothing more ominous than stalling. After a long moment he turned back.

"Whatever your motive, you told me we would talk after this is done," the Admiral said.

"I didn't say *when* we would talk."

Now the Russian swore. "This is a comedy to you?"

"Anything but," Lord assured him. "Actually, I am waiting on you. Counting on you, in fact— "

Ptushko was about to reply when he turned away suddenly and shut his Glossator. *"Da?"*

It was likely Borodin calling. Lord hoped the path between entente and treason was about to widen a little. The Zero-G director watched as the admiral listened intently. Ptushko stared at the man in the space suit and did not look back at Lord until the communication was ended. His expression was unforgiving.

"Three microscopic robots," he said. "That is what Dr. Borodin found on a hair sample he retrieved. They were active—somehow *thickening* the hair sample. Now you will talk."

"Yes," Lord said. "Now I will. Now I *can* talk." He was troubled at the report of three nanites on a single hair; that was more than he had anticipated. It was difficult to imagine how many were still on Cameron. "Tell Dr. Borodin to keep the little robots in an airtight petri dish."

"He did so on his own," Ptushko replied. "Unlike you, Mr. Director, we have strict guidelines for handling foreign materials on this station."

"We had enviable protocols too until this man, *your* man, broke them," Lord replied, indicating Cameron.

Ptushko dismissed the charge with a flick of his hand. "And why are *you* here, if not to investigate us?"

"That's a fair question, but your thesis is incomplete," Lord said. "My personal goal is *pax humana.*"

"Peace for all?" Ptushko laughed. "Global *glasnost*?"

"Interplanetary, and yes," Lord said. "I've spent a lifetime dropping ordnance on war makers. I'm looking for a better way to do things."

"Fine words. But you search under your rules."

"Show me someone who does not, to some degree," Lord replied. They were just trading blows and no point was served. "But let's see if we can trust one another just to deal with the problem at hand. And make no mistake—this is *our* problem—yours, mine, and everyone on board."

Ptushko grunted low in his throat. Lord took that as an accord. But the Russian was actually correct to doubt: the only reason Lord was ready to talk now was because he was no longer revealing something secret. The Russians had discovered the nanites on their own.

There is some level of hypocrisy in that, he had to admit. But Lord himself had betrayed nothing, and no one.

"Admiral," he began, still weighing his words, "these 'microscopic robots' are not themselves biological, though they clearly interact with biological matter."

"Interact how? Apparently not to destroy?"

"No," Lord said. "Not intentionally. They are also not intelligent, though they share programs that—and this was news to us—have been rewritten by subatomic particles of Russian origin."

"Again, you blame us—"

"I *inform* you," Lord gently interrupted. "The particles responsible for this alteration in their program are defective hadrons that infested a portion of our station after hitchhiking on hardware provided to Mr. Cameron by someone in your intelligence service. I did not know that any corrupted nanobots were on this man until we arrived. The fault for *that* was the inability of the *Empyrean* to communicate with the Soyuz."

"The communication you received?"

Lord nodded.

Ptushko considered the information. "So that is why you had this man placed in a space suit," the admiral said. "To contain any more of them?"

"It is."

Ptushko considered this. "You did not answer the question—the robots 'interact' *how*?" the admiral asked.

"I'm getting to that," Lord said. "First—there could be none at all or there could be dozens, hundreds, I don't know. I assume there are a lot since rooting around a single follicle would not have caused him to scream like that. But this is only a temporary solution. To answer the other question, I don't know how long it will take, but that suit is going to fill with new hair and possibly skin particles created by the nanites."

"Cellular factories," Ptushko said.

"Yes," Lord said. "As a result of that, Mr. Cameron will suffocate in time and the suit will eventually burst."

"Then he must be ejected into space at once," Ptushko said. "There is a vent door in the medbay for the disposal of potential biohazards."

Lord regarded him critically, but not with surprise. Ptushko was an exemplar of classic Russian military overkill. He had once famously sunk a yacht that was used as a drug-processing facility by North Korean gangsters. This, despite intelligence that more than a dozen trafficked women were on board being transported to high-end clients.

"Even though the man's a traitor, I'd prefer to seek other options," Lord replied. "We have a little time and the *Empyrean* is searching for answers as we speak."

"What do you mean by 'a little time'?" Ptushko asked.

"I don't know, exactly. Maybe two hours."

It was a wild, very rough guess, but the admiral seemed to accept it. Perhaps he already knew, had been briefed by whoever had been eavesdropping on the call from Carter. From the Russian's expression there were clearly other questions he wanted to ask, felt obliged to ask, but they were less important than figuring out what to do.

"Is it possible that *you* harbor any of these robots in your hair or elsewhere?" the admiral asked. "Or my pilot?"

"Very unlikely," Lord said. "I haven't felt anything, and I'm sure you would have heard from Lieutenant Uralov if she had. I am told they do not generally migrate except on tissue they create, which *could* become airborne if they are shaken loose."

"Airborne—in this enclosed environment," Ptushko said. "Expanding within the filters."

"I know," Lord said. "But the prisoner did not receive a sufficiently strong jolt. Not yet. Which is another reason we have to move cautiously."

Ptushko gave Lord a look—a warning?—that suggested he would not hesitate to push the prisoner, Lord, and Svetlana out the airlock if there were a risk of infestation. But he said nothing, as he also must have realized that such an effort might actually serve to dislodge any nanites.

"Do you want to talk to your scientists about any of this?" Ptushko asked. "I will keep an open channel."

"They promised to let me know if a solution is found," Lord

answered. He did not indicate how many scientists were working on this, which was probably no more than Carter and one or two people at NASA; telling Ptushko that would inform him just how top secret it was. "Is there anything Dr. Borodin can suggest?"

"I'm not at liberty to discuss conversations with my staff," Ptushko replied.

So much for glasnost, *for openness,* Lord thought. The admiral too, was not going to divulge the resources of the station though probably for a very different reason: Borodin's tools were severely limited. The science on board had not been seriously updated since the Russians took over, except for whatever the gangsters had brought up. Lord already knew that, but the admiral was not about to confirm it.

"You know, Director Lord, as I think about this, my inclination is to send you back to your station," Ptushko told him.

"Why?"

"While I respect your stated sentiments about wanting to help, I cannot watch you *and* supervise a situation," Ptushko said.

"I understand, though forget about me—you may want to keep the Soyuz here. In case it's needed."

It took a moment for Ptushko to grasp the implication. In the event the nanites impacted the ship or its crew, the spacecraft was their only lifeboat. At least three people could get away.

"You would be happy to take us in at the *Empyrean,* of course," Ptushko said.

"Actually, that would not be my call," Lord replied, palms raised helplessly. "But doing so would guarantee the safety of your personnel. Would you care to put such a request in to Commander Stanton?"

Lord already knew Ptushko would never do that. He would sooner save three occupants by sending them to Earth. The embarrassment for Moscow of having the entire population of the *Red Giant* "abandon ship" for the American station would be too rich.

"Not at present," Ptushko replied. "Yet once again, you seem to know more than you are saying."

"How so?"

"If I sent you back, it is only a two-hour round-trip to your station," Ptushko said. "Do you have reason to believe that the situation will gravely deteriorate before that? Are these 'nanobots' capable of swifter action than you are saying?"

"I only know what I'm told," Lord said. "These things have written their own program, are creating their own timetable—and, as I said, we have no idea how many of them Mr. Cameron may have picked up."

Ptushko snorted. "I am unimpressed by what the Federal Bureau of Investigation does not know."

The Glossator didn't capture Ptushko's contemptuous tone. But Lord did.

"We've had better days," the Zero-G director admitted with a crooked smile. "We all have."

Ptushko shook his head, openly annoyed and still very guarded. He was about to say something when Lord heard a communication through the man's audible IC. It was Dr. Borodin.

"Admiral, come to the lab!" the scientist told him. "You must see this!"

SEVENTEEN

I HAVE NEVER heard the station so quiet," Janet Grainger remarked. "But it is the loudest quiet I've ever heard."

Even though the Zero-G team was sequestered in the comm, there was tension rippling through the space station, through their ICs. Adsila and the others could sense it, feel it, the way they felt the power of the sun even through the void. In a closed environment like the *Empyrean*, nothing truly happened in isolation.

Having heard nothing at all from Director Lord or Dr. Carter, Adsila was also feeling more than a little at sea. She was picking up activity from the Drum, Stanton preparing to bring down Slammers if needed to seal off the Agro Center, ordering off-duty station workers to stay at their posts. He had not announced a Situational Call for all shuttles public and private to head for the station, which meant that there was no plan yet to evacuate nonessential personnel.

As she listened to routine communiqués on Earth, watched field reports pertaining to satellite assets—her daily morning overviews—an audio message came from Dr. Carter in the Vault. His voice was taut, lacking its usual calm, understated monotone.

"EAD, are Agents McClure and Abernathy present?"

"They are."

"Permission to access."

If Carter had wanted information he could have contacted them directly; this meant he had some kind of duty in mind. Though the medic was a member of the Zero-G team, he was still secondary to the director. In Lord's absence, that meant he needed Adsila's permission to discuss a potential detail.

"Agents McClure and Abernathy," Adsila said, engaging their ICs. "Dr. Carter is on with me."

"We're here, sir," they said in unison, their faces joining the conversation. There was empty space where Carter's image should have been.

Since the only team member excluded was Janet Grainger, Adsila shared her own feed with the communications director, eyes-only. The others would not be aware she was on. Grainger acknowledged the courtesy with a slight nod.

"With your permission, EAD, I would like these men to go to my lab and await instructions," Carter said.

"What is the duty, Doctor?" Adsila asked.

"I'm waiting for permission to brief them," he said.

"Only Agents McClure and Abernathy?" she asked.

"I've included you and Janet in the request, but need-to-know is not my call," he informed her.

Adsila understood. She cocked her head toward the door and both men left quickly, the surge in their excitement palpable as they scooted around their desks with a boost from the station's centripetal force. The pocket door to the comm whooshed to the right, then closed when the men had exited.

"I can see you're in the Agro Center," Adsila said to Dr. Carter. "Stanton has been ordering personnel to that area. Have they also been security cleared?"

"They have, and I repeat: I am not in charge. This is NASA's operation. They have their own criteria."

Criteria. The EAD hated the word. By definition, it was exclusionary. Despite all the progress society had made, there were still clubs within clubs. Stanton's team. NASA's team. Zero-G. Just outside one of the PRiD access doors was a replica of the plaque on the Apollo 11 lander, which read "We Came in Peace for All Mankind"—yet, even now, Lord was spying on the Russians. It was enough to make an idealistic pangender wonder if it would ever be possible for a single human being to be all things to all interests.

That made Adsila think of another plaque, the one over the entrance to Hell in Dante's *Divine Comedy*: "*Lasciate ogne speranza, voi ch'entrate*—Abandon all hope, ye who enter here."

Right now, Carter was probably nearer to that than the other, she thought.

Adsila had spent her lifetime understanding that the different qualities between her male and female aspects had nothing to do with competency or abilities. Her Cherokee parents had decided to have their child genetically pangendered in the womb—not to give her organic options but to grant her wisdom, so she could understand that humans were not their sinew and bones but their spirits. Recently, the CHAI Ziv Levy had proven that flesh was not even required to define a human. He had made love to her with parts that were more cybernetic than flesh.

And yet, ancient judgments are entrenched, calcified like dead tissue, she thought. Like ripples in a pool, biases continued to breed sexual prejudice, nationalism, religious fanaticism, destructive territorialism of every stripe and color. None of which made Adsila want to give up: to the contrary. She was resolved to fight all the harder. That was one reason she had quickly come to respect Samuel Lord. Agree with him or not, he risked life and career to maneuver like a tank over barricades in a search for truth and solutions. He made her realize the irony of another societal head-set, ageism.

Who the hell decided that bottomless, youthful vigor was somehow more desirable than experience, perspective, and cumulative understanding? Zero gravity had cut into that idea even further, since young muscle had virtually no meaning up here and swift, less experienced reflexes—in the wrong direction—could send spacewalkers to their death.

Carter's voice trod heavily on her equitable thoughts.

"EAD, security clearance has been granted to Agents Abernathy and McClure," the doctor told her.

"Acknowledged," Adsila replied.

Grainger's face was in two places: in her IC and right beside her. Both reinforced the . . . *diminution* Adsila felt. That was the only word that seemed to fit.

"Well," Grainger said with barely concealed displeasure, "there's a nice—"

"Bureaucratic decision," Adsila replied, cutting her off. "It's territorial, nothing more."

"Exactly what I was going to say, EAD," Grainger replied. "Wasn't going to say, 'kick in the ass.'"

Adsila looked at Grainger and offered a smile she didn't quite feel. It wouldn't help to have two angry people in the comm.

"It wasn't personal," the EAD insisted. "It's like being angry at a machine."

"Haven't *you* ever kicked a homebot?"

Adsila's smile became sincere. "Just once, when I was a teenager, before the improved iRobot brand was released. It was my mother's. The thing made its way outside and vacuumed the flower beds."

Grainger laughed and wagged a finger. "I remember that first model. When you told it, 'Clean under the bed,' you had to be very specific."

"I learned that and kicked the 'bot when it came inside." Adsila laughed. "But you know what *that* did? Made it cough the rest of the humus into my dad's cherished kitchen. That was when I learned not to kick machinery."

Almost at once, a Wishie appeared in both of their ICs. It was Grainger's; Adsila didn't bother with psychodramatic fluff. The program automatically animated images of a user and depicted it in a wide variety of actions. The components Grainger's program had gathered showed Adsila, as a male, kicking a NASA logo from the *Empyrean* and watching it burn up in the atmosphere.

"Admit it." Grainger laughed, watching the ten-second vignette play out before looking back at the EAD. "Doesn't that make you feel better?"

Adsila's male form was standing sternly at his post in the comm.

"Very," he answered sternly. But it wasn't just rage at NASA that Adsila was keeping under control. It was the experience of every Native American, of every woman, of every gender-diverse person he had ever known, the human struggle against entrenched interests, be they government or private industry. It made Samuel Lord's form of iconoclasm not just appealing but suddenly essential to him.

The two Zero-G officers got serious and went back to work.

Adsila noticed, then, that McClure had "accidentally" left on his IC feed so that the EAD would see whatever the science officer saw. Adsila had a moment of *that's very Sam Lord* before realizing how much trouble McClure could get into for the "oversight."

"Agent McClure, you forgot to shut your IC feed to the comm," Adsila told him as he hustled down the corridor.

"Did I?" he replied. "I'll fix that now, yes?"

"Yes, please," the EAD said. "And thank you."

"You're welcome, sir," McClure replied.

Adsila plugged back into the usual "low-burn" data flow in the comm. He was angry about being sidelined, angrier than he had initially admitted, even to himself. But more than that, he hated to be in the dark about a project that involved most of the six-person team.

That exclusion changed when Stanton called for all standby personnel to report to the Agro Center. Technically, that didn't include Adsila. But it didn't expressly exclude him either. He wasn't going to stay out of a crisis because of a technicality, nor would Stanton have the time or energy to keep him out.

"My hands are just too full of rattlesnake," his grandfather used to say when he was busy.

Adsila was already moving toward the door when he told Grainger, "You've got the comm. I'll be in Agro."

The EAD heard Grainger wish him luck as he jogged into the hallway.

Movement always helped when Adsila's mood soured, and he practically leapt when gravity permitted. He hurried to the elevator and, exiting, Adsila found the green line a veritable highway of people rushing to and from the Agro Center. Stanton wasn't here and he didn't recognize most of the people who were. To his surprise, a number of those standing outside the closed door of the greenhouse were donning hazpacks—pockets that, when pressed, would expand to enclose them in hazmat suits with a two-hour supply of air.

One person Adsila did recognize was Lancaster Liba. The man was seated in a MagChair, a plastic bucket and backrest with magnetic metal skis that traveled by gliding nearly friction-free along similarly charged strips laid in the floor throughout the station. The *Empyrean* was the only space facility fully accessible to people with disabilities.

Liba was sitting away from the seven other people who were suiting up. He was not wearing a hazpack, though he did have a transparent healing blister on a patch of skull behind the ear. The electrogenetic contents stimulated the repair of damaged cells and were commonly used for fractures. Adsila knew from the autobriefing in his IC that Liba had been injured, though he didn't know how or why. Clearly, Liba was not going in, which meant he was likely here in an advisory capacity.

The EAD stepped beside the Gardener.

"How do you feel, Lancaster?" Adsila asked.

It took Liba a moment to recognize Adsila. He was accustomed—and happier, he freely admitted to Lord—when the EAD appeared in female form.

"I feel like I've been struck by lightning and then whammed by the tree it hit."

"Were you?" Adsila asked. He wasn't joking.

He considered that. "You know, Mr. Waters, I can't actually say."

Adsila's mouth twisted. "Meaning—"

Liba just smiled benignly. "If a tree falls in the Vault, it doesn't make a sound if NASA says, 'Shhhh.'"

Still thinking about Sam Lord, Adsila was about to play a card from his deck as a way of obliquely getting information—by asking if his two agents were in any danger—when Liba received a call from Carter. The call was microphone only, Vault security having been intentionally and temporarily breached thanks to a hardwired line run from the Vault to an IC link in the greenhouse. The feed was on audible. Adsila was under no obligation to inform Liba that he could hear, since he didn't report to him. He looked at Adsila in a way that said he knew what was what and didn't care.

There were sounds coming from somewhere inside the Vault. They weren't pleasant sounds: they were sharp, sizzling snaps followed immediately by creaking, cracking groans. Adsila could not imagine what was going on in there. Whatever it was, the word *unhealthy* stuck in his mind, like the hollow, lonely sound he had heard as a child one night of an old, scuttled barge knocking against a wrecked wharf on the shores of the Mississippi River.

Adsila heard Carter shouting inaudible instructions before turning to the call.

"Liba," he said, "while we're waiting for NASA to approve the new people, have you got any weed-killer that doesn't contain organics?"

"Something with just chemical toxins?"

"That's right." The doctor sounded calm, though there was a clipped quality to his voice—as if he were thinking aloud. "You have nothing hidden, illicit?"

Liba actually laughed. "You know I don't," Liba said. "First, NASA screened every ounce of everything that came up here. And second, your kias in the med world banned 'em."

Kia stood for "know-it-all." Liba clearly had it in for the scientists who knew things with certainty and then didn't, by which time they had forced their beliefs on others.

"It was worth a try," Carter said dejectedly. "What I'd give for gly-phosate."

Adsila's drop-down told him that the herbicide blocked the enzyme that helped synthesize tyrosine, phenylalanine, and tryptophan—essential amino acids. The banned compound was deadly to growing plants.

"We've got glyphosoy," Liba told him.

"I know, I checked the inventory," Carter said. "But I can't risk introducing more biological material. Those things may just morph. As it is, they're moving faster than before. Factor of three." He paused. "They're learning, the bastards."

"That'll teach you to make things too well," Liba said.

And then Adsila understood. There were nanites in there, the same kind Carter had used to extract Ziv Levy's robotic spies from his belly, only these nanites were obviously ungovernable for some reason, somehow using or feeding on organic matter. He felt a sudden sickness in his lower abdomen as he hoped that Carter had gotten them all.

Adsila indicated for Liba to cut the microphone function of his IC.

"Are the nanites destroying or reproducing matter?" Adsila asked.

"If I were allowed to answer that question, I'd say the latter," Liba told him.

"What would happen if we introduced the nanites to cells with contradictory instructions?"

"I'm not following you," Liba said.

Adsila shifted to his female form to make his point. "What if they replicated one kind of cell, became acclimated to that . . . and then those cells switched due to some kind of cytoplasmic egg timer. Would hard-turn, conflicting instructions confuse the nanites?"

"Leave them without marching orders, you mean," Liba said thoughtfully. Liba looked intrigued at the thought, and also pleased to see "her." He raised a gnarled finger for silence and switched the audio link back on.

"Hey, Doc? I just had a curious thought," Liba said. "What would your babies do with cells from a pangender?"

Carter was silent for a moment. "Interesting. It would either confuse them into stasis or double their capacity."

"What do you mean double?" Liba asked.

"There would be enough of the old cell structure present so that they would simply adjust to the new material—add it to their cell construction library, as it were."

"Worth trying?" Liba asked. "Should I get a hair sample and send it in?"

Carter was silent again. "Agent McClure? Are you there?"

"Here, Doctor," McClure replied.

"I'm going to ask EAD Waters to go to the lab," he said. "I want you to take a hair sample and introduce it to the petri dish marked B11.16. Report what happens."

"May I brief the EAD about why we are requesting a hair?" McClure asked.

"She already knows," Carter said. "I heard you arrive, EAD. Mr. Liba's feed is both input *and* output."

"Shoot," Liba said. "Well, I'm just a country botanist—what do I know from ICs?"

Adsila was glad Carter had known that but hadn't shut her out. He was a difficult man to get close to, a man of secrets, obviously; it was good to know that he could be a regulation-bending pragmatist when he had to be.

"EAD?" Carter said.

"I'm on my way," Adsila replied, with a glance back at the hazpack team. They were standing at the entrance to the Vault with a variety of cutting tools, doing nothing while NASA performed whatever background checks were required by charter.

Not even fiddling while Rome burns, she thought as she hurried back along the green line. No wonder Stanton resented Lord: the Zero-G director would have found a loophole in the regulations and the team would already be inside the Vault.

Thinking of Lord, Adsila checked her IC as she boarded the

elevator. There were no messages from him. She wasn't expecting any; they had not expected communications from the Russian space station to be plentiful. Still, with so much happening on two fronts, she wished there were more for her to do than just donate a strand of hair.

A part of her too was jealous of his adventure—bold, new, unscripted.

Give it time, she told herself but heard it in her grandfather's voice. *Your greater adventures will come.*

EIGHTEEN

FOLLOWING BORODIN'S URGENT call from his lab, there was an awkward moment as Ptushko turned and Lord moved to follow him.

"No!" the Russian said over his shoulder. "You will remain here."

"Respectfully, Admiral, this is not a time for politics," Lord said. "I might be able to help."

"*How?*" Ptushko demanded, his hands full of the hatch frame.

"Let's find out," Lord implored him. "I cannot leave the station or communicate with *Empyrean*—you lose nothing by letting me come with."

Ptushko didn't have time to argue and, in the moment he took to consider it, he couldn't think of a good reason not to agree—other than the distasteful act of having to agree with his enemy. The admiral pushed himself into the corridor, followed tentatively by Lord, who found the narrow confines and lack of up-and-down a challenge.

Lord had not spent much time in zero gravity—ironic, given the name of the team he commanded. And very little of it was tranquil. More incredibly, to him, his time on the *Red Giant* was already the longest period he had ever been free-floating in space. His four space journeys had been in form-fitting couches with various restraints; the space walk on the *Empyrean*, when he faced down the Chinese Dragon's Eye, was done with magnetic boots and surfaces to adhere to. This was very different. It was a little like swimming, in the sense that he could move any way he wished, but weightlessness wasn't quite like lounging in a bathtub. Here, the muscles quickly learned that they didn't have to work very hard . . . so they relaxed, the entire body relaxed. Even in a seat, everything that wasn't tied down was floating. That included your hair, your clothes, even whatever little bit of saliva was on your tongue if you cleared your throat—which was not uncommon, because the machine-cleaned air tended to be pretty dry. If it weren't for the crisis at hand, Lord would be enjoying the sheer, almost absurd fun of free-floating. Unlike some power climbs and dives he had endured, there was nothing stomach-churning about it. This was liberating. It was especially freeing for his CHAI thigh, since there was no added weight on that side of his body. The only thing he had to watch out for was not to bump the walls with his legs. Moving along without his hind-quarters swinging like a tandem bus took some practice, and he was glad Ptushko was in front of him and not behind. Ptushko also helped to deflect the attention of crew members who otherwise would have been staring at the high-ranking adversary in their midst. Still, a few of the handful managed to steal a glance.

This must be how Adsila feels, being unique, he thought. He was accustomed to being looked at for something he did, for an achievement. He didn't like being ogled for something he *was.* The word *outsider* had been banished in the so-called correctness purge of 2019—along with *alien, foreign,* and many other us-versus-them terms. But human nature had not kept up with linguistic bullying, only made it embarrassing to admit to.

They reached the lab in less than a minute; weightlessness was nothing if not fast. The room was smaller than Dr. Carter's lab, and every millimeter of space was full of something—from test tubes filled with space rock to digital thermometers to a Kozyrev Gas Trap, named for the famed astronomer, which looked like a dunce cap and was used to trap elemental particles in space. There wasn't room for all three men in the tiny cubicle, so Lord hovered in the hallway, sideways, which was easier than trying to turn. It actually gave him a better view since he could adjust easily whenever either man moved.

Borodin looked both alarmed and excited. The scientist took a moment to flash a look at Lord.

"Admiral, I am not sure our guest should see this," Borodin said, his craggy features sagging unhappily.

Lord drifted forward slightly, at an angle, inserting his head in the door. "As I just told the admiral, I may have something to contribute," he said.

"This is not just about you or your contagion," Borodin snapped back.

"What is it about?" Ptushko demanded.

"Admiral, if I tell *you*, then *he* will know!" the exobiologist replied.

"Just go ahead," Ptushko said. "If our station or national security is compromised, we will send him to Earth with his prisoner and let the Kremlin sort it out."

Lord suspected that Ptushko wasn't bluffing. There was room on the Soyuz to do just that, and it wouldn't even cause much of a stir, since a lot of bureaucrats in Washington would be happy to have him lost for a year or two in Moscow or Star City or wherever they would take him.

Still, he was happy to risk it just to find out what had agitated Borodin.

Shaking his head with unhappy resignation, the exobiologist turned to a small transparent container about half the size of a test tube. It was floating above the lab table in some kind of stasis field, probably magnetic. Off to the side was a dish with the sample of Cameron's hair, held to the lab table by what looked like blue gum. Fixed on top of it was the lens of a wireless microscope, undoubtedly plugged directly into Borodin's IC. Lord took a moment to examine the rest of the room and noticed something under the lab table.

"There is something in the cylinder you do not know about, Admiral," Borodin pointed out with a hint of apology.

The admiral did not seem surprised. "Go on."

"I was instructed to tell no one and—"

"Proceed!" Ptushko said impatiently, like a man who understood how the system worked and was in no mood to be accommodating.

Borodin seemed both resigned and absolved. He hooked his gray hair behind both ears and his eyes brightened—like those of a child, Lord thought.

"Admiral, there is a specimen of indigenous Venusian life in the container."

No one moved. The exobiologist waited for his words to take hold. It took longer than he had anticipated. For several seconds there was no change in the expressions of the other two men.

"Is it alive?" Lord asked, the obvious next question occurring to him after the reality tenuously took hold. It was almost an automatic response, forensics trumping all else.

Borodin nodded, once.

"Thank you," Lord said in earnest. "Thank you for sharing this."

"Are you sure?" Ptushko finally asked.

"Confirmed by Dr. Ivan Cherkassov himself at MSU," he said.

"How can *he* be sure if— "

"He hasn't examined the specimen?" Borodin asked. "We've reviewed a great deal of data, ruled out all other options. There is no mistake."

Ptushko seemed to have a sudden understanding—about something. He stared at Borodin, who nodded slightly. Lord wanted to know more about what they weren't saying. Instinct told him it had to do with the Scud launches: they went toward the sun . . . toward Venus. Lord also knew he would have to wait.

"First contact," Ptushko said. "And *we* made it."

Lord had expected some comment like that and deflected it. This was a titanic discovery for all humankind, and he wasn't just saying that because he was on the "losing" side. A door had opened and now anyone could walk through—which was precisely what the Russians feared, he knew. No matter. The universe suddenly seemed more than it had been moments ago, not a cold, dead, gaseous expanse but an incubator.

"What *is* the specimen?" Ptushko asked. "What does it look like?"

The scientist used his IC to project a hologram image, reminiscent of old handheld tablet devices Lord had used decades before, but without a frame. Borodin was being cautious by using the external projection: once the data was plugged into an IC, it was no longer entirely secure, even with Ptushko.

The creature before them looked like a piece of butterscotch-colored rice with eight flanges on its body: one on either side, three standing on the top, three on the bottom. The octet of relative large fingers was extremely active, shivering as though the creature were a cartoon character plugged into an electric socket.

"The Venusian resembles a terrestrial tardigrade, a microbial 'water bull' that dwells in terrestrial moss," Borodin said.

"I'm guessing that would make sense in the soupy atmosphere of Venus," Lord said.

"It would," Borodin acknowledged. "It does." He seemed slightly impressed that Lord had picked up on that.

"How is it surviving outside the atmosphere?" Ptushko asked.

"Microbes are extremely hardy," the scientist said. "This creature has a minimal organ system—its insides seem more like a filtration system with a nerve bundle to control the system—dominated, like many terrestrial invertebrates, by an ovotestis structure for reproduction. It can mate with any other member of its species." Borodin added thoughtfully, "There are many who believe that Earth was seeded by Martian microbes, when that planet still sustained life. Perhaps they came from Venus. Possibly both! The potential for knowledge, for exploration, has just exploded around us!"

"What else do you know that isn't speculation?" Ptushko asked. He was not being critical, just methodical. "Is it toxic?"

"That is unknown," Borodin said. "But—let me show you the reason I called you here." The scientist blinked and moved his eyes. "Admiral—look at these readings."

The image before them changed. Ptushko and Lord saw a series of jagged lines moving right to left, reaching higher and higher like mountain peaks. There were five of them, three red, one yellow, and one blue.

"What you are looking at, here in red, are the activity lines of the nanobots from the prisoner's hair." He pointed with an index finger. "The yellow line is the Venusian." He traced a finger along the graph. The yellow line was rising faster and at a steeper angle than the red lines. Numeric readouts confirmed the relative spikes. "Now, look at this," Borodin said. He blinked hard and the graph flashed backward to the moments before the hair sample containing the nanites was brought into the room. The red lines vanished. The yellow line was calm, showing only low, gentle rises and falls.

"Explain," Ptushko said after failing to grasp what Borodin was showing him.

"They are aware of one another," Lord said.

"Correct, but they are more than aware," Borodin said excitedly, all caution gone.

"You can't be serious," Lord said with sudden understanding.

"About what?" asked a frustrated Ptushko.

"They're communicating, Admiral," Lord said.

"Not exactly, but I think you are close," Borodin replied. "It is my belief that the little robots sensed the microbe and the microbe responded by—well, the readings suggest it screamed at them."

"In what way?" Lord said. "Fear? Rage?" He was thinking aloud, not really asking.

"Who knows?" Borodin replied. "The microbe sent out some kind of sustained energy wave—no, more like a *wall*—that caused the nanites to respond with agitation."

"The cry went *through* the petri dishes and the suspension field you've got it in?" Lord asked, indicating the Venusian microbe.

"Somehow, yes. And you will note," Borodin added, "the response of the microbe appears to be far in excess of the threat posed by the nanites."

"A scorched earth approach?" Lord wondered.

"Possibly. I don't yet know."

"What is the blue line?" Lord asked when he had somewhat absorbed the other data.

"That," Borodin said with something approaching reverence, "is something I have never seen in this form. It is a magnetoencephalographic reading—a response to electrical currents produced by the brain. Only it is not originating with the microbe. This"—he jabbed a finger at the Venusian sample—"is an entirely alien life-form in every sense of the word. One that is actually causing the nanites to rewrite their programming."

"They're trying to find a way in because they could not blow the house down," Lord thought aloud.

"I don't understand," Borodin said.

"Children's story about a big bad wolf," Lord answered.

"I don't know about that," the scientist said, "but your assessment about finding another way in, I believe, is accurate. There is an attraction that seems to be functioning as a dendrite, if you will—the branch of a neuron that conducts impulses."

"In short, Doctor?" Ptushko asked impatiently.

"The nanites want to reach the microbe, but not to destroy it," Borodin said. "I believe they wish to connect with it."

Artificial evolution raised exponentially, Lord thought. *Merger with a life-form they can literally get their pincers around.*

Lord was trying to digest this new information when he hadn't yet fully processed the reality of first contact. He was also still remarkably unfazed that the Russians had made it. Hell, he wasn't even doing his job, probing for information about how, when, and what the Kremlin might be planning to do next. And now he was trying not to be preoccupied by what had just occurred to him, the utterly bizarre notion that there was some kind of conflict or otherworldly romance going on at a molecular level, invisible to the unaided eye.

"It's ironic, isn't it?" Borodin continued with a measure of solemnity. "The first contact between a species from another world and a species from Earth—at least, the first contact we can document—and we are not even part of the conversation."

"My ego is not wounded," Ptushko said, his eyes on the rising lines of the graph. "I want to know what's happening here, how it affects my command."

"I will be working on that," Borodin assured him.

"An understatement," Ptushko replied. He turned to Lord. "Is there anything else you can add? We have been open with you."

"There is nothing," Lord lied. He wasn't about to give Ptushko a reason to throw the microbe out the window as he'd been prepared to do with Cameron and the nanites.

The eyes of the three men remained on the innocent-looking tube that contained the most important discovery since the Neanderthals mastered fire.

"Director Lord," Ptushko said, moving from the lab into the corridor, "this presents a dilemma."

"I recognize that," Lord said amiably.

"I am quite certain that my superiors will not accept, on faith, your word that you would say nothing of this discovery to your government—or refrain from seeking to find out how that discovery was made."

"Nor would I give my word, since I will do exactly what you just described," Lord agreed. "It's pretty much my job description."

"I appreciate your frankness," Ptushko said with an appreciative nod. "But, as you say, you may be of assistance as a liaison with the creator of these nanites."

And with your ability to spy on him, Lord thought. Clearly, Ptushko was also intent on doing *his* job.

"Can we say, then, that rather than send you and the prisoner to Earth, you will remain on the *Red Giant* for the present as our guest?" Ptushko asked. "Would you, would your people, accept that?"

"I accept that," Lord replied. "Besides, there are many who would love to see me take up permanent residence here. Do you have a time frame?" He turned it from a political hot potato to a practical matter by indicating his uniform. "I didn't exactly pack for a long visit."

"I do not," the admiral replied. "As you see, this looks to be a somewhat open-ended project."

"Might it be possible for your pilot to make another trip and gather some belongings? I'll stay here—"

"Unfortunately," Ptushko said, "that isn't something we can do at the moment. Perhaps we can cobble together a kit for you? At least a prograz and your own toothbeam?"

"Admiral, you're very kind. Thank you."

A shave and plaque removal were actually the last things on Lord's mind. He had simply wanted to know, for sure, that the admiral couldn't spare the Soyuz. Ptushko had told Svetlana to prepare for something before he knew about the Venusian. The Zero-G director wanted to know what that was. While he had pretended to sleep in the Soyuz, he checked out the gear—most of it old and outdated—and also watched Svetlana work the ship so he knew its operation. As he suspected, unlike the kites and shuttles, it had limited range, extremely limited capabilities. Lord believed that it was being upgraded for a longer journey. He also believed that now he knew why. So did Ptushko, judging from that silent exchange he'd shared with Borodin.

"I appreciate your understanding," Ptushko said to Lord. At that moment the admiral seemed to let his formal guard down, was more like a man who was talking to a peer now, not to a spy or prisoner.

"I will be no trouble, which is a promise I've never made to my own superior," Lord assured him.

"Thank you. I have troubles enough up here," Ptushko said, with a nod at the module across the corridor at the former American lab Destiny, now the home of the Russian mob.

"Are they currently in residence?" Lord asked.

"One," Ptushko replied, surprising Lord with his candor. The admiral explained why with his next remark: "I would, in fact, welcome any thoughts or information you might care to share."

"Gladly," Lord replied. "The enemy of my enemy is my beef?"

"You might say that," the admiral agreed, after the Glossator had found an appropriate translation for *beef*—best friend. "If I were to send you some files for comment?"

"I will be very happy to help."

"I will send it presently," Ptushko said.

Lord nodded. He wanted to open the file in private, make sure that it could be scanned this far from the comm by elite FBI software that searched for malminds, SimAIs that found a nesting place in the IC and spied without ever being heard from.

This little part of the visit, while a lesser part, was a thrilling chess game for Lord, played with a timer. It was also over. The politeness of the conversation was becoming marginally embarrassing now, almost like Roosevelt, Churchill, and Stalin at Tehran and Yalta. They hated the Axis only marginally more than they mistrusted each other. It was time to move on.

"Where on the *Red Giant* should I place myself, Admiral Ptushko?" Lord asked. "I don't want to be in the way."

Ptushko had a dilemma and Lord was keen to see where the admiral would put him: in the midst of the action where Lord could observe whatever they were doing, even if the Glossator were shut down; or away from the action, where he could spy on them without being watched.

"Why don't you wait with Mr. Cameron?" Ptushko suggested after considering the matter. "That way you can also report any change in his condition."

"Will that inconvenience your medical staff?" Lord asked. "I don't want to crowd them."

Ptushko looked at him wryly. "As you've certainly observed, there *is* no medical staff, Director Lord. Dr. Borodin is our medic."

"I hadn't come to that conclusion," Lord lied. He had noticed an emergency medical kit under Borodin's lab table and had drawn exactly that conclusion.

"You know the way?" Ptushko said, trustingly, with a little bow of his head in the right direction.

"I do, and thank you," Lord said. Not that Ptushko had anything to lose by trusting him. Lord wasn't going anywhere.

As Ptushko moved in one direction, Lord went in the other. The few crew members Lord encountered now ignored him or nodded with a kind of practiced ambivalence and then turned away. He was anything but dismissive of the conflict he represented to them: whether to be a loyal Russian or a good "fellow traveler" in the high frontier. Both attitudes were legitimate and understandable. Unfortunately, they did not mesh well—even with Lord. Nothing had changed the fact that he intended to find out what was going on here, what preparations Svetlana Uralov and others were making, and why. Most intriguingly, why had Ptushko known that he had needed his pilot and a reconfigured Soyuz before knowing about the Venusian life-form?

The answer seemed apparent, even if unconfirmed.

Life has been discovered on another world, Lord thought with renewed awe. *It was a world with which Roscosmos had considerable experience and NASA had none. A world they may have visited without anyone knowing it.*

A world whose secrets any nation on Earth would clearly be wise to seek and understand.

A world to which only one of those countries had access.

Now it was Lord who had a dilemma.

NINETEEN

SAM LORD HAD faced countless difficult, life-and-death decisions since he was a boy.

As a kid with a quarter, he had to decide which gum to buy at the newsstand on Eighth Avenue. As a teenager, whether or not to get involved in preventing a late-night beating on Ninth Avenue, a gay man being assaulted by two no-necks. As an adult, whether to drop ordnance on a school in Mexico where bombs were being made. At the newsstand, he bought one pack and stole another, figuring that the owner ended up even. On Ninth Avenue, he smashed a peepshow window to trigger an alarm that brought the cops. In Mexico, he followed orders and pulverized the school and everyone in it.

Most of those decisions took place in a millisecond. They were either instinct, the result of training, or else cautious self-preservation. None of those decisions had been entirely clean or even right, and how he felt after each informed what he did the next time he was faced with a similar situation.

Don't steal. Defend the helpless. Do what it takes to protect your nation.

This current situation was the first uncharted territory he had faced in a long while. He looked for analogues in past behavior.

As the director of Zero-G, as an American, his job was to help prevent a belligerent government from obtaining any tactical advantage.

A Venusian microbe, especially one that could interact with electronics on some level, was definitely that. And it wasn't just Moscow who would have access to this monumental asset but also The Satellite, the Russian mob. They would have available to them something that could be weaponized, potentially distilled into some insane new drug.

Many possibilities, none of them good.

Yet, as a human being, as a man who aspired to visions of humankind reaching outward into the universe, how could he possibly stand in the way of knowledge?

As Lord floated toward the medbay, he asked himself, *If you had been active in the 1950s, you would have stopped Russia from getting the bomb, wouldn't you? What about when they launched the first satellite,* Sputnik? *Would you have sabotaged that?*

But the atom had already been split and the US was just a few months behind the Soviet Union with *Explorer.* This was different. No one had an extraterrestrial germ in their arsenal. Until now, no one even knew they existed.

Which also brings up the question: How the hell did *the Russians find it?*

The microbe was unlikely to have just drifted over. Though its origin could have been determined from its makeup—elements from the Venusian atmosphere would have been present in its body—the Russian station didn't have equipment sensitive enough to notice something like a microbe.

It could have ridden in on a micrometeoroid, Lord decided. Both the *Red Giant* and the *Empyrean* had EPNs—electromagnetic particle nets—designed to detect and snare dangerously fast pieces of space rock.

But there was something more likely, Lord thought. Remembering the white paper Al-Kazaz had referred to, Sun742, he realized that the Russians might already *be* at Venus. Or preparing to go, on a specific timetable. Ptushko would have known *that* much. And if they were there, they'd pulled it off in secret—perhaps using the old Scud-Fs that Zero-G couldn't quite figure out. If so, it was quite an achievement.

This situation was like the Venusian itself in many respects: it had a lot of arms moving in different directions. It was dissimilar, however, in one major respect: the implications were as incalculably big as the bug was incredibly small.

As Lord neared the medbay, the file on the Russian mob arrived. Lord slowed to have a look at it. The scan software worked, as he suspected it would; designed to reach Earth, it would certainly reach here. Lord opened the file and started reading. He grinned. It was a dossier on a St. Petersburg–born black marketer CHAI named Veronika Astakov. Details about her activities were all there: acknowledgment that she was indeed a member of The Satellite who specialized in the smuggling of cybernetic parts cut from dead bodies. Given the cost of new tech, these retreads, or "reets," were highly prized. The file also contained suspected contacts for freelance work in Israel and India, where she appeared to be developing a network for those nations' cybernetic weapons, firearms, and remote-detonated explosives that were controlled by thought. The only thing missing from the file was something Lord knew: that she had been arrested in Tel Aviv the week before.

Ptushko wants to see if I am aware of that, Lord thought.

Knowing it would tell the admiral that Israel's special investigations unit, Lahav 433, and the FBI were sharing information about Russian mobsters specializing in high-tech. Perhaps he was secretly looking for allies in that struggle. Or perhaps Ptushko wanted access to international traffickers who could get him Chinese or Indian technology for the *Red Giant.* The admiral might be willing to swap information he possessed about The Satellite in exchange for upgrades Roscosmos could not afford.

Lord had drifted to the medbay door, which was still open. He entered with an awkward turn—it wasn't just weightlessness that was a challenge, it was constant spatial disorientation. He ended up going into the room headfirst and did not get a good look at Douglas Cameron until he was almost directly over the man.

The man was still unconscious inside the space suit, but with the dim shadows moving across the faceplate, he was hardly still. Lord cautiously moved closer to the tinted glass, proceeding like a scuba diver approaching a sharp-edged wreck. He saw Cameron asleep inside, breathing easily through external tanks. Lord's eyes moved along the outermost thermal micrometeoroid layer of the garment. He saw it rise and fall as Cameron breathed—then realized that the motion he was seeing was not respiration. The bulging of the space suit was out of synch with his breaths. Cautiously, Lord placed a bare hand on the fabric and felt a rippling motion under the surface, like ocean sands below your feet.

He swore to himself.

In most Russian space suits, a tight but soft inner cloth layer protected the wearer from abrasion and also retained the body's perspiration as a natural coolant. There was a high cotton content in these layers.

Organic matter, he thought, angry that he had not considered that fact. The nanites were replicating it, perhaps drawn there by Cameron's cells, his hair, his perspiration, and they were creating pressure on the outer skin of the suit.

Intentionally? he wondered. *To get out?*

They could not have acquired that level of sentience, they simply could not have. *Unless they had tapped into the man's brain.* He still couldn't believe they had evolved that far, though perhaps they were exhibiting behavior that their fellow nanites had already exhibited in the Vault.

Lord glanced back at the corridor, in the direction of the lab. Dr. Carter had said that the nanites in the Vault still had some kind of connection with the nanite in his lab.

The nanites in Borodin's lab, he thought. *Having hit that energy wall generated by the microbe, were they calling for help to resume their assault on the Venusian?* And if so, why?

Lord pinwheeled toward the door, overrotated, and had to grab the edges to steady himself. He saw a crew member, an engineer, floating upside-down and apparently making repairs on a device.

"Get me the admiral!" he shouted.

The woman looked at him, scowled, shook her head in confusion. *Dammit.* She didn't have a Glossator.

"Ptushko!" Lord shouted, pointing beyond her. *"Ptushko!"*

The woman understood and, after a moment's hesitation, decided the man's tone merited action. She pushed off the wall and headed away like an Olympic swimmer while Lord turned back to the medbay. The space suit was undulating visibly now, even from this distance. He looked around inside to see where the air vents and old computer jacks were. Lord stuck his head in: the intake and exhaust ducts were above the door, oblong vents with vanes to direct the airflow. They would have to be closed tight. There had to be some kind of sealant on board in the event of leaks—

Lord heard a crisp, creaking sound, like leather being stretched, as the space suit began to balloon along the chest and neck.

Cameron started to stir. The floating oxygen tanks banged gently against the table. He tried to raise his arms, found that they—and he— were secured to the table. All the while his upper torso continued to swell.

Ptushko charged down the corridor, twisting and rotating, masterfully moving hand-over-hand using every available surface. He was followed by Borodin and the engineer.

"What is it?" the admiral demanded.

"We've got a little revolution going on," Lord said, and explained briefly as he backed from the hatch, the admiral swinging around to peer into the medbay.

Ptushko was not happy but this was not the time for recriminations. "Do the robots require oxygen?" he demanded.

"No," Lord replied, though in a word he had just intimated where they were designed to function. But he didn't want the Russians to waste time sealing and decompressing the room—and killing Cameron in the process.

"What about heat, cold?" Borodin asked.

"I don't know," Lord lied, attempting to backpedal. The question wasn't relevant at the moment. "Look, they're breaking free of the suit.

Get me some kind of foam to seal the vent. We have to shut the ventilation system here, then find out which wiring conduits connect this room to others and have those terminals plugged."

Ptushko communicated the instructions to the engineer, Olga Novikov.

While the exobiologist hurried to a wall-mounted storage locker located near the docking portal, the engineer consulted her IC and talked to other engineers.

"I told you we should have ejected him," Ptushko said, firing Lord an angry glance. "We may not have time now."

"Murder is a bad precaution," Lord said.

"Not when you consider the alternative, which you apparently did not."

This wasn't the time to argue—especially with a man whose leaders, whose heritage, consisted of just that tactic.

"Admiral, this is a surprise to me too," Lord confessed. He indicated the heavy door. "Give me the sealant then shut this hatch. I'll stay inside with Mr. Cameron and monitor, use the foam to paste them to the gurney—"

"The gurney?" Ptushko said, confused.

A loud pop came from the medbay, causing both Lord and Ptushko to turn sharply in that direction. Appropriately, the botanist's suit had popped open at the neck joint like a wisteria seedpod. Cameron moaned as a very faint cloud of fine, white particles filled the air. The particles looked like snowflakes, but they were half the size and a sickly gray color. The hundreds of particles closed up the space between them, then moved like a slow-motion swarm of bees, collecting low over Cameron's chest and neck.

Lord understood at once that the white in the particles was fabric. The black aspect of the cloud was the nanites. And there was something else. Something Ptushko had become aware of before Lord did.

They're weightless here, the Zero-G director remembered with alarm. *They don't have to crawl.*

The nanites hovered there for a moment. Lord could not see them individually; they simply caused a dark smudge on the view, like a thumbprint on the visor of Lord's flight helmet. After a moment, like the first black cough from an old internal combustion engine, the cloud of nanites began rolling slowly forward, charcoal-gray; they left the white particles of fabric behind, floating formlessly above the gurney. The cloud of nanites did not cohere as such but, rather, each element within seemed to be going in the same general direction.

Toward the science lab of the *Red Giant*. Toward the cry of the nanites in suspension there.

Cameron was dully awake, still moaning and gasping; it was possible that some of the little robots had entered his body, probably through follicles, possibly through the nose, mouth, and ears. Lord had no idea what they intended to seek there, whether organ or sinew or both. Their programming had been to build a vine. Perhaps they would look for the skeletal building blocks of a human being. However, he suspected that, like these nanites, they were on their way out now, answering the call that had clearly summoned the others.

Pushing Lord aside, Ptushko pulled himself into the medbay and grabbed a silver fire extinguisher from the wall, a small oblong unit with Russian markings and a traditional nozzle. The admiral directed it at the murky cloud. Water-based foam blew out toward the nanites, snagging them in midair and carrying them toward a built-in cabinet that looked like a series of white safety deposit boxes. From the various armbands and electrodes poking from it, Lord knew that this was the medical monitoring station. The foam struck the panel and hung there just as Borodin arrived with the sealant. The admiral swapped containers with the scientist and eased deeper into the room. Lord eased in behind him but Borodin remained in the corridor.

Holding the half-meter-long, capsule-shaped red container in one hand, Ptushko used the other hand to negotiate along the wall of the medbay, trying to stay wide of the mass of foam.

"Borodin, are the robots in your lab emitting signals?" Ptushko asked.

"They're creating electronic noise of some kind."

"That these things can understand?"

Borodin looked at Lord, who shrugged. There was no need for him to confirm. The admiral would have to assume the worst.

"Can you block it?" Ptushko said impatiently.

"I have no idea," the exobiologist replied.

"Try!" Ptushko ordered.

Borodin grunted in acknowledgment and hurried off, muttering, "Electronics is *not* my field!"

The milky mass hung against the wall like a cloud on a mountainside, internal bubbles popping now and then and ejecting a watery white plume—a chemical mist that expanded seemingly in slow motion. Below it, the mass was changing shape, rolling, beginning to bulge toward the lab.

"They're tearing free," Ptushko said as he continued moving toward the air vent, his eyes on the lumpy foam.

He was right—but not in the way Lord had been expecting. They were no longer a single mass. Having been snared, moving together, they were dividing into smaller "squadrons." He saw four, then five separate bulges, each moving in a slightly different direction. He hoped—but could not be sure—this was simply the shortest way from the foam and not a tactical adjustment to keep from being captured again. He looked around, wondering if they could wrap something over the fast-budding foam, even the spacesuit, before it came apart.

And then, with a surge, each bud broke free.

"Help me!" Cameron groaned below him. He was more fully awake now, bumping hard from side to side. "In . . . my . . . *skull!*"

Ptushko ignored him. It suddenly made sense to Lord that the nanites would go toward his brain, where the greatest concentration of electrical signals in the human body were. God help them if they were actually seeking to control him.

"Olga, lower the vanes!" Ptushko said, yelling into his IC.

The panels were still horizontal. If Ptushko sprayed the vent now, the foam would simply fill the vent and keep going.

The small globules that had emerged from the foam began to darken as the nanites shed the indigestible mass. Tiny beads of foam floated everywhere, destroying the natural cohesion of the substance. They now represented their own threat to nasal passages and circuits.

"Let me communicate with my station," Lord told Ptushko.

"Don't speak!"

"Admiral, they know more about these—"

"How to shut them down?"

"No," Lord admitted.

Ptushko sneered at him. "Convince me first that you didn't release them on purpose!"

"I'm not suicidal," Lord said.

"Your service record suggests otherwise!" he shouted. "Borodin!"

Lord didn't hear the rest. The admiral had killed the Glossator link.

Lord stayed out of the way. It was true that, in the thrall of conflict, the frenzy of teamwork and inevitable one-upmanship, Lord was often reckless. Anyone who had observed the struggle with the Dragon's Eye, as the Russians surely had, would have known that. But Ptushko's reaction was more than that, more than just the man's prudent suspicion of an American lawman. The Russians had a long history of allowing senior citizens to sacrifice themselves honorably. During World War II, older Russians threw themselves at the Germans, at the turrets of their panzers, to blunt the shells and buy time for the young fighters to take up positions in Stalingrad. Before that, in 1904, elderly Russians on wooden carts were used to transport bullets from train to train across trackless miles of tundra during the war with Japan. If they died, at least soldiers weren't being wasted.

Just because you believe your best years are ahead, "out thataway," it doesn't mean everyone shares that view.

There was a whir and a gentle clack as the vanes of the air vent came down. Gripping the frame of an overhead fluorescent lighting fixture tightly with his left hand—so that he wouldn't go jetting backward—Ptushko wrapped his right arm around the canister and sprayed. His body pinwheeled slightly toward Cameron as the much thicker, off-white foam jetted along a straight path. The admiral coated the narrow rectangular vent with a back-and-forth motion. The sealant formed a lumpy mass over the rectangle.

Moments before Ptushko finished, Lord noticed the nanite clouds shifting behind him. This wasn't a slow, rolling motion like before, it was an explosion toward the vent, like something simultaneously gone wrong with a half dozen pastries in a microwave oven. The nanites rejoined in a thin, serpentine line inches from the admiral. As if he—no, the ear nearest them—were the new target.

Or his brain? Lord said. *Christ, have they evolved enough to recognize and anticipate antagonistic action?*

Ptushko didn't see them; he was busy looking for any cracks in the sealant.

"Watch out!" Lord shouted.

Ptushko responded reflexively to the cry. He looked at Lord, to his right, and not behind him.

With no time to explain, Lord grabbed the sides of the hatch and pulled himself in hard, flying toward the Russian officer. The Zero-G director bull-hugged the man around the legs as his own shoulder hit the wall just under the vent and he bounced back, pulling Ptushko with him.

They avoided the moving spear of nanites—but only for an instant. As if they were a like-minded swarm of bees, they turned toward the open hatch. A Russian crewman, who had paused to watch, leaned in. Still hugging Ptushko with his right arm, Lord extended his left hand and the young man grabbed it. He pulled Lord and the admiral toward him, the two clearing moments before the nanite cloud arrived.

"Don't leave me!" Cameron screamed.

Lord's eyes shifted to the prisoner as he cried out again, inarticulately now. Through the rent in the suit, Lord saw that the contents of the man's throat seemed to be squeezed through his flesh like meat through clenched fingers. Droplets of blood emerged from nanite-inflamed pores and hovered in the air; white, fatty tissue followed in small beads; ruddy esophageal matter came next. The screams stopped, followed by gasps and then silence. The man's fingers curled and clawed but for just a moment. The stream of organic matter that poured from the torn suit was not nanite-driven but the result of a body having been breached in zero gravity.

Lord was strangely transfixed by what followed: when Cameron died, it was not like any of the too numerous combat or civilian deaths he had ever experienced. It was more terrifying than hostility or rage, more frightening than an accident. It was as if a new level of the food chain had been established: we feed them. Lord thought of the CHAI technology in his own leg and remembered what Professor Jacob O'Hara of NYU-Columbia had described in 2032 as "the platinum looking-glass": human creations looking back at humans as inferior.

The moment seemed at once abrupt and eternal and it ended as Ptushko continued moving. Without releasing the container, the admiral snatched the open hatch with his left hand. Because he was moving feet-first toward the corridor, he was able to slam the airtight panel behind him as he exited. The door shut hard, jerking all three men who were still holding it. Ptushko was shaken free of Lord. The crewman released the American. All three men floated outside the stricken medbay.

Ptushko passed the sealant container toward the crewman, who left to put it back in the locker.

"Spasibo," the Russian said, turning his translator back on.

Lord didn't need to hear the Glossator to know that the admiral was thanking him.

Lord nodded in acknowledgment but his eyes were on the hatch, watching the sides cautiously. Not that he would be able to see the nanites if they came through individually.

Ptushko noticed his gaze. "The seal is pure chemistry, no biological material," the admiral assured him.

"So much for the benefits of organics," Lord murmured.

If Ptushko's suspicions weren't entirely put to rest, they were allayed for the moment by the apparent containment of the nanites.

"That was grotesque," Ptushko said, though without emotion. "What in the name of God have you people created?"

Lord had no answer for that and didn't offer one.

"The robots changed their tactics," the admiral went on. "How? *Why?*"

"I don't know," Lord answered. "I don't believe they were haphazardly turning toward the only way out they had left. They seemed to have *known* what we were doing."

"Are you sure?"

"No," Lord confessed. "But when I lunged for you, they *were* headed for your ear."

"The prisoner was yelling about his skull. They don't—eat?"

"No. Just the opposite," Lord said helplessly.

The men hovered there, collecting their breath and their wits. Lord was not ready to share what he was really thinking. It frightened him more than anything that had happened thus far. But before he could be certain of his suspicions, he needed to talk to Dr. Carter on the *Empyrean*.

In the meantime, he had just a single, uncharacteristic thought:

I pray I'm wrong.

TWENTY

EVEN BEFORE THEY had arrived at Dr. Carter's lab, Ed McClure and Michael Abernathy had received their instructions from the biophysicist: to find a way to strengthen—to the point of lethal impermeability, if necessary—the electronic field that defined the Vault.

"Any material related to the vine that tries to get in or out, I want it fried," he had told them.

The agents knew that wouldn't be a simple fix. They both read from the same file to which their new security clearance gave them access: *The six surfaces of the Vault were designed to prevent electrical and magnetic signals from leaving by means of densely particalized metal and nanocrystalline-grain structure held aloft by a variable magnetic field that reacts to the slight but constant variations in the space station's centripetal force.*

As Abernathy observed, "An electronic wheat field is definitely not the death ray Dr. Carter is asking for."

After a quick examination of the specs, the two young men did believe they could increase the pull and polarity of the magnets to turn the vine away from the wall. They were starting to investigate that when they heard from Dr. Carter that EAD Waters was on the way over. They were told to expose the laboratory sample to the pangender's hair.

"Start from a distance and move in," Carter had told them. "Whatever else you try, do not put them together."

Moments later, Adsila arrived, entering the cramped laboratory sideways. McClure killed his IC microphone.

"Do you have any idea what this is about, EAD?" he asked.

"Something that Dr. Carter wants to try, obviously," Adsila replied, also shutting off her IC feed.

"Conflicting biodata overload, I would guess," Abernathy suggested. "Burn out some mollies."

"Yes, that's probably it," Adsila said.

"Which makes sense, but why would they be drawn to *you*?" McClure asked. "They aren't swarming over the team in the Vault, as far as we know."

"There must be something about pangenderism, obviously," she said.

"But the nanites wouldn't know that until you throw the switch, so to speak," McClure said very respectfully. He was treading carefully; Adsila was still his superior.

Adsila looked from one to the other of the agents. This was not the time to be coy.

"It does have to do with memory," she said. "Nanite memory. They've been inside me before, only that's something Dr. Carter couldn't say without revealing my confidential medical history."

Abernathy was visibly embarrassed.

"Sorry, EAD," McClure said quickly.

"No, it's all right," she said. "It may help to know. Carter used them recently to find and eliminate less sophisticated nanite spies planted deep inside by Ziv Levy."

Both men understood. They were more abashed than perplexed by the new wrinkle.

She went on, "I'm guessing that if the nanites perk up, if they remember me, then there may be a way that we can either get them to relocate their original programming or, as you say, confuse them when I switch."

"Very clever," McClure remarked, in as neutral a voice as he could muster.

Adsila plucked a hair and placed it into the tweezers offered by Abernathy. Despite the weeks they had spent in space, it was still surreal to see the single strand move from side to side like a snake charmer's cobra in response to the lesser gravity here and the gentle turn of the station.

At least, Abernathy hoped it was that and not nanites, hidden and hibernating in her hair, coming back online.

Sleeper cells, he thought, giving a very literal meaning to the latter word.

"I don't know what you're discussing in secret, but plug me back in."

It was the voice of Dr. Carter from the Vault. The three Zero-G team members obliged.

"We've just taken a strand of hair from the EAD and are about to put it beside dish B11-16," McClure informed him.

"Start from one hundred millimeters away," Carter advised them. "That's the maximum programmed recognition distance for replication."

They had been planning to utilize a small cylinder on top to introduce the sample. The two-inch-high section functioned as an airlock, keeping the nanites inside by allowing an outer cap to be closed off before opening a small sliding door at the base of the little tower. Instead, McClure removed the stopper while Abernathy employed his IC to measure the distance.

Sensors attached to the dish registered electrical activity inside and fed it to the two scientists. Carter had not bothered to craft a microscopic eyes-on observation system for the activity; he already knew what the nanites looked like, what they did, and how they did it.

McClure shared his IC feed with Adsila. The three watched as the numbers and various graphs changed.

"What am I looking at?" the EAD asked.

"Something very weird," McClure replied. "Dr. Carter?"

"Here."

"I'm assuming the nanites should respond to the presence of familiar organic matter," McClure said.

"That is their default function, yes, when they are functioning correctly," he replied. "Erase their memories and, absent programming that assigns a specific task, they'll go into hibernation."

"Then why are you concerned about them attacking you or the others in the Vault?" Adsila asked. "Why can't you leave?"

"We may have picked up particles of bark or root from the vine," he said. "If there are nanites on us—"

"The process could begin again somewhere else, understood," Adsila said. It chilled her to think about pockets of nanites working unnoticed in dark, hidden corners of the *Empyrean* . . . constructing biological matter in secret until it was too late.

"Agent McClure, are the nanites *not* responding to the hair sample?" Carter asked.

"Sir, the numbers show them going nowhere *near* the hair," McClure said. "It's not that they're avoiding it as such—they just seem to have some other project going."

"That's not possible," Carter said. "Agent Abernathy?"

"Ed is correct," Abernathy replied. "The nanites are clustering toward a specific vector."

"Which is what?" Carter asked.

He overlaid a map of the *Empyrean* on numbers that were clustering in a corner of the IC.

"Align please, Taurgo."

Adsila heard a grunt of acknowledgment. "Taurgo?" she said.

"A talking bull," Abernathy told her. "I always wanted one."

That hadn't shown up in his psych check; the EAD let the SimAI identification pass without comment. Taurgo was correlating the direction of the nanites' motion to the station.

"The Scrub," Taurgo growled. "That where they go."

"Not the Agro Center but the *bar*?" Carter asked.

"It would appear so, Doctor," Abernathy replied.

"Pull back, bigger view," Carter told him.

The Zero-G agent told Taurgo to create a larger map and not to stop until instructed. A fully fleshed but translucent image of the *Empyrean* appeared. The Scrub became smaller as the larger of the station filled their ICs. Then the outside of the *Empyrean* was visible, near-space, Earth—

"Hukin' damn," McClure said after a moment.

"What is it?" Carter asked.

Adsila, Abernathy, and McClure had already seen the location being vectored by the nanites and were trying to absorb the implications.

"Agents, what's going on?" Carter demanded.

Abernathy was about to answer when he heard Carter cry out to someone on his end.

"What *now*?" Carter yelled.

"Dr. Carter?" the science officer asked.

There was no answer, just chaotic shouts.

"*Sir!*" the science officer yelled.

"The damned vine appears to be . . ." Carter said, then waited and confirmed after a moment. "Yes, it's growing faster."

"Pointing in what direction?" McClure asked.

"Different from before—hold on," Carter told him. "It's moving along the ground toward the wall . . . about where the elevator is."

McClure hurriedly highlighted the shaftway on an *Empyrean* schematic. The movement of the vine was in concert with the motion of the nanites in his lab dish.

"If it's any consolation, Doctor," McClure said, "at least the nanites are being consistent."

"In what way?"

"They're all moving in the same direction—which seems to be toward the *Red Giant*." McClure scowled. "Except for some of the nanites in a dish on the bottom shelf marked L207. *They're* moving toward the hair."

"The 207s are Ziv's nanites," Carter said. "Pesky, not so sophisticated as ours, but hardier."

"You have them in sera?" McClure said.

"Their one advantage, and I'm studying it," Carter said. "They can function in fluids. Adsila, will you call over to the station and try to speak with Sam? Find out anything you can. We have to know if the nanites are seeking the station, Cameron, him, or something else."

"I'll call at once."

The EAD quickly arranged the communication through Janet Grainger. The last communiqué she heard from the Agro Center was Lancaster Liba shouting from a distance, "Doc, it sounds like Hell's own rodeo in there!"

When Adsila was connected with the ISS, her own factory-set SimAI reminded her, "Frequency 130.167 MHz is medium bandwidth voice-only—"

Adsila winked off the alert lest it remind her every minute that she was communicating openly on a "hostile frequency." A Russian answered, full audio-visual, and Adsila blinked on her Glossator.

She identified herself and asked to speak with visitor Sam Lord. The Russian radio operator said he would try to find him.

"'Try'?" Abernathy muttered. "You could shout from one end of the ISS to the other and they'd hear you!"

Adsila killed her outgoing link to the rest of the *Empyrean*, except for Carter in the Vault. She did not want the conversation footnoted every time the Russians lied or obfuscated. She was still following local developments on audio.

"The vine is growing fast enough that we can see it happening now," Carter continued. "Agents, we can't let it get out of here again."

"Understood," McClure replied.

Carter began giving orders to the team in the Vault, speaking more urgently than before. He was instructing them to surround the farthest tips of the vine and begin bending it back.

"Taurgo," Abernathy said, "if we want to bake the Vault, what kind of a solar spread can we create using the microvoxels in the Agro windows?"

"Not enough . . . even . . . at . . . maximum . . . spread," the deep, throaty voice replied. "Vault too big. Beams too small."

The microvoxels were tiny, prism-like structures—essentially expandable pixels that permitted *Empyrean* crew members to observe and magnify a view. This could be done by pinching the section and physically widening it or, in the case of the greenhouse, by using the IC to align a segment of the window with a segment of space and programming a percentage. The view would magnify instantly.

"What if we concentrate on just a portion of the floor?" Abernathy pressed. "Maybe we can burn the flora there?"

"Room content . . . insufficiently . . . combustible," the bull answered.

"Taurgo, there *has* to be an incendiary methodology using indigenous content."

"Yes . . . fertilizer . . . cylindrical pressure vessel M735 in water system . . . hydrogen from air duct 119 . . ."

"An anarchist's bomb?" Abernathy said.

"An explosive that will also destroy the greenhouse and depressurize the Agro Center," McClure said.

"Request was . . . incendiary device. I will . . . replay . . ."

"No, never mind, thank you," Abernathy said.

"You start a big fire there, the filters won't be able to vent it fast enough," Adsila said. "You could poison the station with burning petrochemicals."

"Burned nanite particles will be inhaled!" Carter said. "Embedded in lung tissue, they'll be carcinogenic." He was breathing heavily, had obviously been helping to forcibly redirect the vine.

"No fire," Abernathy agreed. "Electrocution?"

McClure had brought up a schematic of the greenhouse and asked for every part of it to be identified. He read the labels quickly, saw the sprinkler system.

"Analysis of water content for solutes and ions," McClure requested.

Abernathy nodded appreciatively. If the levels of both were high enough, the water would become a very significant electrical conductor. Numeric values appeared.

"Is that enough to destroy plant cells?" McClure asked.

The science officer's SimAI was the soft male voice, Edgar, one of the standard options that had been bundled with the FBI program.

"Ohm's law indicates that even at full dispersion of water, total voltage necessary will be insufficient," Edgar replied flatly.

"What if we reroute electrical?"

"It will overload before you achieve electrocution," the voice remarked.

Carter's voice once again cut into the ongoing discussions.

"It's budding again!" the biophysicist said. "Dammit, we turn the tip back and a new branch appears in that direction! EAD, we have to know if Director Lord has any idea why they're trying to head in his direction."

"I'm holding for him," she said.

The delay was frustrating, not just tactically; Adsila did not like feeling helpless.

Just then, Lord came on, audio only.

"I was about to call the doctor," Lord said. "What's going on?"

"He is extremely busy *deep* in Agro at the moment," Adsila said, hoping he got her euphemism for the Vault.

"Understood," Lord replied.

"Director, the objects in the lab and in the agricultural center are both attempting to maneuver in the direction of your location," she said.

"I am not surprised," he replied.

Adsila *was* surprised. "Sir? Can you explain?"

"Nanites that piggybacked here on Mr. Cameron are showing a similar synchronous movement toward a particular local target," Lord said.

Adsila and the others were also surprised to hear him speak so openly. But he had carefully avoided naming the target—unless he was not sure what it was.

"Is there anything we should know about?" Adsila asked, pressing him.

"Only this," Lord said. "I believe that the little troops are being rallied for a common goal."

He said "troops." Is this war? she wondered.

"Rallied," she said.

"Not by my hosts," he assured her.

So a third party or some unspoken, external force of some kind was causing the nanites to coordinate, she thought.

"Anyone we know?" she asked.

"Nothing you know," he replied.

"Nothing." Not a person, then. And he said *"you."* From that she surmised that Lord knew, he just couldn't tell her.

"Do you face an immediate threat?" she asked.

"Already in progress."

"Is Cameron all right?" she asked, still trying to find an answer, a way in that would provide some insight or clarity.

"He wasn't, last I saw of him," Lord replied. "And I can no longer be sure." That suggested either Lord or the crew or both were unable to get to where Cameron was—perhaps for the same reason that more *Empyrean* personnel were not being allowed in the Agro Center: rampaging nanites. Adsila struggled to put it all together. It sounded as if there was something on the *Red Giant* that had excited the local nanites . . . and also here, even from that distance. She couldn't imagine what it was, and that troubled her.

"Sir," she began—

"I'm sorry, EAD, I cannot tell you more," Lord interrupted. "I promised my hosts. But Carter, or someone, *has* to find a way to rewrite the nanite programs. Very, very soon."

There was an urgency in his voice that she had never heard, even at the height of the *Jade Star* crisis. It communicated far more than even the strong words.

"He's working on it with our science team," she assured him.

"Good. Now, what's happening there?" he asked.

"As Mr. Liba put it, 'Hell's own rodeo,'" she replied.

"Obviously he's recovered," Lord said. "But he doesn't have any ideas."

"No sir," she said.

"All those great minds, stymied," Lord said. "Hold on—"

The connection went silent. Adsila checked to see that it was still open.

"Sir?" Adsila said.

"Yes," Lord came back after a moment that seemed much longer. "Still here."

"Did something happen?"

"I was thinking," he said. "That's what happened. Look, I've got to go. I'll be in touch."

TWENTY-ONE

THOUGHT. THAT WAS the key. It *had* to be.

As Lord struggled to connect dots, to unearth clues, he realized that the nanites were probably doing exactly the same thing. To plan, to survive, to grow. To a purely mechanical entity, the capacity to do so—thought, accelerated mental evolution—had to be a next step. They already had mobility. They did not need air or water. With the proper materials, they could manufacture more of themselves—reproduce. What else was there but mind?

His mind spinning even more than his body, the Zero-G director floated back toward the medbay and met Ptushko coming toward him.

"Did you speak to your people?" the admiral asked.

Lord nodded. "The conversation was no help."

"Your team is facing the same problem," he guessed.

"They are," Lord admitted. "But *we* apparently have a more challenging dilemma. Without revealing more than this, I can confirm what Dr. Borodin has already surmised: they are designed to interact with biology. In the case of the Venusian sample, Dr. Borodin mentioned a nerve bundle. I suspect the nanites are drawn to the strong electrical activity of biological intelligence."

"The nerve bundle ... is a rudimentary brain?"

"Just as in certain dinosaurs on Earth," Lord said. He thought back to the Saturdays he spent at the American Museum of Natural History, hearing about Stegosaurus and its two brains—one of which was located in its tail, essentially a packet of biological controls to work its tail. Scientists had attempted to re-create those brains using 3-D plasma sculpting, but surviving fossils contained too little information to make it functional. Lord jerked a thumb behind him, toward the medbay. "Do you realize what that tells us about your alien sample, Admiral? It may be sentient . . . possibly self-aware . . . in a way we don't understand."

"*Intelligent* first contact," Ptushko marveled.

"Exactly."

"And the nanites want to do what—*join* with that creature?"

"It's a theory."

"To what end?" the admiral pressed. "An upgrade?"

"That too is a theory," Lord said.

Ptushko considered the idea. "Then to stop them," he said, thinking like a military man, "all we need do is put the Venusian sample in space—"

"The nanites will go after it there," Lord assured him.

Ptushko's expression showed interest. "But they will be on the outside, no longer a threat," he said. "Isn't that what we want? To eject the nanites into a void?"

"No," Lord replied.

"Why?"

Lord said nothing. Once again, he was not free to tell the admiral that a nanite-Venusian hybrid would duplicate itself endlessly, as if constructing a segment of the space elevator, and then perhaps would do what is also inherent in their programming: try to connect with Earth.

Ptushko waited a moment for a reply, then made a disgusted sound. "Your nationalism is beginning to disgust me, Mr. Director."

"I apologize for that, but between us we know all that is currently known—and I wouldn't betray *your* trust any more than I would that of my superiors."

"You are indeed most capable, Mr. Lord. You manage to position covert activity as integrity."

"Admiral, let's try and stay on topic here, all right?" Lord said, deflecting what was probably a valid point. "Our immediate need is to stop the nanites by understanding their objective. Can we go back to the lab and bring Dr. Borodin in on this discussion?"

Absent other options, the admiral agreed. It wasn't exactly a blink, but Lord had apparently convinced the man there was a line he would not cross, and Ptushko had grasped that he probably couldn't beat this alone.

The two men found Borodin using old-fashioned alligator clamps and strips of metal to try to create electrical impedance, something that would drive the nanite from the side of the dish. An MPL—microscopic plasma lens—was affixed to the top, held there by a neutral resin that did not conduct an electric or magnetic charge. Borodin's dour expression revealed how unsuccessful his efforts had been.

"I must commend the genius who came up with this," the exobiologist said, flinging the back of his hand in the direction of his microscopic captive. His eyes were watery from staring at his captive subjects.

"Borodin, we need solutions, not accolades," Ptushko said.

"Then you'd best get our engineers on it! They're better qualified."

"I have requested assistance," Ptushko said. "I will let you know when it is available."

Lord wasn't entirely sure he believed that; admitting he couldn't handle a situation that had arisen on the *Red Giant* was the quickest way to earn reassignment. Borodin looked as though he wanted to protest but thought better of it. Perhaps the scientist didn't believe him; or perhaps the Russians knew something they weren't willing to share with Lord.

Secrecy is a two-way street, the American thought.

Lord's IC had automatically plugged into the nonsecure MPL at once, and he looked now at what the scientist's microscope revealed. He had no idea what he was seeing, though he did notice a slight, occasional jitter in the gel-like lens and wondered what could be the cause. It was not rhythmic, the way it would be if responding to the humming of nearby electronics. Then he became aware of a dull, irregular sound that came with it. He recognized it from the *Empyrean*. The noise hadn't been there before and seemed to be coming from the direction of the center of the station.

Space walkers working on the station exterior, Lord thought. *That must be where the engineers are.*

There was a short silence, broken when Ptushko spoke.

"What do you both think *would* happen if we put the robot and the microbe together?" the admiral asked.

"Just what we're seeing now," Lord replied truthfully. "A struggle."

"With the addition of a physical component," Ptushko said, "perhaps the Venusian would overpower the nanite."

"Interplanetary warfare as a way of welcoming an alien species?" Borodin said. "No! We cannot do that to the sample. I won't."

"What if I order it?" Ptushko pressed.

The question elicited a look of anguished surprise from Borodin. "Would you jeopardize the greatest scientific find in human history *and* give the nanites what they apparently want?"

"Do you have a better option?"

"Yes, continued, applied reason instead of brute solutions," Borodin said, then looked away with disgust.

"We haven't a lot of time!" Ptushko said.

"Then we must focus," Borodin countered. "The question we should be asking is *why* the nanobots want to get to the microbe."

"Director Lord believes they want to acquire—how would you describe it, a cellular expansion of their intellect?" Ptushko asked.

Lord nodded, his entire body shifting in zero gravity. He steadied himself on the nearest surface, Borodin's shoulder.

"Admiral, what you ask would surely result in injury to, if not the destruction of, the sample," Borodin said. "These robots have pincers. They are not construction tools but deconstruction tools—a means, it appears, of severing soft tissue samples and placing them in a small compartment on the underbelly. A laboratory, Director Lord?"

"I don't know," Lord replied. The answer was truthful, as far as it went: he had no idea how the nanites functioned.

"And to what end?" Borodin continued. "Reproduction or destruction of organic matter?" He regarded Ptushko. "If Mr. Cameron is any indication, the two goals can also be one: the nanites could sample cells and mutate them, cause tumors or disease." Borodin looked back at Lord. "What are they, an artificial means of necrotizing fasciitis?"

Ptushko glared suddenly at Lord. "Is that what these things are?" he demanded. "Flesh-eating robots created by your agency? Did your government design them to destroy brain cells, kill enemies? Or were they created to extract information? Is that how they got into Cameron's head?"

"Admiral, this debate will only reveal the breadth of my ignorance," Lord said. "I urge you to deal with the science and mechanics of the situation, which is precisely what my people are doing."

"You 'urge,'" Ptushko said. "You encourage *glasnost*, yet even in the face of disaster you maintain the stupid, stubborn, self-defeating partisanship that has threatened our species since we inhabited caves."

"Like you, I'm just a cog in the machine of civilization," Lord said. "Striving for tactical advantage is how our species often makes technological progress. Those struggles put us in space."

"And are you satisfied with that state of affairs?" Borodin asked.

"I accept it," Lord said. "Humans are a work in progress."

"But—we have, right now, the three of us, the chance to *change* that," the scientist said.

"All right," Lord said. "Tell me what you're building outside."

"That has nothing to do with the matter at hand," Ptushko said.

"The matter at hand is cooperation. So—cooperate."

There was renewed tension in the small laboratory, as old, enduring rivalries continued to choke higher aspirations, shared needs. Borodin sighed and looked back at the MPL.

"I need more information about these things . . ." the scientist said, his voice trailing off. "I'm out of my depth here."

Ptushko turned to Lord. "All right, Mr. Director. Let's try this. What would you do if the station were under your command?"

Lord's eyes sparked to life. He was impressed with the tactic. Not getting what he wanted, the Russian proved that he had a pragmatic streak.

"Thank you, Admiral," he said. "As it happens, I've been contemplating that very question and have already rejected two ideas. First, we *could* simply swat this nanite, crush it like a mosquito. That might disconnect the others from the Venusian microbe . . . and we still have to deal with the ones inhabiting Douglas Cameron. My concern is that those have tasted blood—Venusian sentient energy. They will continue to try and get here or, worse, if you eject them from the *Red Giant*, they *may* be able to pick up signals from any other microbes 'out there.'"

"On Venus, you mean," Borodin said.

"That's right," Lord said.

"That would be an eco-catastrophe," Borodin said. "Unthinkable."

"I agree," Lord said. "And a real threat to humankind. You both saw enough in the medbay to know that we could end up with a mini-CHAI, a cybernetic nanite-Venusian hybrid. God only knows what that would be like, what it would be capable of doing."

"I am not concerned with what God knows, only what Lord knows," Ptushko pointed out.

Lord ignored the easy dig. "But we do have one advantage," he went on. "As long as this nanite is here, the others have a goal: to support it, to get to this room, to reach the microbe. Distracted, they will probably not turn on the crew as they did on Cameron."

"Probably?" Borodin said.

"They are writing their own new instruction manual," Lord said. "I knew very little before this, and I now know far less than that."

Everyone fell silent. Lord had a feeling that Ptushko was growing desperate—in addition to the threat the nanites posed, he had another project that required his attention—and would act on what his guest recommended. Certainly that would be preferable to possibly losing the *Red Giant*.

"Comrade Lord?" Ptushko pressed again. "Your command solution?"

"Yes," Lord said. "You mentioned the vent door in the medbay. I assume you can decompress the module."

"We can."

"Then, if it were up to me," Lord said, "I would flush the room, remove the microbe from the *Red Giant* to the Soyuz, and lead the nanites into space."

"But you said you didn't want them outside," Ptushko said.

"I said I didn't want them *ejected* into space," Lord told him. "If nothing else, they would eventually de-orbit into the Earth's atmosphere. We can't afford to risk even one surviving reentry. But if we lead them away, like the Pied Piper—that's different."

"To what end?" Borodin asked.

Lord regarded both men in turn. "I don't think they'd survive the heat of the sun."

"Neither will the Venu—" Borodin began, then stopped as he realized what Lord was saying. "The sample will be safe inside the Soyuz."

"That's right."

The admiral was instantly suspicious. "You don't want us to have the nanites. That is why you're proposing this expedition."

"I *don't* want you to have them," Lord agreed. "Frankly, gentlemen, I don't want *anyone* to have them. Not you, not us. If ever there were a good damn reason to go 'back to the drawing board,' this is it. But I'm proposing this idea because no one here or on board the *Empyrean* seems to have a better one."

Ptushko thought for a moment. "Do you seriously expect me to send my only vehicle *and* a team that close to the sun?"

"At least as close as Venus," Lord replied. "You are planning a trip there, are you not?"

Lord had just taken a huge leap, though an educated one. It was met by a stony silence that lasted several seconds. When Ptushko did not deny it, Lord felt that the ground—and the direction he must take—were eminently more solid.

"While I flew over with the lieutenant, I noticed an HR in the Soyuz," Lord continued, referring to a palm-size hand rocket, an air-thruster used for limited movement outside a vehicle. "What I'm thinking is, we craft a very simple mousetrap, from the Kozyrev Gas Trap you've got with one side attached to the HR. You open the hatch and, using the microbe as bait, draw the nanites inside the KGT. When we have them, you seal the trap and launch it toward the sun."

"But not the sample," Borodin said.

"Not the sample," Lord agreed. "First contact should not end in murder."

Borodin nodded in agreement. Ptushko did not.

"Though you will, of course, have your pick of additional specimens," Lord went on. "Directly below the Soyuz. On Venus."

Neither Borodin nor Ptushko rejected the plan, which told Lord something important: that the Russians were *already* at Venus. This microbial sample did not float in on a piece of space rock, like pre-life organic matter found fossilized in rocks collected by robotic Mars missions. As long as they weren't going to jettison this sample before they had another, the scientist seemed on board with the plan.

"Let me think about this," Ptushko said.

"I wouldn't, at least not for very long," Lord said, indicating the nanite in the dish.

"I am aware of my responsibilities," the admiral said.

"While you consider it," Lord said, "add this to the mix. I'm going on this mission."

TWENTY-TWO

DESPITE THE PRESSURES of the moment, Ptushko seemed almost amused by the suggestion.

"What could possibly persuade me to permit you to go with my team?" he asked Lord.

"I am your only conduit to those who are most knowledgeable about the nanites, and are undertaking ongoing research," Lord replied.

"You refer to your team, who cannot stop them," the admiral replied.

"They cannot stop them *yet*," Lord said. "I have confidence they will. And, as a military man, you know as well as I do that it's good to have a backup plan if, say, the HR refuses to fire."

Any trace of Ptushko's amusement was gone now. "This is extortion, Mr. Director."

"Hardly," Lord replied. "I may need information to save lives on my station. I don't know what these morphing nanites will do in space. This is the only way I can be sure to get that information."

"Which, you admit, you will pass along to your superiors, your scientists."

"Admiral, I'm not a physicist, I wouldn't even know what I'm looking at," Lord answered truthfully. "If it makes you feel better, I will cede control of my IC to Lieutenant Uralov—who, I assume, will be piloting this mission. Either we all win or we all do not. And if you're worried about me seeing what you've got going on at Venus, do you really think it will remain a secret for very long?"

As Ptushko listened to Lord's argument, he was busy rushing mentally through the political and logistical pitfalls and seeing no gain for himself. Even dying up here would be preferable to having to face Roscosmos after being ambushed and exposed by the director of Zero-G.

"I cannot permit it," he replied with finality.

"Of course," Lord said. "And if something like a nanite eruption should affect your pilot in transit, who else will be remotely qualified to fly your Soyuz?"

Lord already knew the answer to that from having read the *Red Giant* crew dossiers before leaving the *Empyrean*. There was no one. Otherwise, the discredited Svetlana Uralov herself might not have been asked to fly the craft.

The admiral's smile had not wavered. He was actually grateful for Lord's observation: the American had just insulated him against any political blowback. Still unhappy at having been manipulated—but also in possession of knowledge that Lord did not have, would never have— Ptushko checked the status of the Soyuz upgrade in his IC, saw that it had been completed.

"Lieutenant Svetlana Uralov, report to the medbay," he said.

"At once," she replied.

The admiral continued to regard Lord. "Director Lord, Russia has a tradition of storied exiles like yourself—men and women who triumphed over great adversity, legends dating back to Prince Nevsky in the thirteenth century to Mr. Trotsky in the last century. Even from afar, they managed to upset the order of things."

"For the better with Alexander Nevsky, as I recall," Lord said. "Drove the Teutonic Knights from Mother Rus."

Ptushko nodded. "And Trotsky received an icepick in the brain for crossing Mr. Lenin. Be very certain that you follow the loftier example, Director Lord."

Lord acknowledged the warning with an appreciative nod, though there was something about Ptushko's manner that troubled him: he had surrendered a little too easily at the end, as though he were in fact anxious to have Lord go on this mission.

What's your endgame, Admiral? Lord wondered as Borodin turned his attention to modifying the KGT from fitting on the exterior of the *Red Giant* to being adaptable to the HR.

Like a Valkyrie—Teutonic imagery was still fresh in Lord's mind—Svetlana speared toward them headfirst through the blinking lights of the module. She was wearing a spacefaring undergarment similar to what Lord had on. Arriving breathless from her run, she tucked her legs, found purchase on the wall with her right hand, and swung into position, facing them. She studiously avoided Lord and stared directly at the admiral.

"Lieutenant Uralov, Mission 717 is officially yours," Ptushko announced.

"Yes, sir. *Thank you*, sir," she said, trying hard not to show in her expression the enthusiasm that was in her voice.

Ptushko glanced at a digital readout in his IC. "Commander's log: mark time of transfer of authority at current time." He regarded her like Borodin studying his specimen. "Lieutenant, Director Lord has requested that he accompany you and Dr. Borodin. As commander, the decision is yours."

Lord couldn't decide whether to admire the man's cover-his-ass savvy or detest the abrogation of responsibility. In any event, the maneuver was shamefully blatant.

Svetlana remained frozen. Only a loose strap on her arm and stray hairs were in motion. "What—what reason would I have to bring him?" she asked, though she already seemed to know that whatever answer he provided would be hollow and insufficient.

"The mission parameters have been expanded," he informed her. "Dr. Borodin will brief you." He looked at Lord but was still speaking to Svetlana. "Let me know your decision about the director. I have a crisis to manage."

The admiral's departure left a residue of tense indecision—for which there wasn't time. Only Lord and Borodin knew that.

Svetlana's eyes sought the scientist. He told her briefly what had happened.

"Your scientific assessment of the mission?" she asked him.

"We should undertake the enhanced mission and we should have this man with us," the exobiologist opined. "Now, if you'll excuse me, Lieutenant, I have preparations to make."

The scientist left to go to the small engineering section and finish the unlikely joining of the hand rocket and the Kozyrev Gas Trap. In his absence, the tension immediately thickened. Svetlana studied her companion.

"Games," she said bitterly. "What is yours?"

He shook his head. "None. Dr. Borodin is correct," Lord said. "Your station and mine are both facing the same danger. I must go with you."

"You are not a scientist," she said.

"As I told your colleagues, I am in touch with scientists we require," he said.

"Would you fly an aircraft with secondhand advice?"

"That's how I survived the *Grissom* crash landing," Lord said. "Look, whatever you imagine my motives to be—and some of that may be true—the benefits outweigh whatever you might be risking." He nodded after the vanished Ptushko. "The admiral's maneuver was just a precaution. I'm sure you've seen it before. I have, many times, in too many ranking officers. Don't let that influence you."

"Thank you for the self-serving advice," she said coldly.

"Oh, don't take it that way," he said in a more personable tone. "It wasn't American to Russian, it wasn't veteran to up-and-comer, and it definitely wasn't some alpha male role that most of the civilized world repudiated long ago. It was pilot to pilot. Even if you don't know me, you should know which is the dominant dynamic."

The lieutenant didn't move, but her expression seemed to soften.

"Anyway," Lord said, extending his arms, "I've still got my suit on. I may as well use it."

Svetlana nearly smiled at that—but not because of Lord. She had just reached a decision. There was this mission, of course, but also the one that had been bothering her since she returned from the *Empyrean*, the one she had failed to achieve: getting inside this man's mind and agenda.

"The trip will be eight hours," she said. "I assume, from your background, that you do not suffer from claustrophobia."

"I've flown longer missions in my Vampire, where I had to be very alert all the way," he replied.

"And on the return trip?"

"Even more alert," Lord said. "I had enemy fighters in pursuit."

Svetlana took one more moment to look carefully into his eyes. "All right," she said, turning. "Come with me."

Lord followed her. He did not ask how they would be traveling roughly 106 million miles that quickly. He had an idea.

They floated back through the station, toward Ptushko's office. That was not their destination, however. They returned to the docking module where Lord had first come aboard, a small compartment budded off the center of the main corridor, Earthside. The hatch to the Soyuz was open and a crew member was inside, working off a printed checklist.

Folded inside with whatever Earth-built upgrades they're installing? Lord wondered. Maybe *Red Giant* funding was even worse than Zero-G had thought. Small items like this would be one reason Admiral Ptushko would be reluctant to have an observant FBI officer on hand.

Svetlana moved away but Lord called after her. She paused.

"May I contact my command center?" he asked.

"They have contacted you here with updates?" Svetlana said.

"Yes—"

"Then we will leave the initiative to them," she said.

"*Empyrean* will be tracking your departure anyway," Lord said.

"I cannot control what *they* do, Mr. Director," she replied. "While we are on this mission I will preserve the secrecy of the mission to the best of my ability."

"One more thing, then," he said. "Preparations must be made to eject the nanites. I would like to be involved with that."

She pointed to her IC. "I am told I will be getting a mission update from the admiral while I change," she said. "You will be briefed when your input is required."

"Lieutenant, please—I am not the enemy. I *want* to help," he said.

"I understand," she replied, then added with some steel, "That is an enviable trait in a backup pilot. That, and silence."

He had been put firmly in his place and acceded to it with a gracious little bow. Svetlana continued on her way, leaving Lord where he was.

It was truly heartbreaking to see someone so young, so smart, be so jaded, he thought as she vanished around a corner.

Lord tried to stay out of the way; there was nothing he needed to see here and now. In addition to the man inside the Soyuz, there was a crew member outside. Her eye motions indicated that she was working on her IC, probably a prelaunch checklist interfaced with the Soyuz itself. From his position, Lord could see that a small plastic locker had been added to the gear between the seats. The drop-down translated the label as "food and medical."

Alone with his thoughts, it was the first time he was able to consider the fact that he was going to another planet. Not just the moon, which in itself had been extraordinary, but Venus. For all he knew, he would be the first person in history to do both. As he often did, he took pride and gained perspective from his go-to yardstick for all things: *Not bad for a kid from Hell's Kitchen.*

And yet even with that awareness, there was a strong undercurrent of regret. Humankind was still just getting started in space and Lord very much wanted to see it all. He wouldn't, of course. Not in any conventional sense—and any other method could not be known. That longing reminded him of when he was a kid, and older family members and occasionally an instructor would say some variation on *The more you learn, the more you realize you don't know.* That didn't make sense to Lord, then. Right now, Sam Lord was keenly aware that he was at the absolute zenith of not-knowing. And it wasn't just the universe with magnitude that was obvious and daunting. It was us, with our multitude of needs and views, wounds and strengths, aspirations and inspirations. The whole of it was unchartable, unmanageable.

He almost envied the focus of Svetlana Uralov, who returned dressed in the same space suit she had been wearing in their first flight, the one he himself had on, which would allow them to depressurize and open the hatch of the Soyuz for an hour. All she seemed to want to do was use him to get back to Earth, to recover the life her dossier said she had suddenly left behind. He hoped there was some way he would be able to help her achieve that, without compromising his own objectives.

Svetlana spoke with the woman working outside the craft, then ducked her head into the Soyuz to confer with the man inside. When that was finished, the occupant of the craft exited and, with the other woman, wished Svetlana a safe and prosperous journey. As they were saying their goodbyes, Dr. Borodin arrived, also in a space suit.

There was an unavoidable sense of consequence in the preparations and farewells. Even though they were small, they were highly professional—and solemn. There was seemingly nothing routine, as both of the workers had been extremely intent on their jobs.

The two crew members drifted into the corridor but did not depart; presumably, the Russians would seal the craft once the others were inside. Borodin entered first, carefully clutching a pouch to his chest with one hand, grunting and constantly adjusting his body as he squeezed into the right seat; Lord went in second, in the center, grateful for the lack of gravity that allowed him to float in slowly like a cloud; Svetlana swung in last and with considerably less effort than the older men had required.

The door shut with an easy, weightless *clang* as Svetlana reviewed her drop-down checklist. There was new data there; he could tell from the movements she made in the air and on IC links—small screw-shaped knobs—that had been plugged into the panels.

The feeling in the ship was very different from what it had been only an hour or so before. They were going boldly on a historic journey, and that very much informed their mood. Lord could hear Borodin breathing heavily, saw Svetlana more engaged with the ship than she had been before, and he himself—what was that line from Shakespeare that Erin had once said to him? *Take from my heart all thankfulness!* Zero-G had been a wonderful opportunity; this was an unimaginable perk.

There was a gentle one-g thrust from the small retrorockets that pushed them back into their seats as they uncoupled from the *Red Giant* and turned toward the star side of space. Their trajectory would not be the sun but where Venus would be when they arrived. The area outside the window was dark and clear, the heavens were awash with crisp, distant lights.

Lord was suddenly aware of a familiar and unexpected sound: the sibilant firing-up of zeta-pinch fusion jet engines. He had calculated the time and distance and assumed that was how they'd be making the trip, though he hadn't known that the Russians possessed them. They were the same high-power thrusters that had swiftly propelled the *Grissom* shuttlecraft to the moon in a little over three hours instead of two days. Though the rockets would naturally be silent in space, the dense plasma-to-fusion operation occurred internally and resonated through the craft.

The initial surge quieted as Svetlana effectively idled the craft, waiting.

And then Lord heard a communication that he had been half-expecting but which chilled him nonetheless:

"Vent the medbay."

The Soyuz was in the wrong position to see the expulsion firsthand, but Svetlana had it on her IC and shared the view with the others. The three sat in silence as a hatch opened slowly and the sudden, explosive vacuum caused everything that wasn't welded to a surface to be sucked out. There was a rush of smaller items like bandages and vials and a few instruments, all of them tumbling wildly like a mad little circus parade. And then came the stretcher with the remains of Douglas Cameron, minus the twin oxygen tanks. The semirigid plastic sheet slammed hard against the rectangular opening but it did not go through, lying athwart at a forty-five-degree angle to the opening. The body was still strapped to it, facing outward—but not for long.

The remains of the botanist burst in the vacuum as the pressure within pushed the shroud of flesh toward the void. The rain of body parts bloomed in all directions—but they did not stay dispersed. The particles large and small slowed, then improbably stopped, then finally coalesced into something inhuman, a roiling mass controlled by a very small nanite army. The small robots were working like tugboats, marshaling the larger pieces of Douglas Cameron like an obscene constellation. Almost at once they began to move toward the Soyuz.

"There is no self-propulsion unit that I could detect," Borodin said.

"I cannot say whether they possess one or not," Lord replied truthfully.

The scientist was studying his IC. "Algorithms suggest only one major force at work: gravity. But the nanites are using it ingeniously," Borodin said with amazement. "What they have done is to isolate masses of biological tissue in line with the Soyuz and, in particular, with the microbe. The nanites have orientated themselves along vectors in which all three of those are aligned—human cell contents to the Soyuz to the microbe. And they are being drawn in that direction by our gravitational pull."

Lord knew that the exobiologist wasn't speculating: his own IC had come alive with the same magnetoencephalographic readings that had registered in the *Red Giant* laboratory.

Svetlana watched the coalescing, marionette-like mass of human-biological matter approach, sailing smoothly toward them like a fallen skater on ice.

"We have created something monstrous," the woman said. "All of our collective knowledge culminating in—that."

"I wonder if 'that' has any awareness," Lord found himself thinking aloud.

"It's a grotesque thought," Borodin stated. "Electrons flow as easily in a vacuum as in air."

Now that the nanites were under way, Svetlana turned to her countdown checklist.

"Uralov to *Red Giant*, we are ready for departure," she said. "Running automated engine program."

"Permission granted for fire-up at completion of AEP," replied the radio operator, whose hollow tone suggested that he was seeing everything they saw. He followed that with a gentle "*Удачи!*"

Lord did not have to wait for the translation to know that the man had wished them a heartfelt "Good luck!"

TWENTY-THREE

'M GOING TO the Vault," Adsila Waters announced.

Adsila's pronouncement brought disapproval from nearly everyone on her IC feed.

"Your presence is an absolute negative!" Stanton barked.

"EAD, please *wait*!" Abernathy implored. "Just wait."

"For what?"

"Investigation," he said. "Just a little more."

Agents Abernathy and McClure were still going through Carlton Carter's data in their ICs. The nanite samples on hand had grown increasingly agitated since they'd arrived, causing concern that any course of action might excite them more. Adsila was not opposed to the scientific process, but she was accustomed to reaching a point and then acting—not randomly, but listening to the universe, letting hidden spirits, invisible hands move her, direct her.

"I'm with the EAD," McClure said. "The hair sample was not sufficient to get their attention, but it doesn't mean our thinking is wrong. We don't have time to wait."

"I'm not saying we take a hukin' vacation, but we have to make time to get this *right*," Abernathy said.

McClure was growing impatient. "We need results at best, more data at the very least, and the only way to obtain that is by experimentation."

Abernathy looked at Adsila, who was waiting impatiently beside McClure. "If they recognize you, the nanites could devour you, EAD. Do you understand that?"

"I do, but I agree with Ed," she replied. "We have to start trying things."

"All right, fine—I just want to think this through. A minute, please."

"A minute," McClure said. "That's it."

"Could what you're doing create something *worse* in the process?" Stanton demanded.

"Unlikely," Carter said. "Things are pretty bad right now, Commander."

"I'm thinking about a potential second front," Stanton said. "One with legs, mobility—"

"Nothing is guaranteed," Carter admitted, "except the continued deterioration of the situation if we do nothing."

Abernathy shut out the debate as his eyes ranged through the classified files and unclassified readings coming from the Vault. "What we're seeing is communication *from* biota *to* tech," he said to his teammates. "The result reads like an encephalogram—beta waves at 30 Hz. If you want to block waves in that range—"

"You'd have to surround each nanite with mylar foil on *six* sides," McClure said.

"There has to be another way!" Abernathy shot back.

"Even if there were," McClure explained patiently, "you have to find and identify them all. The signals are merged, impossible to pinpoint. And then there's the problem of adaptability. The files say that Dr. Carter started in the theta range—they've boosted *themselves* higher, not him."

"I still think we should work back and look for oscillation patterns," Abernathy said. "I don't believe these are random. Find the trigger for each one and you stop the waves."

"Yes, if there were time," McClure told him.

"Why are you reluctant to test my hair sample?" Adsila asked.

Abernathy sighed. "Because we don't know what they will do with this information."

"What *could* they do?" she asked.

"What can *x* number of mutating energy feeders-generators do to any potential conduit to more energy?" he asked.

"I'm not following," Adsila said.

"Nor I," McClure said. "Agent Abernathy, the number of qualifiers in that statement makes researching them impossible."

"No, it makes *any* action reckless," Abernathy said. "We have to isolate the what-ifs quickly, yes, but with some certainty."

"EAD, we have to stop this," Carter said, speaking exclusively to Adsila. "The status quo is going to kill us for certain. Whether that happens at the current pace or faster is really of no consequence."

Lacking rank, the biophysicist could not issue that command. Lacking indecision, Adsila did.

"Go ahead with the experiment, Agent McClure," she said firmly.

Abernathy gestured unhappily but with resignation. As he looked on warily, the senior agent inserted the hair in the container and closed the top.

"Air pressure, Dr. Carter?" McClure asked.

"Start with Earth normal," he replied.

"One bar," McClure confirmed, speaking to the cylinder as the Pascal gradations climbed to 100,000 and settled at that level. When he entered the room, the science officer had made sure to auto-add the FID—Fiber Identification Code—of every piece of equipment in the lab to his IC. Descended from security chips introduced nearly forty years before, the FID allowed authorized users to interface with the hair-thin molecular computer embedded in every legal product manufactured on and now off-Earth. McClure had no doubt he would lose access as soon as his security clearance was revoked; until then, he felt as if a secret world was open to him—if he had time to explore it.

"They're ignoring it," Adsila observed.

"Still reaching toward the *Red Giant*—though, hold on: there's been a slight shift in their orientation," McClure noted.

"*Empyrean* just observed a launch from the Russian station," said Grainger, who had been patched into Adsila's IC.

"A Scud?" Adsila asked. She was too busy watching the seemingly empty dish and cylinder with nanite and hair to check her own IC updates, which had been minimized to keep from distracting her.

"No," Grainger replied. "It's their Soyuz."

"That's a *very* quick turnaround after its trip here," Adsila remarked. "Bearing?"

"Ecliptic coordinates currently . . . heliocentric longitude 41.483862 degrees . . . geocentric longitude 292.64251 degrees . . . EAD," Grainger said with some surprise. "EAD—the ship is headed for the inner solar system."

"Speed?" Adsila asked.

"Six thousand, eighty-three miles per second and rising," Grainger said. "That is a very powerful launch . . . tracking four times their launch-approach speed to *Empyrean*."

"What's driving it?" Adsila wondered aloud. Curiosity compelled her to bring up images of the Soyuz docked at the PRiD when Lord boarded. There were no obvious enhancements and anything *not* obvious would have been beyond Russian technology.

McClure interrupted the conversation. "We're getting a reaction," he said. "The hair strand is oscillating."

Adsila moved closer to the container with her hair.

"One Hz . . . two . . . three . . ." McClure said.

"The nanites aren't changing their orientation," Abernathy reported.

"If they're not all interacting, then what's moving the hair sample?" Carter asked.

"I'm trying to figure that out, Doctor," McClure replied.

As McClure was speaking, Adsila felt a punch behind her eyes, one that momentarily turned her world a rusty red. Her head jerked forward. McClure, who was standing between her and Abernathy, saw her jerk. He swiftly turned and put his hands on her shoulders.

"What is it?" the scientist asked.

It took her a moment to respond. She was staring at nothing in particular. "I don't know. I felt—my IC went down and I went with it."

"Is it back?"

She nodded.

"Are you?" he asked.

She looked at him. "Yes. It was as if I . . . rebooted."

"And?" he pressed.

It took her another moment to answer. "There's been an upgrade," she responded.

The laboratory became very quiet.

"Adsila, the nanites couldn't do that," Carter said. "Even if they could get to you through a strand of hair, which is doubtful, they don't have that kind of broadcast amplification."

"Well, something does," she said. "And there's nothing else here."

Her eyes turned to the cylinder. She saw the hair now, clearly; or, rather, she saw a golden vibration that clung to the hair. Her eyes drifted to the petri dish, where there was a red nimbus around the spot where the nanite had to be, pressed to the side of the container.

Suddenly, the red shifted and, like Tinker Bell, floated toward the side of the dish facing her.

McClure watched her eyes drifting. "EAD, what is it?"

"I'm going to the Vault," she replied, and turned.

"Adsila, what's happening?" Carter asked.

"The nanite turned toward me, the same way it shifted toward the Soyuz," she said, exiting the laboratory.

"Turned toward you or whatever it's watching outside the *Empyrean*?" Carter asked.

"I don't know," she said, "and we have to find that out!"

"Mike, keep working on this," McClure said to his subordinate as he followed Adsila.

"Haven't stopped," Abernathy replied, studying a new analysis of the nanite's energetic output. "I can tell you, the bug-bot is getting hotter. Voltage rising, temperature rising. Activity increasing."

"What's it trying to do?" Carter wondered aloud. Then, almost at once, he said, "The vine is changing again. It's moving, expanding faster in a different direction."

"Toward me?" Adsila asked.

She and the others were following her progress through an *Empyrean* schematic she brought up.

"Toward you," Carter said.

"What the hell happened back in the lab?" McClure asked no one in particular. He was struggling to keep up as Adsila swiftly negotiated the shifting gravities on her way to the Agro Center.

"Triangulating the energy readings at the moment the EAD swooned," Abernathy said. "Lags, I don't think she was targeted," he said, using an old acronym for ladies and gentlemen.

"Then what?" McClure asked.

"I think Adsila was speared. Skewered, actually. A far-field electromagnetic wave, an extremely high frequency reading—forty-two gigahertz—was emitted by the retreating Soyuz and struck her from behind. A near-field superhigh frequency, three gigahertz, came at her from the front. There's a faint trace reading, one megahertz, around the hair."

"Were the stronger forces directed at her or at each other?" Carter asked.

"It appears to be the latter, with the EAD at the vertex," Abernathy replied. "The near-field frequency looks like it caromed off the hair. The source here read the EAD's energy, as did the Soyuz energy. On their way to meet each other, they found her, latched on."

"That kind of communication is what the nanites are programmed to do, but only with each other and not at these distances," Carter said.

"So now they're behaving like ants, over long distances," Abernathy said.

"They're just skipping through the evolutionary chain, aren't they?"

"Mike, what did you mean when you said the nanites 'latched on'?" McClure asked, focusing on a development the others seemed to have missed.

"I mean it seems as if the two energy sources are now tracking *her* instead of each other. But—okay, now this isn't possible," Abernathy said.

"*What* isn't?" Carter demanded, even slight delays frustrating him.

"The off-station source does *not* appear to be the Soyuz itself," Abernathy replied.

"Impossible," Carter said.

"Ziv? Other nanites?" Adsila suggested.

"Not on my frequency," Carter said.

"It's crazy," Abernathy went on. "There doesn't seem to be a single point of origin. It's a broad sweep narrowing to a point here."

"From?" Carter asked.

"The flight path of the Soyuz, but from a point outside the vessel," said Grainger, who had the more sophisticated hardware. "The EAD is the vertex of a roughly 130-degree angle between the inner solar system and the Vault."

"What the hell are the Russians doing?" Adsila wondered. "Can't we *see* the Soyuz?"

"It's flying into the sun," Grainger told her. "We're blind."

"Whatever the Russians are doing, whatever the nanites are up to, the vine is getting ugly and more aggressive," Carter said. "We can't control it by hacking."

It took Abernathy and McClure a moment to realize that Carter meant the old-school word, chopping it instead of shutting down the technology.

Adsila refocused on the problem at hand. "Something turned it on, something can turn it off," she said as she took the elevator to the Agro level.

"Is there something you're not sharing, EAD?" McClure asked.

Adsila shook her head. Her face was stern, head throbbing as though she were upside-down and blood was rushing to it. "I just have a feeling I can get the nanites to stop what they're doing."

"How?" Carter asked.

"Commander Stanton?"

"Yes?"

"Send me a security clearance code for the Vault—Cameron's will do, he's not using it."

"What do you need it for?"

"The only tool we haven't tried," she replied. "The one they're asking for."

TWENTY-FOUR

T HIS IS FUN."

Lord's comment, soft and unexpected—even by him—was sincere. As the thrusters sent the Soyuz on its journey, the Zero-G director felt the two-g force temporarily press him back into the cushions. After hours of weightlessness, it felt like much more; with the variable gravity on *Empyrean*, the sustained pressure had a familiar, Earth-like quality that made him smile. He also experienced a wash of humility and camaraderie as he thought of all the pioneers who had been thrust back into this well-worn seat. But most of all, he felt the comfort, warmth, and profound mystery of the looming unknown and it beckoned with a full-throated voice.

This was not a translunar run, it was transplanetary. And it was not a trip into the void, it was a journey toward Sol, Earth's star, the furnace that had birthed these worlds. Eleven years before, the Giant Planet Probe had proved definitively that the outer moons of Jupiter and Saturn were captured asteroids. But everything else in the solar system, from Mercury to Pluto to the recently discovered dark planet Tempestes—a gas giant, apparently a failed star—was born in or spun from the sun.

It was exciting but unnerving to be headed toward the old nursery, like a kid coming home from boarding school. Who knew how the parent would react?

The parent, Lord thought. Sexless. Powerful. Gender suddenly seemed like a disability, not an asset. Something to be evolved out of.

"'Fun,'" Borodin muttered as he finished examining the HR/KGT hybrid and strapped it to a bracket above. "We are being followed by a creature composed of exploded human body parts, controlled by hostile nanobots. This is not like your AppleWorld Park where you can customize every thrill in every attraction."

"I know," Lord replied, smiling. "But this is surprisingly like every time I climbed into a cockpit. Safety was never a guarantee, but *challenge* was. That was what made it fun. You lived each moment at maximum alert."

"Without time to observe, to understand," Borodin said.

"That came later, during debriefing—the one you did and the military conducted," Lord allowed. "In the midst of any action, the brain had to play along with the rest of the body. No special attention to its loftier, contextual functions."

"Like an animal," Borodin said.

"Perhaps that too," Lord agreed.

"Then forgive me," Borodin said, "but that is no way to live."

"In the moment, you mean?" Lord asked.

Borodin grunted, which Lord took as agreement. "You leave nothing behind, pass no learning to the future. Where is the lasting value except—and this is key—except in the warped rearview mirror of memory? Your debriefing is colored by reflection, emotion, time, and distance. It is not reliable."

It was Svetlana who replied. "The shadows of events are still a reflection of those events, Doctor," she said. "The distortion is not so great."

"If I applied those parameters to a microscope, you would think the microbe was a triangle or a noodle."

"And if we stopped to overthink everything," she replied, "humans would still be vainly considering the world from a cave without the hunter-gatherers to map that world."

Lord snickered. "When I was a kid I thought they were called *hunger*-gatherers," he said.

There was no reaction from his companions. It took him a moment to realize why. The words sounded nothing alike in Russian.

"I love this, and I don't just mean the mission," Lord went on enthusiastically. "It's the teamwork." He turned his head slightly so he could see Svetlana over the side of the couch. "Only when you've been there can you know something absolutely." He turned to Borodin. "And only when you've thought about it can you learn from it."

"'Know something absolutely,'" Svetlana said. "Yes, that's accurate. It is a quality missing from the unchanging routine of life in space. In a way, perhaps we have regressed up here. All we *do* is hunt and gather."

Lord suddenly felt a great deal of empathy for the woman. Even though the Glossator replicated the tone, he could hear longing in her natural voice.

"Teams," Borodin grunted again. "In science, it's an oxymoron. We fight each other, form alliances, then fight among those groups. We are better alone. That is where real progress is made."

"Like the sun," Lord said. "A single parent."

Borodin snickered. "Yes. If you cannot use the universe as a model, then there is nothing you can trust."

"Except," Lord said, "if I'm not mistaken, roughly four-fifths of the stars we see in the skies are binary star systems."

"Well, they are parents," he said. "I don't mean the poly-pods you have in America but traditional, Russian parents."

"I'll have to think about that one," Lord admitted. "Because in every system science has ever studied—as far as I'm aware—the planets *do* work together, are interdependent."

"As are galaxies that are drawn together by gravitation," Svetlana added.

"You are obfuscating my scientific approach with faith-based mythologies and fable," he said. "Is the universe run by a single god or no god or by a pantheon? Which civilization got it right? If we are to ever find that out, my method must be applied."

"Or maybe the truth will just be revealed," Lord replied with a smile. "My most epiphanic moments have come when I wasn't expecting them. Test-piloting. Falling asleep. Sex."

"How artfully you evade responsibility," Borodin said.

"Not at all," Lord insisted. "Breakthroughs are as likely staring at the sky—as in 'I want to go *there*!'—as peering through a microscope."

"Or arguing with a harsh pragmatist," Svetlana added.

"Dreamers!" Borodin said distastefully. "The reality of our present situation requires more than wishing and watching. You all give me a pain."

Lord chuckled and Svetlana looked at the American, smiling. The Zero-G director looked out the small window and considered once again where they were going. Many were the times he had flown into the sun aboard his Vampire. Flying *to* the sun—that was a very different thing. The craft was flying itself for the moment, and Lord saw the same look of wonder in Svetlana's face. It *was* fun. Even the sour deconstruction of Borodin couldn't spoil it.

It was going to be a long flight and Lord could not imagine making it in silence. But he felt it was better to react to whatever was said than to initiate conversation and put the others on their guard. He occupied himself by imagining the reaction on the *Empyrean* when they figured out where the Russian vessel was headed. He was sorry he hadn't been able to call the team, but he had no doubt—when they saw the patchwork corpse trailing behind—that they would draw a few generally accurate conclusions.

The initial thrust of the engines had not abated as the Soyuz was propelled toward its full transit speed. The numbers were staggering as he did the mental calculations. Traveling 106 million miles in eight hours meant they would be reaching a top speed of 15 million miles an hour. Just that fact was difficult to process. And they were taking it with an alien life-form.

Borodin is wrong, Lord thought. *When even the parts are inconceivable there is nothing to do but let it all wash over you.*

"Look," Svetlana said, sending an image of her companions to the ICs.

It was Earth slipping into the blackness—still large enough to matter but shrinking by the moment.

"Our guest does not seem to possess a sense of wonder," Borodin said.

Lord thought for a moment that the scientist was inaccurately describing him. Then he noticed that the scientist was looking at the dish—or rather, at the microscopic feed that magnified the contents exclusively for Borodin's IC. Though a sealable mylar pack had been placed in the craft for stowing, just to the man's right, Borodin still held it to his chest.

"What is it doing?" Svetlana asked.

"Hovering in the center of the container like a ferrofluid suspended in a magnetic field," Borodin answered. "It isn't reacting to the nanites or acceleration."

Lord continued to look ahead. "To what, then? To Venus?"

"Perhaps, though we are still too far for that, I should think. The microbe didn't reach in that direction when we were on the *Red Giant.* We are not appreciably closer."

"But we are away from the electrical and biological overstimulation of that environment," Lord said.

Svetlana used her eyes to adjust the rearview. She looked at the macabre shape behind them. Nodes of tissue were growing in all directions, like cancers; and it was nearer than before.

"Director Lord, what do you make of the change in the nanites' proximity?" she asked.

Lord looked. The puppet-Cameron was only about ten meters away. "They're about half as far as when we left," he said with some concern.

"How can that be?" Svetlana asked.

"I don't know," he admitted. "The question is, are they making it happen?"

"They could be reacting to emissions from the zeta-pinch drive, ions in the solar wind, or both," Borodin suggested.

"'Reacting'?" Lord said. "You mean using the backwash to power up?"

"There is no other explanation I can think of," he said. "Is that normal?"

"I don't believe so," Lord said. *They were designed to function in space,* he thought. *Could they be drawing power from solar wind? Was that part of their self-sustaining design?*

"The tissue—is also changing, it seems," Svetlana said. "Director Lord, do you see it?"

"I do," he admitted.

She turned suddenly toward the American. "Is there something you have not told us about them?"

"Nothing that has to do with their operation," he replied. "As we saw in the medbay, they were created to heal injured human tissue."

"Is that all?"

"That's all I can tell you," Lord said. "It's all that's relevant."

"So they are making more biological mass," she said. "From what?"

"From whatever elements are available to them," Lord replied. "Straggling particles of Cameron's cells—"

"But I believe you're wrong, Mr. Director."

"How so?"

"More than what you just described is available to them," Borodin said. "Space is littered with the building blocks of life—carbon, hydrogen, iron. We've been coasting through that marketplace since we departed. To these robots, each particle would be the size of a football. Easy to grab."

The pilot and Lord both seemed concerned by the revelation.

"Doctor, should the director contact his scientists?" Svetlana asked.

"It might be a good precaution," Borodin admitted.

Before Svetlana could contact the *Red Giant*, the mass of biological material changed. All watched as it practically doubled in size, rolling like lava down a peak, cells duplicating, while their root-mass expanded toward the spacecraft.

"They're spinning it out like silk," Svetlana marveled.

"An element-rich environment indeed," Borodin said. "They're still trying to get the microbe."

"But it's not trying to get away," Lord replied. "Why?"

"Maybe it's trying a different tactic," Borodin said. "The flanges have gone very still now."

"Hiding? Stealth mode?" Lord wondered aloud. "Can it possibly know we're using it as bait?"

The question seemed to intrigue Borodin. "If it does, then it would have a higher capacity for reason than I imagined."

"Or else the ability to read the images in our minds," Lord suggested. "This is an alien life-form. Who knows what it's capable of knowing or sensing or foreseeing?"

"Terran or extraterrestrial, it cannot conduct such processes with so rudimentary a brain."

"There may be involuntary reactions buried in its racial memory," Lord said.

"Mystic rubbish."

"I have a Native American officer on my staff who would disagree with you," Lord said. "What about familiar patterns? Relative proximity to the sun, Venus, with charged 'particles' in pursuit."

"Science fiction," Borodin said.

Svetlana wasn't paying attention to the discussion but to the remains of Douglas Cameron. Hanging utterly still between growth spurts, the nanite-infested corpse came even closer to the Soyuz, as though pulled along on an invisible string.

"If escaping detection is the objective, then the microbe has failed," Svetlana observed.

"We need a plan, quickly!" Borodin said.

"Why the urgency?" Svetlana said. "Director Lord, how would they even get in here? There is no biological matter between us and them."

At that moment, there was a flash of static across their ICs. Then another. Then a third.

"It cannot be possible," Lord said. "It just can't be."

"What?" Svetlana asked with alarm.

"Those electrical impulses—Cameron's IC," Lord said. "Is it possible the nanites have plugged into that, are communicating wirelessly with his brain?"

Another silence filled the cabin.

"Even if they did, I repeat, how would they get inside?" Svetlana asked. "How will they reach the microbe?"

"First they'll want to shut us down," Lord said. "Through him they can reach us, our ICs. They can learn the controls, open the hatch."

The woman swore in Russian.

"Lieutenant, you'd better close all your IC links," Lord said. "We all should. Go to full manual."

"We'll lose visual on the nanites," she thought aloud. "And the ability to communicate with the *Red Giant*."

"No choice," he replied.

Svetlana nodded in agreement and did as he suggested. The exterior view gone from the drop-down, the walls of the Soyuz suddenly seemed much more solid, nearer, uninviting. So did the heavy breathing of the exobiologist beside Lord.

That's the problem with reason, Lord thought. *When it fails, panic fills the void.*

"Lieutenant, if they get any closer, can you burn them?" Lord asked.

"No," she replied. "Not burn. The engine averages twenty Kelvins— that's *minus* 473 degrees Fahrenheit."

NASA had wanted to freeze them, Lord remembered. "Is that a directed or dispersed blast?"

"Highly concentrated," she said.

"You maneuver with thrust vectoring," Lord said. That was the ability to move the nozzle itself to change direction.

"Yes," Svetlana answered. "If they're anywhere near the magnetic nozzle, they'll be hit."

"At the very least it will immobilize the medium they're using, the remains of your prisoner," Borodin added.

"Let's do it," Svetlana said. "I'll need my IC to pilot that maneuver."

Lord understood. "When you activate, use it as quickly and sparingly as possible."

That sounded like a command and Lord would apologize later. Svetlana turned just her own IC on with a wink. She looked for a moment, then moved her eyes in slow circles. Her expression showed concern.

"What's wrong?" Lord asked.

"They're gone," she told him.

"How can that be?" Borodin cried.

Svetlana continued using her eyes to adjust the craft's external lens. "They're not behind us—"

There were scratchy little thumps on the metal walls. Lord looked up and felt something unpleasant rise in his throat. He raised a near-weightless arm and pointed at the window.

"They're above us," he said with quiet alarm.

All three ports were covered with near-frozen biological material meshed with new, half-frozen human cellular material: pieces of bone, muscle, skin, organ, blood in a mass that reminded Lord of one of those zombies in TV and film the younger fliers were hooked on in the 2010s. The cyborg had dimly recognizable human forms here and there—a finger, a portion of scalp, a piece of breastbone—and these were animated. But there was no part of the construct that was alive.

"They're still using gravity," Svetlana said.

"I don't know about that," Lord said.

"What else?" Svetlana said.

"The nanites may be capable of rock climbing, in effect," Lord replied. "They have pincers, as Dr. Borodin has seen. The surface of this craft is micropitted—collisions with particles, imperfections, corrosive brushes with the extreme outer atmosphere."

"But they still can't get in," Borodin affirmed. "They can't access the electronics."

"There's still an open channel from the *Red Giant*," Lord said, thinking furiously.

"How does that help them?" Svetlana asked.

"If the nanites have the range, they may be able to use Cameron's IC to plug into the onboard computer, search for data, wavelengths, learn the zeta-pinch schematics—I don't know and I don't want to find out."

"What kind of storage capacity do these things *have*?" Borodin demanded.

"I wish I knew," Lord said. "It seems to be morphing."

"I say we turn back," Borodin announced. "At least we'll be closer to a safe haven."

Svetlana replied, "Doctor, for all we know that is what the robots want . . . if that's even the right word."

"If it looks and smells like sentience . . ." Lord said, his voice trailing off.

"Ridiculous," Borodin said. "They have written a program and are following it. We are in the way. If we go back, we can deal with that corpse."

"And free the nanites and face a greater potential disaster, no!" Lord said.

"Yet you refuse to say what that *is*!" Borodin shot back.

The debate was interrupted when something that looked like a three-fingered hand moved into view. The fingers were ungainly, knuckles turning unnaturally this way and that. All eyes were on it.

"They . . . they are going to try to open the hatch," Borodin said, his voice snagging under his chin.

"A space zombie," Lord muttered. "Yes, yes . . . yes. Where were zombies always vulnerable?"

"What are you talking about?" Borodin said.

"I should have thought of it before!" Lord said excitedly as he turned on his IC.

Svetlana tensed as they were once again linked. "What are you doing?"

Lord raised a finger. "Just a second."

His eyes moved. They didn't move fast enough, so he switched to finger control. His index fingers flew through the air in front of his face, sweeping, swiping, poking.

"What's the thing doing now?" Lord asked.

"Nothing," Borodin replied. "It stopped moving."

Lord gestured again, circling a finger as though he were turning an old rotary phone like his grandmother had.

"Now?"

Svetlana answered with amazement, "It's floating away from the Soyuz. Director Lord, *how*—?"

"Ready the engine," Lord said. "The nanites will be within firing range at any moment. Hit them with a blast—then be prepared to correct course, because I don't know how sustained the burn will have to be or how far off trajectory it might put us."

"It's forward-thrust only," she said.

"Factor in whiplash from the dead man?" Lord asked.

"No," Svetlana said appreciatively. He was correct: that could impact their forward movement.

Except for breathing and an occasional tap from an old relay, the Soyuz was silent. Borodin flipped on his own IC and the three of them watched as the external lens picked up the mass as it floated over the craft toward the metal-mesh dish that formed the nozzle of the drive. The small structure was located just beyond the larger, circular array of "wings" that were the engine's capacitor banks.

"On my mark," Svetlana said—whether intending to or not, reminding Lord that she was still the commander of the mission.

"On your mark," Lord agreed.

The trio continued to watch. There was a slight stretching of the biological mass toward the lower "limbs," but the jumble of cells was too frozen to allow much give. There was a sudden "burp" as new tissue appeared throughout the shape—but they were frozen, in the cold of space, before they could stretch very far . . . or get away.

Lord grimaced—but only on the inside, refusing to let the others see. He continued to work his IC with his fingers.

The remains of Douglas Cameron were pulled behind the Soyuz, to the mouth of the engine, and then the IC lens went a cool orange-white. It flashed for five seconds and then Svetlana ended the burst, leaving behind a corpse coated in a thick gray-white cocoon that obscured whatever was inside.

"That looks pretty solid," Lord said. "I think we're okay."

Svetlana quickly turned to the controls, using the pitch-and-yaw controls to maneuver them back on course.

Lord jerked, then deflated in his seat. But he was careful to make no eye movements until he had used his fingers to disengage from the IC. He did not turn it off, however.

"Are you all right?" Svetlana asked, glancing over.

Lord nodded.

She looked back through the lens. "It's still out there. Doctor, what is the specimen doing?"

Borodin adjusted his IC so he could enlarge the microbe. "It's moving again," he said. "It knows the nanites are no longer a threat." The exobiologist looked over at Lord, his eyes wide with admiration. "Sir, *how* did you do that?"

Lord was still shaken, though he did not want to talk about that. He dared not tell them that his solution had come from the whole-cloth fiction of old zombie movies.

"Something of Cameron was definitely still alive in there," Lord said. "The same brain functions the nanites were able to access and read and keep alive are the same ones I used."

"To do what?" Svetlana asked.

Lord replied, "To put the Mindcuffs back on and hold the son of a bitch still for you."

TWENTY-FIVE

"Y OU MAY *NOT* have that security clearance, EAD Waters!"

Stanton's voice was strident but Adsila found his intractability more annoying.

"If you try to enter, you will be shocked severely unconscious," the commander added.

She killed her connection to Stanton's IC. "Janet?" she said, taking the call private.

"Here."

"What can you do?"

"Lancaster Liba heard all that and just sent me his security authorization," Grainger told her. "But if I use it, Stanton will find out where it came from. His career will be over."

"Cameron passed through comm security," Adsila said.

"Yeah, and using the data we collected will get *you* fired," Grainger pointed out.

"I have to get in," Adsila said. "Don't send it—just don't block me when I go in."

"Won't be watching for you," Grainger replied.

Adsila Waters was about to do something unusual for her, something that was also unacceptable conduct in any FBI field office. Without asking permission from NASA, she was going to enter a top-secret facility with stolen credentials.

But the young pangender was coming to understand that Zero-G was not "any" FBI field office. It was the command of Samuel Lord, a man who had always known the freedom of flight and had come up here to express and expand that idea in every way possible. The EAD was beginning to understand why Lord's methods worked: the building blocks were courage and expediency versus good intentions and bureaucracy.

Adsila had her own fingerprints to put on that approach, starting now. Lord had not just given her the framework to do so, but the courage as well. The good news was, if she failed, she'd probably never hear about it. She would be dead or something monstrous.

Showing her IC ID and walking swiftly through the greenhouse, past sanitation workers doubling as security personnel—many of whom seemed surprised to see her striding through, but none of whom appeared eager to engage her—she was not thinking about PD Al-Kazaz, Stanton, or anyone else. She heard the sinister, malevolent crackling and popping of the vine inside the Vault, the shouting of the team as they moved to get out of its way. She ignored all of it. She was only concerned about her own physical reactions as she neared the Vault.

They were subtle, at first. It began with a tingling in her belly, which had an unexpected familiarity: that was where Ziv's nanites had been inserted and then removed.

"EAD?" It was Abernathy.

"Yes?"

"The Ziv nanites have gone very, very still," he said.

"Response to the EAD's departure," Carter told him.

"I don't understand," Adsila said. "Speak freely, Doctor, I've told everyone."

"Ziv's nanites still have your readings in memory," Carter said, still phrasing his explanation with careful respect for her privacy. "Even at this distance, they've noted the change in your field."

"You mean, the fact that I'm this sudden vertex."

"Exactly."

"They're spies and they're hiding their energy signature," Abernathy realized.

Adsila wasn't surprised at subtle frequencies being read from that distance. She was surprised, and angry, that Carter hadn't informed her as a matter of course. This was still an open-ended research project and she was an unwitting subject.

The Cameron code finished downloading and Adsila resumed her previous pace. The next sensations were not a surprise, though their intensity was: when she reached the entrance to the Vault, her entire organ system seemed to light up. The tingling in her lower abdomen was buried in the buzz, in the low hum that rose from her heart and lungs to her jawline and ears, and another that rolled down to her upper thighs.

Those were the nanites. And she wasn't even *through* the electrical barrier yet.

The snap and rumble from inside was broken by a harsh yell from Commander Stanton.

"Do *not* enter that restricted area, Waters!" he yelled. "You will suffer a concussive electrical blast!"

She turned and saw the officer storming toward her, accompanied by a woman she recognized from the high-security area of the Drum, Zoey Kane. It was illegal to conduct surveillance of *Empyrean* personnel, but Stanton had to have been watching her progress. There was no reason to bring a weapon other than to enforce NASA's authority here. Adsila noticed at once that the petite woman was wearing a P3s Gauntlet, a stun weapon that could knock out an adult bear. Still, it would do less damage than the Vault safeguards—if she were vulnerable to those. And there was one thing the Gauntlet could not do.

Adsila turned and stepped inside the Vault. Stanton shouted for her to stop but he did not give the order to fire, knowing that the blast would be absorbed and bounced back by the electronic doorway.

It took a moment for Adsila's eyes to adjust to the muted light and autumnal hues inside the Vault. It took less time for her to assess the environment of the place: sickly, with a metallic tang to the already over-filtered air.

When she could see clearly, the nanite-construct was the first thing she saw. It literally filled the room. Made of thick, monstrously deformed vines, the spheroid tangle resembled an *Escobaria vivipara* cactus she and her grandfather had once transplanted to their garden. Each of the two dozen or so individual strands also had a faintly electric pulse that fell short of a glow—white pinpoints that reminded her of a dewy spiderweb at sunrise. She heard crackling deep inside the mass, as tendril struggled against tendril, to bud and expand.

Only after she'd taken in the mass that began just a few feet from her did she notice the men and women pressed on either side of it—Dr. Carter among them. They were using tools to hook and turn strands that had broken free, struggling to tuck them back in on themselves. Weight here didn't matter; intrusion into the larger area of the greenhouse and especially the air vents did.

In those moments when Adsila sized up her surroundings, Stanton and Zoey had both walked right up to the door but did not go in.

"You were told to remain outside, Waters!" Stanton shouted through the opaque barrier. "How did you gain access?"

Adsila had no intention of responding. As she stood there, Dr. Carter emerged, sweating, from under a bulging bough. It was writhing like Gulliver under Lilliputian ropes—in this case, being held in place by crew wielding improvised pikes made from support poles for cornstalks while pieces were sliced away using laser axes. It was a losing battle, since the severed sections quickly sprouted their own new extensions.

Even in the shaded darkness of the vine, the perspiration on Carter's taut flesh had an active, glistening sheen. For a flashing moment, Adsila feared that he and everyone in here had been infected with nanites, become part of the vine.

"Dr. Carter, do not let her approach the object!" Stanton yelled. "*Carter?*"

"I'm here," the scientist replied, then added, "It's difficult to avoid contact with anything in the room we have left. To which point, do not think about coming in. Also, you're needed out there."

"I am *quite* aware of the situation," Stanton replied angrily. "We've been listening from the Drum."

"Then you are also aware that we are losing a war in here," Carter told the commander with unaccustomed urgency. "If the EAD can help, we must let her."

"That is for NASA to decide, not you *or* me!" Stanton said.

"Commander, please," Carter said. "No jurisdictional spats—not now. Besides, she's already in here."

"Security breaches are not 'spats,' they are what *put* us in this situation!" Stanton yelled. "What are her special operations skills? My superiors will want to know."

"The nanites know me," Adsila replied. "They may accept my intervention."

"Go on," Stanton said.

"That's it," she replied.

"That isn't a plan!" the commander responded fiercely. "What does that even *mean*?"

"Let me show you," Adsila said.

Carter stepped up to the door. "Sir, we don't have time for a debate. Please let her try."

Stanton calmed somewhat. "Will what she is doing interfere with NASA's efforts?" he asked. "At least point me in a direction."

"Commander, NASA is having no more luck than we are," Carter said. "Speaking of which, McClure? Abernathy? Where are we?"

The voices of the two science operatives came through the makeshift audio feed into the ICs of everyone in the Vault.

"Doctor, the collective nanite brain has set up a variable frequency shield that is both random and deflects nearly one hundred percent of every signal we try to slip through," McClure replied.

"They seem to be applying ten percent of their total electronic resources to this purpose," Abernathy replied. "That leaves ninety percent to control their population and expand their empire sunward. When we strengthen the electric field, they use the bounce-back—our own signal—as part of the interference and deflection."

Stanton snarled, "You did a very good job, Doctor."

"Commander, that isn't all my doing," he said. "These things are getting smarter. Cameron introduced them to a subatomic universe of defective particles and God only knows the chain reaction it started."

"Which is why it's so difficult to get data," McClure said. "They are working with tools we cannot see or track. We can only watch the results and infer causation."

"And based on that deep ignorance you're asking me to approve a new tactic?" Stanton replied.

"It is because of that ignorance we need to try new things," Carter replied.

"Blindly, gropingly?" Stanton said.

Adsila was beginning to realize what Sam Lord had demonstrated during the Dragon's Eye challenge, that treating a crisis response like a tennis match was pointless. The debate was not just about the subject but about the volleying skills of the participants and their standing in the ranks and the endorsement fees at risk. Stanton had three objectives, only one of which was stopping the vine. The other two were serving his bosses at NASA and preserving the hierarchy on the *Empyrean*. She couldn't blame him for his hesitancy: except for the narrow course they'd been following, the objectives were in conflict.

Adsila had to relieve him of the latter two responsibilities. The mention of Cameron gave her the means.

"Commander Stanton," Adsila said, "I am here to collect evidence in our autonomous and ongoing espionage investigation. Permit me to proceed."

Stanton seemed mildly surprised, then impressed. After a moment, he asked, "This is now a joint mission with Zero-G?"

"It is," she found herself replying.

"I see."

Adsila began to wonder if he was surprised or if she was a mental move behind him. Her newly articulated mission had now been captured on the ICs of the two *Empyrean* officials. If her plan worked, the situation would be contained. If it failed, or worsened, that was on her, not him.

"Very well, EAD. My officer and I will remain out here to give Zero-G whatever support it requires in the pursuit of your stated objective," Stanton said. "Dr. Carter, we will also continue to support the danger-resolution program as outlined by NASA."

"Thank you," Adsila acknowledged.

Carter returned to Adsila's side. "What do you need from us?"

"I think I'd like everyone to step away from the vine," she said.

"You realize what that will do?" Carter said. "There will be nothing and no one to turn the vine from whatever direction it chooses to go— toward you, toward the inner solar system."

"Understood. McClure?" Adsila said.

"With you, EAD," he replied.

"Stop all direct research on the nanites," she said. "I don't want them to be distracted."

"Shutting programs," the science officer replied. "Done."

Carter was no longer perspiring. His grave expression was sallow. "Adsila, at least tell *me* what you're planning," he implored.

She looked at him, resolve in her eyes and voice. "They've tasted me—my hair," she said. "If I can get their attention again, I'm going to try to take control of that ten percent of their energy."

"And then what?"

"If I can draw them to me, get them *all* linked to me, and then switch genders—"

It took a moment for Carter to process what was being suggested.

"You'll confuse them," Carter said, his voice rising with hope. "They won't want you *or* the vine."

"And, hopefully, they'll stop building things," Adsila said.

"Dr. Carter, that's assuming your original design framework is still in there," McClure said via the audio link.

"It very much appears to be," Carter said. "The nanites have only been duplicating cells from recognized subjects. Random nanites have approached but not replicated any other tissue."

"So they're not hostile, just picky?" McClure said.

"That's how they were designed," Carter answered. He regarded Adsila. "This could work."

"It had better, hadn't it?" she said.

With that, Adsila Waters walked up to the vine and moved her arms toward the tangle.

TWENTY-SIX

THERE WERE TIMES in Lord's life when language provided insights that visualization could not match. One of those occurred in 2045, when he was present for the original merging of NATO and the United Republics of Eastern Europe into NAREETO. Seated near a French general, the talk turned to space—or, as General Nancy Dupré called it, "l'espace," pronounced with a long, generous "ahhhh" in the middle.

"L'espaaahhhhce." That captured, somehow, the vastness of the place much better than Lord's simple, punchy "space."

With Earth receding and the inner worlds looming—at least, in their ICs—the universe seemed bigger, somehow, than it did when he looked out the great reception-area panoramic window of the *Empyrean.*

And there was something else on his mind. The still-growing mass that had been Douglas Cameron was in itself a small, populated world. It was replete with robotic intelligence—or instinct or programming or however one might understand it—but it was an autonomous little island in the cosmos. He understood the need to destroy it, but was troubled by his right to do so.

Is accidental existence no less legitimate than planned forms of life?

That wasn't all. Right now, this vessel was possibly one of the most unique spots in all of creation, the nexus of three species that had originated in three distinct and different cosmic habitats. Unless there was a convention of alien beings somewhere in the universe, this might be a first in the 15 billion years since the big bang.

What kind of ego does somebody need to say, "One of you has to go"? he wondered.

"I think I'm starting to get Stockholm syndrome for the nanites," Lord finally remarked.

His words disrupted the contemplative silence that had settled on the Soyuz.

"Do not become comfortable with their presence, or complacent," Borodin warned. "Though the nanobots inhabit a new breeding medium, they are still in pursuit of us, of the microbe. Would you hesitate to swat mosquitoes or phage bacteria?"

Phagemids were biologically engineered viruses that attacked specific deadly targets, leaving surrounding cells and microbes intact.

"On Earth, I always tried to trap and relocate spiders and mice," Svetlana said.

"I just ignore bugs or shoo them away," Lord said. "As for microbes—you have a point. Survival of the fittest, I suppose. So far, the nanites have shown no discretion. A human body, a cancer cell—they would duplicate them equally. But it is also true that, absent biological matter, they would not perish."

"Just go dormant," Borodin said.

"I believe so," Lord replied, uncertain whether or not that was true. For all he knew, they might rewrite their programming again to build sandcastles on the moon.

"Doctor, are you suggesting that we should house these nanobots somewhere out of the way?" Svetlana asked.

"I am not," he replied. "It's simply a thought, not a recommendation. You're also suggesting this because they're no longer trying to open the hatch of the Soyuz," Lord pointed out.

"That is not untrue," Borodin agreed. "I am relieved and thinking more objectively now."

Svetlana said, "It was also easy to feel sorrow for polar bears before climate change was reversed and they overpopulated, started showing up in the streets of Yakutsk looking for dogs and children to eat."

"That too is fact," Borodin said. "But, you know—polar bears were not offspring of the human mind. I am questioning, as a scientist, if this is a legitimate form of parenting. Throwing our creations into the sun."

"I believe, Doctor, that I may say without contradiction, we are the grandparents of the ugliest child in the history of our species," Lord said.

Svetlana laughed; Borodin scowled. Lord expected the latter and welcomed the former.

"I wonder, Director Lord, if Stockholm syndrome is a practice you depend on."

Even before he heard the translation, Lord knew it was Admiral Ptushko who was asking about the tendency of a hostage to become sympathetic to a captor's cause.

"I never rely on manipulating others to trust me," Lord replied. "It comes naturally."

"Your manner—"

"It's not only that," Lord interrupted. "Other people have an affable nature, some very bad people do, in fact. I happen to believe in what I'm doing and I trust that other people will as well. In my job, that doesn't always mean siding with the cheerleaders of one side over another."

"Noble words," Ptushko said. "Lieutenant, I am informed you were out of communication with us for a time. Is everything all right?"

"Yes, Admiral," the lieutenant replied.

"I am glad to hear that," Ptushko said. "Dr. Borodin, Moscow is eager to know why the robots are tracking the Venusian."

"I have been trying to determine that with my limited resources here," Borodin replied.

Lord thought with sadness, *And there is the first salvo in the discussion about a potential counterweapon made of Venusian DNA.*

The mood in the Soyuz deflated, its inhabitants resumed their previous silence. Lord had considered, then dismissed, asking Ptushko if he could contact Zero-G. If there were something to report, they would have been in touch and Ptushko would have encouraged a response in order to listen.

The trip continued in relative silence and the reclaimed air began to take a toll on Lord's energy levels. He experienced the same drowsiness, once, with a recycled-air scuba system, which is why he only dove once. Something about inert gases minus CO_2 fudging oxygen intake—he didn't understand and it didn't matter. He had to breathe.

Lord turned his IC to low audio, shut his eyes, then slumbered—which was seductively easy to do when one's entire body was floating.

Sometime later, he woke with a buzzing in his ear—a voice. Lord winked up the volume.

". . . are definitely *after* it and growing toward that end!" Borodin was saying.

"How do you know?" Ptushko answered.

"Our acceleration has been carefully charted and it does *not* match the proximity of the nanite mass. Nor do very minor gravitational fluctuations or the impact of solar wind. They are putting all of their efforts into unidirectional expansion."

"Because of your microbe?" Ptushko asked.

"That is my belief," Borodin said impatiently.

Svetlana was calmly piloting on Lord's left. Lord could see her eyes from the corner of his. They were obviously following drop-down data, probably pertaining to both the ship and the frozen, cometized remains of Douglas Cameron.

Since they were talking about the nanites, Lord accessed the rearview camera of the Soyuz. He must have been asleep quite some time: though pieces of ice still clung to the corpse, it was no longer frozen. Lord's first thought was that the nanites had assigned drone status to some of the workers, enough to pincer their way out. That seemed a little advanced—though not inconceivable—and he wondered instead if the freeze had not gone deep enough, if they had simply continued replicating cells well within the body and burst free. Perhaps the nanites had inadvertently released gas trapped in cells and that had expanded.

Regardless of the reason, the size of Cameron's remains had trebled. They looked even less like a human being than before and more like a grotesque parade balloon, draped with crepe. As Borodin continued to talk, the Zero-G director said nothing, just listened. From the exobiologist's tone, something else had apparently gotten his attention.

"Admiral, we know that the microbe is not unicellular and that the flanges have been almost constantly in motion," Borodin went on. "I told you earlier there is a dominant organ in the Venusian that appears to have a reproductive function. I cannot see it here, now, without my equipment, but the ultraviolet oscillations I *am* reading seem to originate from that area of its anatomy. The readings between three hundred and four hundred nanometers are identical with certain species of concupiscent fish on Earth, which makes sense given the environmental similarities between our seas and the opaque, soupy atmosphere of Venus."

"A Venusian mating call," Ptushko said. "Is that what you are describing?"

"Not as such," Borodin said. "It is more like a signal they would recognize from their programming, from working with cells. A signal they would naturally respond to: the sound of mitosis."

"Cell replication . . . has a sound?"

"In an atmosphere as thick as Venus, where sound carries, very possibly," Borodin said. "But that's not what's important now. The fact that the nanites have been so adamant about reaching this specimen suggests that it seems to have what the nanites want: the Venusian's apparent capacity for functional hermaphroditism, the ability to reproduce without the participation of another partner."

Lord finally spoke up. "You're saying the nanites want to find a way to make more of themselves."

Borodin turned to him. "I am."

"And they will succeed in reaching us again—or rather, our engine—before we reach our destination," Svetlana added.

"Can't you do what you did before?" Ptushko asked. "Freeze the mass?"

"Admiral, the nanites have learned," she said.

"In what way?"

"The front of the dead man is still covered with ice," she replied. "But it is a convex surface, consciously—*intelligently*—formed."

"I'm still not—"

"Sir," Svetlana said, "the nanites have shaped themselves a deflective shield."

TWENTY-SEVEN

G ROWING UP, ADSILA was taught that trees and plants have a mystic connection to humans. This was not solely because of the sustenance and shelter they provided but because of their dual connection with the Upper World and the Lower World—areas largely inaccessible to humans. This sacred status is especially true of flora that remained awake for all seven nights of the Creation, which enabled pine, holly, spruce, cedar, and laurel to retain their leaves throughout the year. It also left them blessed with curative powers, making them essential ingredients in Cherokee medicine and rituals.

The circle too was familiar to her through dance and tribal meetings.

Both factors were emphatically present in this vine, and it was not without respect and humility that Adsila laid her flat palms on the exterior tangle. But she also did so without fear, feeling a sudden kinship with the ancient tribal symbols and believing they would continue to serve and protect her.

At first, the contact was little different from another childhood memory, picking up and handling a tumbleweed. Adsila's little hands would slip inside and writhe around and she would actually savor the scratches she received. She pretended that her fingers were little mice, making their way through the brambles.

The vine was not a tumbleweed. She knew that at once as the flesh of her hands tingled and the hairs on her body all rose as though responding to static electricity. It was not the same feeling she had in the zero-gravity areas of the station where hair floated; it felt as though the individual hairs were being pulled in all directions. Each strand on her head seemed to be reaching away from its follicle, but not in the same direction as the vine.

The local nanites are working independent of the others, she thought. *They are focused on me.* That was as far as her thinking went; she was immediately distracted when she heard the bark beneath her hands begin to crackle.

"Adsila, what's happening?"

Carter's voice was not in her IC, it was in her ears. And it was coming closer.

"We seem to be evaluating each other," she said, half-turning but without breaking contact with the vine.

"What do you mean?"

"I appear to have my own autonomous contingent among the nanites," she said. "It's all right—I'll let you know if it isn't."

Carter stopped but remained where he was. Adsila looked back at the vines as she felt her hands being gripped around the sides, as if in a firm handshake. Even in the dreary light she saw that the surface of the vines around her had—*inflated* was the word that came to mind. They had expanded to hold her in place. That was still the nanites working within the foliage; the tiny robots had not migrated to her, as far she could tell.

I have their attention, she thought.

Exhaling and rolling her shoulders, she managed to snuggle closer to the exterior of the ball. She thrust her palms in deeper, and after several moments, the vine puffed around them once more, actually spilling around her thumbs and pinkies and reaching around to the backs of her hands.

"What is it doing?" Carter yelled.

"Growing around me," she said.

"Around just your hands?"

"Yes."

"Incredible. The nanites are marshaling growth in just one small area," Carter thought aloud.

"To keep her there?" McClure asked in the doctor's ear.

"That would be my guess."

"Why?"

"They know her cells, the structure is in their memory."

"I don't like what I'm hearing, Doctor," Stanton said from the outside. "Waters, *get away!*"

"No!" Carter said. "If this works, we may be able to contain them."

"And if it doesn't?" Stanton asked. "Your colleague is at risk!"

"Let me continue!" Adsila shouted back. "If I stop, we have nothing!"

"If anyone can find a way to reach them, it's the EAD," Carter told him.

Stanton did not appear to be sold, not entirely. He ordered for two of his people inside, two with the improvised pikes, to position themselves on either side of Adsila, but standing several steps back.

The Zero-G officer faced the large spheroid, her forehead against it. Her heart was beginning to race as the cracking sound continued inside the network of thick vines. She hadn't bothered to tell Stanton that she couldn't get away without great exertion: the puffed-out segments held her fingers fast. She didn't know why she had put both of her hands forward except that it was a traditional way of making an offering; she wondered if she were subconsciously showing submission.

To an entity that has no consciousness or reason, she reminded herself. The network before her was still a collective of things working as parasites.

And then, in an instant, she was no longer so sure.

Adsila heard a sound she had only experienced once before, and briefly: it was at the death of her great-grandfather Kanuna—the Bullfrog. Perhaps it was because her entire family was present, or because it was the first death the four-year-old had experienced; whatever the reason, when the frail man breathed his last, and his long white hair seemed to rise from the pillow as his head sank within it, she thought she heard the faraway sound of sacred rattles.

"His ancestors welcome him," her grandfather had said through tears. Yet when he spoke it was a separate sound, a sound of the real world. The rattles were not.

Adsila heard something very much like those rattles now, not in her ears but deep inside her head. It was as if her own flowing blood were making the sounds. Except the beats were higher, faster, more like crickets on a close, warm night. She felt something touch her jaw, swell around it; concurrently, she experienced the same rough movement in and around her hair, pulling it firmly, fixing her where she was.

"Adsila!" It was Carter's voice.

She shouted from deep in her chest so he could hear. "I'm all right . . . sensing some kind of—connection? Probe? I don't know. Let this play out."

Her voice penetrated the knitted cybernetic mesh of the vine; she felt the vibration of it against her forehead. She thought she detected a slight increase in the volume of the clicking sounds.

Pincers? Nanites moving over bark? Chatter? *Were the nanobots talking to one another?*

An instant later it became clear that they had taken the bait. They were transferring attention from the vine to Adsila.

They are on my hair.

The tugging on her long hair became more intense: she could now feel countless numbers of individual strands.

The pulling hurt and her scalp began to tingle with electric current. She felt a tickling on her neck, across her earlobes, a faint scratching around the corners of her eyes, moving inward. Those had to be nanites in motion, and she had an idea where they were headed: toward the strongest electrical current in her body, her brain. It was time to do what she'd come for.

With extreme effort, Adsila wrenched free of the vine.

"Are you all right?" Carter asked.

Adsila wasn't sure so she didn't answer. She was taking stock of her body. The hair pulling had stopped but the follicles were still alive. Not her scalp, but dozens of tiny pockets scattered across the surface. The tickling turned liquid and then it was under her skin.

She looked several feet ahead at the vine. The small portions of bark that had erupted to hold her were expanding now, bubbling slowly toward her. Just those segments and nothing more.

"You've overwritten their previous objective," Carter exclaimed. "How?"

"Because they recognized me—"

"It can't be that simple," Carter said.

"That's not my area," she said. "Now that I have access, let's see what they do with this."

Standing there, feeling the tingle in her head sink deeper—focusing on it, measuring it so she would notice any change—Adsila switched to her male form. She experienced the familiar shift of liquid distribution throughout her body, the alteration in her musculature, the subtle changes in her thought patterns—

"They've stopped moving," Adsila said. He took another moment to be sure. "They were active at the top of my head. Now they're not."

"The vine has stopped moving as well," Carter said with cautious optimism. He came closer, craned his neck to the sides. "The nanites appear to have stopped moving everywhere. McClure?"

"Same here," the science officer said.

Carter approached Adsila, once more the physician. "How do *you* feel?"

"Like I'm watching a feather fall," he said.

"I don't follow."

Adsila replied, "I'm all right, I think."

"But?"

"It's the eagle you should be watching."

Carter came around, looked into his eyes with a physician's practiced skill and concern. "Is this caution or something actionable?"

"I don't know."

"Your shoulders are tense," Carter said.

Adsila relaxed them. The subtle tension did not dissipate. It was like what a predator in the darkness or in the canopy of a tree might feel, something the EAD could not see but could sense. He felt that way because if there *were* no danger, the seconds shouldn't be passing as slowly as they were.

Adsila looked from the ominously dormant vine to Carter. The doctor's eyes were still scrutinizing his colleague, his patient, as though there would be some kind of physical reaction, even just a tic—perhaps an unnaturally swirling hair—if the nanites came back online.

"You don't look like you're willing to accept this as finished either," Adsila said with a little laugh.

"You don't know how very, very hard I'm hoping," Carter said, and his face relaxed a little. In fact, the doctor suddenly looked more at ease than Adsila had ever remembered seeing him.

No one seemed to be moving in the Vault, lest they make a sound that might be mistaken for the vine.

A small, shuddering creak came from the vegetal mass. All eyes shot toward it.

"McClure?" Carter barked.

"Nothing here, the nanite's dormant."

The doctor's eyes scanned the vine. "It's settling," he said. "Remarkable."

"What is settling? And remarkable?" Stanton asked.

They'd forgotten about the commander, who was still outside the Vault.

"The nanites created a division of labor, like bees," Carter said. "None of them is working to support the superstructure anymore."

The silence that followed the sound was deeper than that which had come before it. Now no one seemed to be breathing.

There was another snap, then nothing.

Carter looked back at Adsila. "You haven't moved," he said.

"Afraid to," the EAD replied.

"You're not feeling anything from the nanites, are you?"

Adsila shook his head slowly, paying careful attention to his scalp as he did so. "Not a scratch."

Carter started to breathe more easily. So did Adsila.

"Dr. Carter?" Stanton said.

"They appear quiescent," he replied. "McClure, what are the readings in the lab?"

"Currently at -70 megavolts," he said. "High end was +30 mv."

"Displacement scan covers 100 mv," Carter said. "That's the range of human cell activity. They've lost interaction with Adsila."

"But the nanite here, at least, is still functioning."

"Around fifty volts?" Carter asked.

"Fifty-two," McClure said.

"Normal 'search' reading," Carter said, relief in his voice. "It's looking for something to do."

"You mean, searching for its last biological partner," McClure said.

"Exactly."

Adsila heard the two scientists running through the data but he wasn't paying attention. The EAD was looking at the vine, experiencing a wave of calm, of comfort, he hadn't felt before.

It's the crisis averted, he told himself. *You're standing down.*

But even as he thought it, Adsila wasn't convinced that was true. He had a sudden, unusually insistent urge to switch back to his female identity. He felt it as a burning low in the belly, where Ziv's nanites had been located . . . where Carter used some of these very nanites to draw them out.

It was a sense he did not welcome. A feeling that was unfamiliar.

A very real concern that he was losing control of his body.

TWENTY-EIGHT

EAD?"

Dr. Carter's voice broke sharply in his ear. Adsila looked at him. "Yes?"

"Are you all right?"

Adsila nodded unconvincingly. "What . . . what's happening in the lab?"

"It sounds, from what Ed has to say, like the nanites are scanning, trying to locate you," Carter informed him. "They're looking for an exact match to the hair sample, probably just finding pieces."

Adsila nodded. *Pieces,* he thought. *There are always pieces, missing pieces, even when I'm whole.* Adsila didn't know where that sense of loss was coming from. Whenever the pangender shifted, "he" never missed "her" and "she" didn't miss "him." This was something else.

"Adsila?"

The EAD came out of his head and saw Carter again. "I'm feeling drained."

"Understandable. Commander Stanton?"

"Yes?"

"We can use MaGloves to collect and store the nanites now," Carter said.

"Zoey's getting them," Stanton replied.

At the mention of the MaGloves, Adsila smiled lightly, stopped thinking about his body. He had found Magnetic Gloves a challenge during training. They were designed to handle untethered metal objects in zero gravity. The flux was controlled by IC and Adsila found the poles reversed in his male and female forms. It had something to do with the shifting physicality of pangender cells impacting the vector field. The PGA—the Pangender Alliance—had fought to change the science but failed. One could not argue with electromagnetism. Adsila found it a wry matter, and a metaphor for life itself—wherever he went, people responded to him or her differently. It was archaic on the one hand, but perhaps inescapable.

"Except in special relativity," Dr. Carter had told Adsila during final evaluation. "In that case, magnetic and electric fields are merged as an electromagnetic tensor determined by the relative velocity of the observer and charge . . ."

Meaning it would take a quantum physicist to find a pangender unremarkable as anything but a human.

Carter glanced from Adsila to the vine then back. His expression seemed guarded.

"I think it's safe to get you out of here, to get all of us somewhere else," he said. "At least into the greenhouse, where we can get our ICs connected."

The doctor started to pull away but stopped. Adsila was just looking at him.

"What is it?" he asked.

"Doctor, the nanites are behaving . . . aberrantly," Adsila said.

"Yes," Carter agreed. "But what specifically are *you* referring to?"

"I mean . . . about me," Adsila said. "Why are they searching? Shouldn't they have switched their attention to another object by now? Back to the vine, for example—the way they did from the vine to me."

Carter came back toward her. "That would have been my guess, but you apparently have something they want," he said. "Something their new program isn't willing to give up. I'll have to explore that further under controlled conditions. That's why I want to get you out of here."

"I think I still feel that . . . *pull*," he said.

"Dr. Carter, is there something new I should tell NASA?" Stanton inquired.

"Not yet!" Carter replied. He moved closer, his expression showing concern. "How do you feel it, Adsila? Where?"

"The tugging sensation seems to be centered where Ziv's nanites were."

"Just below the navel."

"Yes."

Carter put an arm around the man's shoulder. "Let's get out of here."

"I don't want to go," Adsila said.

"Why?"

Adsila shook his head. "I don't know."

Carter looked back at the vine. It could have been his imagination, but it didn't look quite as wan and wasted as it had a minute ago. "Mc-Clure?" Carter said.

"Doctor?"

"There's a slap box in the cabinet above you, to the right."

"I see it."

"Get me a pouch labeled 53B," Carter said.

"Got it."

The slaps were skin-absorbed patches made of a derma-absorbed saline-polymer medium infused with dosed pharmaceuticals, based on technology found in illegal labs during the War on Narcotics, a "slap-on" patch that provided an efficient, germ-free way of administering drugs.

"Also," Carter said after a moment, "get a gray pouch labeled 65D. About half the size of the others."

"I see that too."

"Abernathy?" Carter went on. "Bring them to the Vault now. I'll meet you at the entrance."

The men acknowledged and Carter turned back to Adsila. The EAD looked at the doctor.

"What is he bringing?" Adsila asked.

"Low-dose ventilated benzodiazepine derivative in case you need to relax."

"A bender?" Adsila said. "Can't I just have a drink?"

"No," Carter replied as he took the officer's pulse.

"Old-school," Adsila said, smiling thinly at the doctor's fingers on his wrist.

"The modern world hasn't stripped me of all my triage training," he said. "You're slightly elevated. For your male aspect, I mean."

"I don't feel tense—not exactly. A little anxious, maybe?"

"I understand. I just want to make sure you stay that way until I can administer localized hydrotherapy. Are you sure you want to stay here?"

Adsila turned to the vine. "I'm afraid to go."

"Afraid? In what way?"

"I feel like I still have control here."

"Of the vine . . . or yourself?"

"I honestly don't know." The question caused Adsila to scowl. "You asked for two slaps."

"Don't worry about it," Carter replied. "All you have to do is concentrate on being present, in your body."

Adsila nodded and sat, cross-legged, on the warm, mushy soil. He straightened his back, shut his eyes, slowed his breathing to a near-meditative state. The EAD accessed the alpha centers of his brain, a traditional state allowing greater internal insight. Solid red flame grew from the darkness and filled the area behind his eyelids. It shaded prismatically through red, orange, yellow, green, blue, indigo, violet—the flame burning high and fierce all the while.

And then the spectrum rose again, faster, climbing beyond red to a silvery-gray region that Adsila had never experienced—

He opened his eyes, looked around for something familiar. His eyes found Carter, looking down with concern. The doctor knelt and grabbed Adsila's shoulders, steadying him.

"What is it?" the doctor asked.

"Gray," the EAD replied. "I've never seen anything gray in meditation."

"Adsila, you have to stay here, stay present," Carter told him. "Look at me."

Adsila fixed his eyes on those of the doctor. He was vaguely aware of the others in the Vault standing back, at a respectful distance, but watching.

"What do you see?" Carter asked.

"Your eyes."

"Talk it out!" the doctor said. "Whatever words come to mind."

"I see your eyes," Adsila said. "Confident. Certain. Brown. Myself. I see myself. I'm distorted . . . in your iris. Black. White. Male. Male. Male?"

"Yes, you're male!" Carter said, gripping Adsila tightly.

"Male."

Adsila fell silent.

"Adsila! *Male!*" the doctor coaxed.

"Male," the EAD repeated, almost in a whisper. He felt the doctor gripping him tightly. Adsila tried to keep his eyes open but they wanted to return to an alpha state . . . the gray . . .

"*Adsila!*"

When his eyes opened again, the EAD was in her female form. She was fully awake, alert, and conscious of the cries and rushing around her. Carter was still kneeling, holding her, yelling something.

". . . go back!" he was saying. "You have to go back!"

Adsila shucked his hands away. She looked past him, saw the vine writhing like some monstrous amoeba, pulsing everywhere, pushing out.

She heard the doctor talking, couldn't make out the words because he had backed away, then left.

Adsila rose with an uncustomary feeling in her chest. A bond like nothing she had ever experienced.

With the vine?

She shook her head. She didn't want this. The nanites were coming alive again in her scalp. They were playing with her electrical impulses, with her cells. She had to change back. She felt herself growing angry, resentful, violated—the way she had when Ziv had infested her.

"Get *out!*" she growled.

She felt herself begin to switch back . . . and then she hit a place she could not pass, as if she had run to the point of exhaustion and could not take another step. She struggled against it but her muscles were too tired to shift. She watched helplessly as the vine sprouted new growth in a burst of vitality.

"No!" she cried as she fought to regain her male identity, failing as tendrils of silver-brown flora exploded toward her.

And then her world went to a new color: black.

Adsila dropped to the rich humus face-first, moments before Dr. Carter arrived with Abernathy in tow. The young agent stared at the monster uncoiling before him, but only for a moment. They had been delayed by an argument with Stanton about bringing another person into the Vault, but the commander had to grant him access: Carter explained that the nanites had control of Adsila, and either Abernathy brought the pouches in or Carter had to come out. Liberated nanites was something Stanton could not risk.

Carter raced ahead and dropped to Adsila's side, motioning impatiently at Abernathy. The vine was uncoiling like an octopus now, pent-up growth surging unchecked.

"Open 65D!" the doctor yelled.

Abernathy checked the pouches, tore open the gray one. Carter snapped his fingers and the agent handed it over.

"Doctor, what are you doing?" Stanton demanded.

"Not your concern."

Stanton read from his drop-down. "You're administering CEDIM," he said. "A combination of conjugated estrogen and diindolylmethane for androgen suppression."

"That's right."

It took a moment for Stanton to realize what Carter was proposing. "Doctor, you're going to force a gender change?"

"Have to."

"Dammit, that is against the law in *every* quadrant," Stanton said. "You do that and I will arrest you."

"Go ahead," Carter said. "If I don't do it, we die." The doctor palmed the slap with an experienced grip and applied it to Adsila's neck. "Have the other slap ready," he told the Zero-G science agent.

Abernathy complied. Both men watched as the EAD convulsed slightly, then morphed like a time-lapse flower into her male identity. The first slap had already been absorbed when Carter applied the sedative. The EAD relaxed into a dreamless sleep.

Beyond them, the vine crackled almost as quickly to a brittle stop. Carter exhaled, breathed, then put a comforting hand on Adsila's shoulder. He didn't know if the young man would feel it, but he hoped so. Then he looked up at Abernathy.

"Let's get him out of here."

TWENTY-NINE

L ORD BRIEFLY CONSIDERED the reality of both a shield created by the nanites, and the fact that the nanites had been smart enough to do that. The admiral's voice in his Glossator snapped him from his reflections.

"Lieutenant Uralov, Moscow is concerned about the Soyuz and its crew," Ptushko said. "They are recommending that you jettison the Venusian specimen."

"No!" Borodin shouted.

"Sir, I believe that is at the extreme end of what we should be considering," Svetlana said.

"They feel that where there is one there are more," the admiral said. "That is not true of the Soyuz. We only have one."

Lord wondered if Roscosmos and NASA were actually being run by the same lunatic brain trust.

"Lieutenant Uralov," Lord said, "in face of the nanites' new threat formation, I respectfully request that you convene a crew meeting."

Svetlana turned to him with surprise at almost the same time as the admiral answered.

"Director Lord," Ptushko replied, "you do not have that kind of authority. You are not a member of this crew."

"I am more than a passenger and I have mission-specific skills," Lord replied sharply. "If there're other qualifications, I'm not aware of them." He looked over at her. "In any case, as I recall your command designation before departure, Admiral, this is the lieutenant's mission . . . her decision. Is it not?"

The prompt brought a noticeable brightening to the pilot's eyes. Ptushko would have to go on the record now either assuming responsibility or not.

"It is her command," the admiral confirmed.

Lord continued to look at her. "Lieutenant? We need all eyes aboard contributing to a solution."

She thought for a moment, then said, "I am concerned about our status. Dr. Borodin, any thoughts?"

"Nothing remotely helpful," he said apologetically.

"All right," Svetlana said. "I would like to hear what Director Lord has to say. Go ahead, Mr. Director."

Lord thanked her, though he felt somewhat guilty: the truth was, he did not have any solutions or even any idea how to find one. What he had was information and he decided to cycle through it.

"We have to rule out any action with the Venusian specimen," Lord said. "If we jettison it, the nanites will pursue it, and probably get it. We may be ceding an entire world to some martial hybrid. And if we destroy it, we don't know what will happen when we get to Venus. It may be in contact with its comrades. Do we want our actions to be considered an act of war?"

"With microbes?" Ptushko said. "That is absurd."

"Several times in our history, plague and flu have nearly wiped our species from the globe," Lord said. "I am being careful, methodical, Admiral."

"You are being absurd," the admiral said. "Those germs were on Earth."

"How do you know they didn't come from somewhere else?" Borodin asked.

"Now *you're* being ridiculous," Ptushko said.

"Director Lord, please continue," Svetlana said.

Lord swore he could hear the admiral's angry breathing. He was proud of the pilot for taking her mission responsibility seriously, not politically.

"Dr. Borodin, is there *any* way to quarantine the nanite?" Lord asked.

"Nothing we haven't tried," the scientist replied. "Certainly not with the technology we have here."

"That's the problem," Lord said thoughtfully—as though he had considered everything that was coming out of his mouth. "We cannot turn around. That would undermine the reason for going to Venus."

"We are near the point of no return," Svetlana said. "Unless there is a specific tactic for returning—"

"There isn't," Lord said. "Not to the *Red Giant.*"

"You will recommend the *Empyrean*?" Ptushko said.

"No, sir," Lord replied. "The nanites have completely taken over Cameron's brain functions, the Mindcuffs broken. Going anywhere inhabited by humans is too great a risk."

"Can they read or even attack our minds?" Borodin asked, suddenly showing concern.

"I do not know," Lord admitted. "And what would we say to them if we could communicate? We do not negotiate with terrorists, so let's table that."

"There is a lot we do not know," Svetlana said, showing a flash of irritation. "What do we *know*? You suggested there might be a plan."

"What we do know," Lord said, "is that the nanites want the microbe. How is that 'want' manifested? What is a biological equivalent?"

"Lust," Borodin said, frankly and unexpectedly.

Lord liked that. "Lust. And how does one deal with that? We use a cold hose, take a cold shower," he said.

"You are being ridiculous," Ptushko said.

"No," Svetlana told her superior. "He may have something. There is a source we can use to bathe them."

Lord leapt ahead of her; he wanted to imply that it was where he was leading the conversation all along.

"You're referring to the omnidirectional Kurs antenna," he said with a knowing smile.

"I am," she said enthusiastically. "We can't hit them with the engine but we *can* wash them with random, conflicting data as to our exact location—local vertical, local horizontal, torque equilibrium attitude—"

"They won't know where we are or how to pinpoint us," Lord said. "In fact, we won't have changed our trajectory at all."

"Brilliant," Svetlana said as she immediately fed a false program into the antenna that controlled the Soyuz–*Red Giant* docking maneuvers. Watching through the rear lens, Lord saw the half-ice mass wobble in their wake. It was not out of control; to the contrary, it was very much in command of its motions relative to whatever beacon it was using; possibly the sun, more likely a star. But it was unable to get a consistent bead on the Soyuz.

"They are no longer closing the gap between us," Svetlana said with quiet triumph. "The nanite mass is holding at its present distance. You've done it."

"*We've* done it," Lord gently corrected. "The onboard team has done it."

Lord made sure to turn to Borodin, smile, and include him in the victory. The Russian smiled back timidly, aware of exactly nothing that he had contributed but appreciating the inclusion.

Ptushko remained aggressively silent.

Tranquility returned to the cabin as the crew relaxed and Lord, in particular, had to acknowledge that the perspiration levels of these undertakings was becoming higher than in his hotdogging days on Earth.

Either it's getting more difficult—which I doubt—or you are holding on tighter than ever to see what's coming, he told himself.

There was some hard truth to that: when there were only war and missions to look forward to, bailing on life was the understood coin of the realm, the price of frontline vigilance, the cost of a ticket to see more of the same as far ahead as you could imagine.

Here? Lord did not want to die en route to another planet. He wanted to see it. And more of what space had to offer.

After the initial flurry of euphoria and enthusiasm had passed, reality set in with a reminder about the place of Lord and every other human in the cosmos. Interplanetary space passed with an almost expository sameness. It seemed to say to Lord, *You are too small, your steps too minute, to notice any change.*

"I piloted a dead-stick shuttle across the surface of the moon," Lord said matter-of-factly after a long but not uncomfortable silence; everyone seemed to be husbanding their own thoughts. "It's different flying when you have a horizon like that."

"I saw the crash landing," Svetlana said. "It was quite remarkable."

Almost immediately she regretted making that comment. She had confirmed that the *Red Giant* had eyes on the moon and the American Armstrong Base. He would have suspected as much, of course, but she did not have to confirm it.

"I think half the Earth saw it in one form or another," Lord said, quickly covering for her. "At least, that's what the GoVerse said."

"What's the 'GoVerse'?" she asked.

"The Government Universe," he said, wanting to "give" her something he knew the Russians already were aware of. "It's a fast, honest forum for the public to critique high-level decision makers. It's anonymous and takes the place of old-style polling, letting officials know where they stood at any given moment. I guess I rate highly enough so that twenty-odd million people had commented on the action within six hours of its happening."

"This goes all the way to the president?" she asked probingly.

"From me on to the top," Lord said. "It creates a matrix for action, interaction, and planning. Who to embrace, who to avoid, what policies are popular, which are not."

"I would be afraid of getting whiplash," she said. "Does anyone stay the course?"

"Sure," Lord said with a twinkle. "People like me, who mostly ignore it."

"Maybe there is something to it," the pilot said thoughtfully. "To having a consensus rather than a mandate."

The last remark was surprisingly pointed, more for Ptushko's benefit, Lord suspected, than for his own.

"Speaking of my command," Lord said, "do you think it would be possible, now, to communicate with my team? Things were not going very well when I left. I'd like to know how they're doing."

Svetlana passed along Lord's request. It was denied.

"What do I have to do to earn their trust?" Lord wondered. "I won't say anything about the microbe."

"It's the paranoiacs' world," Borodin answered. "The rest of us only live in it."

That was true enough. Lord took some comfort in the fact that there was a good team working on the nanite problem. However green some of them were, they would do what was right. Even Carter, and he threw a lot of weight around at NASA. Besides, he was an optimist by nature; perhaps they had already tamed the things and calmed the situation.

There was a small fire from the pitch-and-yaw jets then and a slight adjustment in trajectory. Like a beacon in the distant star field, the orb of Venus rolled into view from the top of the window to the bottom.

"Oh my," Lord said.

Space—their section of it, the solar system—suddenly seemed very near and very familial.

The trip resumed in a reverent, cathedral-like quiet with the ivory light of Earth's twin growing brighter as the Soyuz headed toward it. Lord began to make out the smudgy pale-gray marks of the clouds, still too far to be distinct but darkly present against the whiteness.

Or are those tears in your eyes? he wondered in earnest. Probably both, he decided as he worked the heel of a glove across his left eye.

As Venus grew larger, a message came in from Admiral Ptushko, who ordered that only the lieutenant be party to the call. She blocked translation and had what sounded, at first, like a spirited exchange—one that swiftly became argumentative. It ended, inevitably, with Svetlana going silent, then sounding contrite before signing off.

Now the ensuing silence *was* uncomfortable.

"Did he ask you to leave me there?" Lord asked rather flippantly.

She hadn't turned the translator back on. She asked Lord to repeat what he had said. He did.

Svetlana listened to what he had to say.

She didn't laugh.

THIRTY

HE SOYUZ WAS suddenly like a kitchen where the gas was leaking: no one moved, nor spoke, for long, long moments, for fear of creating a spark.

Finally, Svetlana said very quietly, "We have a scientific base in the atmosphere of Venus, Director Lord. You will be seeing this soon enough. It is an airship design that was assembled robotically and is presently unoccupied. Initially, this first flight was supposed to bring Dr. Borodin and an engineer to test the systems."

Lord listened with interest, despite his concern about whatever new instructions Ptushko had given her. The base explained all the Scud launches: the Russians were ferrying materiel to the second planet. He had to admire them for taking the lead on another world. America's Mars program had stalled as resources were poured into the moon, which was viewed as a more strategic and financially manageable goal.

Though Lord did not for a moment imagine that the Russian project was pure research. Otherwise, his presence might not have caused such apparent distress. He still didn't know how Ptushko planned to resolve that conflict.

"Very impressive," Lord said. "So I ask again: did Ptushko suggest leaving me there?"

"No," she said. "Though you might like that better."

Svetlana's pronouncement came as a shock. Lord didn't expect to be pushed out the hatch and left to die in space. But Ptushko was apparently more disreputable than Lord had imagined: more dirty work, dirtier work, and he'd passed that too, onto Svetlana.

The pilot killed the radio link to the *Red Giant*. "I was ordered not to discuss this with you until later," she said, "but I have too much respect for you to withhold information."

"Thank you," Lord said, though his gratitude was muted with concern.

"It is the admiral's feeling, echoed by Moscow, that after our mission here is ended, we return you to Earth rather than to the *Red Giant*."

Lord wasn't entirely surprised. "Against my will," he confirmed.

"As our guest," she said.

"A euphemism as old as language," Lord complained.

Svetlana did not address the remark; she knew it to be true. "They request that you board the *Kometa*, which will be waiting to rendezvous with us in the upper atmosphere. It is my understanding, sir, that personnel in your government have approved this plan."

Bastards, Lord thought. He had taken the potential danger represented by the CIA and other security agencies too lightly. He had underestimated the powerful friends that the fallen Colonel Jack Franco had in the Defense Intelligence Agency. It was Lord who brought him down, and that was a debt someone felt had to be paid.

My God, it's worse than the gunslinger mentality my pioneer ancestor Isaiah Lord faced in the Old West, Lord thought. *There, at least, you confronted your enemy at high noon and the survivor was having lunch by 12:01.*

It wasn't just the fate of Colonel Franco behind this, the way Lord had crossed the Thin Black Line to take him down. This had been gestating for over a year. The other American intelligence agencies had agreed not to contest the FBI taking the only available space on the *Empyrean*, expecting that Al-Kazaz's choice—fighter pilot and intelligence newcomer Lord—would go there and fail, preventing the FBI from ever regaining a meaningful foothold. He did the opposite and now they wanted him gone.

But accessories to kidnapping?

That kind of collusion flirted with treason. Lord could not believe that even his worst enemies in government would descend to that level. Would the Russians claim that he had defected? Possibly. But that wouldn't prevent Al-Kazaz from creating a firestorm in the White House and in the newtiae. The claim would be tough to document, support, justify.

No, Lord thought. *There is something else going on.* He didn't believe that Svetlana had been told the entire story. He was beginning to form a general idea what the truth might be, but he needed more time and information to flesh it out. He would also need Svetlana's help. He wasn't sure he could ask. If she agreed, it would cost her dearly.

At the moment, there was nothing Lord could do about any of it and there was still an important mission to complete.

It was momentarily difficult for Lord to recapture the sense of wonder he had felt just minutes before, but not impossible. The Earth was retreating and he had to let these problems recede with it. He had been around the track enough to know that setbacks were of the moment and it was his ingenuity, his resources, his experience that would reverse them.

Borodin had been quiet all the while, working out the logistics of using the microbe to draw the nanites back within range, close enough to affix the HR/KGT and blast them toward the sun. It had to happen far enough from Venus so the nanites would not go there, but close enough to the sun so that they would rapidly be immolated.

Svetlana reopened communications with the *Red Giant*, though she had nothing to say to them. The mood in the Soyuz was lower than it had been at any point of the journey. Lord suspected it wasn't just his fate that troubled the pilot but her own role in it. She had been bullied, successfully, again. He wished there were something he could do to help.

"I don't suppose you can tell me more about the Venus base," Lord said. "I mean, it's not as if I'll be able to tell anyone about it."

Svetlana and Borodin were silent.

"Big airship," he said thoughtfully. "Brilliant multipurposing, now that I think of it. I assume it's the same ellipsoid design as *Kometa*?"

"Please," Svetlana said imploringly. "You know I cannot talk about these things."

"Of course not, the chief's ears are listening," Lord said. He smiled and looked out the window. "I'll stop now."

He did, but only to try something that had been working in the back of his mind. Lord made a point of disconnecting the Glossator from the Soyuz with a finger. At the same time, with his eyes he changed the focus of the translating device, and he used a finger to narrow the wedge of the pie-slice icon floating in front of him until the tip was a needle-fine point. Then, pretending to settle into his couch, he pointed that point directly at a bracket on the wall of the Soyuz: the bracket that contained the Venusian microbe.

Then he turned the Glossator audio to full and switched to a category he had never used, one that was situated beyond Farsi and German, Mandarin and native Hawaiian, Hebrew and Swedish.

It was a setting titled, simply, Unknown.

The Glossator was not a general amplifier. It did not take in all sounds and make them louder. It heard only the targeted language and layered on a translation that was louder than the speaker's natural voice, but still within the user's ambient setting. Volume adjustment allowed the listener to play up or down the original spoken language.

Because the Zero-G Glossator was often used for surveillance, Lord employed a setting to filter out the Soyuz and its two occupants. It was similar to what Lancaster Liba used when he was watering plants in the general areas of the *Empyrean* and wanted to hear what guests were saying in a distant corner. The surveillance wasn't legal but the information was often useful.

The audio went silent except for the beating of his heart. Lord filtered that out as well. He heard nothing after that. But he felt, deep inside his ears, the faintest vibration—like the tinnitus he had suffered before undergoing auditory hair transplants in 2045.

Lord typed a command into his IC, fingers poking through the air; he didn't think Svetlana would stop him, since he was not connected to the *Empyrean*. He asked Red to search for patterns in the sound, to explore decibel variation, to pick out any overlays, then asked for the information to be recorded and also displayed visually so the sound would not be interrupted; Lord quietly blessed the SimAI interpretive function that fixed his imprecise fingering.

Ten columns of very long numbers and technical abbreviations began rolling in front of Lord's eyes, like simultaneous stock prices from around the globe. Beyond them were a variety of graphs depicting what the numbers were describing. And hovering in the foreground, brighter and larger, was his exchange with Red.

There are eight separate tones comprising the one, Red wrote in response to his queries. **You can see them overlaid and in motion in Graph Delta. Each distinct tone is continually changing at a pulse width from .001 to .04 seconds. As far as I can determine from the vibrational spread, the points of origin are the eight flanges of the microbe.**

It's communicating? Lord asked succinctly, after taking a moment to process that information. Was each arm, effectively, a *tongue*?

I believe it is, given the recurring patterns in the vibration. And there is more circumstantial support. I am using Interstellar Medium Pulsar Software to measure the sounds. Based on Doppler waveform decay, the signals are traveling just over 25 million miles in a heliocentric attitude. That is our current distance from Venus.

Is anything coming back? Lord asked with trepidation. This was a lot of information to process, quickly.

Give me a few moments to filter out solar interference based on the old Stanford models, Red replied.

Lord waited, unhappy to find that anxiety was suddenly trumping curiosity. He never thought this could happen to him, especially given all the new hardware he'd had to learn when he was flying: but a few years before, as psychiatrists saw more and more people breaking down, giving up, unable to handle technological progress, they had taken to calling the results a "mindshake." This was surely what Lord was feeling, a complete overload on his mental and psychological systems. Not only was he in space and traveling to another planet—which were considerable adjustments for an octogenarian—but he was facing something more than a new and unknown life-form, a potential new civilization.

Shocks that you will nonetheless have to get over very, very fast, he told himself.

The answer from Red was not unexpected. But it was overwhelming.

I believe there is a response, Sam. Way too much of one for me to chart.

What do you mean?

I mean the reply is too large for me to graph.

THIRTY-ONE

AN ANGRY COMMANDER Curtis James Stanton followed hard on the tread of Carlton Carter as they hurried to the Zero-G medbay.

". . . having violated the rights of and accosted a colleague in the service of the Zero-G Division deployed onboard the *Empyrean*, Dr. Carlton Carter . . ."

Carter paid no attention to the reading of the space station's Miranda Doctrine. He was receiving a constant flow of data from Mike Abernathy while at the same time monitoring the status of his patient, Adsila Waters, who was being transported on a canvas gurney being carried by a pair of cargo bay workers. They were the only people available for the detail; the rest of the makeshift Agro staff had remained behind while Zoey Kane used the MaGloves to scan them and collect the nanites. Though not dormant, they were effectively inactive as they searched for signs of the female Adsila Waters. The nanites were going to be deposited in a gallon-size electromagnetic chamber that McClure had brought from the laboratory. The tight membrane sealing rim had been specially designed by Carter for the transport of active nanites: placed inside, they would be able to duplicate material in a remote location—such as skin on a battlefield or a rare blood type—to render timely medical attention.

Adsila Waters was still unconscious due to the effects of agent 53B, chloral hydrate, which was not just a sedative but specifically slowed the activity of the central nervous system—and Adsila's ability to overcome the gender-transforming effects of 65D, which was testosterone cypionate with a cyclopentylpropionate ester booster.

Under normal clinical conditions, Adsila would sleep, as a male, for four hours with the dosage he used. But he was concerned that Adsila's neurological state was far from normal. Whatever was affecting the EAD, whatever link had been established with the nanites, might still be working inside.

Stanton had finished his recitation by the time the small team crowded into the elevator, the stabilizing mesh holding Adsila on the canvas when it was tilted nearly upright to fit. As they rode up, Abernathy contacted Carter.

"Doctor, I'm starting to see very, very low level activity from the nanite here," the science officer said.

"Where is the activity directed?" Carter asked.

"We're getting it here too," McClure added. "Electromonitor on the EC is reading .1 Hz."

"Same here," Abernathy said.

"That's still within search parameters," Carter informed them both. "If it goes above 3.0, then we can start to worry."

Carter noticed Stanton glaring at him when the doors opened. "With all this, you still aren't sure you've got them shut down?"

"That is correct," the biophysicist said. "Just don't forget, Commander, I'm not the one who breached station security and corrupted the Vault."

Carter had meant the remark to be defensive but it came out as accusatory. All that did was inflame the tension that existed between the two men.

"You will be confined to the medbay," Stanton said as they walked down the corridor. "When NASA has declared the situation stabilized, and your patient can be transferred to the care of the station doctor, you will remain in your quarters until transport to Earth can be arranged."

Carter knew that wasn't true: at the very least there would be a jurisdictional struggle between the *Empyrean* commander and Prime Director Al-Kazaz. Being held in stasis here suited Carter: he did not trust NASA to know when the nanite challenge had been met and conquered.

"I've got a .05 uptick here," Abernathy said.

"No change here," McClure added.

"Acknowledged," Carter said. "Abernathy, count out the numbers for me, even if there's no change."

"Yes, sir," the agent replied. ".15, .15, .15—"

"Doctor, are you worried about something?" Stanton asked from behind.

"—.15, .15, .17—"

"McClure?" Carter barked.

"No change."

"—.18, .18, .18—"

The small team reached the Zero-G medbay. Carter entered first.

"Transfer the EAD to that cot," he said, pointing at the nearer of the two as he continued on to the lab.

"It just hopped to 2.11," Abernathy said, his voice registering concern.

Now that he was back in the lab, Carter had a moment to reactivate his IC. The data feed from the nanite floated front and center. Then he turned to the cargo crew and Stanton, who were standing in the medbay.

"Leave, one by one," Carter told them.

"Explain," Stanton demanded.

"I want to know if any of you is triggering this response," Carter said thickly. "Now go! You first!" he said, pointing to Stanton.

The commander turned smartly and stepped into the corridor. "Farther," Carter said.

The numbers climbed to 2.3 Hz.

"Both of you next," Carter told the men who'd been carrying the gurney.

The duo left, single file.

The numbers rose to 2.7.

"McClure?" Carter asked.

"No change . . . wait!" he said. There was a brief silence. "Just jumped another .64."

Carter joined the others in the hall. As he stood there the numbers climbed another .2. That could only mean one thing: the nanites in the laboratory were scanning Adsila for some reason. The doctor faced Stanton.

"Please go to the Vault and wait there," Carter said.

"What's happening?"

"For some reason, the nanites here appear to be responding to Adsila's proximity," he said. "And he to them."

"Even in her . . . his . . . male form," Stanton qualified.

"That's right," Carter replied. "I have to find out why. *You* have to be ready in case the team there needs a leader."

There was a generous, complimentary quality to the remark and Stanton seemed momentarily appeased. He nodded.

"Good luck, Doctor," Stanton said, then turned to the cargo bay crew. "With me," he told the men as he walked briskly back to the elevator.

Carter went back to the lab. The numbers had gone to 3.54 Hz. Abernathy's young face looked older, and pale. The doctor brought up the virtual image in the transmission electron microscope. He felt as though he'd been hit in the chest.

"It's not scanning anymore," Carter said.

"But the numbers are above—"

"It's active," Carter interrupted the agent. "The damn thing is back to being operational."

"The nanites here are rising too!" McClure said.

"Stay there," Carter informed him. "I need educated eyes-on."

"Yes, sir," the senior agent replied.

Carter leaned his head into the medbay, saw Adsila still in male form. He ducked back into the lab. "How are you doing this?" he said to the nanite. His brain racing, the biophysicist felt sick as he careened into the answer.

"They must know who Adsila is," Abernathy said, speculating aloud.

"They do," Carter replied.

"How?"

He said, "When I pulled these nanites from the EAD, it was in Adsila's male form."

THIRTY-TWO

ORD DECIDED TO say nothing about the audio-visual display he had just experienced with the microbe.

It was difficult—as a human, not as an American—to refrain from sharing the awe that filled him, to deny his cabin-mates the opportunity to hear the greatest symphony ever conceived.

Disconnecting from the microbe, Lord could not help but wonder, now, if Pythagoras had somehow heard Venusians—or others?—conversing when he first posited the existence of *Musica universalis*, the Music of the Spheres, more than 2,500 years ago. It was remarkable—indeed, prophetic. The mathematician had written that interplanetary sounds would be manifest in exactly the three qualities Lord had just witnessed: in numbers, visual depictions, and sounds.

Over the years, those critics who accused Lord of being self-impressed, cocky, never understood that, like his cloud-piercing Vampire, ego had a ceiling. To any open eyes and minds, the vast world, the deep universe, the unprecedented deeds of giants like that ancient Greek, were rich enough and mighty enough to bend *any* knee in humility.

But, as humble and expansive as he felt, Lord was also very much present and in a modified survival mode. He was being held by an enemy he knew he must somehow escape. Information was power and, for the moment, he had a head start on his companions—and, thus, on Admiral Ptushko.

Ptushko, he thought, the very name making him feel as though he'd just base-jumped from the heights of Olympus into a curbside trash can. Lord not only intended to get out of this snare but put the admiral in one.

Lord heard communications, in Russian, between Svetlana and Borodin. Obviously, the Zero-G director was now to be cut from crew chatter as well.

Borodin began to check the joints on his space suit.

"Mr. Director, we are nearing the disengagement coordinates," Svetlana said suddenly. "Please secure your suit."

"Is there anything I can do to help?" Lord asked.

"Thank you, no."

Lord checked his suit, made sure the helmet was secure, determined that the visor seal was one hundred percent. Then he raised the tinted amber polycarbonate. Svetlana was busy so he turned to Borodin.

"May I ask how you intend to attach the device to the nanites?" Lord said.

"Lieutenant Uralov is calculating a small pivot to slow the Soyuz," Borodin said. "When she executes the maneuver, it will hurl the nanite mass forward."

"At an extreme rate of speed," Lord pointed out.

Borodin shook his head. "It will not," the scientist said, indicating his IC. "We worked it out in simulation. At just a .04 angular shift of the Soyuz, the mass will continue forward at a manageable rate."

"Can your jets execute that fine a—"

"Not jets," Borodin said. "Gravity. We vent a small amount of air from the pressure release valve, change our position relative to the sun, and *it* will pull us into the turn." He patted an empty pocket on his arm. "If I miss the first pass I will have the microbe with me as insurance—to turn them back in our direction."

"Impressive," Lord said. He liked seat-of-the-pants flying as much as the next pilot, though there were a lot of moving parts to this maneuver.

Lord pointed to the HR/KGT unit floating above the scientist. "How will you attach it?"

The exobiologist used a finger to turn the weightless device around, revealing a six-inch-by-two-inch strip.

"I've affixed a silicone adhesive patch," Borodin said. "The heat and radiation will not degrade the bond until the mass has been caught in the outer corona of the sun. By then, the body will have burned away and the nanites will be scoria."

Once again, the Russian scientist was not wrong—in theory. Unlike other forms of adhesive, silicone would find purchase on the ice, biological material, or nanites. The maneuver should work as he described.

Lord watched as Borodin began blinking, obviously running the plan again in IC simulation. The Zero-G director did not know if this was a good plan, but he did not have a better one.

Venus glowed brightly from time to time as the Soyuz moved toward it, slight adjustments in trajectory sometimes shifting the planet away from the small viewport. When it was there, the cabin filled with a ghostly pale glow, like vivid moonlight. The cloud-shrouded world itself was a dull pearl hanging in space, a nearly uniform off-white color with faintly darker, slightly tawny bands in the high northern hemisphere and around the southern pole. Lord could not help but think of those clouds bustling with life. He felt sorry for Borodin, whose life's work this was, having to busy himself with the nanites at this point. He wondered if the man would be approaching the world scientifically, philosophically, romantically, or all three.

Impossible not to, Lord decided.

"Five minutes to decompression," Svetlana announced. "Go on internal oxygen."

Lord used the universally color-coded panels in his IC to trigger the process.

The suits were plugged into the Soyuz by hoses attached to the seat.

The software was automatically read by the wearer's IC, which interfaced with both the suit circuitry and the ship. Borodin was in the only seat with an extension hose, since it would be necessary for him to partially exit the craft. The pilot and Lord were fastened to the craft with crisscrossing chest harnesses so they would not be thrust upward by the depressurization. Borodin was hooked to his seat by rubber alloy bands. Like the hose, the straps were long enough to allow him to stand upright.

For a fleeting few moments, Lord felt as though he were back in a pressure suit in a fighter cockpit. Then, of course, he was in control of his environment. Now—

Though shut in layers of fabric and mylar, his vision filtered, hearing limited, touch effectively gone, Lord did not feel alone. Even if he could no longer hear the Venusians, he knew they were out there and listening. Were they also thinking? Or were they creatures of pure instinct? What could they do besides "vibrate" at one another, still tens of millions of miles from Venus?

"One minute to decompression," Svetlana said.

The Soyuz turned and the sun flared brightly through the capsule, like the eye of a giant opening slowly.

"Thirty seconds."

Borodin removed the microbe container from its holder and slipped it into a pouch on the arm of the suit. He carefully patted the Velcro strip closed. Then he plucked the floating HR/KGT unit from above him and peeled the polymer strip from the adhesive. Newer silicone compounds were activated by IC interface and target proximity, but the Russians had not upgraded to the newer versions: they had stockpiled tons of the original adhesives during the silicon shortage of 2046 and were still working through it. That was right before NASA started mining the element from lunar regoliths and preparing vast quantities cheaply with recycled reactants rather than coal.

"Fifteen seconds."

Lord switched to his IC camera interface, saw the misshapen, icy mass that was once a living man. It looked like an ancient hunter who had been frozen in a glacier for thousands of years, scraggly from top to bottom, back to front, alternately bloated and emaciated as he was exposed to the furnace of the sunlight.

Borodin reached up with his left hand while he tucked the propulsion unit against the ribs on his right side. The hatch would pop automatically at zero, opening to the back of the craft: it would serve as something of a shield for him if the nanites hurried forward.

"I wish I'd had time to rehearse this," he said quietly.

"It will all fall into place," Lord assured him.

Borodin looked over and smiled thinly at Lord before turning his attention back to the heavy, curved doorway overhead. Lord could hear him breathing heavily, which was understandable. As long as he didn't hyperventilate. Lord knew that at the very least Borodin had space-walked before. Since the *Red Giant* was so old and in need of overhauls, extravehicular training was mandatory for everyone who lived there. They never knew when a seal or joint might break and their lives might depend upon it.

There was a hiss as the hatch opened, and then an audible rush of air as Borodin stood on his seat and pushed it wider. He turned and faced the rear of the Soyuz construct, staring out over the long girder-like rectangle that contained the power generator. He could just see the top of the nanite mass behind the outward curve of the capacitor banks.

"Preparing to vent—now," Svetlana said.

If the illumination hadn't begun to shift slightly inside the cabin, Lord would not even know they had turned. Somewhere, gas had begun puffing in the smallest whispers through an external port. Lord continued to watch the camera feed.

"The mass is not moving," Borodin reported. "Not moving . . . not moving . . ."

And then, suddenly, it did.

The remains of Douglas Cameron did not thrust forward as planned: it came apart in several dozen small pieces, all of them flying toward the hatch from all sides, like a meteor swarm.

"God!" Borodin screamed as the nanite-driven projectiles flew toward him. "They are *separating* themselves!"

Lord did know whether the nanites had been planning this assault the next time the microbe appeared, or whether they had spontaneously, opportunistically seized upon it. It didn't matter. The Zero-G director rolled to his side as far as his restraints would permit, and grabbed the black, springy straps that were holding Borodin to the sides of his seat. He yanked the weightless man down, the HR/KGT slipping from under his arm and tumbling away as he struck the hatch on his way back down.

"Lord, stop!" Svetlana yelled. "You've doomed—"

She was cut off as the hail of nanite-biomatter started striking the Soyuz, causing it to ring loudly. Lord scrambled over the disoriented Borodin to try to shut the door but the scientist was still partially outside. Several of the projectiles struck the Russian, penetrating the outer layers of his suit.

"Help me! *God, help!*" he screamed.

Lord reached up and grabbed the arm with the pocket that held the microbe and pulled that sleeve down, inside, causing Borodin to come with it. Lord thrust the arm toward Svetlana.

"Grab it!" the American screamed.

Svetlana didn't hesitate, holding it so Lord was free to try to reach the scientist's neck and head and pull them through the hatch. Lord had just gotten his fingers around a shoulder strap when a nanite mass struck the faceplate hard, right below the forehead seal.

The visor cracked, burst outward, and Borodin's face went with it. He was dead before he could even voice a scream, his flesh freezing, eyes popping from the pressure imbalance, mouth locking in a grimace as his saliva turned solid.

Lord turned away from the hatch, looking down, fumbling with the dead man's sleeve to get at the microbe container.

"Let him go!" Svetlana cried, leaning over to release the scientist's straps.

"No, we need the microbe!" Lord cried.

The pilot managed to release the magnetic hooks while the lumpy nanite *things* continued to pelt the Russian's body, several of them landing in his eye sockets, others merging with icy blood and bits of skin and muscle that were stuck inside what was left of the visor. There was no chance to save the body but, fortunately, the nanites were not able to make quick turns to dive inside. His thickly padded fingers finally opened the pocket and removed the microbe.

"Here!" Lord said, thrusting it toward Svetlana.

She took the microbe and hugged it toward her while Lord shoved the dead man through the hatch, his muscle memory feeling as though he were loading a washing machine back on Earth. Borodin floated free, his arms twisting as if performing some obscene T'ai Chi maneuver, and Lord pushed off the hatch, moving back down to his couch as Svetlana auto-closed the hatch.

The gong of the nanite horde continued to ring, but only for a few moments. Then it was silent.

"They're going to re-form around him, aren't they?" Svetlana asked.

"That would be my guess," Lord said. He looked up, tried to see the man's remains through the hatch. But Borodin had drifted off toward a blind spot, even for the cameras.

Ptushko, who had been listening, asked what had happened. Svetlana told him. He received the news without comment and said he would get back to her. Lord did not know whether or not the pilot had intended to let him hear all of that. He had been where she was now: the way she looked and sounded, nothing seemed to matter.

"There was no way you—we—could have anticipated that kind of attack," Lord told her. "This is a new kind of enemy, far more resourceful than I imagined."

"I know that," Svetlana said. She did not appear shaken; just contemplative. "Nonetheless, Dr. Borodin is gone and we've failed."

"Not necessarily," Lord told her.

She glanced at him, not with hope but with a hint of curiosity. "You know something," she said accusingly.

"About what just happened? No," Lord said. "But there's a reason why I wanted to get this." The Zero-G director pointed at the container Svetlana was holding.

"How can that help us?" she asked.

Lord replied, "Let's find out."

THIRTY-THREE

ED MCCLURE STOOD transfixed in the Vault, waiting for the unseen nanites to return to visible functionality. For the science officer and everyone else around him, there was nothing to do *but* wait: they couldn't leave, since there might now be operational nanites on them, and they weren't able to react to a vine that was still apparently dormant. Using the MaGloves was dangerous, since it would draw the small robots to him, with potentially lethal results.

As he looked out at the gnarled, massive obscenity in the center of the Vault, Ed McClure had a flashback to sitting in his pastor father's church, listening to him read from Matthew 13:38. *The weeds are the sons of the evil one.*

The gospel had not been referring to actual weeds, but the metaphor certainly fit. Especially with the humidity in the greenhouse and the roiling sun he knew was just outside the great windows.

The tangled vine popped—suddenly and loudly and in all directions, including down. That gravity-directed thrust actually raised it from the ground on thickened vines, causing the vine to seem even larger. The expansion sounded like a series of sharp whiplashes, one after the other, some overlaid, as the nanites resumed their programming.

"I heard that," Carter said from the lab, only the audio making it through the hastily rigged feed.

"It just pushed out in six directions!" McClure marveled. He and the others stepped back from the growth, all the way to the outer wall of the Vault.

"That probably won't last," Carter replied. "The nanites are just coming back online—getting their bearings, reestablishing their new program parameters. Let me know as soon as you can tell which way it's headed."

"How does that help us?" Stanton demanded from the Drum.

"If they're seeking Adsila, we may have some control," Carter replied. "Grainger, try again to reach Lord, tell the *Red Giant* it's urgent."

"Yes, Doctor."

"Doctor Carter, will the Agro Slammers hold that thing if I drop them?" Stanton asked.

"They won't go in that direction," Carter replied. "There's nothing out there they want. McClure, keep the pikes ready to turn the new growth."

The science officer motioned toward the ad hoc team. There was fear in every face but resolve in the set of each shoulder, in every arm. "We're ready," he said.

"*Red Giant* regrets that the Soyuz is not available," Grainger reported.

"Is that Chinese death ray still out there?" McClure asked.

The question wasn't serious but the relieved chuckles in the Vault were. The Zero-G staff was growing increasingly concerned about the silence of their director, and the void and distances in space—even in local space—had never seemed as insurmountable as at this moment.

"At least the replication hasn't sped up," McClure remarked as time passed and the vine remained unchanged.

"I don't see how it can," Carter said. "The processes require chemical reactions that cannot just 'happen faster.' There's also less raw material in the Vault than there was before."

"I don't know, Doctor," McClure replied.

"What do you mean?"

"We're here," the science officer replied ominously.

Three minutes passed and then the vine grew again.

"It's moving!" McClure shouted as a massive tendril punched from one side, the side ninety degrees from McClure and the other workers, and stretched out like a lance, falling slowly to the ground as the near-Earth gravity tugged at it. "It moved toward the side wall . . . the elevator side."

"How big is the tendril?" Carter asked.

"About four feet," McClure replied.

"No other eruptions?"

"None."

"The damned thing is putting all the nanites to work in one direction," Carter said.

"Go to work!" Stanton ordered the workers.

The team moved forward with their improvised tools, McClure staying back to watch the rest of the vine.

"Abernathy—overlays?" Carter asked.

The agent replied almost at once. "It's moving toward us now, not the Soyuz."

"It can't be just familiarity with Adsila," Carter said. "It's more familiar with the vine!"

"It has to be pangenderism," Abernathy said.

"Reasonable, but not the whole story," Carter said. "That may just be a means to an end."

"A means to what 'end'?" Stanton demanded.

"I'm starting to think that the nanites want to be alive."

"You mean, themselves?" Stanton asked. "As in, *they* want to live?"

"Yes."

"But how did they even conceive of that?" Abernathy asked. "They're not SimAI. They aren't self-aware."

"Not as we know it, but this may be a very strong, energetic, *electric* reaction," Carter said. "The nanites could be responding strictly to a heightened vibrational setting they've experienced, one that briefly caused increased productivity—which is, after all, their basic program.

Abernathy, look at the frequency of the nanites that were exposed to Adsila previously."

"When was this?" Stanton asked.

"Sorry, I'm not free to say," Carter told him.

"You're right," Abernathy replied. "It's the same as they are showing now."

McClure was listening. He did not have to add what Carter and Abernathy both knew: that the nanites were not only familiar with Adsila Waters on a cellular level, they had been sent specifically to remove Ziv's nanites from inside her—from inside his—reproductive organs. They had experienced a kind of signal that was superior to their own and naturally sought that upgrade.

"So from that time, the nanites have equated faster vibration and enhanced functional abilities with the electrical signature of propagation," Abernathy said.

"Very possibly," Carter said. "But my original programming didn't allow them to act on that stored data."

"But there are no fail-safes now," Abernathy said. "They picked up the signal, realized that if they control Adsila they acquire both genders. And then—"

Abernathy stopped, as though he were afraid to articulate the rest.

"The nanites make male and female duplicates of the EAD and use them to reproduce the hybrid nanite-humans," Carter said. "It's a premature and very unformed thesis, but that could very well be it."

"Is that what I'm supposed to tell NASA has been going on?" Stanton asked. "That you've created Pinocchio? And he's in heat?"

"Again, Commander, I created microscopic robots," Carter said. "Defective hadrons did the rest."

McClure was still processing what he'd heard when the vine erupted again, sending a long, sharp spike from the farthest end of the previous growth. Like the earlier extensions, it grew from the point that was most distant from the center of the vine, not from the now-turned tip of the fresh limb. It was a net gain of nearly three feet for the nanites.

"An update from NASA," Stanton said. "They say we should burn or electrocute each new growth."

"I already did the incendiary simulation, sir," Abernathy replied. "We'd be putting six hundred twenty liters of bad air, per second, into a filtration system designed to handle less than half that. And we don't have sufficient water in here to douse ancillary burning due to sparks."

"NASA studied the data too, I'm sure, and decided the current danger is more severe," Stanton said.

"We are not at that point yet," Carter said. "I'm still studying the nanite response."

"As for electrocution," Abernathy said, "there is no guarantee the charge would remain in the tree—not with the humid environment and complex root system. And if it shorts the Vault, growth could accelerate in the fuel-rich contents of the greenhouses."

"Look, NASA does not want the vine killed and I'm not hearing any alternatives!" Stanton yelled.

"Why don't they?" Carter demanded.

"Because they do not feel that all options have been explored and—"

"They do not want program funding cut," Carter said. "They do not want the project delayed. They do not want to have to go back to Congress and explain this."

"Not your problem, not your call," Stanton said. "I want options from the man who built the thing!"

"Here's one," Carter replied thoughtfully.

"I'm listening," Stanton said impatiently.

After a moment, Carter said, "Give the nanites what they want."

THIRTY-FOUR

SVETLANA HAD RESUMED the course to Venus, piloting by rote, pursuing a flight plan that no longer seemed to have merit or urgency. Neither she nor Lord had to look outside the Soyuz to know what was happening. Somewhere along its expansive length, the creature that was nominally Dr. Borodin was being cannibalized and reconstructed by the nanites.

Lord had been where she was now, losing a colleague on a mission. He knew the hit was hard and, as reality settled in, the aftermath was worse. As the seconds passed and the event became more remote, the desperation to reach back across the minutes—mere minutes!—to change the result became stronger. The shock waves were still resonating, you were still in the zone, and then, suddenly, the ripples died and it was gone. You were alone, except for the awful weight of failure.

The Zero-G director gave the pilot a few minutes to get her feet under her. He couldn't see her eyes but he could hear her breathing. He waited for the trembling sound he knew was the emotional dam breaking.

That was when he raised a hand and caught the woman's eye and indicated for her to cut her feed to Ptushko.

"Why?" she asked.

"It's important," he replied.

Numb, but without additional discussion, she killed the link to the *Red Giant*. She turned to him but said nothing.

"I want you to hear something," he said. "Red? Play back most recent Glossator recording."

"You *did* spy on us?" she charged.

"Hold, Red," he said, and turned to Svetlana. "Does it never stop? The suspicion?"

"Typical," she said angrily. "Blame the victim."

"I'm not blaming, or accusing, *or* spying," he replied. "We are sitting here with the greatest scientific discovery since fire and—do you realize we don't know how old our guest is?"

"Your gift for shifting focus is impressive," Svetlana said. "You wanted me to hear something?"

Lord loosened his harness so he could face her. "Yes, but first I want you to hear *this*. We may be hosting a life-form hundreds, maybe thousands of years old. It may have been alive before there was a United States or Russia or a single human being that didn't live on a tree limb. In the face of that, maybe you can retain your geopolitical polestar and cynicism, but I cannot."

The woman was listening but he could not tell if she was hearing him. He also knew that the impediments were greater than they would have been an hour before: a loss like this left you wanting to lash out, to doubt everything, to *hate*, and he was the only target.

"Earlier," Lord went on quietly, "I turned the Glossator on the Venusian life using software that is decades beyond what your unit possesses. I recorded the result and analyzed it so I could share it—with you, with Ptushko, with NASA, with anyone who wants to hear the sound of a living, vital universe and not the croaking of a struggling, hoarse humankind. What I want you to listen to, Svetlana, is this microbe apparently communicating with other microbes on Venus."

The pilot's attitude changed, as if the weight of a living world suddenly bore down on her from its close, silent orbit.

"Is there . . . language?" she asked.

"Not that I could understand," he replied. "I've kept recording and—incredible as it may seem, there are definitely patterns to the tone and colors of the contact." He forced a small half-smile. "Listen now?"

She nodded.

"Red, resume," Lord instructed the SimAI.

The sounds he had recorded filled their ears and the graphs filled the space where their visors would have been. The Soyuz was alive with fellowship—and, this time, Lord no longer felt as if he was on the outside looking in. The shared experience bonded him to Svetlana, to the world outside and closing, to the possibilities inherent in action that was devoid of boundaries and old hatreds and suspicions.

Now, for Svetlana, the tears came. She raised a gloved hand to touch the numbers and bars, to be part of the exchange in some tactile if ephemeral way.

"Tibetan singing bowls," she said almost joyously. "That's what it's like. My mother brought some home from Nepal, played them for me when I was a girl. They . . . elevated me, joined us."

Red dropped a visual into Lord's IC of ancient brass and alloy bowls, with a wand that was run around the rim to create magical sound and visceral healing. The universality of the similarity between these two forms of sound, of music, brought tears to his eyes as well.

Svetlana's hand came down and grasped Lord's. "Thank you," she said.

"You're welcome," he replied.

Svetlana turned her eyes toward the window. Her face was washed in the pale glow of the second planet.

"We were going there to turn the lights on," she said. "Dr. Borodin knew what to do when we reached the station."

"I'm sure the *Red Giant* can brief you," Lord said. "They obviously intend for you to complete the mission. You have not been recalled."

"No," she agreed. "Not yet."

The glow passed, along with Svetlana's briefly uplifted mood.

"What is the name of the station?" Lord asked.

"Lomonosov," she replied.

Lord's drop-down identified the honoree as Mikhail Lomonosov, an eighteenth-century astronomer who discovered the atmosphere of Venus.

"I suspect that will be changed now," Lord said.

"Yes," Svetlana agreed.

The two surviving members of the crew fell into reflection as Svetlana piloted the craft and communicated routine data with the *Red Giant*. Most of that was about Venus, readings that would broaden Roscosmos's understanding of the world and help to chart the movement of the space laboratory. Apparently, they were getting only rudimentary data, which did not include albedo, precise speed, and other orbital data. What Lord could ascertain was that the *vozdushnyy korabl*, the airship, was in a geosynchronous orbit around the planet's equator, turning retrograde with the world and matching its long orbital day of 5,832 hours. It hovered high in the Venusian thermosphere, at 202 miles, where it was able to utilize the sun for power and retain altitude with a minimum of lift.

It was an incredible achievement, especially in that the pieces were launched and assembled robotically.

Another request to communicate with the *Empyrean* was denied, and Lord was convinced more than ever that the refusals had nothing to do with Russian protocols. Nor did the orders that Svetlana had received.

Further analysis and reflection were interrupted by a startling and unfamiliar sound in Lord's IC. It was like corn popping loudly in both ears, and was followed by an image that he hadn't seen since childhood: video snow.

"Are you seeing that?" Svetlana asked, shouting to be heard over the din.

"I am," Lord told her.

The two killed their ICs and looked around, searching for a leak in the Soyuz or sparking circuitry, something to indicate a catastrophic failure that might be affecting the electronics and their ICs. There was no hissing, no scratching, nothing amiss. They looked at each other.

"Are we still on course?" Lord asked.

"Nothing has been affected," Svetlana replied.

"Could it have come from the planet?" he wondered aloud.

The pilot didn't answer. She couldn't.

Lord exhaled loudly. He did not like anomalies that had no immediate explanation other than *This is new*.

"Turning IC back on," he announced.

Svetlana nodded and did the same.

Lord had been half-expecting to see that the glistening snow had coalesced into Venusian microbes, floating in the dense atmosphere and reaching him by some great effort of vibratory mind. That was not what he or Svetlana saw.

The destroyed features of Dr. Gavriil Borodin appeared in their ICs. The mechanics of the engine were behind him, his ice-covered skull was still inside the helmet, the suit still relatively intact. Patches of sinew and splotches of frozen blood clung to the lower portion of what was once a face, including the remnants of lips.

"Dear God," Svetlana said.

But the horror was not just visual: the mouth was attempting to form an ugly semblance of motion.

"What is causing that?" she asked. "There are no muscles remaining—"

"There are nanites with pincers," Lord said.

The Glossator extrapolated a word from their movement and Red translated. Lord felt the kind of nausea he hadn't experienced in decades.

"*Is* he speaking?" Svetlana asked, hearing the SimAI answer in English.

"Apparently," the Zero-G director replied. "He said, 'Alive.'"

THIRTY-FIVE

WHAT DO YOU mean 'give them what they want'?" Commander Stanton asked Dr. Carter.

The Drum of the *Empyrean* had only a skeleton crew as its staff worked other jobs to keep the very short-handed station operational. The command center was a squat, wide cylinder located in the zero-gravity center of the *Empyrean*. Commander Stanton and his officers were able to move easily between stations, with only the wedge being off-limits. That was where officers Lajos Beck and Zoey Kane ran NASA's top-secret Space Intelligence Corps.

Only Beck and Stanton were present now, Kane having returned to the Agro Center to act as intermediary between the personnel inside and the Drum.

Stanton was in constant contact with NASA. High-ranking, security-cleared officials in Houston and Cape Canaveral were able to hear the exchanges between Stanton and Carter; Stanton did not know whether it was the extreme nature of this crisis or an unspoken loss of faith in his ability to command after the Dragon's Eye debacle that now had multiple authorities listening to every word.

Carter's suggestion was not immediately dismissed by the space agency, which alarmed Stanton. The idea of potentially turning a human being over to the nanites and their construct was sickening. Most of the

NASA scientists Stanton had met were not bad people, but they were committed to the expansion of a human presence in space. By definition, that meant risking lives.

"What I mean," Carter explained, "is that Agent Abernathy has been monitoring the electronic output of what I'll call the nanites' operational command nexus in the vine. The human brain runs approximately 1,016 synapse operations every second. That's ten times the amount the nanites are performing."

"Meaning?"

"Bear with me," Carter said. "Each of those operations requires five times ten to fifteen joules. The nanites' molly batteries generate one-fiftieth of that. NASA, are you running those figures?" Carter asked.

Stanton ignored the taunt. "Your point?"

"Adsila can certainly outthink and out process the vine," Carter said. "I'm suggesting that we do what we were doing before: plug her back into the malignancy."

"Won't that expose her to the nanites?" Stanton said. "They can get to her brain."

"That's exactly right," Carter told him. "That's the point. Once there, we run the risk that they take charge of her brain, her body. The alternative view, our view, is that she can control them, fight them. In short, you create a CHAI, without big shiny new bones and joints, but with microscopic robots that can infest and duplicate cells."

"Is she still sedated? Has she—volunteered for this action?" Stanton asked.

"I know her," Carter said. "She will. But before I wake her and ask, I want to know that there is no other option."

"NASA does not discuss their plans, you know that," Stanton said.

"I know," Carter replied. "In which case, I will not present this very risky option to Adsila Waters."

Stanton disliked this game of brinkmanship with the *Empyrean* as a pawn, and he found himself increasingly, actively disquieted by option. He had a bad feeling that NASA would accept it. Even now, he imagined that their CHAI research head was being conferenced into the discussion.

"Is such a CHAI hybrid reversible?" Stanton asked.

"I don't know," Carter admitted. "My goal is to take the nanites' attention away from the vine, put it on Adsila, and buy us time to find out."

A text appeared in an open eyes-only folder of Stanton's IC:

Inform him that NASA is considering it. Wake EAD Waters.

Stanton felt ill. Regardless of what NASA might think in consideration of Adsila possibly agreeing to becoming a guinea pig, the commander was horrified by the option.

"I want to talk to the EAD," Stanton said.

"We'll be expecting you," Carter replied.

Stanton's trip to the smaller of the *Empyrean* medbays was a blur: confusion and anger at Carter for suggesting this, deeper resentment at NASA for even considering it, and disgust with himself for being complicit in the process. He did not understand how, in just a few short weeks, this brilliant assignment, this position in the high frontier, this dream command had turned to ash.

He entered the small room and found Carter standing beside a gurney where Adsila was still sedated, a new slap patch on the inside of his elbow. In the laboratory beyond, Agent Abernathy was working furiously on his IC—eyelids blinking, fingers darting.

There was something calm, almost smug about Carter's bearing.

"What is this?" Stanton demanded.

Carter put an index finger at a temple and rotated his hand—the universal sign for killing an IC.

Stanton obliged.

"What's going on, Doctor?" Stanton asked—more civilly now. He regarded the man for a moment. "You never intended to offer Adsila as a CHAI, did you?"

"Of course not," Carter replied. "I'm a doctor, not an assassin."

Stanton didn't realize he was holding his breath until he released it. "I'm glad to hear you say that. Very glad. Then why am I here?"

"Because we've hit a wall, but I do have a plan," Carter said. "You see, however we try to get back into the nanites' control programs, we fail. There are no links. No back doors. The accident has corrupted their system in a way we cannot even *deduce* because we do not operate at the level of hadrons, defective or otherwise. The only way of getting to them is through a direct plug-in using something they want."

"I thought you just said—"

"I don't need Adsila," Carter assured him.

"Then I don't understand."

"You have to let me back in the Vault," Carter said.

"To do what?"

"To destroy the vine," Carter replied. "Reduce it to dust."

"NASA has already shot that idea down."

"It's the best option I'm aware of," Carter said. "Unless you tell me what they're planning."

"You know I can't do that," Stanton said. "Besides, even if they permitted that, the nanites would still be operational, would they not? Wouldn't they still seek a new medium—migrate from there to here in search of Adsila?"

"That last part is correct," Carter agreed. "But I've got Agent Abernathy working on a Trojan Horse that will hopefully kill that programming."

"Hopefully?"

"We have seen that the artificial evolution of the nanites has created a goal-oriented SimAI, and that goal is expansion," Carter said. "I think there's a blind spot."

" 'Hopefully,' " Stanton said. "You 'think.' NASA says we have about forty-five minutes before the situation in the Vault becomes critical. I cannot authorize time spent on more guesswork."

"Respectfully, let me be the point man on that—not you, not NASA."

"Dr. Carter, you are way outside your authority *and* mine."

"Commander—Curtis, we cannot corral this beast," Carter said.

"The nanites are mutating on a subatomic level and we are not able to get ahead of that. What does NASA have to offer?"

"They're still working on the problem," Stanton said. "Their scientists want more time."

"Is that why they're considering my plan to sacrifice Adsila to the vine?"

Stanton was silent.

"They are considering it, are they not?" Carter asked. "At least, they haven't told you 'no.'"

"Where is this going, Doctor?"

"Tell me what they're planning," Carter said. "Let me weigh whether that, or my other plan, has the best chance of success. I swear to you, I will give you an honest analysis."

Stanton was silent. He was in a miserable corner now: any way he turned was morally corrupt. Either he betrayed his oath to NASA or he risked the safety of his personnel by serving an agency that had an inborn tolerance for high risk.

He thought again of the heroes who gamely flew out to confront the renegade Chinese space station.

This is the reality of command, he thought. *Not only selecting the best of several bad options, but living with the results.*

"NASA is running simulations," Stanton said, then faltered. The taste of dishonor stuck in his gullet. He inhaled, went on. "As I understand it, the tests suggest that gold nuclei colliding head-on will release sufficient kinetic energy, hot quark-gluon plasma, that will destroy the hadrons in ten to twenty-three seconds."

"Commander, we do not presently possess a Relativistic Heavy Ion Collider."

"They believe that exposing the Agro Center to solar wind and using microvoxel refraction combined with—"

"Their solution is to play ionic billiards?" Carter said. The biophysicist half-turned, shaking his head, as he considered the science. "Maybe. *Maybe.* If it works, someone wins a Nobel Prize. If it fails, we die."

"No," Stanton said. "If it fails, *you* gave them a backup plan. Your suggestion actually encouraged them to follow this path."

"The folly of political fiefdoms," Carter said. "We're a few months from the year 2051 and our government still hasn't learned to communicate openly, to avoid needless risk."

"You're the one who turned one option to two," Stanton said.

"Because you won't let me proceed with option number three," Carter said.

"Talk about fiefdoms," Stanton replied. "So far, you haven't even told me what it is."

"Plausible deniability," Carter said.

"You're protecting *me*?" Stanton said.

"I am," Carter told him. "So far, NASA is unaware of any rule you've infracted, such as telling me about their top-secret plan . . . and if Adsila refuses to press charges, I won't be tried for forcing a gender switch. Let me back in the Vault to try this my way. If it succeeds—you can take credit or not, it doesn't matter to me. If it fails, it's a black hole in *my* cosmos and there will still be time for NASA to try their long shot."

"What is your idea?" Stanton asked.

Carter told him. The commander listened with a rising sense of horror. Whatever beauty he had ever seen in the stars, in space itself, would forever be tarnished by what Carter was proposing. He wondered if the *Empyrean* itself would ever be clean after this, and he said so.

"The question, Commander, is not whether the station can overcome this scarring," Carter said solemnly, "though I believe it can, and will. The question is whether it will survive the next hour."

Carter turned to Abernathy and sent him on a mission. When the agent had gone, Carter looked at Adsila.

"You still need his permission," Stanton told him.

"I know," Carter said. He terminated the patch using his IC, causing the fibers to seal with a fine, nonporous aerogel. Almost at once, the EAD began to stir. "I will get it before proceeding."

Stanton seemed satisfied with that. "I'm going back to the Drum," he said. "Clear up the legal matter, obtain a medical release for your plan, and I won't interfere."

Carter's eyes and smile could not conceal the welling of pride he felt in the commander.

"Thank you, Commander," Carter said.

"No, Doctor. Thank you," Stanton said. "Sam Lord wouldn't have bothered to ask."

THIRTY-SIX

LORD DID NOT have to explain to Svetlana that it wasn't Dr. Borodin who was communicating with them, that his brain had frozen and ceased functioning almost immediately—and, with it, his Individual Cloud. However, that did not explain the word that had appeared in his IC.

He considered the situation in silence for quite some time. He also replayed his IC recordings of the single word they had received.

The answer to the immediate problem and the explanation for the actions of the late Dr. Borodin were obvious and disturbing.

"That message had to have come from the *Empyrean*," he said at last.

"How is that possible?"

"They are connected to this co-op thing out there," he said. "They are in communication with the nanites. They have evolved to the point of trying to create rudimentary speech through the only biological creature they've inhabited with that memory, with that capacity."

"Are you saying they're trying to trick us into taking Borodin back inside?"

"I don't think that's it," Lord said. "I don't even think that's what they meant. I believe they are expressing what they wish to be."

"Alive," Svetlana said.

"We already suspect that's why they want the microbe," Lord said. "I have a feeling they're asking for our help."

"Which we will not provide," the pilot confirmed.

"No, of course not," Lord said.

She was looking at him. "But you seem to be considering it."

Lord seemed startled by the remark. He shook his head. "Not that. I'm thinking that if they are still communicating from the *Empyrean*, things are not going well there. Admiral, are you still listening?"

Lord waited. There was no answer.

Svetlana asked. The radio operator said that Ptushko was not presently available.

"No doubt he is discussing the situation with Roscosmos or Moscow," Svetlana said. "Asking what's to be done with me for failing on this mission."

"I'm sure he's more concerned with his own future," Lord said.

Svetlana killed the outgoing link to the *Red Giant*. "True," she said with a hollow laugh. "He's the one who appointed me."

Svetlana decided she would keep the link silent until Ptushko called for her. It wasn't a power play—she had none, she felt; she just didn't want to be caught up in housekeeping communications when there were larger stakes that required her attention.

Lord looked out at the growing world. It now filled a large part of the window. "The mission is hardly over," Lord said. "The planet you are going to is inhabited. Dr. Borodin's loss is tragic, but it was the price of progress. And you will be bringing glory back to Ptushko, to Earth."

"You're forgetting something," she said. "The nanites. We cannot allow them to get anywhere near Venus."

"I've been thinking about that too," Lord said. "Red, how difficult would it be to construct some kind of patterned response to the microbe? Just dots and dashes, that kind of something—something to at least open the door to a dialogue."

"Heck, I can whip something up," Red said, "but I cannot guarantee that the specimen would hear, understand, or respond."

"Go ahead," Lord instructed.

Svetlana looked at Lord as her Glossator translated. "That is your SimAI?"

"It is," he said. "Former wing person—lost her."

"My regrets," Svetlana said sincerely.

"If you're finished," Red said, "I have a waveform that duplicates the most commonly utilized phrase of their exchange. A caveat, though: I have no idea what it is. They could be swearing at each other."

"Try it," Lord said. "On visual: let's see what we get back."

Lord cleared his IC of all open files save the Glossator. Once again, the Soyuz seemed to be filled with palpable anticipation—ironic for a collection of old bolts and plates to rattle with such human energy. He had been in cockpits where he had felt a similar kind of internal and external electricity, but that was about short-term goals, missions with generally familiar parameters. This was new in a way that few humans had ever experienced that word—perhaps Marco Polo, Columbus, Gagarin, Apollos 8 and 11.

The signal went up in the Glossator, a visual repeated three times.

"I think threesies should be enough?" Red said.

Lord didn't answer. He was too busy watching and waiting.

The answer that came back was not what he or Svetlana had been anticipating. It was one color: indigo.

"Red, what's that?" Lord asked.

"Me being overwhelmed," the SimAI replied. "You wanted a message? Or a note? You got an oratorio."

"Explain," Lord said.

"The response is so large and loud that the entire visual reach of the IC, all one hundred forty-eight degrees, can just show the first rush of about ten thousand replies."

"From the planet," Lord confirmed.

"Oh, the microbe you've got is tucked in there—at the bottom," Red said. "Real pile-on."

"What do we do now?" Lord asked.

"Well . . . the fractal we have suggests that they've repeated your message," Red said. "I've selected the next-most-popular wave-form—"

"Send," Lord said enthusiastically.

Red complied. "I've sent this in a narrower bandwidth, only—"

The answer came back swiftly, showing indigo, violet, green, and blue.

"Looks like they've toned down their reply too," Lord said.

"They matched my frequency," Red said. "Very impressive. I'll try another, smaller."

This time the reply resembled the original messages that the Glossator had intercepted.

"I believe we are now talking through the specimen and not through the entire population of Venus," Red speculated.

"Wonderful," Lord said. "Now, how do we actually communicate?"

"I think they're beating you to that," Red said. "Hold."

"This is . . . frightening," Svetlana said. She had searched her brain for a better word but one hadn't emerged.

"It is," Lord said, "but would you miss it?"

"Not for anything," she agreed. "I am only sorry for Dr. Borodin."

"He got to meet an extraterrestrial," Lord said. "He may not have finished his life's work but he fulfilled it."

Red returned before she could reply.

"As far as I can tell, based on a very small sample," the SimAI said, "the Venusians have transmitted the equivalent of an abacus. They are sending out layers of the same signal, but at different densities."

"Can you ascribe numbers to those layers?" Lord asked.

"Already have," Red said. "One through—well, a very high number that is still climbing."

"Suggestions to winnow?" Lord asked.

"Put Venus on the metric system," Red said. "If I attach numerals to the first one hundred signals, we may be able to establish a base-ten form of communication . . . get away from these unmanageably large numbers."

"Do it," Lord said. "Svetlana, how long until we reach the station?"

"Roughly an hour," she replied.

"We'll have to do something about our guest before—"

"I have received a response," Red interrupted. "Can you bring up a topographic map of the planet?"

Lord turned to Svetlana. "I'm sure yours will be better than whatever I have."

The pilot nodded, accessed one, and swiped it over to Lord. A pair of false-color maps appeared, looking like roadkill: each a flattened globe with twelve wedge-shaped pieces projecting from a polar center. The outer fringes of each of the twenty-four slices was the equator.

"Why do you want it, Red?" Lord asked.

"Because a random series of numbers has come back based on tens," the SimAI replied.

"Random—but not meaningless, I am guessing," Lord said.

"Let's see what I can come up with," Red replied. "Also, would you plug me into the ship's sonar and other sensors?"

Svetlana hesitated, but only for a moment.

"Thanks," Red said. "Give me a minute."

"Director Lord—" Svetlana began.

"I think it's time for 'Sam.' "

"All right. Sam: you are allowing that these microbes are intelligent," she said. "That is a big leap based on a series of numbers that has been received and interpreted by your SimAI."

"I'm not so sure it's a big leap," he said. "When I first eavesdropped on them, our friend here"—he pointed to the microbe in the Soyuz—"was feeling an assault from our friends out there." He jerked a thumb toward where Borodin was last seen. "I assume they still know he's there."

"Why?"

"Because we were not the only ones who responded to that word 'Alive,' " Lord said. "I went back and had a look at the recordings of the microbe since I first 'heard' them. There was a spike when that happened."

"I've been studying the numbers from Venus," Red replied. "They are columns thousands of numbers deep. Or rather, thousands of groups of hundreds deep."

"Individual pods of microbes piled one on top of the other?" Lord guessed.

"I can't think of what else they would be," Red replied.

"Meters?" Svetlana suggested.

Lord repeated her comment to Red.

"No," Red replied. "Those would be the same, whether you are measuring vertically or horizontally. These vary and they keep changing. Aha."

"What?" Lord asked.

"The changes match the wind currents in the atmosphere," Red said. "These figures do refer to stacks of microbes."

"So they do dwell in the atmosphere," Svetlana said.

"There does appear to be an anomaly forming," Red observed.

"Tell me," Lord said.

"There's a point in the atmosphere where the numbers are diminishing . . . rapidly," Red said. "With a matching increase in other columns."

"The microbes are migrating?" Lord speculated.

"It would appear so, but in all directions away from a certain point," Red said. "They seem to be calling our attention there."

"Any idea why?" Lord asked.

"If you're asking for their endgame, I couldn't say," Red told him. "But I can tell you this: it's beneath the general location of the Russian airship."

"Define 'general,' " Lord said.

"It's too early to do that," Red replied. "The microbes are apparently rotating in the atmosphere. I suspect they are using the flanges to hold their general position, but it is not being precisely maintained."

"Understood," Lord said.

"This concerns me," Svetlana said.

"Why?" Lord asked.

"If the microbes are aware of the nanites, their electrical energy, then they are surely aware of the laboratory we placed in their atmosphere," Svetlana said. "How do we know they are not drawing us there to destroy it and then send us and our nanites on our way?"

"It's a good point, a reasonable concern," Lord said. "It's also a risk we seem to have to take."

"Always the buccaneer?" she said. It was not an accusation, just a way for her to express incaution personified.

"Perhaps," Lord said. "But for good or ill, we seem to have been given an invitation. As the first ambassadors from our planet, we would be what— rude? Irresponsible, something worse, if we failed to accept?"

"We could be flying into a trap," she said. "Do you think they would have communicated with us were it not for the nanites?"

Lord considered that. "It's a good question. I don't know. In that case, we and Dr. Borodin would have been on board the *Lomonosov* and unable to escape whatever it is."

Svetlana was tempted to contact the *Red Giant* and ask for their opinion. She noted that the radio operator had checked in, requesting a response. The pilot sent an automated signal in reply; they would simply assume she was making preparations to enter orbit and dock with the airship.

"All right," the pilot said. She began entering data into her IC. "We are a go for docking. But what do we do about Borodin? If the nanites infect the atmosphere, who knows what the ramifications will be?"

"There is no doubt of that," Lord agreed. "So we take this a step at a time. Something may occur to us—or be sent to us—as we make our way."

THIRTY-SEVEN

THE SOYUZ WAS just thirty-odd minutes from the Earth's sister world, its face no longer able to fit in the viewport. The Russian pilot was annoyed with herself that after a voyage of more than 100 million miles, circling the sun to reach the clouded world, it was suspicion and not wonder that filled her mind. For Lord, the feeling was exactly the opposite. He was awed and he was prepared to trust the inhabitants of this world. The alternative was a terrestrial plague, something that he did not want to believe existed on another world.

Who is to say they are not equally excited to meet us? he wondered. Then he answered his own question with a flash of guilt and despair: because we brought the nanites.

He could only pray that the Venusians were either simpler or more enlightened than that. Perhaps they wished for nothing more than to survive. He didn't know—there was so damn much they didn't know—but they had to learn. To do so, they had to dare.

A half hour later, the occupants of the Soyuz were the first human beings to go into orbit around an alien world.

Lord could barely breathe when Svetlana cut off the zeta-pinch drive and applied the braking rockets to put them into an orbit that would bring them to the *Lomonosov* in one hour, two minutes.

Svetlana had reestablished communication with the *Red Giant,* informed them that telemetry showed all systems operating as designed. Lord was still plugged into the sensors of the Soyuz. En route to the rendezvous, he saw the remains of the Scud boosters that had brought the components into space. It seemed strange to see those familiar weapons of war out here, discarded, having been retired after completing a mission of peace.

The airship was indeed something of an inflated white pancake. Hovering at the fringes of the planet's impenetrably thick cloud cover, it was a queen at the center of a ring of eighteen retainers: inert metallic boxes with long joined arms and "hands" that resembled Swiss knives, the assembly robots that Svetlana informed him were nicknamed the Charities after the attendants of Venus in Roman mythology.

It was a surprising, pleasing bit of whimsy for a corps of scientists and politicians who historically lacked that attribute.

"The fact that they are still there should be a good sign," Lord said.

Svetlana once again cut off outgoing messages to the *Red Giant*.

"And my first thought was 'bait,'" the pilot replied. "The microbes knew we'd show up in person some day to check our base."

"Also," Red said, "the microbes may not have been able to reach the *Lomonosov*. There is no indication about the depth of the indigenous columns, only their population. The microbes may not be able to reach this altitude, where the exopause and planetocentric distance—"

"Thank you both," Lord said. "My hope and my sense of wonder remain in force. Red, the microbes talked to us about the opening under the airship. There has to be a reason. I see the docking hatch on top—"

"The bay on the bottom is for probes," Svetlana said. "There are none, as yet, on board."

"Probes—to be dropped into the atmosphere," Lord said.

"Yes, of course. Why?"

Lord was shaking his head slowly. "It isn't possible," he said. "Could they be capable of that kind of abstract thought?"

"What are you talking about?" Svetlana asked.

"How long until we dock?"

"Three minutes, twenty-two seconds," Svetlana replied. "Sam?"

He held up a finger, asking her to wait. "Red, has the arrangement of the columns stabilized?"

"It stopped moving within five minutes of having started," the SimAI said.

"When we connect with the docking ring, Red, give me an accurate coordinate for the position of the microbe column array."

"What are you thinking?" Svetlana asked.

"That the microbes have a solution we never considered," Lord replied.

As Svetlana maneuvered the Soyuz into position, the interior of the craft was upside-down relative to the *Lomonosov*. Lord watched the camera in the rear of the craft, saw the long extension of the zeta-pinch engine swing away from the airship.

Lord did not want to disturb Svetlana, but he still saw that dead, half-grinning skull in his IC, hanging in the ether like Marley's Ghost, a dead warning for sins it was not too late to redress. It pursued them using—what? Gravity? Some form of microscopic motility? An energetic connection of some kind to the microbe?

Doc, you've got a lot of explaining to do, Lord thought as he wondered when and if he would get to see Carter again. *One crisis at a time*, he decided. He looked out the porthole, smiled faintly. *One* world *at a time.*

The pitch-and-yaw jets fired small, popping bursts and the descent of the Soyuz slowed as Svetlana maneuvered it toward the docking ring. A ring of green proximity lights came alive around the ring as the spacecraft closed in. The shadow of the Soyuz fell on the smooth, white surface of the airship. It appeared to be made of the same elastomeric aluminum as the outer skin of the *Empyrean*: he would not be surprised to learn that the Russians had appropriated that technology as well.

Lord was recording all of it. NASA should know that they have a leak.

Unless we took it from Roscosmos, he thought as he turned his eyes back to the video feed.

There was a very low, ship-rattling hum as the two vessels kissed; it was followed by a deep *thunk* as the Soyuz's ring snugly entered the port on the *Lomonosov*. It was followed by the same silence Lord had experienced in previous zero-gravity dockings, a tranquility spiced only by the clicks and whirs of internal mechanisms locking them in place. There was also, now, a noticeable pull of gravity.

"Secure," Svetlana said. But the word hadn't quite died when she added, "There is a disturbance below."

"Red?" Lord asked.

"It is a cyclone," Red replied. "A really big one."

"Has previous data showed anything like a storm in the upper atmosphere?" Lord asked.

"I'm checking," Svetlana told him. "Our probes have recorded high-altitude winds that circle the planet in just four days—"

"A constant state of hurricane," Lord remarked.

"The winds below are currently four hundred kilometers an hour—more than twice the speed of the worst storms on Earth. But, Sam, that does not include the new disruption." She looked at him. "That is turning at 554 kilometers an hour."

"Direct sunlight, Red?" Lord asked.

"Not even plausible," the SimAI replied. "You'd need a lens about 1.5 kilometers in diameter, focusing the rays— "

"Thank you," Lord said.

The *Lomonosov* was beginning to shudder from the turbulence and, with it, the Soyuz. Lord looked out at the cadaver hovering behind them. It too was moving.

"Red," Lord said, "is it possible the microbes are doing this? Creating that storm tunnel?"

"There would have to be a lot of microbes moving very fast," Red said.

"There *are* a lot of them," Lord said.

"Are they trying to destroy us?" Svetlana asked.

"I don't think so," Lord replied. "They could have pulled the airship down long before this. I wonder—they've been talking to our friend here, the microbe. Could it have warned them about the nanites?"

"If it did, why would they pull it toward them? Isn't that what it wants?" Svetlana asked.

Just then, the body of Dr. Borodin began to wriggle and jerk violently, like one of those inflatable figures Lord used to see as a child at used car lots. It began to descend, moving away from the zeta-pinch support structure at an angle, dropping in a slow, awkward cartwheel.

"Red," Lord said, "what is the atmospheric pressure on Venus?"

"It is ninety times that of Earth," Red replied.

Lord and Svetlana exchanged glances.

"Before you ask," the SimAI said, "the answer is no. Based on the information I have access to, there is no way the nanites can survive."

The occupants of the Soyuz watched by camera, it and they continuing to quake, and then they observed through the windows the body of Gavriil Borodin pinwheeling toward the planet, drawn by gravity and the high-atmospheric spin of the cyclone. Lord quickly switched on access to the dead man's IC. It broadcast a signal for just a few moments as the body sank deeper, reminding Lord of Gustav Doré's etching of the circling angels from *Paradise Lost*: myriad figures in layer upon layer causing the space within to churn. And then there were pieces of Borodin swirling in the mix, turning and appearing to melt and then vanishing, as telemetry from the IC suddenly ceased. Through the window, they saw the storm continue to spin—and then, after several minutes, it stopped as suddenly as it had begun. The airship and the Soyuz stopped shaking. The exosphere was once again still.

"Threat neutralized," Lord said quietly, almost reverently.

"I think Borodin would have appreciated having his remains end up on another world," Svetlana said. Then her eyes narrowed suddenly. "Hold on."

"What is it?"

"We're not done," Svetlana said, looking at her readouts.

"What do you mean?"

"There's another hole opening up," she said.

"Where?"

Svetlana replied, "Right beneath the *Lomonosov*."

THIRTY-EIGHT

ADSILA AWOKE, ALERT and surprised to see where he was. Almost immediately, Dr. Carter bent over him.

"What's happened?" Adsila asked, his voice raspy. He noticed, then, that he was male. "Did something go wrong?" he asked with alarm.

"The nanites got to you somehow," Carter said.

Adsila's throat tightened as he thought back to the last thing he remembered. "Vibrations," he said. "My abdomen was trembling violently. It triggered the change." He looked at Carter. "How did they do that?"

"The nanites don't have a lot of memory but all of it is attuned to biological matter," Carter said. "They knew what strings to pluck."

"It can't be that simple," the EAD said, flexing his fingers and neck.

"Remote control electronics are actually very simple, some of the earliest we mastered on Earth," Carter said. "We can review that later. Right now, we're pressed for time."

"The vine?"

"Still growing, reaching crisis status," Carter said.

Adsila was alert, focused. He fought the drugs that lingered in his veins. "What do you need from me?"

"Your blood," Carter replied. "I need permission to draw it and use it."

Adsila thought for a moment. "The nanites cannot survive in liquids."

"That's right."

"But the vine," he said. "What will you—"

"I plan to use the blood as the medium to kill it."

Adsila slowly raised himself to an elbow on the thickly padded cot and remained there. "How?"

"With this, EAD," a voice said from the doorway.

It was Mike Abernathy, who had returned from a trip to the Agro Center. In his hand was a large plastic container labeled GECGM.

"What is it?" Adsila asked.

"Genetically Engineered Corn Gluten Meal," Carter said. "Liba keeps it to contain overgrowth of certain species. He assures me that it'll kill most anything with roots."

"More than that," Abernathy said, "it's a wholly biological agent. The vine ingests your blood, replicates the entire concoction, and dies."

Adsila shook off the last of the grogginess. "Very clever. All right. How long *do* we have?"

"About twenty-odd minutes for the vine, much less to stop NASA from trying something radical," Carter told him.

Adsila sat and shifted to his female identity. She always felt better in her dominant form, and that was the identity that had a score to settle—with a plant.

"Take what you need," she told the doctor, hooking back the sleeve of her tunic, "with one rider."

"Which is?"

"I deliver the blood."

Carter hesitated, but only a moment. He began to draw blood with an old-fashioned hypodermic rather than the Splinter, a painless needle 1mm long, 0.1mm diameter, modeled after the proboscis of a mosquito. He needed a larger amount than that fine tube could provide.

"You realize that the vine will go after you the same as before," Carter said. "It may not bother with the sample."

"That thing controlled me," she said. "It compelled me to change. I want to fight that."

"The vine has also grown stronger since then," Carter told her as he finished the extraction.

"So have I," she replied.

After capping the needle, Carter handed the hypodermic to Abernathy. While the agent tweezed granules of GECGM into the shaft, Carter went to the supply cabinet and retrieved an abdomen-size square of gauze with adhesive backing.

"I am sorry that I was forced to intervene, to change you back," Carter said to Adsila. "Technically, I'm under arrest for that."

"You made the call you had to make," Adsila said. "All I care about is that we go back and fix this."

Carter still hesitated. "Bravado isn't going to get this done. That is a very powerful creation in there."

Adsila tugged down her sleeve. "I'm not just crowing, Doctor," she said. "But I am affirming our charter here. If we didn't learn something from that encounter, then we are not worthy of being the vanguard of order up here." She slid from the cot. "Is NASA running this operation or is Zero-G?"

Carter smiled for the first time in a while. "We are."

The three set out briskly for the Agro Center, Adsila setting the pace as McClure informed them that in three or four more growth spurts they would be forced from the Vault.

"And make no mistake, it's coming for you," the science officer added. "Every limb of this monstrosity is being thrust in the direction of the medbay."

"We will be there in two minutes," Carter assured him.

As he followed the EAD, the scientist overcame some of his natural pragmatism to embrace the welcome hubris Adsila had displayed—perhaps had borrowed from Sam Lord. The doctor flashed back to words he had memorized when he was being homeschooled by his British-born mother at Naval Station Newport in Rhode Island, a speech that Winston Churchill had given to the House of Commons in 1940: "We shall defend our island . . . we shall fight on the beaches, we shall fight on the landing grounds, we shall fight in the fields and in the streets, we shall fight in the hills. . . ."

The closet pacifist in him could not help but wonder, and mourn. *Is there never to be an end to struggle?*

Charging from the elevator, they heard the vine and the shouts of the Vault personnel before they even reached the greenhouse.

"McClure!" Carter said into the audio feed.

"We've got one more expansion!" the science officer said. "In three minutes the arms are coming through the Vault wall!"

"No," Carter said. "They'll turn to us when we arrive. That buys us about ten minutes more."

"It does not," Stanton informed them. "I'm coming down—NASA will be ready to execute their plan in five minutes. That's how much time you have."

They were moving so fast that the green line beneath them seemed like a writhing snake as they wound through the corridor. Reaching the Agro Center, Adsila half-walked, half-leapt through the greenhouse toward the Vault. Carter was trying hard to keep up.

"Wait out here, in case we need anything," the doctor told Abernathy.

The agent slowed near the Vault door as the ICs of the other two clicked them through. The crisis had a surreal quality, especially when Stanton arrived. Abernathy had been in the comm during the *Jade Star* crisis, removed from the action. This was real and immediate, with a sense of personal danger that made the seconds crawl.

It was as though his brain were drawing out every moment of life in a situation where life could end at any instant.

Stanton remained beside the agent but was unaware of him, his attention entirely on the opaque electronic doorway of the Vault. The commander seemed to want to speak but, like Abernathy, just listened.

Just four feet away, Adsila Waters and Dr. Carlton Carter stood facing the monstrous bramble. The tip of the large arm was facing away from them to the left, but within moments it had sprouted new growth from the sides: a long, thin tendril that covered half the twenty-odd feet between the vine and Adsila in a single surge.

While the rest of the crew crowded behind them in what little free space remained, Carter injected the blood-GECGM compound into the gauze while Adsila looked for the best place to make a move.

"It doesn't matter where I place this," Carter said, indicating the patch. "But I don't want the blood to turn the nanites toward me, so while I get as close to the trunk as I can, you—"

"The new growth is aware of me, so that's where I'm going," she decided.

"It will be sprouting!" Carter called after her.

"Let it!" she shouted back.

Adsila crossed the brittle, ground-hugging portions of the vine that had fallen when the nanites were briefly dormant. Her eyes were on the tendril that had lanced toward her, and she approached it without reserve. Slowed by the tangle beneath her feet, she reached the vine as it sprouted again with a brittle, echoing sound. It came directly toward her, hip-high. She stood inches from the pointed end, her arms stiff at her sides, glaring down.

"Adsila! You can back away!"

She glanced behind her and saw Carter on his knees, holding the large white patch against the trunk nearest the roots. She turned back to the vine.

"Not yet!" she said.

The tip of the branch began to vibrate. This was the closest she had seen it, was able to see the nascent growth beginning again. She felt the same familiar tingling in her belly as it tried to establish contact, establish—

"Ga-no-du." She said the Cherokee softly, almost reverently.

And the Vault began to shake from the ground up.

"Carter?" Stanton cried in her ears. "What's happening?"

"We're coming out!" the doctor cried. "Everyone, *out*! Adsila, come!"

The EAD watched as the stalk standing proud and rigid before her began to bleed. Mist and then droplets of blood pushed through tiny cracks in the bark; at first it was a slow drip, like sap, causing those rents to expand and the limb to quiver. The red liquid spilled over the sides of that arm in thin rivulets, which quickly began to pulse and then pour from the branch. She turned and saw it running from all the tangled parts of the vine.

Dr. Carter was beside her, his arms gentle on her shoulders.

"Adsila, come with me," he said.

"Why is it coming so quickly?" she asked.

"Not now," he told her.

Adsila's eyes roamed across the heaving vegetation, red streams running and pooling, the vine itself turning from greenish-brown to black as the toxins choked it of air and life. Yet the blood continued to flow until the nanites that were producing it drowned in their own issue.

Carter and Adsila remained just within the door, watching as large pieces of the vine crashed to the ground. The biggest, oldest sections crashed first as support structures nearest the patch perished quickly.

"Doctor?" Stanton said. "It sounds like your plan worked!"

"It worked," Carter replied.

"I'll make sure that everyone at NASA understands that there was no time to do anything else," Stanton said. "Thank you, Doctor. Looks like you'll have bragging rights on this one, not your director."

Carter was too drained to reply, too overwhelmed to speak. Whatever it was or would have become, a life was ending in brutal, unpleasant fashion before them—and hundreds of artificially evolved nanites were perishing as well. The biophysicist did not know the level their self-awareness had achieved; he hoped it was insufficient to grasp any concept of death.

He saw Adsila transfixed beside him, seeing something that he apparently did not.

"When you were standing there, you said something," Carter said. "Something in Cherokee?"

"Yes," she answered quietly. After a moment, she looked at him sadly. "I said *ga-no-du*. It means *life*."

"What prompted you to say that?" he asked.

"The vine did. The nanites did, Doctor." She touched her belly. "I felt it here."

"Felt what?"

"That they wanted *my* cells above all else," she told him.

Carter didn't understand at first—and then, suddenly he did. The nanites had experienced her body, one body with two sexes.

God help them, the nanites *had* gained some level of sentience. They did not want simply to replicate.

They had wanted to reproduce.

THIRTY-NINE

THE NEW DISTURBANCE beneath the *Lomonosov* was less violent than the last one. It was also less than a quarter of the diameter of the one that had pulled Borodin toward the surface.

"Do you think they are inviting us down?" Svetlana asked.

"I wouldn't think so," Lord replied. "They saw what happened to Dr. Borodin."

"It is not for you," Red said.

"What, then?" Lord asked.

"The draw of this whirlpool is not designed for a mass the size of the last one," the SimAI replied.

"Then what do they want?" Lord wondered aloud, trying to comprehend this "communication by windstorms." Then his eyes settled on the container and he answered his own question. "By God," he said, "that has to be it. The reason for the very small torque, beneath the hatch." He regarded Svetlana with sudden feeling of humility and pride as he answered her curious stare. "Svetlana, they're telling us that they want their comrade back."

Telling the *Red Giant* nothing more than that she was going to enter the *Lomonosov*, Svetlana turned on the airship systems. She did not mention that Lord would be joining her. When the "all functional" signal was received, she twisted around and opened the hatch of the Soyuz. Snuggling through, she opened the hatch of the *Lo-monosov* and used the overhead handholds to swing in. There was just one-quarter Earth gravity on board, but it was insufficient to float around. She used her IC to access the controls of the station. Soft white lights came on and the pilot turned to help Lord through the narrow opening. When she saw him, he was smiling and holding the container before him.

"The honored guest before the ride-along."

She accepted the container and put it in the sleeve pocket of her space suit then took Lord's gloved hand and helped him in.

The air was thin and warm but breathable. Except for the life-support equipment that had been sealed inside during assembly, the interior of the airship was empty, unformed. There were naked girders crisscrossing like giant Xs to support the outer structure, with rungs between them for maneuverability around the station.

Svetlana was a few feet above Lord as he grabbed the nearest "ladder," just inside the entrance. Looking down, he saw the dark, circular hatch. The ladder they were on would take them directly to it.

He was about to speak when Svetlana held up a finger.

"We board this planetary base *Lomonosov* with gratitude, and a desire to learn from those who have come before us, both human and extraterrestrial," she said solemnly.

Lord smiled proudly and nodded his approval. Nodding back, Svetlana closed the hatch after telling Lord to descend. She followed him down and they stood on a narrow plastic walkway that surrounded the hatch. Standing here, they could feel the powerful churning of the mini-storm below.

Svetlana knelt and used her IC to open the inner hatch of the airlock, which slid silently into the floor. Then she removed the microbe dish and looked at it.

"Second thoughts?" Lord asked.

"We know so little about them," she said.

"True, but this is our chance to learn," Lord said. "The Venusians have, I think, just extended the—the flange of friendship. It's an invitation to return in peace."

With a tight smile, Svetlana gently placed the dish in the compartment. The atmospheric pressure would take care of releasing its occupant. She shut the inner hatch, opened the outer panel, and dropped to all fours to brace herself as the winds swirled through the chamber. Lord had to grab the ladder to keep from falling.

A sensor indicated that the compartment was empty. Svetlana shut the outer panel. The winds slowed . . . and, a moment later, they ceased entirely.

Still on her knees, Svetlana said, "My God, this is what it could be like out here."

"Even we're on the same side right now," Lord noted.

He offered a hand to help her up, which she accepted. "I'm sorry about what has to be," she said.

"Do you know, for a fact, what that is?" Lord asked.

"What do you mean?"

"I have a favor to ask," he said. "A very big one."

Svetlana's features darkened.

"I cannot take you back to the *Empyrean* or the *Red Giant*," she said. "I cannot disobey a command." It wasn't that she was immune to the man or to his admittedly agreeable bewitchery, but at this moment Ptushko was holding her career, her life, hostage.

"I wasn't going to ask any of that," he said with a sweep of his hand. "Nothing like that."

"What, then?"

"I would like you to contact Roscosmos directly," Lord said. "Find out who, there, authorized my removal to Earth."

"Doing so, I would be going over my commander's head," she said.

"Not doing so, you would be endangering my life and your reputation."

"How?" she asked suspiciously.

"Put in the request," Lord told her. "Say that the admiral neglected to create a data trail—which is true—and that this is potentially too big a move for you to make without one. Which is also true. You know, I *am* a field director of the Federal Bureau of Investigation. In any case, they will not react kindly to my being detained."

Though unsure whether she was being offered sound advice or a subtle seduction, Svetlana decided that the query had some legitimacy. With reluctance, she used the communication system of the *Lomonosov* to bypass the *Red Giant* and contact the Russian space agency directly.

While Svetlana raised Roscosmos, Lord moved up and then laterally, shifting himself along the windows that ringed the airship. Outside, the construction robots rested like silent, obedient sentinels. Lord wondered if the microbes had the ability to interact with them, control them the way the nanites had sought to control the microbes.

It was a disturbing thought. He had taken a big step toward trust without ascertaining whether it was wise. With those robots, with a spacecraft like the Soyuz, the microbes could travel to Earth much as humans had reached Venus.

We may have just rolled out the carpet for an interplanetary plague invasion, he thought. But he didn't want to think so, he didn't want to believe so. With that kind of thinking, the great frontier here would hold very little promise. *You've read too many science fiction novels in ready rooms,* he told himself. *We get farther from the caves the closer we get to the stars. Other species* must *feel the same way.*

He was rapt, in space, in the thoughts that space inspired, and did not hear Svetlana's approach.

"You knew," she said.

"I suspected," Lord replied. "What did you find out?"

"They did not request the transfer, nor do they know anything about it."

"On the *Red Giant*, orders could only come from the space agency or—"

Lord did not bother to finish.

Svetlana stood on the ladder beside him, shaking her head. "But it makes sense, now that I think back," she said. "Everything he did was verbal, and I cannot say I ever saw corroborating orders from Roscosmos."

"Because Ptushko does not report to them directly," Lord said. "I suspected as much ever since I saw the door across from his office."

"I bring people up," Svetlana said. "They use it."

"They take orders from Ptushko," Lord replied.

"Speculation," she said with disbelief.

"I watched Borodin on the *Red Giant,*" Lord said. "He was afraid of telling Ptushko too much, probably of seeing his discovery weaponized."

"More speculation." It wasn't an accusation as much as a hope.

Lord moved closer. He flashed a finger, transmitting the file Ptushko had given him on CHAI black marketer Veronika Astakov. "The admiral gave me this, minus key information, hoping I could fill it in. Yet it contains data that even your Federal Agency of Governmental Communications and Information does not possess. I know because I saw their file. Svetlana, Ptushko works with The Satellite. *He* is their man on the *Red Giant.*"

Svetlana did not protest a third time.

"There is something else," Lord said. "The reason he has been so encouraging toward you. Everyone you brought up—did you ever ferry a space pilot to the *Red Giant*?"

She considered that. "Not that I'm aware."

"I suspect he has been maneuvering you into a political and professional corner," Lord said. "He wants to leave you no out except to join him." He watched her expression sour inside her helmet. "I wish that weren't true—I do. I wish that we could return to the *Red Giant*, you would take me back to the *Empyrean*, you would be recommissioned on Earth, and all would be well. But that won't happen. I have a job, but he has a plan—and that is to extend Satellite control to space using the bankrupt Roscosmos as a stepping stone."

Svetlana was very still. She was no longer weighing his argument but what to do about it.

"I am going to finish checking the systems, doing what I was sent here to do," she told him. "Then we leave. Please wait in the Soyuz."

"You're the commander," he said.

Svetlana opened the hatch remotely and Lord returned to his couch, uncertain what she would do. They were still technically adversaries in a cold war that was more than a century old, a war that had ebbed and flowed but had never gone away. But they were also the representatives of a species that was no longer alone in the cosmos—a species that had just been saved from technological haste and folly by a race they knew virtually nothing about.

As Lord plugged himself back into the Soyuz, he prayed not for his own fate but for the fate of humankind.

Which will it be, Svetlana Uralov? he thought. *The cave or the stars?*

FORTY

I T TOOK SEVERAL hours for Ed McClure to MaGlove the straggling nanites from the occupants of the Vault. The nanites were dormant, their brain center having been destroyed by the cocktail Abernathy had dubbed Auntie Flora. "A sweet, biological mix that seemed like a birthday gift from a trusted relative," he said. "Then it killed you."

The nanites collected from the blood mixture were not only inoperative, they were inoperable; examining one, Carter found their interior workings shorted and beyond analysis.

The biophysicist was working alone in his lab when Stanton came to see him.

"Have you slept at all?" the commander asked.

"I will," Carter said, studying the samples in his IC. Without looking away, he asked, "How are you?"

"Good," Stanton said. "NASA says I—we—made 'an understandable and reasonable' on-site call."

Carter looked at him and snickered. "Polite way of saying it's not the way they wanted this to go."

"Right, but it protects me," Stanton said. "Just barely, but enough. I thank you again."

Carter shook his head. "I don't deserve it. I should have had more safeguards in place. And I huking blew my responsibility to a patient."

"We all learned a lot from this," Stanton said.

"Did we? Did NASA?"

"Cameron got Russian tech into the Vault," Stanton said. "We all have to boost our rockets if we're going to prevent this in the future."

Carter seemed unconvinced. "Well—whether we do or not, we all get to fight another day."

"What will you do with these?" Stanton asked, indicating the nanites.

"Take a closer look at the Israeli samples," he said. "Maybe they knew something I didn't about giving them too much power. They stopped short of the tipping point where artificial evolution could take place. That may not have been a technological limitation but a very, very smart choice."

"I hope not," Stanton said as the Drum called him. "I like the idea of quantum leaps in technology."

"Literally," Carter said, thinking about the elusiveness of the particles that caused this misadventure . . . and the potential dangers of having opened that particular Pandora's Box.

"Yes, Lajos?" Stanton said to his secure transmission specialist.

"Commander, we have a communication from the Russian Soyuz."

"Lord?" Stanton asked.

Carter sat up straight, suddenly looking like a well-rested man. Stanton shared the message.

"I don't know," Lajos went on. "It's not a radio message, it's a—it's an SOS."

"No radio or IC access?" Stanton asked.

"No, sir. They are not answering anybody, not even the *Red Giant*," Lajos said. "We scanned the craft, there doesn't seem to be any local or structural distress. Thermal readings suggest two occupants, one of which fits the contours of Samuel Lord."

"Permission to dock granted," Stanton said.

It was an unnecessary order since, by mutual pact between the spacefaring nations, a request for "emergency berthing" on a spacecraft, space station, or space base could not be denied. However, if the emergency proved to be false—and this had the earmarks of being that—the repercussions could include confiscation of the vessel.

"How soon will they arrive?" Stanton asked.

"Sixty-five minutes, sir," Lajos replied.

"PRiD1 and I'll be there, then," Stanton said. He winked off and looked at Carter. "How is Adsila?"

"Generally, all right," Carter said.

"I suppose there will be some physical blow-back from the back-and-forthing," he said.

"She went through some stresses," Carter agreed. "Allowed to de-medicate and free of nanite influence, she'll be fine."

"I assume she's not resting?" Stanton said.

"She is not," Carter replied. "She's at the comm, on modified observational duty. AEAD Grainger is in command. I imagine Adsila will be at the PRiD when the Soyuz arrives."

Stanton nodded then offered his hand. It was the first time Carter could remember shaking it since they met. The commander left smartly, some of his old confidence restored. Carter wished he felt the same. He had tried to maneuver between the scientific, political, and intelligence communities and he had managed to lose sight of who he was and what was important. It would take him a while to rediscover that; it had been years since pure science and responsible research had been his motivation. Perhaps this crisis, coming hard upon the calamity aboard *Jade Star*, would give everyone a reason to hit an emergency stop button.

A reason but not a resolution, Carter thought sadly.

It would be business as usual, though he had to rethink his place in that. Hopefully, his affiliation with Zero-G would give him the new direction he had been avoiding, new goals. Different goals.

Wiser goals.

■ ■

It was the bump of the docking that nudged Sam Lord awake.

He had been sleeping—for real, this time—and dreaming about the

New York of his youth. It had shaped his worldview, the idea that authority was there to be circumvented, was too busy to pay close attention. He was going from store to store, sampling, stealing, staring at girls without being seen, slick in his evasion of shopkeepers, police, his parents—

He was being the Sammy Lord who matured—somewhat, in the essential ways—to became Sam Lord who became Colonel Samuel Lord who became Director Samuel Lord. He had not become Erin's husband, but wherever they were docking now, he had been content with all the other iterations.

It took him a moment to look over at Svetlana. Wherever he went, he wanted to remember the trusting visionary he had finally gotten to meet as they neared another world.

When he finally turned to thank her for this adventure, he saw her looking at him. He knew at once, from her resolute expression, what she had done and where they were.

"We have just docked at the *Empyrean*," he said.

"Yes," Svetlana said. "If you don't mind, I'd like to talk for a moment before you go."

"You talk—I'm speechless," was all he could think to say.

That was true. The *Empyrean* was still here, still operational, and he could not wait to hear what had happened. But the pilot had not opened the hatch, so whatever she had to say must be important. Not only had the woman earned the right to be heard, he owed her the benefit of whatever counsel he could provide—including asylum, if she asked, despite the problems that would cause.

"I have had a lot of time to think about what I wanted to say," she said. "I am aware that this will create a political and diplomatic row, not only when our governments learn what you and I shared but because your people will see the engine that we probably did not design."

"I don't have to tell them much," he said. "And—you need not go back."

"I must," Svetlana said, "and I believe it's important that you do tell everything we experienced. We have an unprecedented opportunity to make a new beginning for our nations, especially when the world"—she paused, smiled—"*our* world, I mean, learns what has been discovered out there."

"That will shake things up," he admitted.

"I don't believe Roscosmos would have said anything, and that would be criminal," she said. "But I am afraid of the personal repercussions. Ptushko has a great deal of influence."

"I suspect," Lord said, "that he may not be quite as vindictive as you are expecting. When he learns what you know—and you must tell him—he will understand that *I* know it too. He won't be repentant or cowed, but I suspect he will return you to Earth with high commendations, just to keep you out of his business." Lord smiled. "That is not something he can do with me and my team."

"I understand, but you must not use this leverage for nationalistic gains," she said. "That is a personal pledge you must make to me."

"I promise," he said, raising two fingers. "I am not a company man. I am up here because the opportunities for his kind must be narrowed and choked—on all fronts, on every side. They will be. My team and I will help see to that."

"I hope you are right," she said.

"I usually am," he assured her with a wink.

"Are you, then?"

"Svetlana, you don't reach my age, survive wars and crashes, go from Hell's Kitchen to Heaven's Gate, without acquiring a very, very good instinct for things." He took her gloved hand. "And if you can't believe the only human in history to have visited Earth, the moon, and Venus, who can you believe?"

Svetlana smiled warmly, squeezed his hand back, then released it to pop the hatch. "Good luck, Sam."

He beamed at her as the hatch opened, then pulled himself from his couch and tasted the familiar, welcoming, machine-processed air of the *Empyrean*.

FORTY-ONE

"Y OU HAVE SOME explaining to do, Doctor," Lord said.

The entire Zero-G team was sitting at the largest table in the Scrub. After briefing Al-Kazaz, Lord had been ordered to give the team a full day off.

"It's not entirely benevolent of me, and don't expect a repetition," the prime director had informed him during the debriefing in the LOO. "I can't afford to have you all punchy with exhaustion, distraction, and drugs."

"Thank you," Lord had told him. "For the record, Peter, I'd have given that same order without you."

"Can't let me have even that," Al-Kazaz had snorted.

"It's yours," Lord had replied. "I'm just affirming the great wisdom of your call."

So they sat, eating a meal without vegetables—not only were they in short supply at the moment, but no one particularly wanted them— and enjoying a bottle of wine from Stanton's private store.

"You know, sir, this is the first time we have all socialized," McClure said. "Why don't we save the postmortems for another time?"

"Actually, I'd like to talk about it, if you don't mind," Carter said. "All of this has been in my head for such a long time I think it would be good to talk about it."

"What about the security aspects?" McClure asked.

"Our clearances were never revoked," Abernathy pointed out.

"I trust you all," Carter said. "And if that's not good enough for NASA, they can prosecute."

"Bravo," Grainger said quietly.

"Besides, we are still sitting on the biggest secret in history," Abernathy went on, "knowledge of an alien life-form. I think we can be trusted with a few secrets that no longer matter."

McClure raised a glass and the others followed. "To nonsecrets . . . and our new planetary neighbors. Hell, being able to say that makes me *very* happy."

"See if you feel the same when they come after us in very, very tiny spaceships that we can't see," Abernathy replied.

"They won't," McClure said. "Not if the rock guys of Mercury have anything to say about it."

"I'd like to interrupt with my own toast," Lord said, lifting his glass.

"Please do." Grainger grinned at the two science officers.

"To a team that works miracles," Lord said.

Everyone joined that salutation in silent gratitude and with long looks of mutual respect and admiration.

"Until the invasion comes," McClure continued. "Then . . . we'll see how smart we truly are."

"We'll crush them," Abernathy replied confidently.

"*Anyway*, if we can table the fable," Carter said, "I know we're not supposed to be working, but there are some things I'm still working out. Such as the degree of artificial evolution that took place and how it manifested itself. In the Vault, the blood and GECGM were reproduced exponentially faster than the initial growth of the vine. When the memories of the individual nanites were linked, that capacity grew into a kind of shared mind—with groups of nanites calling the shots while the processors in the rest were turned solely to manufacturing cells."

"Like a beehive and honey," Grainger said.

"Exactly like that," Carter said.

"How did that happen?" McClure asked. "What was the mechanism?"

"I don't know yet," Carter admitted. "The real question we should probably be asking is how could it *not*? We make these machines smarter and smarter—there has to be a tipping point between 'calculation' and 'sentience.' Something happening at the molly level, a process we had damn well better understand before we make these things too capable."

"From two-bit video games to artificial intelligence in one lifetime," Lord said. "Incredible."

"Maybe humans were always meant to be just a means to an end, an interim 'technology' to make the machines possible," McClure suggested.

"A sobering thought," Lord said.

"As for the nanites pursuing this—Venusian," Carter continued, stopping and finally showing his own sense of awe. "As for that pursuit, I'm pretty certain it was some kind of electromagnetic attachment to the Soyuz or its radio signals," he continued. "They could sense the biological material, but that would not exert the kind of pull you experienced, Sam."

"Would that kind of attraction hold at those incredible speeds?" Lord asked.

"Without friction, absolutely," Carter said. "Which may be a safeguard I can build into any future iterations of nanites. Remotely operated brakes to stop them from moving."

"You intend to continue this research?" Grainger asked.

"As I told Stanton repeatedly, it wasn't the technology that was bad, it was the corruption caused by defective hadrons."

"With respect, Doctor," McClure said, "in our lifetimes I am not sure we will have control over quarks and the composite particles they comprise."

"The Venusians might," Abernathy said. "And *that's* not a fable, Doctor."

"Agent, you might very well be right about that," Lord said, thinking back to the way these mites had controlled the mighty atmosphere of Venus. "I wish I could have recorded what I saw. What I felt."

"There was a lot going on," Carter said. "You were closer to the heat and storms of the sun, and the winds of Venus are dramatic—there is no indication that microbes could affect that."

"Oh, they affected it, Doctor," Lord said. "It changed below me."

"Maybe it was the planet, not the microbes," Abernathy said. "Maybe *it's* alive, talking through the microbes."

Lord grinned. "Oddly, Agent—*that* makes some sense." His eyes shifted to Adsila. "EAD? You've been quiet."

The woman was sitting tall on her stool, her mind clearly elsewhere.

"Honestly, sir, it's what Ed said in his toast," she said. "The Venusians. They exist. They have probably existed for a long time. And it's not just the fact of them that I can't quite process."

"What do you mean?" Grainger asked.

"I'm overwhelmed by the reality that an entire planet, a whole world, has a life-form that is more like me than it is like any other human on Earth," Adsila said. "I can't help but wonder if my kind, pangenders, may turn out to be the majority life-form in the universe."

Grainger raised her glass. "I'll drink to that. To the evolution of our own perceptions, may they never grow complacent or stale."

Glasses were raised again, and while Abernathy speculated on what evolved humans might be—and McClure and Carter and Grainger strongly disagreed—Sam Lord made a silent toast to Svetlana Uralov, who might already be on that ascended road. Then he drained his glass, crossed his arms, and enjoyed the company of some of the most wonderful contemporary humans he had ever known.

EPILOGUE

THE ODDS WOULD have been considerable, if anyone had been present to calculate them.

Moving at slightly more than 15 million miles an hour, the object penetrated the virtually nonexistent atmosphere and struck the barren world a skidding blow, one that caused it to break apart as it dug a long, white scratch across the gray surface. Each piece, no more than a particle, came to tumbling stops and were slowly covered by some of the smaller motes of dust they had knocked toward the black sky. Most of those grains fell wide of the landed particles, and slowly, finding little gravity to draw them back home.

The concussions raised no sound, attracted no attention, disturbed nothing beyond the few square yards of terrain they impacted.

And then, there was movement.

Microscopic, tentative, almost insignificant. But not quite.

The infinitesimal fragments of Douglas Cameron were barely sufficient to be identified as such, were anyone there to identify them. But the nanites inside began to seek whatever cellular matter they could find around them. And there, beneath the burning eye of the sun, on the surface of the planet Mercury, the little robots resumed their work....

ACKNOWLEDGMENTS

I must acknowledge Carmen La Via, my long-, long-, long-, longtime literary agent, whose opinion I respect and ignore, who has great judgment that I never follow, and whose friendship I count on through all these long years. I bow deeply in respect to Jeff Rovin.